Praise for *Homeward Hound*

"Readers will be charmed by Brown's endearing characters, animal and human, all of whom are given to philosophizing on the state of the world." —*Publishers Weekly*

"Those in the fox-hunting and adjacent horse-fancying worlds . . . can appreciate Brown's eye for accurate details throughout." —*Kirkus Reviews*

Praise for *Crazy Like a Fox*

"If you can pick up *Crazy Like a Fox* and recognize the voices of Comet, a wise old gray fox; Dasher, a hound at the top of his game; and Golliwog, a snippy calico cat, you qualify as a member of the pack that surrounds Sister Jane Arnold, Master of Jefferson Hunt and the sleuth in Rita Mae Brown's enchanting novels set in the Virginia horse country. . . . Just the kind of story that adds to the charm of Brown's whimsical mysteries, with their thrilling hunts and intelligent animals." —*The New York Times Book Review*

"Brown's animal characters, including horses, hounds, and foxes, have as much to say as the people, and Brown never misses an opportunity to interject her own social commentary. This will appeal . . . to fans of Brown's Sneaky Pie novels." —*Publishers Weekly*

Praise for *Let Sleeping Dogs Lie*

"A knotty murder mystery . . . Cunning foxes, sensible hounds, and sweet-tempered horses are among the sparkling conversationalists in this charming series starring Jane (Sister) Arnold. . . . The biggest thrills are riding out with Sister and her chatty hounds on a cold, crisp morning." —*The New York Times Book Review*

"[Rita Mae Brown] combines a clever plot, cherished characters and the beauty of nature and rural life to provide an entertaining whodunit." —*Richmond Times-Dispatch*

"Sister remains an intriguing and challenging sleuth. . . . [Brown's] foxhunting titles are great for readers who like gentility with a wicked little twist." —*Library Journal*

"Enjoyable [and] pleasurable . . . Enough with the demographics of foxhunting as most people view it; if I've learned one thing from reading Rita Mae Brown, it is to expect the unexpected!"

—*The Huntington News*

"Whether you're a fox chaser or not, Brown's storytelling skills will keep you entertained throughout." —*In & Around Horse Country*

"As usual, Brown is at her best when relaying the animals' quirks and conversations, and mischievous foxes are a delight."

—*Publishers Weekly*

"Fun . . . [*Let Sleeping Dogs Lie* takes] readers on an adventure."

—*RT Book Reviews*

Praise for *Fox Tracks*

"Sister Jane makes for a memorable amateur sleuth, and the pack of animals sure added a new level of delight."

—*Cozy Mystery Book Reviews*

"An enjoyable whodunit . . . Series fans will enjoy Sister's sleuthing."

—*The Mystery Gazette*

Praise for *Hounded to Death*

"The fun of Brown's series is the wealth of foxhunting lore, the spot-on portrayal of Virginians . . . and the evocative descriptions of the Blue Ridge Mountains. . . . And then there's Sister, the seventy-three-year-old heroine who becomes even more appealing with each successive book. Brown has a winner in this memorable character." —*Richmond Times-Dispatch*

"Will surely please fans of the series. The mystery is fast-paced and filled with scenes from the world of fox hunting. . . . Brown delivers the brush." —*The Baltimore Sun*

"[A] paw-turner." —*Dog Fancy*

"Anyone interested in rural sleuths, animals, Virginia, hunting, or horses will enjoy the engaging story, its countryside and its characters, all wrapped up in a high-quality modern cozy mystery."

—*Booklist*

Praise for *The Tell-Tale Horse*

"Intriguing . . . Fans of the series will be fascinated with Jane's evolution under Brown's hand. With each book, Jane becomes more real—and more human—in the reader's imagination."

—*Richmond Times-Dispatch*

"Grabs readers from the opening scene and gallops through to the very surprising end." —*Horse Illustrated*

Praise for *The Hounds and the Fury*

"With a natural touch at dialogue, a sense of humor and a deep knowledge of country life, Brown creates an engaging novel and a worthy entry into an absorbing series." —*Richmond Times-Dispatch*

"A genteel Virginia foxhunting club makes a delicious setting for murder. How pleasant to linger among the settees and brandy snifters waiting for the bodies to pile up!"

—Memphis *Commercial Appeal*

Praise for *The Hunt Ball*

"The hunt must go on, its grace and glory personified by the foxes, hounds and horses that provide these thrilling scenes with their on-the-ground perspective." —*The New York Times Book Review*

"Score another triumph for [Rita Mae] Brown—and for 'Sister,' who helps run another two-legged predator to ground."

—*Richmond Times-Dispatch*

Praise for *Full Cry*

"A solidly crafted mystery with interesting characters and a nice sense of place. The rolling hills of the Virginia hunt country are beautiful, and all the gentility makes a perfect place to plop a dead body." —*The Globe and Mail*

"A great ride with heroine 'Sister' Jane Arnold."

—*Pittsburgh Post-Gazette*

"A quality tale that is over all too soon."

—Charleston *Post and Courier*

Praise for *Hotspur*

"Dashing and vibrant . . . The reader will romp through the book like a hunter on a thoroughbred, never stopping for a meal or a night's sleep." —*Publishers Weekly* (starred review)

"Brown combines her strengths—exploring southern families, manners, and rituals as well as the human-animal bond—to bring in a winner."
—*Booklist*

Praise for *Outfoxed*

"Compelling . . . engaging . . . [a] sly whodunit . . . [Brown] succeeds in conjuring a world in which prey are meant to survive the chase and foxes are knowing collaborators (with hunters and hounds) in the rarefied rituals that define the sport."
—*People*

"A rich, atmospheric murder mystery . . . rife with love, scandal, anger, transgression, redemption, greed, and nobility, all of which make good reading."
—San Jose *Mercury News*

The Sister Jane series

Outfoxed
Hotspur
Full Cry
The Hunt Ball
The Hounds and the Fury
The Tell-Tale Horse
Hounded to Death
Fox Tracks
Let Sleeping Dogs Lie
Crazy Like a Fox
Homeward Hound

Books by Rita Mae Brown with Sneaky Pie Brown

Wish You Were Here
Rest in Pieces
Murder at Monticello
Pay Dirt
Murder, She Meowed
Murder on the Prowl
Cat on the Scent
Sneaky Pie's Cookbook for Mystery Lovers
Pawing Through the Past
Claws and Effect
Catch as Cat Can
The Tail of the Tip-Off
Whisker of Evil
Cat's Eyewitness
Sour Puss
Puss 'n Cahoots
The Purrfect Murder
Santa Clawed
Cat of the Century
Hiss of Death
The Big Cat Nap
Sneaky Pie for President
The Litter of the Law
Nine Lives to Die
Tail Gate
Tall Tail
A Hiss Before Dying
Probable Claws
Whiskers in the Dark

The Nevada series

A Nose for Justice
Murder Unleashed

Books by Rita Mae Brown

Animal Magnetism: My Life with Creatures Great and Small
The Hand That Cradles the Rock
Songs to a Handsome Woman
The Plain Brown Rapper
Rubyfruit Jungle
In Her Day
Six of One
Southern Discomfort
Sudden Death
High Hearts
Started from Scratch: A Different Kind of Writer's Manual
Bingo
Venus Envy
Dolley: A Novel of Dolley Madison in Love and War
Riding Shotgun
Rita Will: Memoir of a Literary Rabble-Rouser
Loose Lips
Alma Mater
The Sand Castle
Cakewalk

HOMEWARD HOUND

HOMEWARD HOUND

A NOVEL

RITA MAE BROWN

ILLUSTRATED BY LEE GILDEA, JR.

BALLANTINE BOOKS
NEW YORK

Homeward Hound is a work of fiction. Names, characters, places, and incidents are the products of the author's imagination or are used fictitiously. Any resemblance to actual events, locales, or persons, living or dead, is entirely coincidental.

2019 Ballantine Books Trade Paperback Edition

Published in the United States by Ballantine Books, an imprint of Random House, a division of Penguin Random House LLC, New York.

BALLANTINE and the HOUSE colophon are registered trademarks of Penguin Random House LLC.

Originally published in hardcover in the United States by Ballantine Books, an imprint of Random House, a division of Penguin Random House LLC, in 2018.

LIBRARY OF CONGRESS CATALOGING-IN-PUBLICATION DATA
Names: Brown, Rita Mae, author. | Gildea, Lee, Jr., illustrator.
Title: Homeward hound: a novel / Rita Mae Brown; illustrated by Lee Gildea.
Description: First edition. | New York: Ballantine Books [2018] |
Series: The Sister Jane series; 11 Identifiers: LCCN 2018031900 | ISBN 9780399178399 (trade paperback) | ISBN 9780399178382 (ebook)
Subjects: LCSH: Arnold, Jane (Fictitious character)—Fiction. | Fox hunting—Fiction. | Hunters (Horses)—Fiction. | Foxes—Fiction. | Murder—Investigation—Fiction. |
BISAC: FICTION / Suspense. | GSAFD: Suspense fiction.
Classification: LCC PS3552.R698 H59 2018 | DDC 813/.54—dc23
LC record available at lccn.loc.gov/2018031900

Printed in the United States of America on acid-free paper

randomhousebooks.com

2 4 6 8 9 7 5 3 1

Dedicated to Mr. and Mrs. James Evert,
who taught us at South Side tennis courts and
later at Holiday Park tennis courts that it is
the Ten Commandments not the Ten Suggestions

CAST OF CHARACTERS

THE HUMANS

Jane Arnold, MFH, "Sister," runs The Jefferson Hunt. MFH stands for Master of Foxhounds, the individual who runs the hunt, deals with every crisis both on and off the field. She is strong, bold, loves her horses and her hounds. In 1974, her fourteen-year-old son was killed in a tractor accident. That loss deepened her, taught her to cherish every minute. She's had lots of minutes as she's in her early seventies, but she has no concept of age.

Shaker Crown hunts the hounds. He tries to live up to the traditions of this ancient sport, which goes back to the pharaohs. He and Sister work well together, truly enjoy each other. He is in his mid-forties. Divorced for many years and a bit gun-shy.

Gray Lorillard isn't cautious in the hunt field, but he is cautious off it as he was a partner in one of the most prestigious accounting firms in D.C. He knows how the world really works and, although retired, is often asked to solve problems at his former firm. He is smart, handsome, in his early sixties, and is African American.

Crawford Howard is best described by Aunt Daniella who commented, “There’s a great deal to be said about new money and Crawford means to say it all.” He started an outlaw pack of hounds when Sister did not ask him to be her Joint Master. Slowly, he is realizing you can’t push people around in this part of the world. Fundamentally, he is a decent and generous man.

Sam Lorillard is Gray’s younger brother. Sam Lorillard works at Crawford’s stables. Crawford hired Sam when no one else would, so Sam is loyal. He blew a full scholarship to Harvard thanks to the bottle. He’s good with horses. His brother saved him and he’s clean, but so many people feel bad about what might have been. He focuses on the future.

Daniella Laprade is Gray and Sam’s aunt. She is an extremely healthy nonagenarian who isn’t above shaving a year or two off her age. She may even be older than her stated ninety-four. Her past is dotted with three husbands and numerous affairs, all carried out with discretion.

Anne Harris, “Tootie,” left Princeton in her freshman year as she missed foxhunting in Virginia so very much. Her father had a cow, cut her out of his will. She takes classes at the University of Virginia and is now twenty-two and shockingly beautiful. She is African American.

Yvonne Harris, Tootie’s mother, is a former model who has fled Chicago and her marriage. She’s filed for divorce from Victor Harris, a hard-driving businessman who built an African American media empire. She built it with him. She is trying to understand Tootie, feels she was not so much a bad mother as an absent one. Her experience has been different from her daughter’s and Tootie’s freedoms were won by Yvonne’s generation and those prior. Yvonne doesn’t understand that Tootie doesn’t understand.

Alfred and Binky DuCharme are two brothers in their early seventies who hate each other so much they haven't spoken for over fifty years. This is because Binky stole and married Alfred's girlfriend.

Margaret DuCharme, M.D., is Alfred's daughter and she's acted as a go-between for her father and uncle since childhood. Her cousin, Binky's son Arthur, also acts as a go-between and both the cousins are just fed up with it. They are in their early forties, Margaret being more successful than Arthur but he's happy enough.

Walter Lungrun, M.D., JT-MFH, is a cardiologist who has hunted with Sister since his boyhood. He is the late Raymond Arnold's son, which Sister knows. No one talks about it and Walter's father always acted as though he were Walter's father. It's the way things are done around here. Let sleeping dogs lie.

Betty Franklin is an honorary whipper-in, which means she doesn't get paid. Whippers-in emit a glamorous sheen to other foxhunters and it is a daring task. One must know a great deal and be able to ride hard, jump high, think in a split second. She is Sister's best friend and in her mid-fifties. Everyone loves Betty.

Bobby Franklin especially loves Betty as he is her husband. He leads Second Flight, those riders who may take modest jumps but not the big ones. He and Betty own a small printing press and nearly lost their shirts when computers started printing out stuff. But people have returned to true printing, fine papers, etc. They're doing okay.

Kasmir Barbhaiya made his money in India in pharmaceuticals. Educated in an English public school, thence on to Oxford, he is highly intelligent and tremendously wealthy. Widowed, he moved to Virginia to be close to an old Oxford classmate and his wife. He owns marvelous horses and rides them well. He thought he would forever be alone but the Fates thought otherwise. Love has found him in the form of Alida Dalzell.

Edward and Tedi Bancroft, in their eighties, are stalwarts of The Jefferson Hunt and dear friends of Sister's. Evangelista, Edward's deceased sister, had an affair with Weevil's grandfather, although hushed up, it caused uproar in the Bancroft family.

Ben Sidell is the county sheriff, who is learning to hunt and loves it. Nonni, his horse, takes good care of him. He learns far more about the county by hunting than if he just stayed in his squad car. He dates Margaret DuCharme, M.D., an unlikely pairing that works.

Cynthia Skiff Cane hunts Crawford's outlaw pack. He's gone through three other huntsmen but she can handle him. Sam Lorillard helps, too.

Cindy Chandler owns Foxglove Farm, one of The Jefferson Hunt's fixtures. She's not much in evidence in this volume but, like all landowners, she is important.

Victor Harris is Tootie's father. Jerk doesn't begin to cover it.

Cecil and Violet Van Dorn, in their middle eighties, own Beveridge Hundred. No longer hunting, they remain members of the club.

Dewey Milford is president of Milford Enterprises, the largest real estate firm in the county. Helpful in the hunt field, a good rider. Most people like him.

Charlotte Abruza, in her early thirties, at least, is a historical researcher. She understands the latest methods, can use technologies not available until recently.

Gregory Luckham heads Soliden, a huge energy company headquartered in Richmond, Virginia. He foxhunts with the hunt outside of the capital city. Smooth, well-educated, he understands profit, the core of business.

Jude Hevener
Jackie Fugate
Carson Blanton
Sheriff Sidell's new young assistants

Rory Boone is Sam Lorillard's best friend. He also works for Crawford Howard.

THE AMERICAN FOXHOUNDS

Lighter than the English foxhound, with a somewhat slimmer head, they have formidable powers of endurance and remarkable noses.

Cora is the head female. What she says goes.

Asa is the oldest hunting male hound, and he is wise.

Diana is steady, in the prime of her life, and brilliant. There's no other word for her but "brilliant."

Dasher is Diana's littermate and often overshadowed by his sister, but he sticks to business and is coming into his own.

Dragon is also a littermate of the above D hounds. He is arrogant, can lose his concentration, and tries to lord it over other hounds.

Dreamboat is of the same breeding as Diana, Dasher, and Dragon, but a few years younger.

Hounds take the first initial of their mother's name. Following are hounds ordered from older to younger. No unentered hounds are included in this list. An unentered hound is not yet on the Master of Foxhounds stud books and not yet hunting with the pack. They are in essence kindergartners. **Trinity, Tinsel, Trident, Ardent, Thimble, Twist, Tootsie, Trooper, Taz, Tatoo, Parker, Pickens, Zane, Zorro, Zandy, Giorgio, Pookah, Pansy, Audrey, Aero, Angle, Aces.**

THE HORSES

Keepsake, TB/QH, Bay; **Lafayette,** TB, Gray; **Rickyroo,** TB, Bay; **Aztec,** TB, Chestnut; **Matador,** TB, Flea-bitten Gray. All are Sister's geldings. **Showboat, Hojo, Gunpowder,** and **Kilowatt,** all TBs, are Shaker's horses.

Outlaw, QH, Buckskin, and **Magellan,** TB, Dark Bay (which is really black), are Betty's horses.

Wolsey, TB, Flaming Chestnut, is Gray's horse. His red coat gave him his name for Cardinal Wolsey.

Iota, TB, Bay, is Tootie's horse.

Matchplay and **Midshipman** are young Thoroughbreds of Sister's that are being brought along. Takes good time to make a solid foxhunter. Sister never hurries a horse or a hound in its schooling.

Trocadero is young, smart; being trained by Sam Lorillard.

Old Buster has become a babysitter. Owned like Trocadero by Crawford Howard, Sam uses him for Yvonne Harris.

Pokerface and **Corporal** carry Ronnie Haslip. If a guest is a strong rider Ronnie will lend Pokerface. They are good horses.

Bosco, big, kind, carries Dewey, who knows what a good hunter Bosco is. He's part Warmblood, not as fast as a Thoroughbred.

THE FOXES

Reds

Aunt Netty, older, lives at Pattypan Forge. She is overly tidy and likes to give orders.

Uncle Yancy is Aunt Netty's husband but he can't stand her anymore. He lives at the Lorillard farm, has all manner of dens and cubbyholes.

Charlene lives at After All Farm. She comes and goes.

Target is Charlene's mate but he stays at After All. The food supply is steady and he likes the other animals.

Earl has the restored stone stables at Old Paradise all to himself. He has a den in a stall but also makes use of the tack room. He likes the smell of the leather.

Sarge is half-grown. He found a den in big boulders at Old Paradise thanks to help from a doe. It's cozy with straw, old clothing bits, and even a few toys.

James lives behind the mill at Mill Ruins. He is not very social but from time to time will give the hounds a good run.

Ewald is a youngster who was directed to a den in an outbuilding during a hunt. Poor fellow didn't know where he was. The outbuilding at Mill Ruins will be a wonderful home as long as he steers clear of James.

Mr. Nash, young, lives at Close Shave, a farm about six miles from Chapel Cross. Given the housing possibilities and the good food, he is drawn to Old Paradise being restored by Crawford Howard.

Grays

Comet knows everybody and everything. He lives in the old stone foundation part of the rebuilt log-and-frame cottage at Roughneck Farm.

Inky is so dark she's black and she lives in the apple orchard across from the above cottage. She knows the hunt schedule and rarely gives hounds a run. They can just chase someone else.

Georgia moved to the old schoolhouse at Foxglove Farm.

Grenville lives at Mill Ruins, in the back in a big storage shed. This part of the estate is called Shootrough.

Gris lives at Tollbooth Farm in the Chapel Cross area. He's very clever and can slip hounds in the batting of an eye.

Hortensia also lives at Mill Ruins. She's in another outbuilding. All are well constructed and all but the big hay sheds have doors that close, which is wonderful in bad weather.

Vi, young, is the mate of Gris, also young. They live at Tollbooth Farm in pleasant circumstances.

THE BIRDS

Athena, the great horned owl, is two and a half feet tall with a four-foot wingspan. She has many places where she will hole up but her true nest is in Pattypan Forge. It really beats being in a tree hollow. She's gotten spoiled.

Bitsy is eight and a half inches tall with a twenty-inch wingspan. Her considerable lungs make up for her tiny size as she is a screech owl, aptly named. Like Athena, she'll never live in a tree again because she's living in the rafters of Sister's stable. Mice come in to eat the fallen grain. Bitsy feels like she's living in a supermarket.

St. Just, a foot and a half in height with a surprising wingspan of three feet, is a jet-black crow. He hates foxes but is usually sociable with other birds.

SISTER'S HOUSE PETS

Raleigh, a sleek, highly intelligent Doberman, likes to be with Sister. He gets along with the hounds, walks out with them. He tries to get along with the cat, but she's such a snob.

Rooster is a harrier bequeathed to Sister by a dear friend. He likes riding in the car, walking out with hounds, watching everybody and everything. The cat drives him crazy.

Golliwog, or "Golly," is a long-haired calico. All other creatures are lower life-forms. She knows Sister does her best, but still. Golly is Queen of All She Surveys.

SOME USEFUL TERMS

Away. A fox has gone away when he has left the covert. Hounds are away when they have left the covert on the line of the fox.

Brush. The fox's tail.

Burning scent. Scent so strong or hot that hounds pursue the line without hesitation.

Bye day. A day not regularly on the fixture card.

Cap. The fee nonmembers pay to hunt for that day's sport.

Carry a good head. When hounds run well together to a good scent, a scent spread wide enough for the whole pack to feel it.

Carry a line. When hounds follow the scent. This is also called working a line.

Cast. Hounds spread out in search of scent. They may cast themselves or be cast by the huntsman.

Charlie. A term for a fox. A fox may also be called **Reynard.**

Check. When hounds lose the scent and stop. The field must wait quietly while the hounds search for the scent.

Colors. A distinguishing color, usually worn on the collar but sometimes on the facings of a coat, that identifies a hunt. Colors can be awarded only by the Master and can be worn only in the field.

Coop. A jump resembling a chicken coop.

Couple straps. Two-strap hound collars connected by a swivel link. Some members of staff will carry these on the right rear of the saddle. Since the days of the pharaohs in ancient Egypt, hounds have been brought to the meets coupled. Hounds are always spoken of and counted in couples. Today, hounds walk or are driven to the meets. Rarely, if ever, are they coupled, but a whipper-in still carries couple straps should a hound need assistance.

Covert. A patch of woods or bushes where a fox might hide. Pronounced "cover."

Cry. How one hound tells another what is happening. The sound will differ according to the various stages of the chase. It's also called giving tongue and should occur when a hound is working a line.

Cub hunting. The informal hunting of young foxes in the late summer and early fall, before formal hunting. The main purpose is to enter young hounds into the pack. Until recently only the most knowledgeable members were invited to cub hunt, since they would not interfere with young hounds.

Dog fox. The male fox.

Dog hound. The male hound.

Double. A series of short, sharp notes blown on the horn to alert all that a fox is afoot. The gone away series of notes is a form of doubling the horn.

Draft. To acquire hounds from another hunt is to accept a draft.

Draw. The plan by which a fox is hunted or searched for in a certain area, such as a covert.

Draw over the fox. Hounds go through a covert where the fox is but cannot pick up his scent. The only creature who understands how this is possible is the fox.

Drive. The desire to push the fox, to get up with the line. It's a very desirable trait in hounds, so long as they remain obedient.

Dually. A one-ton pickup truck with double wheels in back.

Dwell. To hunt without getting forward. A hound who dwells is a bit of a putterer.

Enter. Hounds are entered into the pack when they first hunt, usually during cubbing season.

Field. The group of people riding to hounds, exclusive of the Master and hunt staff.

Field Master. The person appointed by the Master to control the field. Often it is the Master him- or herself.

Fixture. A card sent to all dues-paying members, stating when and where the hounds will meet. A fixture card properly received is an invitation to hunt. This means the card would be mailed or handed to a member by the Master.

Flea-bitten. A gray horse with spots or ticking that can be black or chestnut.

Gone away. The call on the horn when the fox leaves the covert.

Gone to ground. A fox who has ducked into his den, or some other refuge, has gone to ground.

Good night. The traditional farewell to the Master after the hunt, regardless of the time of day.

Gyp. The female hound.

Hilltopper. A rider who follows the hunt but does not jump. Hilltoppers are also called the Second Flight. The jumpers are called the First Flight.

Hoick. The huntsman's cheer to the hounds. It is derived from the Latin *hic haec hoc,* which means "here."

Hold hard. To stop immediately.

Huntsman. The person in charge of the hounds, in the field and in the kennel.

Kennelman. A hunt staff member who feeds the hounds and cleans the kennels. In wealthy hunts there may be a number of kennelmen. In hunts with a modest budget, the huntsman or even the Master cleans the kennels and feeds the hounds.

Lark. To jump fences unnecessarily when hounds aren't running. Masters frown on this, since it is often an invitation to an accident.

Lieu in. Norman term for go in.

Lift. To take the hounds from a lost scent in the hopes of finding a better scent farther on.

Line. The scent trail of the fox.

Livery. The uniform worn by the professional members of the hunt staff. Usually it is scarlet, but blue, yellow, brown, and gray are also used. The recent dominance of scarlet has to do with people buying coats off the rack as opposed to having tailors cut them. (When anything is mass-produced, the choices usually dwindle, and such is the case with livery.)

Mask. The fox's head.

Meet. The site where the day's hunting begins.

MFH. The Master of Foxhounds; the individual in charge of the hunt: hiring, firing, landowner relations, opening territory (in large hunts this is the job of the hunt secretary), developing the pack of hounds, and determining the first cast of each meet. As in any leadership position, the Master is also the lightning rod for criticism. The Master may hunt the hounds, although this is usually done by a professional huntsman, who is also responsible for the hounds in the field and at the kennels. A long relationship between a Master and a huntsman allows the hunt to develop and grow.

Nose. The scenting ability of a hound.

Override. To press hounds too closely.

Overrun. When hounds shoot past the line of a scent. Often the scent has been diverted or foiled by a clever fox.

Ratcatcher. Informal dress worn during cubbing season and bye days.

Stern. A hound's tail.

Stiff-necked fox. One who runs in a straight line.

Strike hounds. Those hounds that, through keenness, nose, and often higher intelligence, find the scent first and press it.

Tail hounds. Those hounds running at the rear of the pack. This is not necessarily because they aren't keen; they may be older hounds.

Tallyho. The cheer when the fox is viewed. Derived from the Norman *ty a hillaut,* thus coming into the English language in 1066.

Tongue. To vocally pursue a fox.

View halloo (halloa). The cry given by a staff member who sees a fox. Staff may also say tallyho or, should the fox turn back, tally-back. One reason a different cry may be used by staff, especially in territory where the huntsman can't see the staff, is that the field in their enthusiasm may cheer something other than a fox.

Vixen. The female fox.

Walk. Puppies are walked out in the summer and fall of their first year. It's part of their education and a delight for both puppies and staff.

Whippers-in. Also called whips, these are the staff members who assist the huntsman, who make sure the hounds "do right."

HOMEWARD HOUND

CHAPTER 1

"Ouch, dammit." Sister Jane stepped down from the small stool. "Sorry." She patted Aztec's neck, her chestnut gelding.

"I thought you were apologizing to us." Betty Franklin, also braiding her horse, Outlaw, leaned over his neck to look at her friend and master.

Sister Jane Arnold was master of The Jefferson Hunt, had been for over forty years. She loved being a master, making decisions, solving problems. She did not love braiding, however.

"I can do that for you." Tootie Harris, early twenties, a whipper-in, offered.

"I know you can, Angel, but I think I should braid my own horse."

"Arthritis." Her huntsman, Shaker Crown, braiding his horse, teased her. "I'm starting to get it. Anyway, I thought this is what children are for, braiding."

"You know, he has a point." Betty was standing on her low stool to reach the mane, a small bit of thick mane between her fingers, the clipped yarn in her mouth, which she took out to speak.

"Think it will be a lot of people tomorrow?" Weevil, the new, gorgeous, male whipper-in, hailing from Canada, asked.

"Weevil, usually is." Sister climbed back up on the stool. "Matador is standing nicely for you."

"He's a good boy with a silky mane. Makes it easy," the handsome blond replied.

"Just think, everyone who will hunt tomorrow is doing as we're doing. I like to think of that, all of us trying to make our horses beautiful for Christmas Hunt," Betty said.

The large end stable doors opened, Sam Lorillard with Rory Boone came in, shutting the doors behind them.

Sam pulled off his lumberjack cap. "Cold out there. Got off work early."

"Cold enough in here." Shaker tugged at Showboat's mane with a short metal comb.

"We're here to polish the tack. If you all are determined to braid your horses, we might as well get working on the tack."

"The only reason you two are doing the tack, and there's a mess of it, is it's warmer in the tack room," Betty good-naturedly said.

Sam, the brother of Sister's gentleman friend, grinned. "That's why we're doing it."

The two men, friends from their days spent living under the downtown bridge by the train station, stripped off their coats, walked into the paneled tack room. Both men had endured detox and counseling, although at different times. Neither of them could get a good job once clean because too many people remembered their misdeeds when drunk. Both wound up working for Crawford Howard, a man with an outlaw pack of hounds. As he hailed from Indiana, he took a chance on them and both Sam and Rory were grateful. Crawford and Sister, often crossways with each other, declared a truce thanks to Sam's steady work and putting in a good word for Sister. Sam and Gray, his brother, had known the tall, slender woman most of their lives. She and her late husband would give them horses to ride as kids. Sam, younger, went to Harvard. Gray, a few years older, in his middle sixties now, had received a full scholarship to the Darden School of Business at the University of Virginia and from thence to a large accounting firm in D.C. where he rose to partner. Gray, one of the first African American men to reach such power in our nation's capitol, wore it lightly. The Lorillards were bright people, as was their aunt Daniella Laprade, often married, each husband richer than the last. God knows, in her nineties she might do it again.

Tootie ducked into the tack room for a moment. "Sam, go light on the oil."

"Will do." He smiled at the beautiful young woman, almost a carbon copy of her knockout mother.

Tootie returned to Iota, her horse.

"Master, thank you again for loaning me Matador." Weevil, finishing the braiding, picked up the stool, placing it alongside the stall. "He's got so much scope."

He used the term meaning "the horse could jump both high and wide," much desired in the hunt field.

"It's good for him to be ridden," Sister replied. "I only hunt him about once every two weeks. That will change next season because I really must retire Lafayette."

The gray Thoroughbred, in his stall, shouted, *"I am not retiring. I can still outrun any horse on this farm. Just forget the retirement crap."*

Raleigh, a Doberman, and Rooster, a harrier, Sister's house dogs, both stretched out on benches, tormented the older horse. *"Retire. Eat apples and carrots all day. Hey, maybe you can take up golf."* Raleigh bedeviled him.

"Horses don't play golf, idiot," Lafayette answered quickly.

"I know that," the sleek Doberman, wearing his blue jacket, fired back. *"You can escape and run all over the golf course. Think of the newspaper coverage."*

Rooster joined in. *"Loose horse destroys greens, tears up Ninth Hole."*

"Claims he was chasing a fox," Raleigh added.

Lafayette snorted. *"Better that than dog poop."*

Before this could further develop, Sister's cellphone rang. She stepped down, punched the icon, walked into the tack room.

"You're going in there to get warm," Betty called after her, "leaving us out here to freeze."

"Ronnie? What's up?" she asked the hunt club's treasurer on the line. Although a lawyer, Ronnie liked being treasurer, though he had Gray's help when needed.

"Forgive me, last minute but I'd like to bring a guest from Deep Run."

She dropped into a director's chair while Sam and Rory dismantled a bridle each to completely clean it and shine the bit. No shortcuts.

"Of course, you know I love Deep Run." She did, too, as Deep Run was the grand and glamorous hunt outside Richmond. "Anyone I know?"

"I don't think so. Gregory Luckham. I'm lending him Pokerface." He named one of his horses.

Sister sat up a little straighter. "*The* Gregory Luckham?"

Now both Sam and Rory turned to look at her.

"Yes, we worked together in Richmond, both of us on the Side by Side fundraiser. I found out he hunted. Would you like to join us for dinner at Farmington Country Club?"

"Thank you, Ronnie, no. You know how crazy it gets before one of the big hunts but of course, he is welcome. I look forward to meeting him. Before I forget, Betty and Tootie talked me into braiding with red and green yarn for Christmas. You know I'm not much for that kind of thing but they told me I was an old fart. To my face. Well, Betty, not Tootie, so I relented."

Ronnie, one of Sister's late son's best friends, stifled a laugh. "You are always correct and I try to live up to your standards, but a little bit of Christmas cheer isn't too much a violation of tradition. Good decision."

"You really think so?"

"Sister, you always make the right decision. Which reminds me. Have you looked at the Weather Channel?"

"The snowstorm?"

"They're predicting it for tomorrow afternoon."

"I saw that, too, so I figure we'll hunt for two hours, two and a half, then turn back. I spoke to Kasmir about it and we both decided to move the Christmas breakfast to Boxing Day. This way people can get home ahead of the storm. You know how weathermen dramatize any hint of trouble, so this should calm the nervous."

"Good plan. You were smart to send the email early."

"Ronnie, instant communication means everyone wants a decision pronto. How do I know what will happen tomorrow? The Weather Channel predicts a giant snowflake will fall upon Albemarle County. Everyone panics. I like to think things through and one thing I know I can't think through is the weather. Have you ever noticed how wrong those forecasts usually are?"

He laughed. "I have, but still you were smart. And as I said, you always make the right decision."

She hung up the phone feeling a bit elated.

Sam, rubbing down a rein, said, "The president of Soliden, the big energy company? Gregory Luckham?"

"Yes." She stood up, slipping the phone in her jeans back pocket. "Why?"

Rory answered. "He's a brave man coming here, the outrage over the pipeline."

Sam filled in. "I don't think anyone will do something stupid at the hunt but you never know. People are really passionate about this, cutting trees, violating a national park, harming the environment. And one of the projected paths dips right over the Blue Ridge, tears up Old Paradise, goes across Tattenhall Station straight through Beveridge Hundred. It's lethal." He named beautiful Hunt Club fixtures.

Rory provided the other side. "Jobs. Lots of jobs. Everything is shareholder value. Soliden doesn't care what is ruined, what animals harmed."

"Obviously I'm against the destruction, but I can't believe someone would make a fuss at Christmas Hunt." Sister wondered why so many people were so passive about such things.

"Outsiders?" Sam raised his eyebrows.

"Sam, I truly doubt that Gregory Luckham is advertising that he is coming to Jefferson Hunt's Christmas Hunt." Sister paused. "At least, I hope he's not advertising."

Back in the aisle she mentioned Ronnie's call and heard the same concerns she'd just heard in the tack room.

"Everything will be fine. Come on, it's Christmas." She smiled, climbing back up on the low stepladder. "I don't remember finishing the braids. They're so tight."

No one said a word.

Weevil had finished her braids while she was in the tack room. Took him no time at all.

She led Aztec back into his stall, arranged his good rug on him, walked out sliding the door behind her.

"I don't know which one of you finished my job but I do thank you. My fingers aren't what they once were."

Shaker smiled. "Ah, but Boss, you can still outride any of us."

She laughed. "Now that is a lie. I keep up. And, in truth, I love it. I'm most alive on a horse. Aren't you all?"

They agreed.

Weevil, who was learning to love her, lifted an eyebrow. "Christmas. The birth of our dear Lord." They stopped to look at him. "I believe if Jesus lived here he would be a foxhunter. Scenting is no good in Galilee. But Jesus was a sportsman. He was a fisherman."

They laughed, happy in one another's company. Weevil reminded Sister of her late son, RayRay, Raymond, who died in a farming accident at fourteen in 1974. Weevil possessed Ray's quick way with words, his sense of humor, his love of hounds and hunting. You go on. No matter what happens you go on. She knew despite all, she was a lucky woman. Her husband, Big Ray, was also gone. Ray's boyhood friends, in their fifties now, stayed close to her. And she didn't care if it sounded like wish fulfillment, she could feel her husband's love and her son's love. She never stopped loving them and would love them until the day she died. She could even feel horses, hounds, house dogs, and cats who loved her.

As she swept her eyes over the people in the barn, she thought to herself, *Love is all that matters. It's so simple. Why do people make life so hard?*

Betty interrupted this reverie. "You're wearing garters tomorrow, aren't you?"

"Of course. Why are you asking me?"

"So I'll wear mine. They cut." Betty complained.

"Then put moleskin under your breeches, twit." Sister teased her.

"That's a good idea." Weevil found garters to rub, too.

Sister tapped her head. "You'd be surprised what's up there." Then she thought to herself, *Amor Vincit Omnia. Bless Ovid. Love conquers all.*

CHAPTER 2

Festooned, a huge, perfect Christmas tree commanded the anteroom before the formal dining room. Christmas balls from the 1920s, glittering new balls, angels, all testified to the longevity of Farmington Country Club, plus why throw holiday decorations away? This redbrick Georgian structure, a hint of Palladio, had been designed by Thomas Jefferson as a private residence before politics overtook his life. Like so many old houses, places, it survived tumultuous times, some up, many down, only to fall into the hands of a few who wished to save it. No one could imagine living there as a family, it was simply too enormous, having been built when one housed one's immediate family, often one's in-laws plus every shirttail cousin within a hundred-mile radius. Housing for slaves needed to stand the test of time and they did. Farmington was built to last. The way to save it was to turn it into a country club, which was done in 1927.

Naturally, many were shocked—a commercial venture, how crude. Those many, however, didn't really have two nickels to rub together, much less what it would take to preserve this elegant place. And so Farmington Country Club inched Albemarle County a bit further toward the New South, which, of course, remained the Old South in ways both laudable and detestable.

The club flourished thanks in no small part to a fabulous golf course, expanded over the decades. The old course, built before land became outrageously expensive, could boast par fives, par fours, and this course did that. The shrubs, old trees, exquisite plantings made golfing as much a joy as possible, although clubs still landed in the ponds.

The formal dining room, painted in eighteenth-century subdued colors, remained a steadfast glory, and it was in this glory that a few Jefferson Hunt members gathered before tomorrow's Christmas Hunt.

Ronnie had called together people to meet Gregory Luckham. Dewey Milford, ever at nonprofit fundraisers, was acquainted with Luckham. Ronnie believed more was accomplished socially than was ever accomplished at corporate meetings or on the floor of Congress. So he had invited people who could make a difference.

Gregory, a full head of ginger hair, sat next to Marty Howard, middle-aged, attractive. Marty knew how to get things done. Next to Marty sat Cecil Van Dorn, in his middle eighties, next to him was his wife, Violet Van Dorn. Sometimes they needed to help each other. Crawford was next to Charlotte Abruza, a historian he had hired to firmly place Old Paradise on the historic register as well as fight the pipeline. Old Paradise, founded in 1812 by a beautiful woman raiding the British supply trade, had a great history of feminist values. Sitting next to Charlotte was Dewey Milford, forties, perhaps the county's most successful real estate developer, and then next to Ronnie glowed Yvonne Harris, the former runway model, one of the first African American models to make the cover of *Vogue,* who could destroy a man with one smoldering look.

One tried to seat girl-boy-girl-boy and Ronnie did his best. Given that he was gay, he thought he provided ballast. He wasn't aggressive about being gay; he just was who he was, which was delightful.

"Crawford, I do wish you would hunt tomorrow. For all we know the fox will flee over to Old Paradise. You'll be right at home." Ronnie encouraged him.

Marty smiled. "We'll be there to see you off. Neither Crawford nor I like the cold weather and it's going to be frigid tomorrow, plus the threat of a storm. I just feel that moisture in my bones."

Cecil laughed. "Funny how that happens."

The first round of drinks raised spirits. Everyone reordered, returning to chat.

Crawford, restoring Old Paradise, lived with Marty in a home they had built not far from Sister's place. No one knew if they would move from Beasley Hall to Old Paradise when it was brought back to life. They kept their cards close to their chest but were against the pipeline for obvious reasons. Crawford reluctantly agreed to attend the dinner prodded by Marty. Her lure was that they should meet the enemy face-to-face. Also Charlotte might get a feel for him, as well.

Dewey, single malt scotch in hand, returned to the weather. "You know, Cecil, I think you're right. My broken bones are more accurate than the radar. I'm riding though. Wouldn't miss Christmas Hunt."

Yvonne smiled at Dewey. "My daughter told me you broke your leg last season protecting Freddie Thomas."

"Oh, I wouldn't go that far." He demurred.

"Tootie said Freddie, who is a good rider, skidded into a big jump, her horse lost his footing, and she sailed over the jump as everyone was galloping to it. She said you hauled in your horse, leapt off to turn people away and to see if Freddie was okay when another rider's horse skidded and you were pinned to the jump. The horse kicked your leg. She said it was awful."

"Ah well, that's hunting. We were all lucky it wasn't worse. Freddie was on her feet. I was not." He joked.

Gregory Luckham joined in. "Hunting is not for the faint-hearted. My wife worries about me but I tell her golfing can be dangerous, too. A mis-hit ball or a tossed club can do damage."

They all laughed politely.

Charlotte, in her late twenties, leaned toward Gregory. "Ronnie may have told you, but I am researching the history of Old Paradise. It's fascinating, encompasses so much of not just Virginia's history but our nation's. We will be using ground-penetrating radar once the ground thaws a little. There must be many bodies buried out there, unmarked."

"Some might be Monacans. They lived there before we moved this far west. Dolley Madison mentioned the Monacans." Violet, who was an avid reader and a member of The Colonial Dames, evidenced an interest in tribal Virginians.

Gregory, knowing what such a finding could do to the projected pipeline route, replied noncommittally, "I'll eagerly await your findings."

"I often wonder what's under the ground at our place?" Cecil spoke for Beveridge Hundred, his estate, which had started as a log cabin after the Revolutionary War.

Crawford looked at Gregory. "If we find bodies, you'll wind up with miles of rerouting. Isn't the pipeline now six hundred miles?"

"It is. You know the Army Corps of Engineers, the Virginia State Water Control Board, other agencies will review every inch."

"Doesn't that depend on how much Soliden pays them under the table?" Crawford threw down the gauntlet.

Gregory reddened. "Soliden would never do that."

"At five million eight hundred thirty-three dollars a mile, the hell you wouldn't."

"Crawford." Marty placed her hand on his forearm.

"Marty, we've poured seven million dollars to date on Old Paradise's restoration. I'll be damned if I'm going to see it torn up. Plus that doesn't consider what I paid for it initially."

"I heard you stole it." Gregory was now angry.

"Let me tell you something, asshole. If you try to put that pipeline through Old Paradise, I won't shoot your surveyors or workmen. I'll shoot you and that's a promise. Come on, Honey." He grabbed her hand, lifting her out of the chair.

As Crawford and Marty charged out, Charlotte excused herself to follow. The other diners, breathless with suppressed excitement, were already texting their friends.

Gregory, motionless for a moment, then knocked back his drink. "I apologize. I should never have let him get to me. I don't need to tell you how volatile a subject the pipeline is. That man may be rich and smart, wanted me to know he's spoiling for a fight. He's a bully, which means maybe he isn't all that smart."

"He reminds me of my ex-husband, a driven man with no sense about other people. People like that only see their goal." Yvonne paused. "Mind you, Mr. Luckham, although I am a newcomer, the pipeline does seem extreme. Surely there has to be a way to accomplish what you need to do without so much, well, drama."

Dazzled, Gregory took a deep breath. "I hope so. I don't get up in the morning and say, 'How can I upset people today? How can I ruin Virginia's environment or heritage?' But we need to cut our dependency on foreign oil. The pipeline is a way to do that, I truly believe this or I wouldn't push for it. As president of Soliden I may be able to sway the board regarding routes, but one way or another the pipeline will be built, all six hundred or more miles of it. One of the reasons I came here apart from wanting to hunt behind Sister Jane was I wanted to see this territory with my own eyes. I've pored over U.S. Geological Survey maps, Googled everything including Old Paradise. It's not the same as hunting where you truly see the spine of the land, so to speak." He kept his left hand under the table as he had cut his palm yesterday, so he wore a thin cotton glove over the bandage. No one asked about it, although they noticed. The outline of a pinky ring could be seen.

"You will see it indeed," Ronnie promised.

"I am so glad to hear you say that," Violet quietly said. "You see a bit of your pipeline, the northernmost route, would traverse our land."

"You have been kind not to be angry with me." He smiled at the lovely older woman.

Dewey spoke. "The Van Dorns own Beveridge Hundred, which is seven hundred acres. It's impeccably preserved. I call upon Cecil and Violet for their excellent company but also to hear the stories of the place. And, I believe, Yvonne, you rent the dependency?" He knew she did, of course.

"I do," she affirmed.

"Seven hundred acres is quite a lot to manage." Gregory nodded to the Van Dorns. "More power to you."

"Truthfully, it's getting to be a bit much," Cecil confessed. "Crawford has five thousand acres across the road plus the land he owns east of here, another five or six hundred acres. And as you also probably know, Kasmir Barbhaiya owns two thousand acres, which abuts Beveridge Hundred. Chapel Crossroads is one of the last places in this country where large estates remain intact."

Dewey, second drink in hand, then added, "You can understand why the Chapel Crossroads area is of such importance."

"Yes, I can." Gregory reached for his second drink being handed to him from the tray. "Ronnie, you've put me in the lion's den."

"No," Ronnie quickly rejoined. "I work for you. We will defend you in court and you know there will be lawsuits, although I hope no need for any here. I wanted you to sit with my neighbors. Of course, you can understand there is emotion, but then again, the final route is not yet agreed upon. As for Crawford, I actually thought he would behave. He's not going to have another opportunity like this."

"Well, perhaps neither am I," Gregory ruefully said.

"Surely, you'll return. For one thing, you haven't met Aunt Daniella." Yvonne smiled at him.

"Aunt Daniella?"

"A great beauty in her day," Ronnie told him.

"And still not bad to look at. She admits to being ninety-four." Yvonne threw that in. "But she knows so much of the real history of these places. The stuff that doesn't make it into the history books. The stuff that young research lady will never uncover."

"Ronnie, every old place has a story about treasure or murder or both." Violet looked up as her first course was delivered. "Beveridge Hundred is supposed to contain a fortune in silver stolen from Mexicans during the Mexican-American War. I suppose even then Mexico was famous for its silver and silversmiths. Mind you, Cecil and I have never found so much as a fork."

They all laughed. Conversation, more relaxed now, included the latest on the news, what films they had seen, books read, as well as hunting in central Virginia.

After dessert, as they walked through the anteroom, Gregory promised them. "Please call upon me anytime. Don't think of me as a bad guy or your enemy. I will listen to everything you say and we are not committed to this being the final route. I will do my best to help you preserve your estates, to keep the beauty of this place."

Yvonne, walking close to him, remarked, "Does this make it more difficult for you? Yes, we want to keep things as they are, but you can also call upon us."

"Thank you." Gregory looked to Ronnie. "This is where you are invaluable. It isn't just dollars and cents. It's public relations. Soliden has been a leader in the state in contributing to the arts, to education. I think we can find a way to protect your environment and history. We need to work together."

"Well said." Dewey's deep voice carried throughout the room.

"You know, we're always the bad guys—our entire industry. But this nation runs on oil and gas. For all the talk about alternative energy, and we are making some progress, we are utterly dependent on gas and oil." Gregory pulled a beautiful ribbed gold cigarette case from his inside pocket, offering anyone a cigarette as they would soon be outside. They refused. He slipped the case back into the inside pocket of his coat.

"Yes, we are." Ronnie flatly agreed, as did Dewey.

Gregory walked with them, although he was staying at the country club. At the front door he mentioned to the Van Dorns and Yvonne, "Perhaps I will see Beveridge Hundred tomorrow."

"Up to the fox." Ronnie laughed.

"Doesn't mean we can't all have a drink at the house after the hunt. Our little two-stall barn is empty. You can put your horses in there and then drive home." Cecil smiled.

"Perfect." Gregory smiled.

CHAPTER 3

Rainbow splinters, brilliant shards of purple, blue, green, yellow, orange, and red dazzled the eye as they flew off horses' hooves, rose up behind hound paws. Christmas Hunt, Saturday, December 23, got off to a perfect start from Tattenhall Station, the revitalized formerly abandoned train station in the westernmost part of the county. Snow clung to the Victorian bric-a-brac, horse trailers filled the old parking lot, a few old hitching posts still intact. Kasmir Barbhaiya, a fabulously wealthy middle-aged man from India, educated in England, bought all the land from the railroad, restoring the station as a clubhouse for The Jefferson Hunt. He built a true Virginia clapboard farmhouse for himself, elegant, modest, historically correct at the highest point of the land, some two thousand acres.

Christmas Hunt is the third of the High Holy Days in foxhunting. Opening Hunt is the first, then Thanksgiving, also often the children's hunt, and lastly New Year's Hunt. A High Holy Day involved wearing one's most formal attire, a shadbelly or weazlebelly, a tailcoat for women and men respectively, a glossy top hat, boots polished to such a shine a man could shave using them. The tack on the horses evidenced not so much as a smudge. Bits gleamed, as did spurs, and every single horse was braided, eight braids for a gelding, nine braids for a mare, and the Master counted. If something was amiss, Sister proved gentle about it. Sister would never criticize someone in front of others. Actually, she didn't have to do so. Every hunt field in every foxhunting club in North America contains fashionistas, usually a woman of middle years or beyond who recalled the glories of Mainbocher or Balenciaga. Somewhat younger women might know Saint Laurent, Halston, or de Givenchy and those even younger focused on Jil Sander. A whisper from one of "the dragons," as they were referred to behind their backs, usually had the corrective effect.

A gentleman noticing a misplaced stock tie pin, or gloves the wrong color, usually tried to buttonhole the offender at the trailer for a confidential word and often a loan of proper gear. Experienced foxhunters carried all manner of goods in their trailers and trucks: extra gloves (never black), most especially string gloves for under one's stirrup leathers placed with the rear of the glove facing the front. Almost everyone stashed extra stock ties because was there ever a hunt when someone didn't stab themselves, blood spurting over the shockingly white tie? Many a rider rode out with thumbs like a pincushion, for those damned pins were lethal. However, properly placed, the pins looked divine and held down one's tie, a four in hand no less.

A High Holy Day created stress. People expanded their vocabulary of abuse while their horses simply turned their heads in amusement. Humans were a volatile lot.

But it mattered. Why? Because those people in the hunt field measured up to sartorial tradition close to four hundred years in practice. Before that, there was hunting on horseback for stag, boar. Fox was considered inferior game to the first two creatures but one just doesn't blow off four hundred years, and the fox moved up in status by the early eighteenth century. At least one didn't blow off tradition when riding with The Jefferson Hunt.

As the ninety-some people trotted out behind Tattenhall Station, with three inches of powdery snow on the ground that only enhanced their turnout, an observer could easily think this was the eighteenth century. Some people from "other parts," as was said in central Virginia, felt they were still living in the same. No one argued the point. Why lower yourself?

The dots of scarlet weazlebellys, scarlet frock coats for the men who had earned their colors, caused Charlotte to exclaim, "How beautiful."

"Never fails to impress." Marty Howard thought the black shadbellys on the ladies quite slimming.

Hands in pockets, the cold seeped into one's bones. Crawford nodded to people once mounted. Over the last year he, thanks to Marty, Sam, and Skiff, his huntswoman, reached a workable accord with Jefferson Hunt.

Sister, happy to have Sam in her hunt field, settling a youngster for Crawford, kept the relationship friendly. She invited Skiff to bring Crawford's outlaw pack to her farm in the summers once a week so they could walk out with her hounds. She planned a joint meet with his hounds in her territory and vice versa. This last consideration violated Master of Foxhound of America rules about outlaw packs.

The MFHA forbade recognized packs and their members from congress with outlaw packs. Well and good, but Crawford lay smack in her best territory, and his portfolio burst as did his bank account. Best you reach a working accord with such a person.

Crawford, too, began to see the wisdom of assistance from someone who knew as much as Sister. Also, some of these people were his neighbors.

"Perhaps I should add foxhunting to my research," Charlotte said. "I bet Sophie Marquet hunted."

"She had her own pack." Crawford knew a bit about the fabled founder of Old Paradise, her fortune made from her beauty and raiding British supply and payroll wagons during the War of 1812.

"As do you, Darling." Marty slipped her arm through his.

Crawford stiffened, having just caught sight of a smartly turned-out Gregory Luckham. "That man is either thickheaded or impossibly arrogant or both. To show up here."

"You knew he was riding," Marty, voice calm, cooed. "Why dignify him with noticing?"

Crawford grunted.

Charlotte, taking her cue from Marty, said, "Seeing how incredible this territory is, how much land is out here in the Chapel Crossroads area, he might realize he's facing an expensive, toxic even, fight."

"Toxic. Good word." Crawford grinned. "Where's Sam?"

"Coming up beside Gray. Trocadero looks calm. Sam is good for him." Marty praised Sam.

"He does look calm." Crawford wanted to hunt the flashy youngster next season.

Gregory Luckham chatted up Kasmir, remarking on how Tattenhall Station looked like something out of a Victorian photograph.

Kasmir, smiling and subtle, acknowledged the compliment, adding, "My wish is it will remain so, a step back in time."

That was much better than growling, "No pipeline."

Crawford's other stableman—not a rider, more of a cleaner, repairman, turning horses in and out—had his hand on Sam's foot. The two laughed about something. Then Rory moved through the people, walking over to Crawford, Marty, and Charlotte.

"Storm's not supposed to hit until later but you can feel the mercury dropping," the barrel-chested fellow declared. "Glad I put on extra layers."

"Glad I'm not riding," Crawford said. "My feet are cold enough now and these Eddie Bauer boots are supposed to stay warm up to minus twenty degrees Fahrenheit."

"My feet are cold, too," Marty agreed. "Why don't we get in our cars?"

"You girls go ahead," Crawford advised. "Rory and I will take a look at the Carriage House. I want to make sure the delivered lumber is all inside. I didn't spend all that money to have it ruined by weather."

He and Rory headed for his Range Rover while the women eagerly piled into her Range Rover. Marty cut on the motor and the heat. They watched the hunt move off. Then they headed back to the Howards' big estate.

The sky, slate gray, seemed to darken a bit.

As the riders moved south, behind the station, the sound of hoofbeats muffled by the snow still provided that rhythm of horse gaits, a rhythm put to good effect by the Roman poet Horace and many poets later. Poetry and music mimic natural sounds and rhythms.

Funny what goes through your head, Sister thought to herself as she held the reins lightly in her begloved hands, mustard colored. If the weather turned wet she'd reach under her saddle flap, leg forward, pull out a string glove from under the stirrup leathers, put it on, repeat the procedure for the opposite side. Her hands would get wet but the string gloves would not slide on the leather reins. You could keep your grip. Sister had hunted as a child. It came as easily as breathing, and along with it came a deep appreciation and love of nature, as well as the fact that no human being, hound, or horse was as intelligent as the fox.

Off they rode. Ronnie Haslip rode alongside Gregory Luckham, his scarlet tails faded to perfection, which meant a long-lived foxhunter. His boots, made by Henry Maxwell, an English company, cost about seven thousand dollars new if bespoke: a subtle reminder of status, but a reminder nonetheless.

No one said a word about the pipeline uproar even though most of those mounted people felt queasy about it. As hounds were not yet cast, whispered conversation could commence. These little moments usually involved a comment about your neighbor's horse, hounds, or the weather. You could be next to an Oscar winner and what would you say? "Nice horse. Good mover."

If ever there was a sport that practiced equality, it was foxhunting. You could either ride the horse or you couldn't. There were people out there in the invigorating air—they said invigorating but it was damned cold—who barely had two nickels to rub together. There were people like Kasmir who had billions and many who had a million or two, but most of these riders were middle-class whites and blacks, passionate about the game, adrenaline pumping.

In the old days, during slavery and after, the African Americans rode as grooms, which meant they had to extricate their white employer or owner from trouble. Times had changed, perhaps not as fast as some would have it, but they had changed for the better.

Following along in Daniella Laprade's big-ass Range Rover—it was a vehicle made for country life so many people owned one—was Yvonne Harris. A conservative estimate was that Yvonne was worth double-digit millions having built an entertainment empire with her despised ex-husband in Chicago. Being driven, Aunt Daniella, who was coy about her age, smiled seraphically when people waved at her.

And you'd better wave at Aunt Dan. A word from this formidable lady could make or break you.

"Who is that with Ronnie?" Aunt Dan inquired.

Yvonne replied, "Gregory Luckham, the president of Soliden Company, the big oil company embroiled in the fracking uproar. Had dinner with him and the Van Dorns last night. I'll tell you about it as we drive along."

"Good for Ronnie, having him over land that is endangered." Aunt Dan, eyesight good, squinted. "Why do people think we can enjoy all our comforts, electricity, cars, you name it, without despoiling the environment? If it isn't oil it's coal and if it's windmills then it kills the birds in flight. People don't want to face the truth."

Dewey Milford waved at Aunt Dan, who waved back. "Sneakiest real estate agent in Virginia, I swear. Just has an instinct for what the new people want."

"Oh, Aunt Dan, who is that with Sam?"

Gray Lorillard, Sister's partner—her generation would not say lover—and Gray's brother, Sam, were Daniella's nephews, her son having died two years ago. She was always close to her nephews but now closer.

"The slight fellow?"

"Yes."

"That's Raymie Woolfe."

"He looks comfortable."

"Steeplechase jockey. He and Sam competed against each other when young, then Sam went off to Harvard and"—a long breath—"came home from Harvard."

Yvonne had heard all this before for Sam, alcoholic, lost his scholarship at Harvard as well as his discipline. He slunk home in disgrace, found jobs working with horses, but wound up living at the train station with the rest of the drunks. His brother saved him by throwing him into a program in Greenville, North Carolina. Gray paid for it, too. Never threw it up in his brother's face. Sam had been sober for over a decade and was now Yvonne's riding instructor, for Crawford built a huge indoor arena big enough for indoor polo. She was determined to ride.

Aunt Dan, noticing the conspicuous silence, grumbled. "Threw away a brilliant future. Brilliant."

"He has restored himself. He's a good man, Aunt Dan. You can be proud of him. Do we need another asshole lawyer from Harvard?"

At this the older woman exploded in laughter. "You're sweet on him."

"I am not. I am never having another man in my life again."

"Well, baby girl, send them to me. I might be old but I can still wear their ass out. I've lost count of my husbands but I could handle another—if the price is right."

They both laughed as the field broke into a slow canter; all conversation stopped.

Shaker Crown, the huntsman in his middle forties, rode ahead of Sister and the field. The hounds, eager, in front of him, picked up scent. As the snow lay on the ground but lightly, the fox would not be hampered. If so, Sister would have canceled the hunt. One must always give the quarry a sporting chance, which is why if a fox is spotted one hollers, "Tallyho" after counting to twenty. Actually only a flight leader or a whipper-in should do that, but in the excitement of seeing an insouciant fox, they are all insouciant, the person bellows, hat off pointing in the direction the fox was moving. If they wear a cap with a strap then they stretch out their hand using a handkerchief or their crop.

The fox probably would have preferred hearing, "Isn't he handsome?" but "Tallyho" would do.

Looking down, Shaker noticed fresh tracks. Scent held, not hot but not fading. Promising.

He didn't blow his horn. Their noses were down. Why bring them up? He couldn't stand a noisy huntsman. Shaker, set in his ways, thought only of his hounds. Never bring their noses up. He would call or blow a bit more often in rough territory or heavy woods just to let his whippers-in know where he or Sister was. As the Blue Ridge Mountains loomed to his right, to the west, one could easily ride into a ravine; sound would bounce around. Now with the leaves off the deciduous trees, sound carried much better, but sound and wind by the mountains could play tricks on you. Even the hounds with their fabulous hearing might pause, listen more intently.

"He turned here." Dasher leapt, turning himself in midair.

A trusted hound, the others followed suit and now hounds ran. A lope, not a flat-out gallop, but the field awakened, a stiff coop loomed up ahead. Sister, an Episcopalian, nonetheless carried rosary beads. This jump did not elicit a call to the Blessed Virgin Mother but she needed to take it seriously. Actually, the jumps that often caused the most problems were smaller jumps because the rider didn't take them seriously and then neither did the horse.

Up and over she sailed on Aztec, such a handy chestnut Thoroughbred. Handy, sensible, loved leading the field and he loved Sister; the two of them made a wonderful team.

Sarge, the young fox, heard the hounds, zigzagged, crossed the tertiary road.

"Tallyho!" Aunt Dan beamed as Yvonne stopped, the fox forty yards ahead.

"He's a little fellow. What a gorgeous coat," Yvonne, learning about foxhunting, exclaimed. "I think he's the one who visits my doghouse."

"Young. He'll get bigger. Maybe eight or nine pounds when he's done. And that winter coat is lush. Oh dear."

A visitor's horse refused the jump so the lady, put out, had to ride to the rear of the field and give everyone else the chance to go over. If a horse refuses, it gives the other horses ideas. Best to get someone over right away, which almost always takes care of that.

"Nice jump. That Luckham fellow can ride," Yvonne noticed.

"Ronnie introduced us when I arrived. Perfectly calm given that this is the eye of the hurricane."

"Honey, every man wants to meet you."

"I am done with men. You mark my words."

"I am. I am." The older woman, her silver-domed earrings highlighted by her silver hair, grinned. "Stop. Don't move."

"What?" Yvonne, confused, asked.

"Second Flight is coming up behind you."

Checking her rearview mirror, sure enough, the long line of those who did not jump trotted on the road.

"Toughest job in foxhunting, leading Second Flight. Bobby Franklin has done it for years. He gets the sick, the lame, and the halt." Aunt Daniella smiled again. "Well, I'm being a tiny bit sarcastic, but it can be difficult. Sister has the best riders in First Flight. But sometimes when one ages or is on a green horse, you go out with Second Flight."

"Sam says that's where I will start."

"No one is better than Bobby. He'll get you as close to the action as possible."

The hounds moved closer to the action so Sarge picked up speed. He sailed over the stone fence enclosing Old Paradise pastures, the estate, having endured as much tragedy as joy.

The white field, open, meant he'd better step on it. No point in being out in the open any longer than possible. The two women in the car could clearly see him hook left heading toward woods' edge, where boulder outcroppings were glimpsed between trees.

Flying now, hounds closed with their quarry. Sarge, with a good head start, easily vaulted onto a large rock, then another, finally slipping into a crevice large enough for him but not a hound. His den, a little cave, filled with straw, old towels, old dog toys he stole from the farms around the area, provided cozy quarters from wind, rain, sleet, snow, for the main opening faced east and weather usually came from the west. Another exit, way in the rear, off to the side, also kept out the weather. And just in case, the little fellow had a backup den forty yards away under a huge fallen tree.

The hounds leapt onto the rocks, only a few at a time, for it wasn't broad enough for the pack.

Trident, a young hound, called down. *"We know you're in there."*

"What are you going to do about it?" Sarge taunted.

"Well—" The young hound wrinkled his brow.

"Don't encourage a smart mouth." Diana, a lead hound, chastised the youngster. *"Come on. Get down. We might get one more cast for the weather is changing."*

The clouds, stacking up on the west side of the Blue Ridge Mountains, were fifteen minutes away from peeping over the top and then another fifteen before they swept down, the wind moaning before the snow arrived, early.

Sister rode up as Shaker had dismounted to blow "Gone to Ground."

The hounds wiggled in excitement. They had done their job after all.

"The Weather Channel predicted the snow would arrive early afternoon. I say we hunt back. We've got some time."

"Yes, madam." Shaker, who had known Sister for decades, addressed her correctly in the hunt field.

Wesley Blackford, "Weevil," held Shaker's horse. The older man mounted with ease. Weevil then fell back as he rode today as third whipper-in. Tootie Harris, Yvonne's daughter, rode as second whipper-in on the left while Betty Franklin, first whipper-in, rode on the right. The side they covered had nothing to do with their ranking and both ladies were honorary, which is to say amateurs. They knew their stuff. Weevil was paid, therefore professional. Betty, in her fifties, had the territory memorized plus she remembered the great-great-grandparents of some of the hounds. Family traits passed. And most of all, she knew Sister. Their friendship, deep and loving, carried both through life's sorrows and joys.

Sister watched Weevil, thirty, perhaps a year or two over the 0, ride to the rear. He carried himself on the ground or on a horse with a peculiar masculine grace. Every action appeared effortless. He hunted with Toronto–North York where he learned how to do things properly, winding up in Virginia through fate. His grandfather had hunted the Jefferson Hounds back in the early fifties. While one rarely describes a man as beautiful, he was beautiful and quite unaware of it.

"Come along," Shaker called to the hounds.

They moved to the edge of the pasture, jumped a tiger trap that was built like a coop but with logs facing upward, stacked next to one another. Snow rested in the crevices between the logs, which gave a few horses pause. The riders kept their leg on and everyone popped over.

"Lieu in," Shaker called out using the ancient Norman term meaning "Go in, get in the covert, and find your fox."

If it was good enough for William the Conqueror, it was good enough for modern foxhunters.

The hounds fanned out, noses down. Nothing doing. Pookah, another younger hound, drifted toward woods' edge. Another huntsman would have thought the hound was trailing off skirting, but Shaker knew his hounds. Pookah stopped. His stern wagged. He sniffed. More tail work.

His sister, Pansy, called out. *"What do you think?"*

"An old line. But maybe it will heat up."

Gregory Luckham, next to Ronnie, as the field had pulled up, said low, "Skirting."

Ronnie shook his head. "No. Shaker makes a loose cast. We can in this territory. That's a blue-chip hound."

How wise of Ronnie to call attention to both the hound and the fabulous territory.

A loose cast was a bit like throwing your hounds on the ground like dice. Fixtures crisscrossed with roads, too much traffic, demanded that hounds stay more tightly together. This was hard on hounds, huntsmen, and staff, to say nothing of wildlife pressured by too many humans.

"Got 'em," Pookah finally sang out.

The hounds rushed to him, noses down. Everyone trusted the hound even though young and yes, they had a good line. All sang out at once. A sound that makes the hair on the back of your neck stand up.

Sister grinned, kicked into a canter, a low dip ahead; she leaned back in the saddle, her legs a bit ahead of the girth.

Raymie, the steeplechase rider, had his legs even farther ahead. He considered it his insurance policy. The man had cleared so many big fences, one would think he wouldn't pay attention, but he did pay attention, which was why he was still riding in his eighth decade, riding hard.

On they thundered, coming within sight of the Corinthian columns of Old Paradise, forlorn standards of a different time. Hounds cut right. The field also cut right and then they heard the wind, which sounded as though someone turned on a radio dial. Silence except for hoofbeats and hound music and all of a sudden, a low, loud moan. Trees began to bend.

Sister looked up. The clouds, gunmetal gray, skidded down the east side of the Blue Ridge as though on a roller coaster, opened.

They were a good four miles from Tattenhall Station. The snow started heavy but the wind proved the initial problem. For one thing it blew the scent to bits. Hounds stopped running, searched. What scent there was was already a hundred yards to their east. Not that it would hold.

To the side of those Corinthian columns stood the rehabilitated stone stable and to the left of that, in a line, Crawford and Rory stood in the Carriage House, which was being rehabilitated.

The lumber, neatly stacked, would be protected from the elements, but Crawford's wrath exploded when he heard hounds.

"Goddammit, I want that fool off my property! I never said Luckham could come onto Old Paradise." He strode toward the imposing double doors.

Rory, behind him, didn't argue but said, "The fox doesn't know that."

"No, but Sister should!"

Trying to defuse his boss's fury, Rory stepped next to Crawford, who already had his hand on the one-foot-tall wrought-iron door handle. The double doors measured a story, impressive, but then everything was impressive at Old Paradise.

"Boss, you know Sister would never cross you." Not entirely true but Rory sounded convincing. "She can't turn around and throw Luckham out of the hunt field. For one thing, it's against MFHA rules."

This stopped Crawford for a moment. "I'm not a member of the goddamned MFHA. To hell with their rules."

"You're smart to avoid all that." Rory fibbed. "But if a hunt has permission to hunt a fixture, the landowner can't deny a rider access to their land even if they hate that person. No one would be able to hunt anywhere."

"Not my problem. I can throw off anyone." He pulled open one door still rolling after two centuries of use. "What the hell?"

A blast of strong wind forced him to take a step back when it hit him in the face.

Shaker blew hounds to him. Three longish blasts. He turned, hounds behind him, his whippers-in turning with him.

Reaching his Master, he leaned forward, shouting, so he could be heard. "Madam."

"We've got to get back before trees come down." The weather felt like a cold, hard slap in the face. "They'll be uprooted," she shouted.

As Master and huntsman realized the danger of the situation, Crawford, head down, pushed to his Range Rover. Rory closed the door behind him, then hurried over to the passenger side, where he got in.

"Wind about tore the door off." He gasped.

Crawford, windshield wipers on high, crept down the farm road, snow sweeping across it. "I am going to tear that son of a bitch off his horse. He's not hunting on my land."

Crawford lowered his window an inch. The wind whistled but he could make out the horn, which was close. Impulsively, Crawford put the car in park, got out. Rory, surprised, sat a moment. Then he, too, got out. The snow, already thick and blowing, obscured everything, although he could hear the horn. Hounds brushed by Rory, who stood still, looking for Crawford. He stretched out his arms to make himself look bigger and riders, coming up on him, swerved.

A country boy, Rory knew if he didn't find Crawford, if they didn't get out of there, perhaps they never would. Crawford was out of his element.

Rory heard the horn moving away, knew riders were close but no longer could see them. He heard an *umph* sound.

"Crawford."

No response. Thinking his boss might have been knocked down by a horse, Rory raised his voice, called again.

"Boss." He yelled for all he was worth.

"Where are you?" Crawford called back, sounded to Rory's right near the sound of the *umph*.

"To your left. I'll yodel. Come to the sound."

A grateful Crawford finally appeared, snow encrusted on his eyebrows. Rory grabbed his hand. They both turned around, hoping to see the car. The lights were on and they could just make out the reflection on the snow.

That was the only time Rory was ever glad for lights on during the daytime. You couldn't turn them off. Together, the two men, arm in arm, battled their way back to the car, motor running. Feeling the car, each man reached his door, opened it with difficulty, then slumped in the seat.

"I've never seen anything come up like that in all my life," Crawford gasped. "Didn't know you could yodel."

"Some." Rory grinned.

"This is impossible." The windshield wipers couldn't keep up with the snow. "I'm heading home."

"Good idea. When you pass Tattenhall Station, let me out. I'll help Sam with Trocadero. No point having him drive the horse trailer alone in this."

"Christ, I don't even know if I can see Tattenhall Station."

"There. I can just make it out. Can't see anyone in yet." Rory hopped out as Crawford stopped, then slowly drove away.

Sister turned Aztec, trotted toward Chapel Cross for Tattenhall Station. It sat on the southeastern corner of that old crossroads, the chapel on the southwest corner. It took her fifteen minutes to reach the road. She'd heard Crawford's car in the distance, barely, but she couldn't see it. He was ahead of the riders. By the time they reached Chapel Cross, the cross on top of the dark blue steeple couldn't be seen. The world turned white, biting white.

Sister was having ample time to repent of her decision. Then again, the Weather Channel mistimed the arrival of the storm.

The wind howled. People could barely make one another out even though close. They reached the trailers.

People dismounted, wincing when their feet hit the ground as their feet had gotten cold and the ground stung when you hit it. Dewey Milford, next to Freddie's trailer, helped her load. They both drove out as soon as the horses were on their respective trailers. Dewey, confused by the snow, realized it, crawled to Beveridge Hundred, where he could turn around the trailer, and headed back. The wind shook the heavy trailer. Untacking horses, throwing blankets on, staff horses were led into the trailer. Sister did not take the saddle off Aztec. She thought keeping the saddle on helped keep his back warm. She put on his blanket. Betty did the same for Outlaw, who was grateful. Each of the staff members took care of horses or hounds. Weevil took Shaker's horse while the older man loaded up the hounds with Tootie's help. Betty had Tootie's horse. The staff had the drill down. People got into their trucks, turned on the lights, which reflected off the snow. Slowly, carefully they drove out while others, slower, hurried to get all done so they, too, could get on the road. Sam, unaware that Rory intended to help him, didn't see anyone so he drove out praying he'd make it.

Staff knew they would be the last ones out. All hounds, accounted for, snuggled into their trailer, which had plastic inserts in the long openings on the top. These were for air circulation but in winter, clear plastic, like glass only it wouldn't shatter, was slid in and on the back door, too. The trailer, straw piled deep, allowed hounds to bed down. That and their shared body heat would keep them warm until they reached the kennels, which would take longer than usual.

Horses loaded up, Sister kept her hand on the horse trailer as she walked toward the truck. A figure ahead of her appeared out of the snow.

"Sister!"

"Ronnie."

"Gregory's horse came back but he's not here." He stopped, took a breath. "I thought he was with me. I could hear Pokerface snort, but I didn't look behind me."

"Wait here." Sister reached the hound trailer as Shaker

loaded his horse onto the back of the hound trailer. Tootie and Weevil's horses, along with Betty's, were already on Sister's four-horse trailer. "Shaker, we have a missing person. Ronnie's guest."

"Jesus Christ," Shaker muttered.

"Come with me. Take your horn." She walked back to her trailer, where Betty, Tootie, and Weevil waited.

"Folks, Ronnie's guest is missing." She turned to Ronnie. "Where did you last see him?"

"I thought he was with me when we rode by the chapel. He was a little behind me. I noticed I couldn't see the cross. I didn't think to look back."

Shaker interposed. "You wouldn't have seen him anyway. We're lucky we got here."

"I can't leave him," Ronnie said, desperate.

Weevil, although the newest staff member, spoke up. "This is the beginning of a blizzard. If we all go out looking for him, we can become disoriented in minutes. It's death. Trust me. I'm Canadian."

"Ronnie, call the rescue squad. Betty, call Ben Sidell, the sheriff. God, I wish he could have hunted today. Report this. Shaker, blow your horn. With God's grace he might hear it and come to the horn."

The two made the required phone calls.

"Ben said they'd get here as soon as they can. Accidents everywhere. Trees are coming down. He ordered me to order you to go home. If we don't go now, we'll be stuck here."

"At least we can go into the station," Tootie thought out loud.

"The horses can't." Weevil smiled at her. "Hounds could but we can't leave the horses in the trailer in these winds. We've got to do what the sheriff ordered."

Tears came to Ronnie's eyes.

"Why don't you follow us, Ronnie? You can stay in the house with Gray and me. No point trying to get to your barn alone."

"I can't leave him. If he's out there alone, he could die."

"Ronnie"—Betty knew him well—"there's no choice. This is getting worse by the minute. Come on, I'll ride with you."

Weevil and Shaker rode together while Tootie and Sister drove. Although only eleven miles away, it took them forty-five minutes to reach Roughneck Farm, Sister's farm.

Hounds unloaded, horses put into the barn including Ronnie's, and Pokerface, the horse he had lent to Greg.

"We're lucky we made it." Sister meant that as they could hear trees cracking in the woods. "Weevil, you'd best stay here, too. Even though your cottage isn't far."

His cottage was at After All, the adjoining farm.

"He can stay with me," Tootie offered. "Come on, Weevil. I need to call Mom and make sure she and Daniella got home."

Betty and Ronnie also walked up to Sister's house, which they did as a human chain, for you couldn't see a thing now. Once in the house, Gray was on the phone, for he had come in early, figuring he'd better get the house ready for stranded people.

He looked up. "Aunt Dan's with Tootie's mother. Everyone is bunked up with someone."

Shaker made it to his cottage as Weevil and Tootie, heads down against the wind, made it to hers.

At Sister's each person used the tall bootjack to pull off boots. Coats hung on pegs in the mudroom. Soon they were dripping melted snow. Betty noticed tears in Ronnie's eyes. He wasn't a man afraid to show emotion. She put an arm around his waist. He returned the gesture and they stepped into the kitchen.

The two house dogs and the cat observed all this as the house shook from the assaulting winds. Gray had a big pot of tea boiling. They could worry about supper once they got warm.

Sister, out in the mudroom, took coats as they were handed to her, lined up boots. She couldn't help herself. She opened the mudroom door to the outside for a moment; then it slammed shut from the force of the wind.

Snow-blind, she thought to herself, and she also thought that if Gregory Luckham hadn't tucked up somewhere, he would freeze to death. No rescue team could find anyone in conditions like these.

Snow-blind.

CHAPTER 4

Tired as they were, everyone rose at first light. Sister threw on her robe, looked out the window. Snowdrifts piled up on the north side of buildings and trees. Snow continued to fall now as big lazy snowflakes. At least she could see and what she saw were trees snapped in half, others uprooted, those being mostly pines due to their small root-balls. Snow covered each roof so if there was damage she couldn't see it. At least, no part of any roof had blown off.

The old curving back wooden stairway led down to the kitchen where Golly commanded the kitchen table. Raleigh and Rooster followed Sister, their claws clicking on the worn steps.

Golly put on her loving face. *"I'm hungry."*

Sister filled a bowl, mixing kibble with canned cat food. She put it up on the corner of the counter so the dogs wouldn't get it. Then she quickly filled their bowls, placing them on the floor by the back stairway. She then filled up the water bowls, grateful that she still had power, a miracle considering the force of the wind.

Footsteps down the hallway pattered into the country kitchen.

"Scrambled egg or over?" Betty, who knew the house as well as her own, pulled a large iron skillet, number 5, out from a cabinet.

"You make scrambled for those who want that. I'll make the easy over. Gray can make biscuits." Sister pulled out another iron skillet.

"He makes the best." Betty dropped butter in the skillet.

"Aunt Daniella's recipe. I'm glad she stayed with Yvonne. Neither one of those ladies is a fool." The phone rang, the landline. "Hello." A silence followed as Sister listened.

The sheriff, Ben Sidell, informed her about road conditions. "Some of the roads are passable. The interstate has been plowed throughout the night. Slow going. Route 250 is being cleared of trees. Stay put."

"What about Soldier Road?" She asked about a state east-west road on the north side of the high plateau on her property called Hangman's Ridge for that's where colonials, found guilty, were hanged.

"Clearing. Plows behind the chain saw crew."

"Shall I assume no one has looked for Gregory Luckham yet?"

"That's why I called. Obviously, no one could do anything last night. It's still coming down. I commandeered a snowplow to get us to Chapel Cross. The board of supervisors was too overwhelmed to argue. Wires came down out there so Central Virginia Electric Cooperative is there. They've called in repairmen from other states. The damage throughout central Virginia all the way up through Pennsylvania seems to be severe."

"Anyone killed on the roads?"

"Thank God, no. When the governor told people to stay home, off the roads, they listened. But a missing person means we'll have our search team out there, so tell me what you know."

"Started behind Tattenhall Station, headed south toward

Beveridge Hundred, but we never got there. Picked up a fading line, which fortunately heated up. Crossed the road. Took the tiger trap and wound up at the large rock outcroppings. You know the place."

"Den there." He did know the place.

"It was cold but the weather held. The forecast was that the storm would come in after noontime. Anyway, I wasn't worried, so after putting that red to ground, we headed west toward Chapel Cross. We hit again and ran within sight of Old Paradise, could see the columns in the distance and then lost. I have no idea why. That's when, almost as if the sky had been unzipped, no warning, really, the snow came down and thick. The clouds were so low, you could almost touch them, but Ben, it truly happened so fast. The wind screamed. So Shaker picked them up, we headed back for Tattenhall Station. Everything seemed to be in order. I didn't turn around and count heads. If something is amiss, someone rides up to tell me. We were all on so to speak like the hounds, all on, or so I thought."

"Were people riding in twos or in groups?"

"Twos, groups, whatever. Heads down against the wind. The snow became so thick but there were no stragglers and Bobby Franklin brought up the rear with Second Flight. How he did it, I have no idea. Everything seemed to be in order."

"What about the whippers-in?"

"They had moved close to the pack. By then we couldn't really see. A hound could get swallowed up so all three whippers-in rode up close to hounds to make sure they packed up, but Ben, by the time we reached the chapel we couldn't even see the cross on top. I could barely see Shaker and I could just see Weevil, who rode at the rear of the pack."

"No shouts or anything like that? Anyone falling off?"

"No. Everyone realized this could be dangerous and everyone wanted to get on the road and home before trees came down, accidents. We made it to Tattenhall Station. I could see trailers once I was upon them. It was a blizzard. A true blizzard."

"Then what?"

"Blankets on horses, loaded, people began to pull out. Shaker and Tootie got the hounds up. Betty and I loaded staff horses. Shaker loaded Showboat"—she mentioned his horse—"onto the hound trailer. Weevil rode in the truck with Shaker. Ronnie, Tootie, and I would drive back in the horse trailer, but before I climbed into the rig, Ronnie came over, upset. Now Ronnie is usually a cool customer, as you know. His guest was missing but the horse came back."

"And he just noticed?"

"Yes. He said the horse was right behind him. He didn't turn to see if Gregory Luckham was on but he said even if he were, he might not have seen him."

"Wouldn't he have heard him if he fell off? Or perhaps someone behind hear?"

"I actually don't think anyone would have heard a thing because of the wind. I had to shout just to try to talk to Weevil as we crossed Chapel Crossroads. And Weevil really couldn't hear me. If Gregory fell off and was hurt or knocked unconscious, no one would have known."

"And if so he's dead by now." Ben spoke honestly, but he could to Sister.

"I don't see how anyone could live in that blizzard. Even if he wasn't hurt, was mobile, he wouldn't see where to go. You couldn't see the hand in front of your face."

"Let me be clear, you or Ronnie last saw him where?"

"I last saw him with Ronnie when hounds threw up at Old Paradise, the columns in the distance. Then I turned for Chapel Cross. I didn't look behind."

"Did Ronnie say where he last saw him?"

"Around the same place. He couldn't pinpoint it and he

faults himself. No one was riding holding hands. He's, well, you know, he's beating himself up."

"I'll need to talk to him. Did he go home?"

"No. No one did from those last two trailers, well our last two trailers and then Ronnie's. Everyone is here still asleep except for Betty and me."

"Once he's awake, have him call me on my cell."

"I will."

"Everyone else okay? Hounds? Horses?"

"Yes." She hung up the phone. Betty, hearing the conversation, asked no questions, as she cracked eggs.

Sister hovered over the second skillet. "Betty, I don't know what to do."

"There's nothing you can do."

She waved her hand. "I know, I know, but I don't know what to do for Ronnie."

Betty walked over and placed her hand on her friend's shoulder. "We're here. That's the best we can do."

"When RayRay was killed, Ronnie and Xavier"—Sister named another of her deceased son's best friends—"visited me. Came to the house, did chores. Stacked the hayloft, and then, as they moved through high school, they invited me to their football games, to their graduations." She swallowed hard. "I don't know what's got into me. I hate to see Ronnie upset."

"Ronnie and Xavier look on you as another mother, I think, and you, well, you love them. You think of them as your boys." Betty smiled. "Your boys who are now in their mid-fifties."

Sister, too, began to crack eggs. "Betty, where does the time go?"

"I don't know but if I find out, I'll go bring some back."

Sister leaned over and kissed Betty on the cheek.

The smells were bringing everyone down. Whatever happened, they'd face it together.

CHAPTER 5

"Honey, drink your coffee and eat your eggs. You'll feel a little better. Your mind will wake up." Sister sat across from Ronnie, normally fastidious but today with morning stubble.

Gray sat next to him after putting a plate of biscuits on the table.

The old friends ate. Ronnie gulped his coffee, hoping it would help. Betty rose and refilled his cup.

A lovely small bone china creamer sat on the table filled with real cream. Sister always put the heavy-duty stuff on the table. Her theory was if you eat or drink fat in the morning, rich stuff, you won't get so hungry the rest of the day. Sure worked for her.

Gray glanced out the wavy glass windows, from the late eighteenth century. "This won't let up."

"At least it's not so heavy," Betty replied. "Spoke to my best husband this morning. He said the drifts were piled against the door."

"Do you have a second-best husband?" Sister teased her.

"Oh, there are days." Betty smiled. "I don't know how he

shepherded Second Flight back yesterday. We have a few nervous Nellies in that group."

"Well, I was in First Flight and felt like a nervous Nellie," Gray confessed. "I don't know what it is, but I think of the times we have run into trouble at Old Paradise."

"Given that it's five thousand acres, I suppose that increases the chances for trouble." Sister nibbled sausage, succulent farm sausage, a bit browned on the edges.

"Oh, I sometimes think Sophie Marquet cursed the place." Betty also savored her food. "Dashing as her life was in wartime, peacetime had to be one problem after another, especially after she married."

"Didn't she shoot him?" Gray wondered.

"He lived. She caught him in flagrante delicto." Betty did so like gossip, especially old gossip, because no one would fuss at you for retelling it. "She swore she forgave him and he wandered no more."

"Would you?" Ronnie livened a bit.

"That's a very loaded question." Gray got up to refill everyone's cups, tea for Sister.

"Do you think people can truly forgive?" Betty asked. "I mean especially something like that, something where you are publicly humiliated? I mean sooner or later it always comes out."

"I don't know, Betty, Aunt Daniella has held her cards close to that famous bosom for decades, must be seven decades now because she sprang into action in her late teens." Gray smiled. "If anyone can understand the long departed Sophie, it's my aunt."

"You've got us there but"—Sister drew this out so they all leaned toward her—"she came close to spilling some of the beans when she saw Weevil. Melted. Just melted. He is the spitting image of an old flame."

"Most women melt when they meet your newest professional whipper-in." Betty thought him gorgeous.

"Well." Sister shrugged. "My only paid whipper-in. You have done unpaid service for over thirty years."

"Yes, I started whipping-in to the Jefferson Hounds at age six."

This brought a roar of laughter. Even Ronnie, distracted as he was, appreciated and loved Betty. Old friends, dear friends, age gaps between them only tightening the bonds. Gray and Sister had known each other for most of their adult lives although Gray, after graduate school, spent the weeks in D.C., married to a socially conscious woman who felt central Virginia much beneath her. After producing a son, they both raised him. She decamped to New York City where her light would shine more brightly. The son, a bovine veterinarian in Colorado, had started practice in Nebraska, and was considered one of the leading veterinarians in the country. So whatever the then married Lorillards did, they raised a good son. The lightning struck Sister and Gray twelve years ago. A surprise to all, especially them.

Betty, having grown up in Orange County, knew of Sister. Once she married Bobby and they started their printing business, she came into the orbit. Ronnie grew up with Sister. He couldn't imagine life without her, nor she him.

Old friends. Old friends who knew one another's good points and not so good points. Somehow the non-perfections only made them all more lovable.

"I am wide awake. Your usual magical breakfast." Ronnie looked at Sister. "I'm ready to call Ben now."

"Would you like to use the landline in the library? It will be private."

"No. I'll use the phone here. I don't mind if you hear me. Maybe you can help me remember what I said. When I get rattled I can forget what I've just said or done."

"Of course." Sister agreed.

Ronnie moved his chair to the phone on the kitchen

counter. Golly, reposing there, lifted her head for Ronnie to pet. She knew him. He stroked her, which calmed him a little.

Raleigh and Rooster on the floor moved to sit down by him. They felt his unease, his worry.

"Ben."

"Ronnie. We're out here now. It's heavy going."

"Deep snow. But can you see one another?"

"We can. We're working quadrants based on Sister's report about the storm coming up while you were at Old Paradise. She said the columns loomed in the distance so we started there. I've got one man on the road. One to my south, Jackie in front of me, and Carson back at Tattenhall Station moving around the buildings checking everything."

"Tattenhall?"

"It's possible he slipped or slipped away as you approached the station. Sister said you told her you didn't look back until you reached the station. Tell me what you did, what you saw."

Ronnie repeated what he had told Sister. "Pokerface was right behind me. I could just see him and he was on Corporal's flank." He named his two horses. "So I didn't know Greg was gone until Pokerface came alongside me at the trailer."

"Taking a rough gauge of distance, you rode for about four miles without looking behind?"

"If I retrace my steps, we turned toward Chapel Cross once the snow came down, all at once. No warning. I'd say we rode toward the road maybe a mile. We were pretty deep into Old Paradise. We saw the Corinthian columns, after all, as I said. Sister picked up a trot. We made it to the road oh, fifteen, twenty minutes. We were in the front of First Flight. Second Flight had more people, they fell back. I heard a car, then nothing as we neared the road. Couldn't see. I don't know how long it took them. But I was up front. I couldn't hear anyone's voice, front or rear. Anyway, we knew we were on the road even if we couldn't quite see it because a few people waded through the drainage ditch filling up with snow. They stepped off the road by mistake. The snow had to be coming down at least three inches an hour. By the time we reached Chapel Cross, you couldn't see the cross on the steeple. I kept my head down. The wind was howling but I knew Pokerface was at my flank. He kept his nose close to Corporal's hindquarters. Couldn't hear anything, as I said. I'm repeating myself. Sorry. Couldn't see Sister ahead of me. Then we reached Tattenhall Station."

Ronnie could hear Ben's labored breathing as he pushed through the snow. "What is your relationship to Gregory Luckham?"

"Business friendly. Our law firm represents Soliden Enterprises. My specialty is protecting historic sites, that sort of thing, and usually our firm works out accommodation between say a cemetery and a developer. Sometimes it's simply money changing hands. If a family is involved like over a cemetery, it can drag on and become emotional. A wants the money from the developer. B thinks Great-aunt Gertrude must rest in peace forever."

"And were you involved in something like this for Soliden?"

"Greg was anticipating trouble. The final route of the pipeline, still in flux, needed to consider drawn-out lawsuits. The state issues were pretty much cleared by the McAuliffe administration." Ronnie named a former governor of Virginia who supported the pipeline as great for Virginia business, job creation. "I wanted Greg to really see the territory and what better way to see it than to ride it?"

Ben, who read the papers avidly, understood what was at stake, including what wasn't said. Careers.

The sheriff stopped to catch his breath. "Did Mr. Luckham know of your historical and environmental concerns?"

"He did. He was a very good CEO. He could incorporate opposing views, make room for same. I would not, could not unless I resigned my own position, work against Soliden, pipeline or no pipeline. He knew that. I think that's why he wanted to know what I thought. Where the historical hot spots rested. Perhaps that's why he agreed to be my guest at Christmas Hunt. I could point out significant areas."

"Did you?"

"Yes. For every change the company makes for the route, I know or can quickly find out what is at issue. This is still hanging. Naturally, I hope to divert the route for many reasons, not the least of which is the incredible historical value of an undisturbed Old Paradise, Beveridge Hundred, or Tattenhall Station."

"You developed enough of a friendship where you'd lend him a good horse to hunt? Pokerface is a saint."

"He hunts with Deep Run. He can ride and ride well."

"Was that all? I know you well enough, Ronnie, to think you had a card up your sleeve."

"Yes and no. Crawford Howard and Kasmir Barbhaiya made common cause, hired McGuire Woods"—he named a powerful mid-Atlantic law firm—"to make certain the pipeline did not come through here. Each man had received a letter declaring a surveyor would be on their property and that did it. Given that their combined wealth is probably half the budget of the state of Virginia, my law firm would like to avoid a protracted lawsuit. McGuire Woods is a very good firm."

"Made the papers. Kasmir and Crawford," Ben recalled.

"Crawford Howard, much as he respected McGuire Woods, hired Charlotte Abruza. He would have them in reserve if it came to that. Crawford even brought her to a dinner I hosted for Gregory at Farmington Country Club where Gregory was staying.

"As for Kasmir, he donated handsomely to the Virginia Outdoor Foundation, Piedmont Environmental Council, anything that preserved the beauty of this part of the world. Having been raised in India, he was keenly aware of what happens when 'progress,' in quotes, is the only value. He made common cause with Crawford.

"I wanted him to really see this area. He'd been driven through it but if he rode it, met the people, he'd understand the passion, the resolve to turn that pipeline away."

"And?"

Ronnie waited a bit. "Well, we had two good runs. He rode over hill and dale, got within sight of those Corinthian columns. I think he was impressed. He had a big smile on his face. A good run will do that."

"I see." And Ben did.

"I figured Greg would have a terrific time at Tattenhall Station. Then I'd get him, not on horseback, to see the restoration Crawford is doing. Also show him old photography of Tattenhall Station, how it was once a small nerve center in central Virginia."

"You're not worried about your law firm?"

"No. I am working for our client. If I can save the client protracted lawsuits and bad publicity, my God, they've had enough, I am doing my job."

"Is there a route that won't raise hackles?"

"No, but this can be made much easier if the company will utilize existing rights-of-way. Yes, it will make it a longer route if they abandon their route. There are other paths. It will add to the cost but so will lawsuits. Truthfully, Ben, they've done a piss-poor job of protecting themselves, of reaching the public."

"Yes. You'd think a company that big would have a better public relations department."

"They're living in the nineteen seventies and eighties. No concept of how quickly news disseminates today. And if this grows worse, Gregory Luckham will be out of a job. The blame will fall on him."

"Would it matter?"

"Ben, you hunt now. You didn't when you took the job as county sheriff. What do you think? What have you learned?"

"I see. Okay, better to have a foxhunter running a huge company than not, even though profits must trump everything."

"This really must be fought by individuals. The federal and state governments rolled over and played dead."

"Did he ever mention to you fear he would be killed?"

"Yes. He had received death threats."

"Someone would have to be highly motivated to venture out in a blizzard to kill him."

"Not if they were riding with the hunt. Someone could have ridden up beside him, stuck a knife in his ribs, pulled him off Pokerface. At that point no one would have heard him or seen him. I don't like to think of such things, but I've been thinking of nothing else."

A few more exchanges and Ronnie hung up the phone to confront three silent people staring at him.

He squared his shoulders. "It's the only thing I can think of."

"It does make sense, but who in the field is that impassioned about the pipeline?" Sister replied. "Irrational enough to kill if that's what they did."

"What if they are impassioned about something else?" Gray leaned back in his chair.

They each looked at one another.

"An irate husband?" Betty half whispered.

"A woman who has been what, pushed around. Felt he was a predator. Oh, it's all too far-fetched. Not out there in the hunt field." Sister threw up her hands.

Ronnie rejoined them after giving Golly another stroke under her chin. "People do crazy things."

"That's the truth," Betty declared with feeling. "I have an older daughter in jail who blew up her life with drugs. And another who graduated summa cum laude from Colby College. You never know."

"Betty, Sarah had help."

"Ronnie, you are kind but no one puts a gun to your head and says you will take drugs."

"People don't just disappear in the middle of a hunt." Ronnie felt so frustrated.

But they do.

CHAPTER 6

Blue shimmered off the snow, the glaze of ice adding to the shine. Sarge poked his head out of his den now that the snow finally stopped. The ice, thick enough to support his weight, still wasn't inviting. Lifting his head, he sniffed. Deer had passed perhaps at sunrise but few scents enticed him. Hunger enticed him, drove him on. As everything was covered with deep snow, so were his caches. No point trying to dig them out.

The footing was good thanks to the glaze. He headed east toward Beveridge Hundred. Mice lived in the outbuildings; often the garbage wasn't secured. Little things were beginning to get away from the Van Dorns like pressing down hard on the garbage cans. Better yet, the human in the dependency, the perfect cottage, put out treats. She even purchased a doghouse, the door facing away from the northwestern winds. Sarge was especially grateful for the treats and the deep straw bedding.

Moving quickly, the light wind biting, he reached Beveridge Hundred in ten minutes at an easy lope. Running kept him warm. He noticed few tracks on the way. Knowing every shortcut for a good two-mile radius from his den, not only could he dump the hounds, he could visit other creatures along the way if he had a mind to, but today no one was lounging at a den's opening, sitting in a tree, or nestling in a stall. The Van Dorns kept a tidy two-horse stable even though they no longer rode, age overtaking their ability to do so.

A curl of smoke, the wood smelling wonderful, rose from Yvonne's chimney. Tootie stacked up a full load of wood for her mother. As Yvonne was not a country girl, she had no idea what she would need. Tootie and Weevil brought over two truckloads for her with Sister's permission. The wood was from Sister's farm. Tootie, handy with chores, cut up the fallen trees while Weevil split them. Naturally, they also created a huge pile for the Master, stacking it in her woodhouse at the corner of the entrance to the mudroom. The last thing anyone wants to do in bad weather is walk far for wood.

Sarge stopped to peer into the living room windows. Yvonne, a Christmas tree in the corner of the room, presents under the tree, sat in a chair as she read. Yvonne was not handy but she could throw together clothing in five minutes, walk out looking beautiful, which she was clothed or unclothed.

Good woman that she was, the cozy doghouse had kibble, little milk bones, tiny grape candies, and Jolly Ranchers. Sarge loved candy. Tootie told her mother that foxes often had a sweet tooth as she helped her mother set up the doghouse.

Out of the corner of her eye she saw Sarge. He darted into the doghouse, having to plow his way through a small drift to get into the house. The blizzard's swirling winds created interesting shapes, opened some areas, closed up others. Yvonne watched the young red fox enjoy the kibble while plucking at candies. She had to smile.

"Merry Christmas, little one," she said.

Christmas brought back memories as it created new ones.

Yvonne wasn't enamored of the holidays, but she had agreed to go to Aunt Daniella's for a holiday drink. Sam, Gray, and Sister would be there along with Tootie, Weevil, and Weevil's mother, who had flown in from Toronto before the storm.

After this, they would drive to Sister's for a big Christmas dinner, more drinks, endless gossip from prior decades, some from this one.

In Chicago when Yvonne socialized with white people, it was always business. Victor, her husband, would push her to sweep the girls for business tidbits, little observations that could help him. This she did. She even liked some of the people but felt she would never be close to them. It was always business with Vic.

She didn't bother to call him for Christmas. Why would she? But it infuriated her that he didn't call their daughter. Yes, she'd walked away with half the money she helped him make, but somehow that wasn't enough. She still wanted to hurt him. Was it a waste of time? It was but the unchristian part of her wanted to see him writhe. Tootie, on the other hand, couldn't have cared less about her father. She'd written him off by the time she reached tenth grade. Pleasant, quiet, she didn't cross him but went her own way. He was too self-centered to see he'd lost his daughter, but then so was she and she regretted that, was trying to make amends.

Sarge, on the other hand, was unwrapping Jolly Ranchers. Marriage never occurred to him. Mating might and a few other foxes at the edge of his territory told him the season usually started in December. Started a few weeks earlier for the grays. Well, a mate might be a good thing to have but he was still on the small side. How was he going to best a big, fully mature red fox? Plus he hadn't found a girlfriend yet, although some unattached females were around.

Popping a lemon Jolly Rancher in his mouth, he looked up at the cottage again to see Yvonne staring at him. She didn't frighten him. Sometimes a young woman was with her. Sarge could hear them talk when the windows were open on those delicious warm fall days. They spoke with the same cadence.

He curled up, just for a minute, then he noticed a shiny ball in the corner. Shiny things intrigued him. Little shiny bits he brought to his den. One belt buckle, a curb chain that he dragged from Tattenhall Station, and a streamer of bright green ribbon. If he sat on it it crinkled. This was a perfect ball.

Yvonne put in a Christmas ball for him because Tootie told her some foxes were scavengers, liked toys, liked old sweaters, too. Sarge awoke when Yvonne started her car engine. A small garage by the cottage protected the car. The roads, not cleared this far out, had packed down a little. Cecil and Violet Van Dorn kept a fellow on payroll with a snowplow. He also mowed the considerable lawns and hayed the fields in summer.

Sarge wanted to take the Christmas ball home but it was too big. Rousing himself, he walked back to the two-stall stable, doors shut. The place could be easily entered if one was a fox or small animal.

A barn owl reposed in the rafters. One eye opened up.

"There's food in the doghouse."

"H-mm," the bird replied. *"Terrible storm, wasn't it? Never heard the winds howl like that. Old birds used to tell stories about the banshee. Now I think I know what a banshee sounded like."*

Sarge, not knowing of those stories, asked, *"Any mice?"*

"A few." She paused. *"Enough."*

The fox looked around. An object at the corner of a stall caught his eye. He walked over to bat it. Then he picked it up.

"Did you see this?"

The bird looked down, both eyes open now. *"Did."*

Sarge picked it up. *"This has a stag's head with antlers."*

"A ring." The bird had floated down for a closer look. As the barn owl was stout, claws formidable, and beak likewise, she wasn't

worried about Sarge grabbing her and he wasn't worried about her grabbing him. He was big enough to take care of himself.

"It's pretty." Sarge peered at it with the owl.

"Gold. Oak leaf on the side. Think this has some religious significance."

"Because of the cross?"

"Yes." She hooked a claw in the ring, bringing it up to her golden eye. *"They're superstitious, humans. I watch them usually from the belfry in the chapel. They do things in unison. A cross is carried down the center aisle and there's one on a table up front with a bigger gold cross, has to mean something."*

"Between antlers?" Sarge questioned.

"Yes."

"Did you see the human who lost this?"

"No. I managed to get home a bit after the snow started. Why a human would be in here I don't know." She opened her beak. *"You're young. I've been watching humans for years. They are highly peculiar creatures. Whoever lost this ring will be back for it if he or she can remember where they were. Had to be during the bad snow."*

"Do you want it?"

"No," the owl replied.

"Then I'll take it." Sarge put it in his mouth, left the stable, but it was so cold that the ring hurt his tongue.

He returned to the doghouse, dug a bit in the straw, leaving the ring there.

CHAPTER 7

A fox topped the huge Christmas tree in place of a star. Garlands swirled around the conifer, sweet smelling. The decorations were hand-painted clothespins; each looked like a hunt member as well as their horse. Christmas balls also hung on the tree.

Tattenhall Station, filled with people, reverberated with sound, talk, music, glass tinkling. The breakfast moved from Christmas Hunt was now in full swing on Boxing Day, December 26.

The road, not plowed but tamped down, could easily be driven. Kasmir had the parking lot plowed out, huge pile of snow at the edge. If anyone stepped outside, which smokers did, they noted the size of the snow pile. They all smoked faster than usual for it was too cold to stay out for a languid smoke.

Sister stood by the tree, her champagne glass in hand. Gray pulled up a chair for her as she had been on her feet for an hour already.

Freddie Thomas pulled up a chair to sit next to her. "Refresh your champagne?"

"No thanks. You know I'm not much of a drinker, but it's hard to resist Cristal."

A big smile, Freddie nodded, then smile fading. "You've fielded so many questions about Gregory Luckham, would you like me to run interference?"

"Freddie, thank you. People are concerned. All I can do is listen." Relief flooded her face for she was grateful to Freddie and more stressed than she realized.

"People don't mean to be a pest. Even though Ben Sidell is a member, being questioned by the sheriff, m-m-m"—she held up her hands, palms upward—"discomforting."

"I'm getting a small taste of what Ben deals with daily." Sister finished her divine champagne.

"We're lucky to have him. Everyone thinks this is about the pipeline, not that everyone wishes him dead, but it is the overriding issue."

"Yes." Sister exhaled. "Freddie, it seems to me no matter what the issue is these days, people take sides and are uncompromising."

Dewey walked over noticing Sister's empty glass. "Madam?"

"No thank you, Dewey."

"I'm running interference." Freddie smiled at Dewey.

"I've noticed everyone all over our Master." He shifted his weight to the other foot. "I liked him. I'd see him at big fundraisers in Richmond. He'd tease me that I was trolling for clients so I'd ask him if he wanted to buy a home in the country. Didn't know him in a business sense like Ronnie, but I thought he was a good guy."

"Let's hope he still is," Sister piped up. "Perhaps he's safe somewhere but unable to contact anyone."

"Really?" Freddie was intrigued.

"What if he suffered a concussion? Lost his memory?" Sister

opined. "Look at all that stuff now publicized about football players."

Freddie replied. "I was reading, maybe it was in the *Wall Street Journal.* It was some time back but there are far more concussions in women's sports, much higher numbers."

Dewey, clearing his throat, said, "I'm sorry to hear that. Excuse me, maybe someone wants to buy or sell property."

"So you are trolling." Freddie looked up at him.

"Just testing the market." He executed a small bow and left.

"Tough business, real estate," Sister commented.

"Any time you work on commission, it's tough," Freddie wisely agreed.

Everyone wondered when they would be hunting again and their Master reassured them that if they could get their trailer in and out, they'd hunt so long as the snow could support fox and hounds. Had to give your game a sporting chance.

Aunt Daniella, next to the bar in an upholstered chair, held court, tumbler of fine bourbon in hand. Sam and Gray kept their eyes on that glass, refilling it when necessary. One needed to keep the old lady happy. And she was, laughing, telling stories, flirting with Weevil, offering advice to Tootie about careers. Aunt Daniella expressed an opinion on everything.

Then again, she'd lived long enough to have one on just about anything.

Ben Sidell leaned against the bar, Ronnie with him. People came by, talked about the bizarre disappearance of Gregory Luckham, then moved on.

"Ronnie, I wish I had something to tell you." Ben looked out toward the large railroad station door. "Who knows when this snow will melt? And now the weatherman is calling for more. We'll keep searching. You know that."

"You think he's out there under a snowdrift?"

Ben thought a moment. "That would be the logical conclusion. However, I've been in law enforcement long enough to keep the door open. Most crimes are straightforward. Some are not. There really is such a thing as a criminal genius. He could be held somewhere for reasons unknown to us. Until we find a body, pick up hard information, I try to keep an open mind."

"The pipeline problem brought death threats. He didn't belabor it but people were stupid enough to threaten the pipeline, the workers, the surveyors, and be quoted in the newspaper or on TV."

"The feds are looking into that. My area is Gregory himself. Plus those guys don't think local law enforcement is worth a damn."

"Waco put paid to that." Ronnie's lips snapped shut.

He referred to the incident in 1993 in Texas when a religious community, nutcases to be sure, were stormed by the feds who didn't listen to the Texas Rangers, or the truly local people like a sheriff, etc. No, they did it the Washington way, the we-are-your-government-you-peon way. Result, a lot of dead people including children.

"Hell, Ronnie, no one learned a damn thing," Ben replied. "Plus it's a new generation. By now Americans are used to centralized government. We locals are just for speeding tickets."

"Nah. I know better than that or you'd have written me a ticket for when I cut you off in the hunt field." Their amusement lightened the moment.

"The obvious cause is the man had a heart attack or a stroke, fell off. However, it is possible that someone could have been waiting for him. The blizzard gave them a rare opportunity for murder or kidnapping," Ben said.

"The question is, how could anyone pull him off, drag him to wherever? You'd think that person would have gotten lost in the snowstorm."

"What if they weren't alone? Or what if they remained mounted? What if they knew the territory as well as, say, Sister?" Ben posed the question. "The crossroad would have been a good place to rendezvous, for lack of a better word. That or one of the outbuildings at Old Paradise. The storm came up so fast but they could have made it out of Old Paradise before you couldn't see the horse in front of you."

"Like a tag team?" Ronnie wondered.

"Yes. Given the weather conditions, it would be difficult but not impossible. The Richmond police questioned his wife. She was in shock."

"I keep thinking, 'Why didn't I turn around?' "

"Ronnie, even if you turned around, what would you have seen?" Ben replied. "He didn't bring his cellphone while hunting. He left it in his car. He couldn't call you or anyone."

"Right."

Ronnie swirled his glass around. "Old Paradise has kept secrets since 1814 when Sophie laid the cornerstone of the house. She bought all the land in 1812 but was prudent enough to wait until the war had shifted farther south. Maybe it had other secrets before that time. Now perhaps there is another one."

Crawford, disturbed but not miserable by Luckham's disappearance, had attended the Boxing Day breakfast to hear what others said.

Ben smiled at him. "Where were you at Christmas Hunt?"

Crawford smiled back. "Waving them off. Then Rory and I checked out the Carriage House. I drove home. He wanted to help with the horses. Today is his day off. You might call him tomorrow. Perhaps he saw something."

The men exchanged a few words, Crawford keenly aware that he had a strong motive if there was murder.

In the corner Charlotte Abruza asked Tootie, "How long have you known Old Paradise?"

"Almost six years. I hunted here while at private school."

"Have you ever come upon old gravestones, markers, in the woods?"

"No."

"A glimpse, maybe old grave markers that are worn down. Look like stones?"

"No. Miss Abruza, there are five thousand acres there. Whole sections are wooded, overgrown. Land changes over the centuries. Anything could be out there."

"Yes. I've convinced Crawford to use ground-penetrating radar. If there are old graves, that should find them," Charlotte answered. "The Monacans were here first, ancestral lands." A somber look crossed Charlotte's face. "Spirits."

"Were you at the station when the storm hit?"

"No. I'd gone back. I never imagined such ferocity," Charlotte replied. "I was lucky to make it back to my office."

"Not at Old Paradise?"

"No. I have an office with electricity, heat, furniture in the guesthouse at Beasley Hall. If I were at Old Paradise, those necessities would be missing."

"The stables?"

"Better where I was. Thought I might find Crawford but he was out. I'd never seen a hunt before. He suggested I go with Marty to view one. He was right. It's quite impressive and colorful."

CHAPTER 8

Clytemnestra was such a cow. Glaring at everyone, she murmured threats to anyone should they enter her paddock. No one wanted to go near her but she shook her head anyway. Her son, Orestes, contentedly chewed small squares of chopped hay sprinkled with a handful of grain. He didn't need to eat. He had grown larger than his mother, but both bovines, bored in their well-built cow barn, walked through the snow, now packing down with a good glaze on top.

Cindy Chandler, owner of Foxglove Farm, also owner of the two cantankerous animals, left the door open to their walk-in area. They didn't have stalls like the horses but they did need some sort of indoor pen so they could eat in peace, out of the weather. Put out together, there was no peace because even though Orestes now outweighed his mother, she would boss him around.

Cindy, perfectly turned out as always, rode by her two cows on Special Agent. There was no love lost.

"Cud breath," the small elegant Thoroughbred remarked.

"Asshole," Orestes spat back.

"I didn't teach you to talk like that." Clytemnestra chided her son. *"If you're going to insult him, then really insult him."* She took a breath. *"You wall-eyed son of a bitch. Your pasterns are too long, your brain too tiny. You are so stupid you let a human on your back and she tells you what to do."* She then faced her son. *"That's a proper insult. Specific to the object. Never rely on the generic insult. It marks you as common."*

"Why do you let her talk like that?" Lafayette, Sister's rangy gray Thoroughbred, her oldest horse, asked Special Agent.

"She amuses me. Putting on airs. Everyone knows cows aren't as smart as horses. That's why she's careful with her vocabulary. She's still a stupid cow." Special Agent blew wind out of his nostrils.

"She can say anything she wants." Magellan, loaned to Weevil for he was Betty's second horse, jumped in the conversation. *"When you're that big you can do and say what you want. Can you imagine the damage she could do if she got out of there?"*

None of the horses around them said anything because they all were imagining the damage Clytemnestra could do, worse if she blasted out of her paddock in tandem with Orestes.

Special Agent and Lafayette, old friends, matched each other's stride. Sister, on Lafayette, chatted with Cindy. They were riding to the first cast; chatting was not out of order.

Even though cold, snow on the ground, twenty people rode out this Tuesday. Sister could have canceled the hunt but she felt her hounds needed to get out of the kennels, the hunt horses out of the stables, and she, more than anyone, out of the house.

Keeping warm on those crystal clear winter days called for the old coats from England. Secondhand tack shops did a brisk business in the old coats, the weave being almost impregnable to the elements. One had to search for the old coats at the Crozet tack shop or at the Middleburg Tack Exchange in Middleburg, Virginia. Even if the wool got wet, one could stay warm. What suffered were your hands and feet. For all the decades that Jane Arnold had hunted, she never really could keep her hands and feet warm. If hiking boot makers could put Thinsulate into those boots, she grumbled, why couldn't Dehner or Vogel? She did not mention Lobb's in England because those bespoke boots started at $7,300. And Maxwell's nudged right behind. Shocking.

"But Dehner's does put Thinsulate in their boots if you order it," Cindy informed Sister, who had been grousing.

"Do they really?"

"Sure. You'll pay more but then again Dehner's is in Omaha, Nebraska. They know about winter."

"I always wonder how Genesee Valley"—Sister named the famed upper New York state hunt—"or Toronto–North York can do it."

"Me, too," Cindy confessed. "But I think there are times when the weather is so ferocious, even they have to stop. I always heard Genesee Valley stops when the river freezes."

"God bless them all. It's bad enough here, although I do like looking at it and it is bracing. I wonder about people who only remain in comfort, don't you?"

Cindy nodded yes, then stopped, as did Sister, who nodded in return to her dear friend, rode slightly ahead, given that she was leading the field and hounds were about to be cast.

As Jefferson Hunt was on Cindy's property, she could ride up front. Given her years of hunting, protocol would have dictated this anyway. But the landowner does have pride of place should the landowner be in the field. As Cindy had won the Eclipse Award twice in her life, the Oscars for horsemen, she would have been invited up front anywhere. She was far too modest to mention her awards or her hunt team victories in her youth. In Cindy and Sister's world, only the insecure cited their achievements.

Betty, home today with a nasty cold, called before the hunt beseeching Sister to call her the minute she was back in the house and tell her everything, everything.

Weevil took Betty's place on the right while Tootie rode on the left. Sister noted how the blond young man, seemingly born on a horse, looked at Tootie. Tootie inherited her mother's beauty but not her mother's ways. She seemed to evidence no interest in romance with any gender and yet, ah, and yet, Sister hoped. To be young and in love, euphoric, painful, everything at once, is one of life's great introductions to the irrational, to a connection that can't really be explained, only felt. She wished it for this young woman she had now known for six years. And as she was beginning to know the young man, gentlemanly, responsible, and bold, she hoped it for him, too.

This reverie was broken. "Master."

"Huntsman, forgive me. My mind wandered."

"As long as your body didn't wander with it." Shaker teased his boss. "As you see, the waterfalls are frozen. I would like to continue to the top of the hill and cast at the old schoolhouse."

"Good." She smiled at him.

The small waterfalls flowed from two ponds, one higher than the other and each containing a pipe, the upper flowing into the lower and the lower's pipe discharging directly into the lower stream. The upper stream ran underground into the upper pond, so only the lower stream was visible and it usually ran vigorously.

Cindy discovered all this while overseeding these pastures. A thin vein of quartz ran toward a piddling pond. Knowing land, soils, and flora, she felt sure an underground stream could be induced to fill an enlarged pond. Then she got the idea for a lower pond and to open a water course up below it. The sound of the spilling water soothed her. Quartz was often a sign of underground water.

Between the ponds a wide path, wide enough for a tractor, allowed one to ride.

The foxes used the ponds to drink, to gather and gossip in warmer weather. Cindy often found fox prints everywhere.

Upon reaching the schoolhouse, the whippers-in moved somewhat away from the pack.

"Lieu in," Shaker called.

Hounds surged forward to the schoolhouse for Georgia, a gray, lived inside. She actually lived in the rooms, having entrances in the basement. Cindy, knowing she had a fox there, installed a cat door in the basement door. Georgia lived the high life because treats were also available. But Cindy placed them far enough away from the house so Georgia would leave scent.

"What do you think?" Asa, the oldest hound in the pack, asked, his nose to one of Georgia's entrances.

"She's still living here." Dreamboat, one of the "D's," answered.

"The way to find out if she's there is to track her line"—Diana stood on the line—*"away from the house. If it heats up in that direction, she's gone out. If it fades, she's in the house. No chance to bolt her out of there."*

"Right." Everyone agreed, casting themselves in a large semicircle just in case Georgia cut right or left.

A line of scent track stayed straight but it was fading.

Diana stopped, looked up at the sky. No help there for a clear, bright day made her work harder.

Parker, wise beyond his years, suggested, *"She's inside. Why don't we go into the woods? Maybe we'll have better luck there."*

Hounds circled the house. Shaker came to the same decision as Parker. He blew a little toot.

"Come along." He turned toward the woods below the schoolhouse, to the right of the waterfalls.

The snow crunched underfoot. A light wind came out of the west, cold on faces. Down they walked, a slip here and there until into the heavy woods. The hickories, oaks, sycamores, gum trees had shed their leaves, the sky bright blue between their branches. All the pines, some boughs lower because of the snow still on them, provided a bit of protection from the wind. As they walked farther down, all finally were free of the wind, a relief.

A thin creek flowed, ice at the edges, where it was more shallow, solid ice. This creek dipped underground at the edge of the woods and that was the water feeding the ponds. Hounds moved on both sides of the creek.

Trooper stopped, sniffed a large fallen tree trunk. *"Been here."*

Diana checked it. *"Long time ago."*

Still hounds spread out hoping for scent. Perhaps whoever sat on the tree trunk left a warmer line, but it was too old.

Deer tracks, easily spotted, dotted the paths, yet not a deer was in sight. Possum and raccoon prints meandered along creekside. Birds remained in their nests, some in tree trunks. All creatures lived on the south side of their trees, nests, wherever, for the wind almost always cut down from the northwest. Those animals like Georgia, residing in human-built structures, could make them even cozier. One could drag in rags, bits of discarded clothing. Georgia even had a stolen down vest she filched from the barn years ago when Cindy Chandler left it on a tack trunk. The vest was perfect. Mating season, beginning, would bring gentlemen foxes to her door. Georgia, at this moment, evidenced no interest. For one thing, she rather liked having everything to herself. Cindy's barns delighted her. The horses spilled feed. Cindy might leave out crackers, mostly saltines. Every now and then if the weather turned ugly, Cindy would place a bucket of high-protein, high-fat dog kibble inside the schoolhouse. She'd open the door to the schoolhouse, set the bucket to the side of the door, then close it. Georgia had become so accustomed to the human she'd sometimes sit while Cindy placed the bucket in the adjoining room. Cindy could see her through that open door and vice versa. A few pleasantries were exchanged, then the human would leave. Georgia would make up her mind about mating when she was good and ready.

The gray could hear hounds down in the woods. Occasionally a hound spoke. Nothing came of it. The weather, too harsh, kept the males in their own dens. As soon as things improved they would be traveling. The smart ones brought little gifts. The dumb ones just showed up at your door assuming a female would be thrilled to see him. Females are picky regardless of species.

Twenty minutes of hunt-and-peck. Nothing. The treetops bent lower. Shaker looked up. Best to keep in the woods. Sister looked up, too, as the sound of wind in pines is distinctive, a *whoosh.* She knew the minute they left the woods they'd feel that wind clear to their bones.

The creek meandered east. So did the hounds, but it really was useless. The huntsman asked them to keep looking so they did.

Pookah, a youngster, puzzled, asked Ardent, an older hound, *"Don't they know there's no scent?"*

Ardent, lifting his head a moment, replied, *"The smart ones do but they can't smell. They know from memory."*

"A lot to remember," the sweet boy said.

"Well, yes, but they have good memories. Not as good as the horses but good especially about things they want to remember," Ardent answered. *"Ah, here's a whiff."*

Pookah put his nose down. *"Not a fox."*

"Bobcat." Ardent took a few more steps. The bobcat had dipped down over the side of the swale.

The bobcat tracks, out of sight to the huntsman, disappeared quickly, for the animal climbed a tree, came down on the other side, then repaired to his own living quarters. Hunting in such weather meant you went hungry a lot unless food was left out for you, and humans did not put food out for bobcats.

Another twenty minutes passed. Shaker turned back after crossing the creek at a flat place, ice crunching with each step. The cracking scared some horses in the field but their equine buddies in the field got them through it.

Emerging from the woods, a blast of icy air hit everyone

smack in the face. Hounds turned upward, with the wind in their faces, too.

Sister rode up to Shaker. "Bluebird day. Let's go in."

"Well, we've had a bit of exercise and they tried. Can't ask for more than that."

"Can't."

Bluebird day meant a blank day, nothing a huntsman wants but it does happen.

Once back at the trailers, Lafayette noticed that Clytemnestra and Orestes, snug in their barn, didn't pay attention to them. Clytemnestra may have been a cow but she was not stupid where her creature comforts were concerned. Cindy left the doors open to their big indoor living quarters so they could come and go. As night approached she would shut the doors, plug in the water trough heaters. Anything that broke the wind kept one a bit warmer, and the cattle barn did just that.

Blankets now on the horses, the hounds on the party wagon with lots of straw so they could curl up in it, the people walked to Cindy's house.

The aroma of food and hot coffee greeted them.

Warming their hands around hot cups of tea, Sister and Cindy wondered what the rest of the weather would be like for the remainder of the week.

"Just seems like there's one storm after another lining up in the Midwest."

Sister nodded. "Cindy, can you imagine what it feels like to live next to one of the Great Lakes? We think we get snow and cold. Gotta be tough to live out there."

Cindy agreed. "Remember when you and I drove out there to hunt in Michigan? I gained new respect for everyone, including the foxes."

"Where does the time go?" Sister mused. "How about last year when we had ten days of seventy degree temperatures in February? That was crazy. My forsythias bloomed." She laughed. "I bloomed. But it did interrupt breeding when the cold snapped right back. The foxes didn't know what to do and neither did I."

"It's odd, though. I know animals can sense weather better than we can. Do you think there was a time when we could do it, too?"

"I often wonder about that. Have all our advancements blunted our senses, our animal vigor, so to speak."

Her phone rang. Cindy clicked mugs with her and walked away to talk to other hunters.

"Hello," Sister answered. "We missed you today."

"What did I miss?" She heard Kasmir's voice, his light accent.

"Raw cold."

"Then I don't feel so bad. Alida and I decided we'd pick up all the things left here from the breakfast before we misplaced them."

"How about I pick them up in forty-five minutes?"

"We'll be here."

Sister clicked off, walked over to Shaker and Weevil. "Fellows, I'm going to Tattenhall Station to pick up whatever was left at the Boxing Day party. Can you take the hounds back without me"—she paused—"or with Tootie in case there's a lot to carry?"

"We'll be fine," Shaker said.

"Come on." Sister put her hand under Tootie's elbow. "I need you to go with me to Tattenhall Station. I forgot to ask Kasmir how much was left over from the party. Just in case it was a lot, I'll make use of your youthful vigor." She teased her.

Grabbing their scarves, their tweeds not really keeping out the cold, Sister cut on the engine and the heater.

"Stop by the hound truck for a minute, will you? I want to pick up my down jacket."

"Right. I always carry one in this car, keep one in the old truck, too. The weather can change on you in an instant." As Tootie got out, grabbed her jacket, slid back in, Sister said, "I need to pick up Raleigh and Rooster. Haven't given them a ride for a few days because of the weather."

"You spoil those dogs."

"I know."

"I've been thinking about getting Mom a dog. There's a fox who visits the doghouse in the back, which we put up for the fox. Now she wants me to open up the back, put in double mudflaps, so if he should get caught in there he can get out. Well, anyway, she's out there all alone. Do you think a dog would bother her fox? She thinks of it as her fox."

"Depends on the dog and it depends on whether she puts in a dog door for the dog."

"Something small and sweet," Tootie replied.

"That wouldn't be too much work for her. As for the fox, of course, I want that fox to stay healthy and safe, so why don't you fix up the dog box as you said and then build a dog yard for whatever you get your mother. That way the animals can coexist, but my bet is that the dog will stay inside with your mother most of the time or drive around with her in the car."

"Good idea." Tootie brightened. "Chapel Crossroads is kind of sparse. There aren't a lot of people around that are close. I mean there's the Van Dorns but she doesn't see much of them."

"Age is catching up with them." Sister inhaled. "I never thought about your mother out there alone. Has she said anything about it?"

"No. I was just thinking. Apart from the Van Dorns, Mom would need to drive to Kasmir and Alida. There's no one at Old Paradise but workmen. All the other places are either up or down the road, miles away."

"You're right. It's a good idea, assuming she'd like a dog. How small?"

"Small enough to crawl into her lap."

"I think she'd be pleased that you're thinking about her. You two seem to be getting along."

"I've spent more time with Mom here than I did all through grade school in Chicago. It's funny to be in my twenties learning about my mother."

"She's learning about you. I expect your whole family has paid a high price for all that success."

While a good crust covered the snow, one could still break through, snow up to your ankles. The ground exhausted you. After two hours of meticulous searching, Ben Sidell and his team rendezvoused at Chapel Crossroads.

"Let's duck into the vestibule of the church," Ben advised. "We'll be okay. I know the sexton, Adolfo Vega."

He did know the sexton. He knew Adolfo would be half in the bag by now, sound asleep. Did the priest know of this affliction? Yes, but the older man kept the grounds and the tiny church in good order. He was never sloppy or rude when he's had one too many. Also where would Adolfo go? Christian charity demanded he be kept on.

The small vestibule, two benches along the sides, unadorned, felt warm. Heat, kept at fifty degrees to keep pipes from freezing, felt like the subtropics at this moment. The four dropped down.

"Whew." Carson Blanton plopped on the seat.

"It's a real winter," Jude Hevener, another young man in the department, said.

Ben, early forties, liked working with young officers. He was impressed by their training, their calmness under most situations, just as he was surprised by what they didn't know. Usually what they didn't know was how politics worked. As a sheriff's department, funded by the county, politics intruded on their work. It certainly controlled their budget. Still a bit idealistic, the two young men would become furious, spoke freely to Ben, about how when anything went wrong they were blamed. It was always the sheriff's department's fault.

Ben would nod in agreement, then reply, "Get used to it."

Jackie Fugate, late twenties, never expressed that frustration. Her father, retired now, had worked his way up to detective. She grew up with all this and understood it. Smart, cool, quick on her feet, Ben kept his eye on her as he felt this youngster would climb. Maybe she would be the first female sheriff in Albemarle County, although the county commissioners would have to go through the theater of an outside search first.

Ben's focus was on the best people. He didn't care about race, background, or gender, but a little part of him liked seeing those who had been denied these opportunities win them. His department had good people. They worked well together. He sidestepped the problems of large police departments, city departments where quotas, enforced as part of the legislation, created more problems than they solved. He was grateful he didn't have to deal with that. He wanted good people and that was that. And right now he wanted Gregory Luckham.

"Sheriff." Jackie always addressed him by his title. "What about retracing the hunt from Tattenhall Station to where we started looking? Go backward."

"Not a bad idea."

She unzipped her heavy parka and smiled.

"It will still be hard to see anything. I mean the surface of the snow is smooth. No big lumps." Carson sank farther into the bench. "If he was grabbed, if he slipped off, well, you'd think some part of him would be showing by now. The snow is packed down."

"A human body would be packed down, too," Ben told him. "It's possible wind might have blown more snow on parts of the body. That's why we're here."

"Wouldn't foragers smell him?" Jackie asked.

"Any form of canine would." Ben slapped his gloves in his

lap. "Yesterday, maybe not, but today they'd be out. Perhaps not for a long time but it's possible some creature is digging for him."

Carson wrinkled his nose. "Like what?"

"Coyote, a dog, even a fox. Canines have incredible noses. The cold won't make scenting easier, but they will know long before we do." Ben absorbed his lessons from hunting with Sister.

"When we do, it's the worst." Carson wrinkled his nose again.

"The carbon cycle." Jackie shrugged.

"Well, let's walk back to the SUV. Why don't we go through the graveyard since we didn't have the opportunity to do that before? This is on the way back. It's possible he might have crawled in by a tombstone, been covered up."

Ben stood up. The three rose with him.

Jude opened the door. "It's worse."

The wind had picked up.

"All right. Carson, take the northernmost. Jackie, the middle, Jude the southernmost. I'll walk along the roadside ditch."

At Tattenhall Station, Kasmir, seeing Sister pull in, was already out the door, large carton in his arms.

Sister jumped out, lifting the back door. "Raleigh, Rooster. Stay."

"I don't want to sit next to a carton," Rooster complained.

"Give it a minute. We'll jump out when she's distracted," the normally obedient Raleigh suggested.

Alida came alongside as she carried a slightly smaller carton. "Fuzzy hats, gloves, scarves." She placed the carton in the back. "Kasmir carried the heavier stuff. A lot of people left their serving dishes. Too much party." She grinned.

Tootie and Sister followed them inside as there was more to come. The fireplace crackled.

"Sheriff's SUV?" Sister inquired.

"Ben popped his head in. They'll keep looking, especially

now that the weather is calm. Still cold but at least calm," Kasmir answered.

Sister picked up a smaller box, looked inside, plucked up an ID chain. "You'd think someone would have called about this."

Alida chimed in. "Earrings in this one. More gloves. Lipstick. It's amazing what people leave behind."

"No phones?" Sister asked.

"Oh, they would have bugged us right away for that." Alida smiled. "People's entire schedules, every phone number they know are on those cellphones. Mine's sure full."

They walked back outside to put the boxes in the back. The dogs still sat there looking sweet.

"Honey, what's the man's name who's missing? I should remember but I don't." Alida slid the small carton next to Raleigh.

"Luckham. Gregory Luckham. He's the president of Soliden."

"Yes, of course." She stopped for a moment, puffs of cold air coming from her mouth. "It's almost as if he's a phantom."

"Given the heated emotions about the pipeline, I don't see how this can come to a good end," Kasmir added.

"True." Sister agreed. "Yet there is something strange. Alida is right. It's like he's a phantom. We have a good start, good run, finally wind up on Old Paradise, the storm hits up in minutes and then, gone. No sign of him. No sight of him or anyone else either."

"What troubles me is we were on Old Paradise," Kasmir said.

"Crawford wasn't going to fuss, not for Christmas Hunt. I spoke to him the night before, asking for permission should the fox turn that way."

"And the fox did." Alida put her arms around herself, for even with her jacket, the cold seeped through.

"And so did Gregory Luckham." Kasmir glanced across the road at the chapel, could see the sheriff's people. "Crawford is dead set against this pipeline. Granted, he and I have worked together and he's been reasonable, but he isn't a man who knows or obeys foxhunting protocol."

"What do you mean?" Sister asked, an idea beginning to form in her mind.

"If he knew, and he had to know, Luckham was on his land, he might have blown a fuse."

"Kasmir, you mean kill him?" Alida was aghast.

"Rage can throw anyone off track," Kasmir answered.

"Yes it can, but I think if Crawford wanted to kill someone, he'd contain the rage and pay to have it done. Why risk everything he's worked for? He's a highly intelligent man despite his vanities," Sister said.

Tootie also noticed the people at the chapel, Ben coming down over the bank toward the road. Sister walked toward him and the dogs jumped down to accompany her.

Alida waved. "I'm going back inside."

Sister waved back. "Thanks for picking that stuff up." Kasmir joined Alida. He, too, smiled and waved. "Come in and sit down if you like. We can always find something to talk about."

Seeing this welcoming party, the dogs bounding toward him, Ben neglected to look down. The ground appeared smooth enough. But the snow filled up the drainage ditches along the road and, now softening a bit, he stepped right into it. He fell in up to his waist and couldn't free himself.

"We'll get you out," Sister promised as she and Tootie reached him.

Each woman took an arm, but he was deeper than they anticipated.

Carson, Jude, and Jackie slid over the side of the embankment of the graveyard to help their boss.

With all of them carefully pulling his arms, they began to

wedge Ben upward. Finally they did get him out. He slid out on his stomach with two people on each arm and Jackie ready to jump into the ditch to hoist him up if need be.

"Treacherous," Ben panted.

"It is." Sister agreed as she helped brush him off. "Looks level."

The two dogs sniffed him, then turned their attention to the ditch.

"Not much scent," Raleigh observed.

"A hint." Rooster gleefully started digging.

"Boys." Sister chided them as plumes of snow flew from their paws.

"Mom, something's dead here. Not even a hint of decay," Rooster happily informed her.

"You shouldn't have mentioned decay. They can't stand it." Raleigh dug alongside Rooster.

The two dogs, side by side in the tight space, grew more excited.

"Raleigh, Rooster. Out. Out now."

With misery on their reluctant faces, they did as they were told.

Carson slid down where the dogs had been. With his gloved hands he began brushing the snow. A blue down jacket appeared, the front of one. Carson slowly continued. The others watched, frozen in fascination and horror.

"Frozen stiff. He'll thaw out. We can help." Rooster inched toward the edge where Sister grabbed his collar.

"No. No means no."

He sat down next to Sister with a whimper.

Carson now scooped snow in his gloved hands. "There's no room for anyone else. This might take a while."

Ten minutes later, a chest appeared. It could be a man but a down jacket is unisex.

"Could it be Luckham?" Jude wondered.

"He was in hunt kit," Sister, voice low, told him. "I would think if it's Luckham, the coat would be scarlet."

Finally a man's face appeared. The lower jaw, hint of beard underneath the skin. Carson continued almost tenderly until the entire face was visible.

He wasn't Gregory Luckham.

CHAPTER 9

Rooster whined as Raleigh nudged Rory's face with his nose. The Doberman vainly tried to bring him back to life.

"Oh, no!" Tears filled Sister's eyes.

Ben, thinking quickly, put his hand on her arm as she began to kneel down. "Don't, Sister. I am so sorry but you can't touch him. He will need to go to the medical examiner's. I have to treat this as a possible wrongful death."

She bowed her head, couldn't fight the tears, so now her dogs licked her face. "Of course. Forgive me. Ben, he fought so hard. He fought long odds."

Tootie, horrified, couldn't speak.

The sheriff, fond of this woman whom he greatly respected, draped his arm over her heaving shoulders. "I am sorry. What can I do to help you?"

She lifted her head, wiped her tears. "Let me tell Gray first so Gray can go to his brother. This will devastate Sam. They went through hell and high water together."

"Yes. Anything you ask. I will need to speak to Sam as soon as possible. So often, well, in the case of murder or an accident, the first responses from friends and family can be helpful. Before they are completely composed."

She nodded. "You understand my worry."

"I do indeed." He looked into those eyes, eyes you could fall into. "Sometimes I hate my job."

She brushed a cold, gloved hand against his cheek. "I know you do. You're a good man. We're lucky to have you in this county."

The mudroom door opened, then closed. Raleigh and Rooster pushed through the doggie door. Sister followed once her gear hung on the pegs. Tootie had returned to her cottage.

Golly looked up from her plush bed in the corner, prepared to say something hateful to the dogs but immediately knew something was wrong. The dogs told her what they knew.

Sister walked down the hall, the long Persian runner absorbing her steps. Gray, at the desk in the library, looked up.

"Honey." He was on his feet.

Her posture, her face, alerted him. He thought perhaps one of the horses had died or a hound. Sister took those losses as hard as those of her human friends.

"Gray, Rory is dead."

"Dear God." Gray's face became ashen. "He, he"—he swallowed—"was he drunk?"

She shook her head. "No one will know until the medical examiner is finished with the body." She sat on the sofa, folded her hands in her lap, as he sat next to her. "Ben and his crew were back at Tattenhall Station. Tootie was with me to pick up leftover stuff from Boxing Day. We saw the SUV. Well, I figured rightly that Ben and his people returned as the weather cleared. Anyway, Ben had fallen in the ditch alongside Chapel Cross, which I saw as we left Kasmir and Alida. He couldn't get out. Tootie and I pulled but Jackie, Carson, and Jude ran out from the graveyard. Finally we got him out and then Raleigh and Rooster leapt into where he had just been and started digging better than two backhoes. Carson got into the ditch and started removing snow with his hands. I couldn't breathe. I thought 'Gregory Luckham' but he wasn't wearing a parka. He was in hunt kit, at least the last time anyone saw him. This entire episode is, well, no matter. It was Rory. He was not a natural color, frozen as he is, but he looked"—she paused—"he looked peaceful."

"I need to go to Sam. He's at work. Will you call Crawford? Given the circumstances, I'm sure he will let me take my brother home."

"Of course."

Gray left the library, grabbed his heavy coat, and was down the drive while Sister called Crawford, who was shocked, mentioned that he hadn't seen Rory since Christmas Hunt but that wasn't unusual given his work schedule and yesterday was his day off.

"Hey." Sam looked up as his brother strode into the barn. "Brushing the snow off before I put him in his stall. Damn stuff sticks like Silly Putty so I guess I'm not brushing I'm dislodging it. What's the matter? You look awful. Did Aunt Dan die?"

Gray shook his head. "She's eternal. Rory."

Sam suddenly stopped. "No. That can't be true."

"I'll put the horse up. Get your coat. We're going home."

"I can handle it." Sam's lower jaw jutted out.

"Maybe you can handle it but I can't."

Sam didn't realize he was shaking. Ice cold, mind numbed, he simply stood rooted.

Gray took the kind gelding, Trocadero, put him in his stall, went into the tack room, got his brother's heavy Woolrich red plaid coat, made Sam put it on, shepherded him to the Land Cruiser, put him in the car, shut the door.

Sam, seeming to awaken, grabbed the handle. "I need to tell Crawford."

"Sister called him."

"Sister?"

Gray then told his brother how she, Tootie, and the dogs found Rory.

Within twenty minutes, a bit slow going on the roads, the brothers drove down the long snow-covered path to the Old Lorillard place, which they were restoring. Gray lived there half the week, then half with Sister. It worked out for all parties.

As Gray parked the big SUV he assured Sam. "We'll get your truck tomorrow."

"Just drop me off at work tomorrow. I am not leaving Crawford in the lurch or Skiff."

He named the female huntsman Crawford had hired for his outlaw pack. Much as this might cost her down the road, for the MFHA viewed outlaw packs with hostility, she needed the work. She and Sam worked easily together.

"Whatever you say. Come on, let's get the fire started."

They walked through the back door, small mudroom with a high shelf over the door into the kitchen, a true old Virginia farmhouse, neither one noticing Uncle Yancy, the red fox, stretched out on that shelf.

Sound asleep, he heard the humans too late so he stayed as still as a rock. They passed right under him.

While the two men crumpled up newspaper, grabbed sticks of fatback, and arranged the logs, Sister, back at her farm, called Aunt Daniella.

She told her what happened.

"Where's Sam now?"

"With Gray, who picked him up from work. They're home now and Gray will stay with him. If there's any doubt, Gray will pick it up first."

"U-m-m," Aunt Daniella muttered, knowing what "doubt" meant.

Sam, sober for over a decade, was facing a terrible blow. No one wanted him to drink.

"I think he will bear it." Sister sighed. "There are so many questions. They're running through my brain."

"Mine, too." The old woman agreed.

"Rory was a good man. He was probably helping someone. I saw him when we first rode out but not when we returned. Well, when we returned you couldn't see anything."

"Yes." A moment, then Aunt Daniella said, "Did you see his body?"

"No. I saw the front of his parka, then his face. He looked at peace, Aunt Daniella."

"If he was injured, shot, say, you wouldn't have known?"

"No. Something is wrong here, something widening, like ripples in a pond. One man disappears. Another is found dead. One is rich and powerful. The other is anything but, but he had friends, good friends and given his background that says a lot."

"Does. His people were violent drunks. That child was beaten simply for breathing. Well, he grew into a big, strong fellow, but the damage was done. I thought of him as a small miracle. And you know it was Sam, once sober, who worked like a dog to send Rory to the same clinic. I never really gave Sam credit for that." She inhaled. "What's to be done?"

"I don't know. If I hear anything I'll call you."

"Ditto." Aunt Daniella hung up the phone, and with the wisdom of the old she dialed again.

"Aunt Dan." A voice happy to hear hers responded.

"Yvonne, I need your help."

Aunt Daniella told Yvonne everything she knew plus how Sam saved Rory. A silence followed when she finished.

"What can I do?"

"Take more lessons. I'll pay. I need to keep him busy."

"You aren't paying and that's the end of that."

"I need you to join us for suppers, here, at Sister's, at your house, and even at the old home place. When Sam suffers he doesn't eat. He needs to eat. He needs people around him. He tells me about your progress riding. I am involving you in our family. I am asking a lot."

"You are asking very little. I would be honored to help. You've helped me. I've been self-involved about my divorce, final, thank heavens. You listen and your silences are as instructive as your words. I'm in, Aunt Dan." She thought a moment. "What is it the foxhunters say?"

"All on."

"All on," Yvonne repeated.

CHAPTER 10

"Possibly a jolt of terrible pain. He didn't know what hit him." Ben looked at the plume from his cup of hot chocolate.

"Poor Rory." Betty shook her head.

Ben stopped by after calling on Gray and Sam. Sister asked, for he called first to see if she was home, if Betty could be there since she had known Rory since his childhood. She might have an idea, an insight.

Golly wedged herself next to the Doberman, wedged next to Sister's leg. She remained quiet, not being ugly or taunting the dogs. She knew they were distressed. She really loved these two dumb dogs. She just didn't want them to know it, that's all.

"So whoever killed him was strong?" Sister dropped her hand onto Raleigh's head.

"Strong enough. He'd been struck with a blunt object. Once the body is thoroughly examined we'll know, but his was not a natural death."

"How long?" Sister asked.

"Winters are not as busy as warm months. Ten days I think at the most. The media will keep attention on this for a bit also because Luckham is still missing. Potential serial killer, that sort of thing. As the media is not responsible to citizens, they can conjure up anything. Aliens."

Betty returned to the last moments of Rory's life. "Really? You think one terrible moment of pain followed by death?"

"Yes." He reassured her.

"Pain is one thing. Terror another," Sister interjected.

"The second issue is was he drunk?" Betty said what they all thought.

"If he were blind drunk, then maybe he would have simply fallen into the ditch. I'm not saying he couldn't have been drunk, but his death was a deliberate act. I asked Sam and Gray, now you two. Did you ever think Rory could have been involved in something illegal?"

"Rory?" Sister's eyebrows arched upward. "Like what?"

"Well, as an alcoholic, a former alcoholic—"

Betty interrupted Ben. "They all tell you they are alcoholic, even if they've been sober for thirty years."

"They do, don't they?" He nodded. "Well, as an alcoholic, who would know better where thirst is? I refer to our profitable stills in the county. If there's one thing Virginians can do, it's make astonishing white lightning. Load up trucks and carry it north of the Mason-Dixon Line. No taxes. Paid in cash. Quite a business."

"All that beautiful water cascading down the Blue Ridge Mountains. Nothing like it," Sister said.

"So you have sampled same?" He half smiled at her.

"Of course not." She smiled back. "Okay, what else?"

"Drugs, prostitution, child pornography."

"Never." Betty defended Rory. "Never. Never. Never."

"Horse stealing. It still goes on. Maybe doesn't make as much money as during the last century, but it still does go on, as do theft, breaking and entering. Silver is easy to sell."

"If he was making money in an illegal fashion, wouldn't we have seen some improvement in his circumstances? That old car of his was held together with duct tape." Sister stated the obvious.

"We'll investigate his bank account. The usual stuff. But you're right. One would think there would be some improvement. He lived in the little apartment over Crawford's stable. Sam wasn't worried about him. His car was gone and Monday is his day off. He thought maybe Rory took time after Christmas Hunt, sort of a long weekend thing. He lived simply." Ben paused. "Yes, we've been through the apartment. No TV. No computer. A few books. A twin bed and a wardrobe with a couple of shirts and a decent raincoat, Barbour, a gift from Crawford to whom we've also spoken. He had four sweatshirts, two sweaters, one nice. A pair of work boots and two pairs of worn cowboy boots. The refrigerator contained milk, eggs, a small steak. The cupboard had two boxes of cereal and one can of McCann's Irish oatmeal. Again, not much. No mail, no bills, no credit cards. Rory was truly off the grid. Oh, he owned a razor, shaving cream, a bar of oatmeal soap, a jar of shampoo, and a small bottle of cologne."

"Beloved," Sister said.

"How did you know?"

"Gray gave it to him for Christmas. It's expensive. Gray wanted him to have something nice and since he didn't know the true cost of the cologne, he readily accepted it. He would have been embarrassed to own a bottle like that, near to four hundred dollars I think."

"No kidding?" Betty was aghast.

Sister smiled. "Gray, mostly prudent, has his ways. He tells me our lives as foxhunters revolve around scent so he will give off the best scent. You should see his bathroom. He has even more cologne at Old Lorillard."

"Sweet of him to think of Rory." Betty then turned to Ben. "Rory's mother is still alive. Steel yourself. She's awful."

"She is. I sent Jackie out to visit her. Women can be better at these things. She came back and said his mother asked nothing about him. She only wanted to know, or rather she wanted the county to know, she didn't have the money to bury him. And Jackie also said she'd never seen a wastebasket so overflowing with bottles."

"Rory had a hard life. He made something of himself. It took Sam's help and most people would only see a day laborer, a poor white man. I saw a success. His murder makes no sense." Sister finished her hot chocolate, needing a pick-me-up.

"If he were involved in something illegal, it might make sense. He was killed to shut him up or so someone else would reap all the profits."

"That might also apply if he found out about someone else. Rory wouldn't tolerate something criminal. Illegal liquor, yes, but that's a way of life here. No one thinks of it as criminal except the feds."

"Yes." Ben waited a beat, then agreed.

Betty added, "What if he came upon someone committing a crime?"

"Anything is possible." Ben twirled his cup in his hands. "I don't feel good about this. Sorry that sounds odd. No one feels good about a murder, but usually we have at least one obvious suspect, other persons of interest. Not always but usually. We have nothing. Nothing but snow." He paused. "Crawford told us Rory had been at the Carriage House with him checking on lumber. The storm came up and Rory asked to be dropped at Tattenhall Station. He said he didn't want Sam to drive alone hauling Trocadero in that storm. I spoke to Sam, who said he never saw Rory. Knew nothing about it. All we know is he did make it to Tattenhall Station."

Betty, thinking out loud, asked, "Could this be related to Luckham's disappearance?"

Sister interjected. "Rory didn't know Gregory Luckham. How could he be involved?"

"Maybe he wasn't involved, you know, part of what surely has to be a crime. But what if he saw something?"

Sister considered this. "Anything is possible, although I don't know how he could see something when none of us could see."

Ben, carefully choosing his words, said, "Betty, we are not ruling out some connection to Gregory Luckham. Sister is correct in that everyone we have spoken to so far feels certain that Rory and Gregory didn't know each other. And all recognize either the coincidence or noncoincidence of one man missing and another found dead near where Gregory was last seen. Granted it's about four miles from the Corinthian columns to Chapel Cross, but Rory was with Crawford at Old Paradise. He may have been closer to the event, for lack of a better word, than we know."

After Ben left, the two washed cups at the sink.

"I'll forever see him. The shock of seeing his face appear under the snow," Sister said.

"I wish there was something I could do." Betty's voice sounded hopeless.

"There is." Sister's voice was firm. "We can find his killer."

CHAPTER 11

The much vaunted January thaw warmed Saturday the sixth. Warm being relative, it was 46°F, which felt marvelous the last few weeks of ferocious winter. Roads plowed meant you could actually drive from point A to point B. However, back roads and farm roads remained spotty, which forced Sister to shift New Year's Hunt, the last of the High Holy Days, to this Saturday since more people can hunt as opposed to a weekday. As the search was still continuing for Gregory Luckham, she chose not to schedule New Year's Hunt near the Chapel Cross area.

Parking big rigs was possible there for the owners of Welsh Harp, well off, had snowplows, big John Deere tractors, any kind of implement a farmer or gentleman farmer could want. The new fixture also housed foxes, both reds and grays.

The pack, deep into the Pippin apple orchard for which the property was famous in the late nineteenth and mid-twentieth centuries, had lost a good line.

Giorgio, a newer bloodline Sister was developing, raised his head. *"He didn't head into the wind. He's not stupid."*

Dragon agreed. *"None of them are. The older they get, the smarter they get."*

Taz, another male, moved off toward the middle of the orchard.

"Taz, what are you doing?" Giorgio asked.

"What if he has a disguised den in the middle of the orchard? It's so barren, the humans wouldn't think to look."

The apple trees, limbs gnarled, ice having melted, looked black, appeared fairy tale–like and, Taz was right, barren. One could imagine fairies or worse watching from the branches.

Nose down, Taz returned to where they lost the scent and cast in a wide circle. Shaker, on Hojo, ready to blow the hounds together to move on, observed. He had faith in Taz, now in his prime. Taz, steady, patient, could save the day while the other hounds could get fussy. Zane, a younger hound, followed Taz. Then his littermate, Zorro, tagged along.

"This has to be him." Zorro inhaled. *"Faint though."*

Rivulets of melted snow ran between the apple rows as the land tilted just slightly. The fox had run into the water, to weaken his scent.

"It is him!" Taz was now obsessed.

Shaker, silent, walked slowly toward and behind the three hounds. The other hounds followed, soon helping Taz, Zorro, and Zane. This scent line taunted them but hounds solve problems. The whole pack became determined.

Diana and Dreamboat pushed. Finally they stopped at a large puddle in front of an ancient walnut tree in the middle of the orchard. This majestic tree commanded the area. The owners gave it plenty of room respecting the giant's years.

"He's here," Taz declared with authority.

"Where?" Little Pookah, not the brightest bulb on the Christmas tree, wondered.

"Get your feet wet, Kiddo." Dreamboat teased the youngster as the larger, bold hound splashed through the puddle, deeper than anticipated.

"Puddle, hell," Giorgio complained.

A visible hole at the base of the tree emitted heavy gray fox scent. Their quarry built his den in the tree and he was so clever that he could climb up inside if need be and emerge out on mighty branches as thick as other tree trunks. Some had become so heavy they bent, dipping to the ground. The interior of the walnut allowed him to create different levels, for the hollowing out wasn't complete. Various natural levels existed inside. The gray fox, secure in his lodgings, considered going out on a branch to torment the peons below but figured they'd stay longer if he did that. Better they go away.

Weevil had ridden up beside Shaker in case he chose to dismount. Betty and Tootie remained on their sides in case Shaker cast from the tree or the fox bolted, doubtful, but you never know with a fox. Foxes never read hunting books so they do exactly as they please, every moment being ad hoc. Drives humans crazy for humans like patterns and predictability.

Reposing on his third floor, the gray, coat luxurious, listened to the confusion and talk outside. *"Idiots."*

"Good hounds. Good hounds." Shaker beamed.

Sister brought the field up closer to view the tree. What a sight they made in their formal attire contrasting against the black fruit trees, the packed-down, melting snow on the earth.

"Just makes me want to read *Aesop's Fables* tonight." Sister grinned for she was bursting with pride at the detective work of Taz, Zane, and Zorro. She loved a stayer, human, horse, or hound. Any creature that wouldn't give up, that pressed on despite the odds, touched her heart, and these three showed off the work ethic of those bloodlines she prized. Not that she'd brag. Sister was a lady. However, if anyone praised her hounds, he or she would receive a warm thank-you and the Master would remember someone who paid attention to hound work.

"What do you think?" Shaker leaned toward her as he'd remounted after blowing "Gone to Ground."

"Everyone still looks fresh. How about you cast toward the caves?"

"As you wish." He teased her, using the command from a fairy tale.

As Weevil, this being his first year whipping-in to the pack, didn't know this territory, Sister simply pointed her crop to the west. "The caves run along the base of the mountains at this point. There's an underground stream in there runs maybe a quarter mile, then comes out not far from the house."

"Thank you." He followed Shaker as she dropped back. Then he did, too. The huntsman picked up a trot to hustle out of the orchard. A large pasture abutted the orchard and then a narrow strip of woods, mostly pines.

Sam, riding with his brother, watched a well-fed sharp-shinned hawk. Game was plentiful here for small to medium-sized predators.

Gray, on Cardinal Wolsey, relaxed a bit. Sam, though grieving, showed no signs of self-destructive behavior. He couldn't bring himself to clean out Rory's meager possessions, though, so Gray and Skiff, along with Marty, Crawford's wife, sorted through belongings, thoroughly cleaning everything for the next occupant, no one in mind at the present.

Bobby Franklin, bringing up Second Flight, stopped, pulled off his cap, counted twenty, then bellowed "Tallyho."

A fox coming out of the woods, bursting through the still nasty thornbushes, shot alongside Second Flight, heading toward the orchard.

Shaker turned the pack, galloped to where he could see the

Second Flight leader, dropped the pack along the parallel of Bobby's arm. Within less than a minute the pack screamed for the scent, fresh, only got fresher.

As the terrain sloped down, hilly in spots, Sister unconsciously slipped her leg a bit forward. Not show ring position but it sure could keep you in the saddle if you ran over sloping ground or took a drop jump, which loomed straight ahead. First the hounds cleared it, picture perfect, then Shaker, then Weevil, such a beautiful rider that Sister forced herself to take her eyes off him as the stout coop drew ever closer. Rickyroo, smooth, rather enjoyed drop jumps. He came up, rated by Sister, found the perfect spot, and sailed over. The landing, good, still proved a little slippery. His front legs skidded along, his hindquarters sank low, and so did Sister. Leaning back, she laughed. Rickyroo, a fabulously balanced horse, truly was worth his weight in gold, one of the reasons she rarely interfered with him. Sister usually let her mount pick the takeoff spot. Not only because he knew his job but he could feel the earth better than she. All she ever had to do was rate him if he wanted to pick up speed before she did. In her mind, why ride a horse if you don't trust him? In his mind, why take care of a human if you didn't love her?

The fox, a brilliant red, put on the afterburners. He hadn't been hunted all season. He'd become a trifle lazy. The speed of the pack pressed him so evasive maneuvers were in order. Knowing where the gray lived, he blew through the orchard, right by the walnut, hoping the heavy scent would split the pack, especially the young entry. Wrong. Hounds stuck together. As the old saying goes, "You could have thrown a blanket over them."

Past the tree, he flew on until he came out of the orchard and then, devil in his eye, he shot straight for the trailers. Not only did he go through the parking, he even dashed in and out of one trailer. So did the hounds. This bought him just enough time to charge by a slew of outbuildings, all painted and prim, until he popped into his den under the children's playhouse, a replica of the main house.

Hounds reached this charming structure about four minutes later. Shaker, long a huntsman, knew he had to get his hounds away from the little house. They were so keyed up, they'd jump through windows, smashing them, or they'd plow through gardens, which, covered in snow, still contained bulbs ready to show themselves come March or April. It was a sure bet those bulbs had been planted by the children, too.

He blew three blasts, then motioned for his whippers-in to close in. Betty knew exactly what ran through his mind. Neither Tootie nor Weevil did but you do as the huntsman commands, so they surrounded the hounds, pushing them back from the house, while Shaker turned to ride away. Usually hounds follow the huntsman. Sister pulled up about forty yards back. The ground had been torn up enough. No point in dragging the field through it. As it was she would offer any restoration that might be needed.

"Why is he leaving? The fox is here!" Pansy, Pookah's sister, was aghast.

"Yeah!" Angle, young entry, wondered.

"Just do it," Dreamboat ordered the youngsters.

Doing as told, the young ones bitched and moaned as they walked, plodded really, every step a torture, toward their huntsman. Once far enough away, Shaker stopped, praised his hounds for their good work. He couldn't help but notice the baleful looks from the P's and Angle.

Sister, Shaker, Betty, Tootie, and Weevil walked them throughout the off-season, groomed them, wormed them, fed them, played with them. Their attitude was easy to read.

"Shaker, let's call it a day." Sister smiled at him, both knowing it had been a decent day. Stop while you're ahead.

The breakfast, in the house, found everyone in a good mood, although the subject of the still missing man and the discovery of

Rory somewhat muted the vigor of a decent day. Welsh Harp's owners were thrilled to see everyone in their best kit.

Sister apologized to the hosts concerning the grounds by the playhouse. They told her not to worry, but she whispered to Walter later that they needed to buy bulbs, lots of bulbs, and even help the kids plant them.

Her Joint Master agreed. Walter possessed a sure touch with people. As a cardiologist, he needed it.

Aunt Daniella and Yvonne enlivened the group along with other "muffin hounds."

Yvonne walked over to Sam. "A good day to start the second half of the season?"

"It was. You'll be out here next year."

"I will. Your aunt, per usual, gave me a running commentary on the history of the place. She said during the war, German P.O.W.s were held here and picked apples."

"Before my time but you know fifty years after the war, a lot of them came back to visit here, to see the Americans who imprisoned them but took care of them. It was quite an emotional event and they all wanted to see the orchards. A lot of tears."

Yvonne put her hand on Sam's forearm, voice low. "Sometimes I forget what we mean to other people. We, as Americans. You just reminded me."

He nodded. "Bad news sells. If there isn't any, make it up or drag down anyone who ever accomplished anything. You don't read about the good we've done and do."

People interrupted them, some to express their condolences, for most of the foxhunters knew what Sam and Rory had lived through. Most of those who lived in the territory had done so, but those who traveled on weekends had not.

Once together again, Yvonne reminded him, "Aunt Dan says she's making spoon bread. Don't be late."

"I won't. You all have been good to me. Everyone has been

good to me." He sighed. "Finding out that Rory had no alcohol in his system has helped a little."

Freddie Thomas, another accountant, was deep in discussion with Gray and Ronnie. Sister didn't intrude but she did signal to Weevil and Tootie, also deep in conversation, to join her.

"Clever." Tootie smiled. "I have never seen a den in a tree like that."

Sister, glad to talk about foxes, related. "Sometimes a fox will create a den under a large fallen log. The exits and entrances are around it, some at a distance, and there's usually one in the middle of the log's bottom. You can't see it from outside. Just looks like a big log."

"That drop jump brought people to the Lord." Weevil laughed.

"I got to go over the coop at the far end of the pasture but I could see everyone else. The shock was, no one came off."

"Surprised me, too. Tomorrow let's do the kennel chores, give the kids a good rest, take three horses and go to Tattenhall Station. I know Ben Sidell has been over it and I know he'll go back until he's satisfied they haven't missed something. Maybe we can be of some help. We'll be looking at it with new eyes. Preys on my mind, Rory and Gregory, too, short though our acquaintance was. It's like finding scent, you know. Surely we'll get a whiff of something."

CHAPTER 12

The first thing Sister, Tootie, and Weevil noticed was the place where Rory was found had been carefully dug out. Snow had been removed onto the road as well as up on the land above the ditch. Ben and his crew tried to examine everything.

Kasmir offered to join them but she asked if she and her staff might repair to the station when finished. He readily agreed, promising to join them.

Sister looked up from the excavation to the church. "Ben and his people have gone all through the grounds, had Adolfo open all the outbuildings as well as the church. Let us first ride through Tollbooth."

Tollbooth, a sizable farm—they all were this far out—lay immediately to the east of Chapel Cross, next to the chapel grounds and another fixture, Old Orchard. Nothing grand, clean simple structures from the mid-eighteenth century survived. The earlier ones had been replaced but drawings were made that hung in the center hallway of the main house, a large clapboard with the additions that accrue over decades.

As there was no traffic, they rode down the center of the road, turning left into the drive. A dangerously leaning tollbooth listed to port. It needed restoration but the owners, quite precise about these things, wouldn't do so until the head of the architectural history department from the University of Virginia visited this structure. They also wanted someone from the Virginia Historical Society to see it. Unique though it was, no other tollbooths being around or discovered, these things take time when schedules are crammed.

"What do you think they charged?" Weevil asked.

"It varied a lot throughout the eighteenth century in Virginia, as the conditions of the roads varied a lot. When the Valley Turnpike was built, it would cost about four dollars and forty cents in overall tolls to travel from the north end in Winchester all of the sixty-eight miles to Harrisonburg on the southern end," Tootie replied having studied a bit of early area history. "It crept up over time."

"Inflation is nothing new." Sister patted Aztec's neck as his ears swiveled forward.

"Doesn't sound like much," Weevil replied, "but I guess it was at the time."

"The toll would have equaled about seventy-eight dollars in 2007 dollars," Tootie informed him.

"The going rate, I expect," Sister added. "When you think about it, it paid for all this over those early decades."

"Weevil, this was the only path from east to west until you got up to what is now Ruckersville and south down to what is now Lynchburg. North and south travel proved so much easier and I expect it was the same for Canada, too. It's the way North America is made."

"Did you two know that we reached the West Coast before Lewis and Clark?" Weevil allowed himself a flash of pride.

"I did." Sister smiled. "What courage. Well, what courage they all had back then."

"I didn't know that," Tootie confessed.

"I'll give you a book." Out of the corner of his eye, Weevil saw Gris. "Tallyho," he quietly said.

"Gris." Sister grinned. "Gris, we know it's you."

"Doesn't mean I'm going to stop and talk."

He walked at a leisurely pace to make his point, then ducked into his den in the equipment shed with the sliding doors. So what if they saw him? They knew where he lived as he'd given them a few merry chases over the years.

"More people?" His mate, Vi, swept her whiskers forward.

"Too many lately." He snuggled next to her. *"It's easy to baffle the hounds and I don't mind the people who live in the big house, but for the last two weeks cars with flashing lights, people over there at the chapel. People at the station for the big hunt, too much."*

"Who is out there now?" Vi asked.

"The Master and the two young assistants. Young, pretty. I sometimes forget that humans can be good to look at. But if the Master is here without the hounds, that means either she's looking to improve the fixture or something really is wrong."

"How do you know all this?" she said admiringly.

"I've watched them for two years. Sometimes I like to give them a run. It's really fun when the humans fall off and their horses run away."

She licked his face. Gris, a year older than his mate, thought she hung the sun and the moon. It took him until he was three to find a mate. His first year used so much energy. Being a young male, he had to find a place to live, safe, warm, but where he could observe goings-on. Then digging, expanding the space, creating hidden entrances and exits, figuring out the food supply and the territory of the other foxes. He had no time for romance.

Once he could search, he had to convince this very pretty

vixen that he was the one. She had suitors from as far away as five miles. Fortunately he was large and not afraid of a fight, but he still had to convince her. Finally, tipped off by the half-grown Sarge, half-grown at the time, he visited the special doghouse at Beveridge Hundred, bringing Vi wrapped grape gumballs. Any fox who could perform such a feat could certainly provide protection and food. Gris, being no fool, would visit that doghouse about once every two weeks.

The owners of Tollbooth Farm allowed a thorough search by the sheriff's department, which yielded nothing.

The ride yielded nothing for Sister and her two whippers-in either. They rode out as they had come.

"Let's try Mud Fence."

This property, so named because the original owners couldn't afford fencing or the labor to cut their timber, built mud fences. In time finances improved. They built wood fences. Slowly they prospered, getting enough money to hire a Cherokee indentured servant.

Mud Fence abutted the chapel. Over the years acreage had been sold off in the bad times until the thousands of acres whittled down to three hundred and fifty. Most of Mud Fence's former acreage provided Old Paradise's northern border.

One house, one small barn, one outbuilding had withstood the ravages of time being built of brick, easy material to make in this part of the world. Ben crawled all over Mud Fence's buildings as well as Tollbooth.

They covered the three hundred and fifty acres in an hour. The footing was slick. Nothing unusual appeared. No scrap of clothing now visible in the melting snow, no vultures pointing the way. They rode back to the border with the chapel, Adolfo Vega's little house, small equipment shed, and the tombstones visible.

Turning to her companions Sister asked, "How far do you think the chapel is from here?"

Weevil said, "One hundred yards."

"Close enough. Now how far do you think the chapel is from the ditch, from the road?"

"It's hard to tell." Tootie spoke up. "The land rises a little."

"Enough to hide behind a tombstone?" Sister wondered.

"Sure, but the snow was so thick, why hide?" Weevil thought. "Plus if you really wanted to hide, wouldn't it make more sense to hide in the woods between Tollbooth and the place where Rory was found?"

"Yes, but if you wanted to get away, you would need to pass Tattenhall Station and we were there."

"Sister, I said 'found,' not 'killed.' He could have been killed and dropped there. There were enough leaves in the ditch to cover a body and the snow did the rest."

"Risky, Weevil, very risky."

"But we were out hunting. Someone could have killed him as it started to snow. Who would know?"

"Weevil, there are always a few people left at the trailers, grooms who don't ride or hunt, husbands who fall asleep in the cab of the truck the minute the field is out of sight. It's possible they might remember a vehicle passing by. Not a lot of people out this way. A strange truck or car would be noticed."

"But what good would it be to come back here?" Weevil asked.

"If you had hidden your car, say behind the small barn at Mud Fence, you could drive out north and no one would see."

Tootie piped up. "But Sister, that's just it. No one could see. The snow came on like"—she thought—"*boom.* Just like that. The killer wouldn't be able to see either. Let's say he got into his car or truck. He wouldn't be able to see for some time. You'd be driving at about ten miles an hour."

Sister considered this. "You're right. I'm trying everything." She tapped her helmet with her crop. "But the killer could have stayed in his car until the snow slowed enough to see."

"But it didn't for a day." Weevil wasn't being argumentative.

"I know. I know." She appreciated that they wanted to figure this out. "I can't stand that nothing makes sense."

They'd ridden, looked, pondered for two hours. Back at the station, horses tied to the rig, blankets on, hay bags full, they sat in the inviting station where Kasmir had brought them lunch from the house and made a pot of coffee as well as tea. The six of them drew diagrams on large sheets of paper, threw out all manner of scenarios no matter how absurd. Dewey had joined Kasmir and Alida when he saw the station light on. He'd come out to check on the Van Dorns.

Sister changed the subject. "Dewey, we missed you at Welsh Harp. The hounds put a gray in his den, which happened to be in the big old walnut tree trunk."

"No kidding? Sorry I missed that. The company had its New Year's party."

"How many people work at Milford Enterprises now?" Kasmir asked.

"Fifteen sales people, all high end. I've got a small construction crew but I usually job the work out. I like to go over potential development areas with my people though. Can save you a bundle when the real work starts. Construction costs can get away from you superfast."

"People padding the bill?" Alida asked.

"When I first started out I got taken to the cleaners a couple of times by that. But I've learned with the help of my small crew to be pretty accurate about supply costs. What can blindside you is a spike in oil costs or even something like copper."

"Copper roof?" Sister asked.

"The old farmhouse look, a copper roof or standing seam tin. These days anything that's metal costs." Dewey shifted his weight in his chair.

"I'm curious. Never asked you." Kasmir looked at the big

man. "How do you know where to build? Sometimes you have to put in roads and that's expensive."

Dewey enjoyed describing his business. "The very first thing I look at is topography. Is there a pleasing aspect to the land? Are there mountain views? Perhaps some running water or a place where I can create a small lake? People like water." He paused. "Given escalating expenses, I create syndicates for various developments. Nothing elaborate, but this reduces cost to me, provides profit to others. Some syndicates have more than one project but anything, anything on water is so much more expensive to buy."

"Never thought of that," Alida confessed as Weevil and Tootie also paid more attention.

"The Virginia Department of Transportation has maps in Richmond identifying future expansion, often with a timeline. When I started out I'd have to drive to Richmond to see them. Now you can pull it up on your computer. But those offer clues to development possibilities. Will the roads be good? How far are you from the interstate? Stuff like that."

"Schools?" Tootie finally spoke.

"Critical." Dewey nodded, thinking how much she resembled her mother. "But really the main thing is the land. People want to live someplace pretty. Of course, I intend to build them beautiful houses, but what's more beautiful than a view of the Blue Ridge Mountains?"

"We certainly have that here." Kasmir beamed.

"You have one of the best views in the state of Virginia," Dewey complimented him.

Kasmir grinned. "I have that when I look at my beautiful Alida."

"Will you stop!" She blushed.

Weevil stared at Tootie, then looked away.

Dewey teased him. "I know what you're thinking, brother."

Tootie, embarrassed, said, "Mom's the looker."

Sister patted her shoulder. "Tootie, the apple did not fall far from the tree." She glanced up at the old railroad clock running as good as it did seventy years ago. "We'd better head out. Kasmir, Alida, thank you, as always, for your hospitality."

"Yes." Dewey stood also.

"Our pleasure." Kasmir stood, too, then said, "We're all troubled by these terrible events."

Kasmir tidied up the papers, offering them to Sister.

"Thank you. No. We aren't any closer than when we started and we've come up with everything except Martians landing in the blizzard."

"There is one other possibility." The others leaned forward. "What if Rory was killed by one of us? Someone in Jefferson Hunt. We all know this territory and even in a snowstorm, close to the station, someone could have slipped off, killed him—why he was there is another issue—but killed him and then walked his horse across the road as though coming back with everyone. A man off a horse in a blizzard walking to the trailer and close to the trailers would not be suspicious. Even if we saw him, would we know who he was in those conditions?" Tootie surprised them, normally quiet as she was, with this disturbing idea.

"That's hard to believe. I can't believe anyone in our hunt club would kill," Dewey replied.

"Who has the most to lose by the pipeline?" Kasmir said to his guest. "I do. Crawford. To a lesser extent the Van Dorns. Certainly not Rory, although I doubt he wanted to see the land torn up."

"What you say is logical, Kasmir. It's impossible for me, at least, to think any of us, especially you, Kasmir, would kill over the pipeline." Sister didn't want to believe it.

Dewey nodded in agreement, then grew serious. "It is impossible, but something has gone terribly wrong and it keeps coming back to that damned pipeline."

"When we find out, we'll be shocked," Sister said.

"We may never find out," Alida replied.

As this impromptu lunch was occurring, Ronnie Haslip sat in Gray and Sam's kitchen. He had called first. Sam was at work and Gray was home, tools out, repairing a hole in the floor by the back door he hoped hadn't been caused by a leak.

They sat at the small kitchen table, Ronnie having passed on a drink.

"I couldn't talk on the phone. Too many ears, you know?"

"A law firm is filled with people who want to know or think they should know." Gray smiled.

"The acting president of Soliden and I had lunch yesterday at Sunset Grill in Manakin Sabot, far enough away from Richmond," Ronnie said.

Gray sat upright. "It's noisy in there and the food is good, just in case he or you might be recognized. Good food is always an excuse."

"Fortunately my work to identify historic sites, potential problems, and"—Ronnie turned up his hand—"broker payoffs is a good cover. Manakin Sabot is full of historic sites. Bill wants me to find a crackerjack accountant. That's you, Gray. What if Gregory found embezzlement or theft in Soliden or, worse, if he was stealing?"

Bill McBryde was Soliden's acting president.

"Thank you, but Ronnie, by the time I stepped off that elevator, someone at Soliden would know."

"I've thought of that and so has Bill. We send in Freddie Thomas to visit a friend."

"Well—"

"Gray, Freddie has a lot of friends and if she doesn't have one there, Bill will find a woman in accounting to be one."

"All right." Gray intently listened.

"Women are less threatening. Freddie is quite attractive, middle-aged, and smart, very smart. She can feed into your computers. For one thing, if you can't ferret out what we need, then the next step presents itself. Soliden calls in the police."

"Hold on, Ronnie. If the numbers we need we can't get, we're locked out, that's a red flag. This isn't my first time at the rodeo. My work involved entire federal bureaucratic divisions. Careers were at stake as well as party trust. You can get killed doing this. If Gregory is dead, and I think he is, it's possible an enormous amount of money is at stake."

"I'm sorry. This is out of my field. You know I wouldn't—"

Gray was quick to put him at ease. "I know. I need to meet with Bill McBryde. Not here. Not at Soliden."

Gray took a deep breath. "I hate to drag Freddie into something like this. She can smell an accounting error but she hasn't been in situations where people are willing to kill. An error in the books, you're okay. Embezzlement, you're not."

"She's a terrific cover. She's brave in the hunt field. She'll be brave off."

"She never sucks back from a stiff fence." Gray smiled at memories of Freddie flying over when others dropped back to Bobby Franklin.

On those hunts when but a handful of people finished in First Flight, one of that handful was always Freddie.

Gray smiled. "Next question, what does the bank know?"

"Only that there was a glitch in payroll, which Soliden immediately covered. There was a seemingly small error in a check to the power company. The head of payroll took responsibility for what is being presented as a small error."

"Small? Their monthly bill has to be five figures at least."

"About forty-five thousand dollars a month to the power company." Ronnie filled in the number. "No one admitted to human error, but it was promptly paid."

"Most people who steal from the company where they work steal from one department, or they are in accounting where an intelligent thief can shift monies at will, cover up tracks sometimes for years. Sooner or later it does show up. White-collar crime is rarely impulsive. It is well planned and well executed. If done a year before retirement, the culprit often gets away with it." Gray was intrigued. "Make the call and get back to me."

"Sam doing okay?"

"I think so. Everyone has been great. I can leave him now and return to my regular routine."

"Was being a tax expert your cover?" Ronnie bluntly asked.

Gray laughed. "I really am a tax expert, but when I was young, my bosses realized I could do a lot more. That's when I started finding the thieves, so to speak. In time I became a partner in the firm. I advised the FBI but I wasn't an agent. Our firm was called on for the long cases, the sensitive cases. The wrongdoers were forced into resignation. Publicity would have hurt everyone. The infected agency, the political party to which the thief belonged, sometimes it could go all the way up to the close advisers to the president, who rarely knew anything about embezzlement or selling information. It would be a foolish president to sell information, buy sensitive stocks while in office. They cash in after they leave, most of them," he continued.

"One of my biggest cases was nailing an important person at the Federal Reserve who was selling interest rate changes before they were made public. Made a fortune. None of this could be made public. Citizens need to trust the Federal Reserve. He quietly left."

"It's a sordid ballet, politics." Ronnie listened intently. "You were a good dancer."

Gray snorted. "I despised those men, always men but perhaps women will catch up. I did my job. Do I think those people belong behind bars? I do, but will it serve the public good?"

"Corruption greases the wheels of state." Ronnie sighed.

"Ronnie, more than you know. I content myself that we're not as bad as Brazil." He paused. "If there's a rat at Soliden, I'll flush them out."

"Hmm. Do you think, Gray, that women will be truly equal when they commit as many crimes as men, especially at a high level?"

"I never thought of that, but I guess it makes sense."

CHAPTER 13

"You've learned to build a fire, Mom." Tootie complimented her mother on the fire she'd built, flames roaring upward in the old stone fireplace.

"Good thing." She smiled. "Thanks again for bringing more wood. I didn't think I needed it."

"You will. This week, m-m-m, weatherman says the January thaw will end, then winter will slam us again. Look how much wood you've used already."

"Not quite half."

"The worst is always January and February. Can get bad storms in March, but it's so bitter especially in February. Funny though, the night sky is beautiful in February."

Yvonne smiled. "I wouldn't know. I never saw the night sky all those decades in Chicago. Seems like eons, and then other times I can feel the wind off the lake. That I do miss, looking out on Lake Michigan from our thirtieth-floor apartment. The calm calmed me and when the waves rolled in I wondered should I be more energetic, too." She stopped, shrugged. "Silly."

"I never miss it. I don't belong in cities." Tootie sat in a comfortable club chair by the fireplace. She could see out the window. She placed her hands on the padded arms of the chair covered in chintz, lifting herself up but not standing, hovering for a moment before dropping back. "We placed that dog box exactly right. Does it need fresh straw?"

"No. I fluffed it up plus I threw in some old towels."

"Mom, you don't have any old towels."

Yvonne waved her right hand. "I have towels that displeased me so I bought new ones, a sort of mango shade, so when I dry off I hold it up to my face and like the reflection."

"Mom."

"The small red fox that visits me likes the towels. Sometimes he curls up on the towels and the straw for a nap. He sure eats a lot of grape balls and Jolly Ranchers. Sometimes I see a gray fox in and out, but that one doesn't usually stay. The red fox seems like a visitor."

"What about the Van Dorns' dog?"

"Misty? She's two years older than God. I don't think she even has the will to bark anymore." She paused. "Although Misty can eat."

"Springer spaniels are such a beautiful color."

"Tootie, I'm surprised you don't have a dog. Everyone else does. You certainly live in the right place for one. Don't you ever get lonely? Strike that. You don't. I pushed you too much to be social."

"Raleigh and Rooster visit me, plus I work with all the foxhounds. Maybe when I'm finished with school. Or a cat. I like cats. Don't you like to watch the red and the gray that come here?"

"Very much. I never realized how beautiful they were until I viewed them close up. Are you sure you don't want something to drink or a sandwich?"

She considered this for a moment. "If you have a ginger ale, I'd drink it."

"Well, I do." Yvonne got up, walked into the small country kitchen, grabbed a Canadian Dry out of the fridge, popped the cap, threw ice in a glass, poured it, then thought she'd have one herself. She carried the drinks in on a little tray.

"Mom, you're getting fancy."

"I was always fancy. I had servants to do all this then. I really don't miss that. I never knew what peace and privacy was until I left your father. Course I never knew how much work the average person did either."

Tootie drank her ginger ale, feeling the bubbles tickle her tongue. "Forgot to tell you. Dad texted me."

"What?"

"This morning. I didn't know he could text."

"I'm sure one of his new girlfriends has taught him how. She must be all of eighteen." Yvonne couldn't help it then. She laughed. "Sorry."

Tootie intellectually understood how brutal the divorce was, how emotional, but it was the emotions she couldn't fathom. How could you let anyone under your skin like that? Then again, Tootie had remained remarkably free of romantic entanglements, even though in her early twenties. She had a capacity for deep friendship. It was the love stuff that she shied away from.

"Could be. Anyway, he apologized for asking me to choose sides, for cutting me out of his will. Not that I believe him."

"I hate that bastard, but for your sake I hope the day comes when he actually acts like a father."

Tootie didn't care what he did. "He wanted to know if you've invested any of your money. He wanted to know if you were buying a house. Stuff like that."

"Ha. Our monies were together but I kept a small account of

my own, an investment account. I did pretty good if I do say so myself. He never gave me credit for it. Well, did you text him back?"

Tootie nodded as she reached for her soda again. "I didn't say much but I told him I had no idea what you were doing with your money. Then he texted right back saying you never told him anything about your gambles—"

"Gambles! I put money on Facebook straight up. I also pulled my money out of Enron before there was a hint of trouble. I can't explain it. I just had a feeling."

"The other thing he said was he read about Gregory Luckham disappearing. He thinks the pipeline will depress land values badly if it goes through."

"That means he has money in drilling stock, energy stocks. He's afraid they'll be volatile. He's so transparent." She knocked back her soda. "But the threat of the pipeline has frozen people buying. No one knows what to do. Betty Franklin and I talk about it."

"Sister, Weevil, and I rode over Tollbooth Farm and Mud Fence Farm yesterday. Sister figured we knew that territory better than the people who own it. Well, not Weevil, but he's learning. Nothing, although we did see a gray fox at Tollbooth. It was creepy seeing where they'd dug out Rory."

"Yes it is. I try not to look at it when I drive to town. Much of it is melted down now. Oh, look." Yvonne put her fingers to her lips.

Sarge slipped in the dog box. The two women slowly rose, slowly walked to the window to watch the little fellow eat kibble sprinkled with dog food. Now that it was warmer, Yvonne scooped out a bit of canned food because it wouldn't freeze. He chewed away, blissfully happy, then he batted around one of the old rubber balls she'd thrown in there.

"Now what's he doing?" Yvonne wondered.

"Batting something around, something like a tiny hockey

puck. He likes to play. I think most animals do. We do." Tootie grinned, watching the happy fox who at that moment looked up, saw both of them, stopped, thought about it, then returned to the tiny puck. He'd swat it against the side of the dog box, dig in the straw to recover it, place it between his paws, throw it upward. He'd miss it, try again, and when he connected he'd really give it a swat.

The puck was the Saint Hubert's ring, although Tootie and Yvonne couldn't see that. What he was playing with looked like a small stone. They sat back down.

"Another?"

"No thanks. I can't drink as much in winter as summer."

"I guess I'll find out. My first Virginia summer." Yvonne leaned back, content to hear the fire's crackle, happy that her daughter visited her.

"You like it out here at Chapel Crossroads, don't you?"

"You know, I really do. If someone had told me I'd be sitting in the sticks of central Virginia in my fiftieth year and loving it, I would have said they were crazy."

A wry smile played on Tootie's beautiful lips. "Mom, you've been spending too much time with Aunt Dan."

A pause followed this observation. "All right, just a year off—or two. Fifty-two."

They both laughed.

"How are your lessons?"

"Cold. I don't see how you can ride in winter. I'm in that indoor arena and my hands are ice."

"Sam's a good teacher."

"Old Buster is a good horse."

Tootie looked at the old wall clock. "Gets dark so early. I can never get used to it. Maybe you need a dog, Mom."

"Maybe. Once I really feel settled I'll think about it. Right now I have a fox."

Yvonne got up to look at the doghouse. Sarge had gone. "Back to his den, I expect." She sat back down. "How are you and Weevil working together?"

"Pretty good. I tell him about each fixture before we get there. He's an incredible rider. Amazing really."

Yvonne asked no more. It was obvious to her that Weevil was dazzled by Tootie, but then most men were, just as most women swooned for Weevil, who was drop-dead gorgeous. Yvonne was not one to push Tootie, but as her mother she prayed the day would come when what her own mother called "a suitable boy" would show up. No parent wants their child alone in life. She thought Weevil was playing the long game.

So was the killer.

CHAPTER 14

Bible open, reading glasses perched above the tip of her nose, Aunt Daniella read the page of Luke, chapter 5, verses 36–39. A knock on the door lifted her eyes.

The door opened. Sam, carrying two bags of groceries, stared at his nonreligious aunt. "What are you doing?"

"Cramming."

He laughed. "You'd have to, Aunt Dan."

"I never broke the Ten Commandments."

"What about 'Thou shalt not covet thy neighbor's wife'?" He carried the bags into her spotless kitchen as he called over his shoulder.

"I never coveted my neighbor's wife." She sounded ever so prim and full of herself at the same time.

"You should have been a lawyer." He unpacked her groceries as she walked into the kitchen.

"Thank you for shopping for me. I hate to drive in bad weather."

"You should give me the keys to your car."

"No. I can still drive. Furthermore, I don't get tickets."

"Of course you don't. The sheriff's department is scared to death of you."

She pulled out a kitchen chair. "Can I fix you anything to eat?"

"No. I brought roasted chicken for both of us, a side salad. Thought about macaroni but decided against it. You eat like a bird."

"Birds actually eat a lot." She smiled. "I can eat. After you finish I will clean up. A human Hoover. Although that expression applies to cocaine." She got up to set the table.

"How do you know these things?"

"I read, Sam, plus I watch some shows. After you and Gray bought me that big-screen TV and a DVD player I watch Netflix stuff. I like to watch old movies like *Raisin in the Sun, Notorious,* the good stuff. Movie stars had faces then. Now actors want to look real. I don't want them to look real. I want them to look like gods."

"Okay." He sliced the chicken, pulled the plastic top off the salads. "What kind of dressing do you want?"

"Oil and vinegar. There by the stove."

"Yes, ma'am." He opened the fridge and took out a bottle of ranch for himself, then sat down.

"How was the hunt yesterday?"

"Not bad. Awful footing. The packed snow was better than this slop, but then it always is. People put studs on their horses' shoes but studs don't do you but so much good in mud."

"Mercer used to say that." She mentioned her son, who died two years ago.

"He was always trying to dress me. I never had the money for his kind of clothes. Mercer had an uncanny knack for picking colors, all that stuff."

"I was happy to divide his clothes between you and Gray. Funny that you three were close in size. No one porked up. God knows my third husband did." She raised an eyebrow. "I finally told him he had to lose weight because I couldn't find his member."

Sam, mouth full, swallowed hard, then laughed. "That would motivate a husband. Aunt Dan, thank you for having me over a lot of nights, for arranging dinners and stuff. Gray, Sister, Yvonne, even Tootie and Weevil, have been great. Crawford's huntsman has been kind, too. Her romance with Shaker is good, I guess."

"Makes sense. He's been divorced long enough to recover. They like the same things. Yvonne will recover, too. What a nasty piece of business that was."

"I'd have shot the son of a bitch."

"Then I'm grateful you were not married to him." She speared a crisp carrot. "How are you, really?"

"I'm . . . I don't know. There are so many questions galloping through my mind."

"That was a remarkable thing you did for him, working extra jobs so you could send him to rehab. I've never told you how much I admire you for that. Have you ever noticed white people bugle blast anything they do for one of our people but what we do for them: silence?"

"Not Rory."

"No." She hunted down another carrot. "Do you think alcoholism supersedes just about everything else, class, race, gender, all the stuff that fills the news? I don't read any solutions to all those things, by the way."

"There are solutions for being a drunk but you have to want to do it, you have to work at it every day. We need to support each other and I pray. I pray a lot, Aunt Dan."

"I do, too. I'd rather people not know about it." She grinned.

"What haunts me is I didn't know he'd come back to drive Trocadero to Crawford's with me. On the big days people always need help and Crawford is good about letting us earn extra money.

Since Crawford wasn't going, not that we expected him to, he allowed us to go. I hunted that four-year-old he wants me to bring along. The guy's got the bone to carry him but he'll have to adjust to Crawford, who is anything but a soft rider. He does try. But Rory usually told me what he was thinking. Did he decide to have a look at the gelding during the hunt? I can't get it out of my head. Same questions over and over."

She cut her chicken into small squares. "Was he in money trouble?"

"He would have told me."

She nodded. "I'm sure Ben has questioned everybody as well as Sister, too. People might talk to her before the sheriff."

"I've even thought what if he was killed elsewhere and dumped in the ditch? He had to have been killed close to Tattenhall Station."

"I think so, too. Maybe he got in the way. Gregory Luckham is still missing and presumed dead. Maybe Rory took a notion to come by at exactly the wrong time. That's the only thing I can think of."

"The medical examiner's report specified Rory was killed on the day of Christmas Hunt. Ben called me. He knew I was tortured by this. Everyone's afraid I'll drink again." He leveled his gaze right at her.

"It's not an unreasonable fear, Sam."

"I would never do that, not after what Rory and I went through. It would break his heart if he knew his death sent me back to the bottle."

"Yes." She said this with feeling. "There are promises we make to the dead. I promised your mother I would watch over you and Gray, grown men that you were, when she passed. She was so sweet. I'd fret over her. She believed there was good in everybody. It's a wonder she wasn't cheated daily. The Good Lord protected her."

"I often wish I was more like her." He drank a tonic water with a wedge of lime.

Aunt Daniella enjoyed her usual bourbon. She drank in front of him even right when he came back from rehab. She swore he had to get used to it or he'd never go to a party again and what fun was that?

"To change the subject, how is Yvonne doing, really?"

"Long leg, natural rhythm. If she sticks to it she'll be pretty good. After all, Tootie got her athletic ability honestly."

"M-m-m." She returned to Rory. "Sam, I think about Rory, I do. Gregory Luckham is still out there, I expect. He came as Ronnie's guest."

"Right."

"Could Ronnie be in danger?"

CHAPTER 15

Ronnie, standing next to Sister Jane, held Pokerface by a lead rope under the lights of his small barn.

"I didn't notice it until I pulled him out to refresh his trace clip."

She moved to Pokerface's right side where a semicircular arc of fur was marked.

Running her fingers over the fur, Pokerface flinched slightly. She said, "No cut. More like his fur was slightly clipped."

"Trimmed. Could a spur have done that?"

"Go get a pair." She took the lead rope while he darted into his small, immaculate tack room. Everything of Ronnie's was immaculate.

Returning with a polished pair of hammerhead spurs, he showed his friend. She ran her thumb over the edge.

"Not exactly sharp as a blade, but let's see. I'll hold him."

Ronnie, spur edge facing outward, moved to the good boy's side, swept the spur along it.

Pokerface flinched slightly. *"Hey."*

"Good fellow, I won't do it again." He took the lead rope from Sister, who examined where the spur rubbed against Pokerface's fur.

"Faint. Of course, anytime anything sharp, a branch, a spur, touches his ribs he'll flinch but I can see a faint mark."

"If Gregory came off with great force, the mark would be deeper than what I just did. At least that's what I think."

"I'll put him in his stall. You fetch a treat."

She walked the 16.2-hand fellow a few steps, slid open a stall door, top half iron railings so Pokerface could see out. Ronnie walked inside as she turned the horse around.

"Your fave."

Pokerface, polite, swept the two delicious Mrs. Field's cookies out of Ronnie's opened palm.

"Hey," Corporal in the next stall complained.

Ronnie, trained by his horses, stepped into Corporal's stall with two cookies for him.

The humans retired to the tack room. The barn shut up for the night, wind rattling the large doors to the outside.

"Would you like a drink? We can go up to the house."

"No thanks. I've got to get home. Tomorrow we'll hunt from After All. I hope this wind has died down by then."

He took out a bottle of water for himself and sat in a small but cozy chair facing Sister, who sat in its mate.

"Well, you can always stay in the covered bridge." He smiled.

"I can never look at that bridge or walk through it without thinking how useful covered bridges were in the past, not for protection against the weather but for 'romance.' "

"Never thought of it." He unscrewed the bottle cap.

"Well, that explains everything." She teased him, then became a bit somber. "How well did you know Gregory?"

"Ben asked me that, too. I knew him as a client of our firm. A very important client, and he was a foxhunter so I thought to kill two birds with one stone." An uncomfortable expression crossed his face. "Under the circumstances, that was the wrong thing to say."

"Not to me. Did you suspect Gregory might be more than a foxhunter? Say, a man on the down low? You have the radar, or is it gaydar?"

He shook his head. "I don't have it, whatever you call it. I took him at face value, a middle-aged man, good looking, driven, obviously successful. Big career, I think he also made good investments. I knew he was married but he didn't talk much about his wife and children. Some men do. The few times he mentioned Liz, it was complimentary."

She folded her hands in her lap after unzipping her thin but warm parka. "I'm always a little suspicious when people constantly bring up their spouses. It's one thing if you know them, but when you don't I figure it's parading heterosexual credentials." Then she laughed. "Why bother? None of us will ever catch up with Aunt Daniella."

"She'll outlive us all." He, too, adored the old lady. "I've gone over in my mind, over and over, did I miss anything? I can't see that I did but when the little arc on Pokerface caught my attention, I wondered."

"Show it to Ben. He'll know better than we do."

"I will. My relationship with Gregory was business and you know I wanted him to enjoy a terrific hunt in fabulous territory. I'm worried about the pipeline. Soliden is keeping their cards close to their chest, which makes it worse. Realtors are up in the air. Potential sellers and buyers are up in the air. Maybe considering expensive material improvements to their property if it's in the line of fire has to hold off. Or why buy until you know the final route? Too many big questions. This hurts more than Realtors or those with houses on the market."

"The 'No Pipeline' signs certainly had to reach him."

"He didn't mention them." Ronnie sank a bit deeper in the chair. "God knows there are enough of them and they're big. Thought it would help especially if he saw Tattenhall Station, Old Paradise, Chapel Cross, everything near the crossroad."

"It's impressive territory."

"If I can steer a client toward a less destructive path, less publicity, I've helped my client and protected land. Once the pipeline is done it can't be undone, Sister. And if I can divert the pipeline, better yet get Soliden to use existing rights-of-way, our law firm will benefit enormously."

"Yes it will. Those damn pipes burst. There is no foolproof system for conveying anything liquid or gas under high pressure for hundreds, thousands of miles. We all know that, but we also know this country does not need to be batted around by OPEC. If, indeed, the gas would be used on our shores, not shipped to China."

Ronnie shrugged. "I'm doing what I can with what I have and given the wildly shifting international situation, who knows? Just Saudi Arabia alone, who knows? Those were, I should say, critical issues that the CEO of Soliden must consider. The wrong call, billions! Billions!"

"Needs a crystal ball."

"Anyone doing business with other countries does. Can you imagine being a car manufacturer? Parts are made all over the world. The public is fickle. SUVs and trucks for a couple of years, a spike in gas prices, they sit on the lot with the dealers paying monthly interest on every unsold vehicle. Gas prices drop. Sedans sit on the lot. If I can steer Soliden toward, shall we say, a more neutral path, suggest just who their interest and market is, plus competition, I have served our client well. This is about more than profit."

"I respect anyone trying to make a go of it." She unfolded her hands, leaning toward him. "Ronnie, maybe this has nothing to do with the pipeline. Soliden does business overseas. Doesn't Soliden have a small position in British gas companies?"

"Does. But I doubt anyone from Britain came here to kill him. This has to be something or someone close."

"That seems likely. Maybe we're barking up the wrong tree. Not that I wish harm on a man I met but once, it's Rory's death that keeps me awake at night. I can think of no reason why he was killed unless it was bad timing."

"Me, too."

As she drove away in her one-year-old Tahoe, already getting beat up, Corporal and Pokerface observed the lights snaking down the drive.

"You couldn't see anything, right?" Corporal asked.

"Like I told you when I came alongside you at the trailers, I couldn't see, my eyelashes were stuck with snow."

"Mine, too. Never hunted in anything like that storm. Couldn't hear. The only way I knew you were behind me was your nose was on my flank."

"Couldn't smell either. All that snow blowing up my nose. I felt him go, I told you that when I got in. Just felt him ripped right off me, but I couldn't see or smell who was there."

"We were single file. No one to bump into us. I don't much care but it bothers Ronnie. I like it when he's happy," Corporal said.

"Me, too, but I do wonder why there?" Pokerface admitted.

"I don't know, but that place has hidden secrets for hundreds of years." Corporal half-closed his eyes as the wind whistled outside.

CHAPTER 16

Sun on frost turned the silver to pink, then gold. Jefferson Hunt at ten A.M. gathered at Close Shave, north of Chapel Cross by six miles. One turned right at the chapel and continued until seeing a hanging sign, CLOSE SHAVE. A man's lathered face adorned the sign.

Terrain, rough toward the west, rolled nicely by the road. Trailers parked in a neat row alongside the farm road. The solid brick house, in the distance, seemed impervious to harsh weather. Just a big old brick block but it had stood not quite as long as Old Paradise, started in 1812, Beveridge Hundred following in 1820. By 1825 money fluttered on pastures, streets, everywhere. Close Shave started during those good times then endured some tight ones, hence the name Close Shave. The Elliotts dug the first chunk of earth up for the brick house and it stayed in the family until after World War I when the line petered out. Owned now by the Winsetts, the fixture was secure or as secure as any land holding could be.

Sister nodded to Shaker, who cast hounds straight up toward

the north. The sun rose higher, the frost began to melt on high ground, good conditions.

Trident, the pack kleptomaniac, stopped to pick up a deer antler.

"Leave it," Shaker sternly commanded.

"Bone is good for my teeth," Trident sassed.

"Don't piss him off. We've just started. Drop the antler," Diana ordered, fangs bared.

Trident, as though in excruciating pain, dropped the antler.

Audrey, young, moved quickly, nose down. Her littermate, Angle, joined her.

The older hounds observed the youngsters but chose not to follow too closely. They were young. No one opened. Then Angle did.

Pickens hurried over to check. *"Red. Don't know who."*

In the blink of an eye, scent warmed, bursting into hound noses. They sang out at once and the walk turned into a flat-out gallop.

Charging north, a three-board fence line ahead, ground still more frozen than not, Sister and Matador jumped the simple coop, the easiest jump to build.

The field, small this Thursday, January eleventh, followed.

The fox running straight turned left, or at least his scent did. No one viewed. Another jump appeared, another coop. Up and over. Betty, on the right, kept her eye on a line of woods. Were she a fox she would have ducked in there. Tootie, on the left, all open, kept up as speed increased. Weevil, in the rear, didn't want to crowd hounds, but he didn't want to slacken the pace either.

The red male fox, well ahead, ignored the woods, cut sharply left, and ran for all he was worth toward Chapel Cross. Hounds, now stretched to their fullest, presented a beautiful sight over the golden ground, frost sparkling on the west side of small hills, swales. The cold air prickling in lungs human, horse, and hound.

Running, running, running, they reached the crossroads within twenty minutes. Were it not for the fences, the jumps, the occasional obstacle, this flat-out run would have taken fifteen minutes.

Then *poof.* Nothing. Hounds whined searching for the scent, the cross glittering on the top of the chapel to their left across the road.

Sister and the field halted, glad to catch their breath.

For all the decades Sister had hunted, she still muttered to herself, "How does he do it?"

Shaker, quietly sitting, giving his hounds time to work it out, pushed his cap back up on his head as he was sweating. Wiping his brow, he then patted on the neck Kilowatt, another of his horses, a gift to the hunt from Kasmir. Kilowatt, a talented Thoroughbred, was barely winded, but then that's why one rides a Thoroughbred, provided they're in condition.

Finally the huntsman rode over to his Master. "Damned if I know."

"Let me ask Kasmir if he minds if we go behind Tattenhall Station. There's no point in doubling back. We would know." She was right because the hounds would have told her.

Acknowledging, smiling to Alida, Freddie, Walter, Margaret DuCharme, out today, another doctor, Bobby, and Sam, she stopped before Kasmir.

"Madam." He touched his cap with his crop, always correct.

"Would you mind if we cast behind Tattenhall? No point doubling back."

"Of course."

Turning, she remarked to Sam as she passed, "Crawford must be serious about this horse. You've been out on him every hunt since New Year's."

Sam inclined his head. "He's an appendix that I think will suit Crawford better than some speedster."

"He keeps up well enough." Sister complimented the Thoroughbred/Quarter Horse cross, hence the name Appendix.

"Poco Bueno blood back there along with Icecapade." Sam cited a strong Quarter Horse line with a fabulous Thoroughbred line.

Sister's eyebrows immediately raised up. "If he doesn't work out, let me know."

"Yes, ma'am."

Back at the hounds impatiently waiting, she nodded to her huntsman. "Good to go."

They crossed the road, passed the distinctive Victorian train station, nudged just up the slight rise behind the station, Kasmir's simple house in sight.

"Lieu in."

They fanned out, eager, noses down. Reaching the top of the rise, a delicious odor curled into their nostrils. *Bam.* Off again. This was turning into a terrific day.

The footing, slippery, kept everyone alert. Hounds flew to the woods' edge, the heavy woods wherein many a fox had dumped them figuratively and literally.

Branches smacked them as the field took the narrow path since that's where the fox had gone. A perfect broad path bisected the middle of these woods but no, this fellow had to take the tough one. A stand of old conifers blocked the light for a moment, a small, ice-covered pond down below. Hounds ran to the pond. The fox had circled it, wisely leaving heavy scent; then he tiptoed through running cedar just south of it, making scent difficult. Foxes knew everything and were not above rolling in cow dung if that's what it took.

"Dammit!" Zandy cursed.

"Stick to it." Cora, an experienced female, encouraged him.

Hounds picked their way through the natural, lovely, snow-sprinkled running cedar ground cover notorious for fouling scent.

Finally on the other side of this big patch they cast themselves all around it, just eating up time, which, of course, was the point.

Sister patiently watched, proud of their work ethic. She bred them, trained them with her staff, and loved good hound work. Naturally she loved her hounds best, but she loved anybody's good hound work, including the night hunters'.

A whine here and there testified to frustration.

"Good hounds. Good hounds," Shaker sang out to them.

Sister gave a small prayer of thanks that she had changed the fixture for today. It was to be at After All but the Bancrofts changed it due to a loose board in the covered bridge that was being fixed today. They'd hunt from After All Saturday. The fixture, tended over decades, always drew a large crowd. It teamed with foxes who knew every inch of After All, the Old Lorillard and Roughneck Farm as well as Hangman's Ridge, as all were connected.

Large fixtures usually provide large sport and that's what was happening today. Finally, Tinsel's stern wagged, then Trident's, antler long forgotten, then Pansy. Soon the pack steadily pushed a faded scent but one warming a bit. It occurred to Cora that this was not the hunted fox, but why spoil it? The hunted fox made fools of them. So hunt what you can.

Pickens broke into a trot. The others followed. Soon enough they ran through the woods again, bursting out at the edge of Beveridge Hundred where old Misty, sitting in the window of the main house, awakened and gave out a perfunctory bark.

Skirting the house and the dependency wherein Yvonne was watching, they kept straight ahead. A number of old estates fanned out along the southern road, but this fox wasn't going there. He was a visiting fox. He turned away, going straight back toward Tattenhall Station using the heavy woods wherein he headed west. Now they really had to fight their way because the paths in the woods ran north and south with only one going east and west. Of course, you had to find it.

Shaker, right behind his hounds, hit away branches with his crop, as did Weevil. Betty, on the edge of the woods, quite far out, was spared. Knowing the territory, she had the sense not to tie herself up. It's easier to come in than to run out. Tootie, however, found herself blocked by a gum tree that had fallen across the little deer path she traveled. The tree hadn't come down all the way so she plunged through the vines, the damn things never die, to get around. By that time hounds were almost on the road.

Kasmir had built stiff jumps all along his fence line on that part of his considerable estate. On the other side of the road reposed Old Paradise, and as they had run there on the day the storm came up, Sister hoped they would not be doing so again. Crawford had been sensible about it, but two times on Old Paradise without asking permission was one time too many.

Hounds stopped cold at the fence line, then followed it toward Chapel Cross a few miles away. They passed the front drive into Beveridge Hundred, moved into Kasmir's land. Working but not speaking, they couldn't do much. What scent there was didn't hold and where that fox went, who knew? But someone was here about dawn perhaps. They pushed.

Once Kasmir's house was in sight they pushed harder but to no avail. They reached the station, crossed the road, stopping at the spot where Rory was found. Little bits of snow lay in the ditch.

Shaker called them away. Hounds and the field headed toward Close Shave. A tiny burst as they neared the farm offered hope of another run, but that was it.

Back at the trailers, the air brisk but not bitter, the small group gathered around Betty Franklin's yellow Bronco, old but tough. She'd lifted up the back so people put in sandwiches, deviled eggs, brownies for the impromptu hunt breakfast. The drinks rested in the bed of Walter's truck, hot thermoses of coffee and tea, water and soda, plus a bottle or two of spirits in case someone needed an early dose for medicinal purposes only.

"Thank you, Kasmir. I'd like to know just who that fox is."

He smiled, his teeth brilliant white. "A Romeo."

"We see them at dusk, sometimes in the morning, walking about, fearless." Alida held up a cup of coffee. She had moved up from North Carolina, settled in recently. Things were working out and Kasmir was in a state of bliss. Then again, so was Alida. They were meant for each other.

"Have you all seen the route, one route, of the proposed pipeline?" Sister asked Kasmir. "Just cuts up Old Paradise, cuts a diagonal across your southernmost land. Doesn't make sense, especially if you know this land."

This immediately aroused the attention of the small group.

Freddie Thomas, Alida's good friend, remarked, "I've seen it. Some is in floodplain down by the creek. Whoever did this has no idea of soils here or how the water flows."

"Crawford and I lobbied our lawmakers as well as Soliden." Kasmir paused. "I found Gregory easy to talk with, opaque, which is what one would expect. Crawford, which you would also expect, was anything but opaque."

"Threats?" Walter asked.

"Veiled but he alluded to upcoming elections and, given his finances, he could bankroll any opposing candidate as well as hire a good PR firm."

"Didn't do Eric Cantor any good," Sam, sharp although usually circumspect, observed.

Eric Cantor, a Republican congressman from Virginia's Seventh Congressional District, had a big war chest, lots of coverage, and lost to a college professor, Dave Brat.

"Happens." Freddie leaned against the side of the Bronco. "You forget your constituency and you'll be sent packing."

"Therein lies the problem with the pipeline." Walter had thought about this. "In theory we are all in favor of disengaging from the Saudis. We're all in favor of jobs, although how long those construction jobs last is a murky issue and never addressed by Soliden. However, when the pipeline goes through your land, it is an entirely different issue. Your land value will never recover. The twenty years or thirty years, whatever they say it will be today, will be a scar on your property. If a pipeline blows it's your fields that will be ruined. And you won't be able to clean them up."

"I suspect the powers that be at Soliden, including the missing president, looked at a map of our county, saw huge tracts of undeveloped land, by their standards, and figured, 'Aha!' Easy peasy." Betty hated this whole thing. "They don't care about potential damage."

"They underestimated us." Kasmir grinned.

"They underestimated you and Crawford." Sister laughed.

"Yes but"—Freddie raised her voice slightly—"what if they still come down over the mountains here and instead of going straight through the land they follow the road. There is a right-of-way. It's better than nothing but still not great. A pipeline can rupture just as easy using a right-of-way as on private land."

"I think they'll swing through Nelson County." Bobby Franklin crossed his arms over his chest. "Small population, not a lot of wealth, lower educational level. They'll steamroll 'em."

Margaret DuCharme, specialty sports medicine, shook her head. "I hope not. It's such beautiful country. So many of those old apple orchards still exist, still giving us apples."

Sister, knowing Margaret since she was a child, said, "You know Old Paradise better than anyone. Given the mysteries that still surround that land, even the old curse, I suspect the pipeline would be full of holes before it got into the ground."

"People have threatened not to shoot the workers but to destroy equipment, expose the pipeline once it's running, shoot into it. Can you imagine the explosion?" Margaret said. "I look at Old Paradise and wonder if this is the curse."

Bobby spoke clearly. "You don't mess around with country people. Or people with a great passion, which the environmental groups have. I respect them even if I think sometimes they go over the top. And you can't dig up graves."

"You might be surprised to hear this from me—after all I am a doctor—but I don't think you disturb the dead," Walter said.

"You know that's a taboo almost every culture observes, no matter the country or the century. It's thousands of years old," Kasmir announced.

"You have dual citizenship, right?" Sam smiled, and when Kasmir nodded he suggested, "You could shoot the pipeline, anyone, go back to India. You wouldn't be extradited."

Kasmir, surprised, rejoined, "No, but I wouldn't be hunting with Jefferson. I'd never risk that."

"What is worth that risk? What could provoke you to kill?" Bobby wondered.

"Well, we'd all agree danger to our families, perhaps even to our way of life." Betty put her two cents in.

"Was Rory killed over danger to someone's family?" Sam couldn't help saying that. "Or someone's way of life?"

"If profit counts as a way of life, it is possible." Margaret picked up a deviled egg. "Think of the crimes, thefts, drama that have happened here. We can start with Sophie Marquet, my illustrious ancestor. Her husband became a liability. After all manner of disagreement he disappeared. And then what happened to all the silver and much of the family jewelry after 1865? The Yankees never found it. Who knows?"

Walter smiled. "There isn't one old place in this county that doesn't have some story about murder or buried treasure."

"Don't forget the illegal stills." Bobby laughed.

"Best country water in the South," Margaret said with pride, using the term for moonshine.

If you said "moonshine," it meant you were a little suspicious. If you used "illegal liquor" or any such flabby term, you were especially suspicious.

"We're all standing here. Some of you were at Christmas Hunt. Does any of this make sense?" Sister wondered. "A wonderful man, a man who pulled himself through hell and high water is killed, and another powerful man disappears at the same location, or so we believe."

"Gregory Luckham has to be dead." Betty noticed the sun dipping behind a large cumulus cloud.

"We don't know that," Walter offered. "We're standing here assuming this is about the pipeline. Maybe it is and maybe it isn't. But until Gregory Luckham is found, I wouldn't bet on anything."

CHAPTER 17

"I can't do this as long as the ground is frozen." Tootie held a two-by-four, leaning it on the doghouse.

"I know but we can look at it." Yvonne, scarf wrapped around her neck, held a mudflap. "We can fix up a back door, double flaps to keep out the wind. Come spring, I can add up on the doghouse."

"Mom, the fox doesn't really need a tower." Tootie knelt down on the cold ground, began sawing a back door.

"But won't it be fun if I build a tower off this back door? He can climb up, look out. No one will be able to get to him if by chance he's trapped in here."

"That's why I'm putting in this back door. Doesn't have to be big, just has to be secure." She lifted up her hand for a first mudflap.

Yvonne leaned the two-by-four against the doghouse, walked to her small wooden box, plucked out a second mudflap. She'd bought a big wooden toy chest, bought mudflaps, bought more sweets for the fox.

Tootie carefully nailed in the top of the mudflap, then placed a quarter round along the top once she affixed the second mudflap. Surely this would keep out the wind.

"What about if I build a fence in springtime?"

"No. He doesn't need a fence. He needs to come and go and not become trapped in here. It's not just hunting. There are other animals that like treats—raccoons, possums. You're starting a restaurant in here." Tootie stood up, checked her handiwork.

She knelt back down and pushed the flaps again. Satisfied, she stood up.

Now Yvonne knelt down, the cold earth hard beneath her knees. She reached all the way to the back of the doghouse—she was almost flat on her stomach—and she pushed the mudflaps from inside. "There."

Tootie, now standing over her mother, waited for her to rise. Then she knelt down to test it from the inside. A metal food bowl clanked.

"Empty."

"I know. I have kibble in the toy chest. Gumdrops, too."

On her hands and knees, Tootie picked up the food bowl, handing it behind her while still down. Her mother took it. Tootie smoothed out the straw, fluffed the old, well, not so old towels. The Saint Hubert's ring fell out of a plush towel. She picked it up, backed out.

"Mom, what's this?"

"I don't know." Yvonne held out her gloved palm wherein Tootie dropped the lovely ring. "It's a deer, a cross between the antlers."

"Saint Hubert."

"You're right." Yvonne, a Catholic, remembered her saints.

"Let's put the two-by-fours in the mudroom." Tootie picked one up.

Yvonne carried her toy chest while Tootie made the trips to put the four two-by-fours in the mudroom. They took off their coats, gloves in the pockets. Yvonne pulled the ring out of her coat pocket. Once in the kitchen, she placed it on the kitchen table.

"The metalwork is beautiful. I think this must have been done by hand. It's too detailed for a stamp."

Tootie picked it up, turning it in her fingers. "It is beautiful. I like the oak leaves on the side facing upward and the acorns on the sides. I wonder how it got into the doghouse." She stared again at the top of the ring, a ten-point buck, his noble head looking left, the cross between those august antlers.

Yvonne then asked, "Anyone in the hunt club wear a Saint Hubert's ring?"

"Not that I recall," Tootie added. "But then everyone wears gloves even at the outdoor tailgates, because it's cold."

"Rory?" Yvonne inquired.

"Oh, Mom, he could never have afforded a gold ring."

"A gift?"

"I would have noticed. I'd see Rory once or twice a month. He'd drop by, usually with Sam. Sam would come by for Gray and to see Sister. Sometimes we'd talk about restoring the home place, about the foxes there."

"I like that old wraparound porch," Yvonne mentioned.

"Remember the story of Saint Hubert?" Tootie asked her mother.

Twirling the ring in her fingers, Yvonne proclaimed, "I do. All those years of Catholic school, I know my saints. He was a rich kid, a pagan his mother had converted to Christianity and this was the eighth century in Belgium, much of which was still pagan. Anyway, his mother begged him to go to church with her on Good Friday. He refused, going hunting instead. The church bells could be heard in the forest at three P.M. ringing to signify the time of Jesus's death. An enormous stag walked in front of him, turned his head, and the crucifixion cross shone between his antlers. That's how Hubert converted. He wound up being the bishop of Maastricht and Liege. Kept on hunting but not on Sundays or Holy Days." She laughed.

"Think those stories are true?"

"I expect there are elements of truth in all the saints' stories. Mostly they provide examples. When you think of the suffering some of these people willingly endured." She shrugged. "I'm not that good a Christian. Actually, I'm quite an awful one. I wish mountains of misery on your father."

"He keeps texting me."

"Why?" Her eyes widened.

"Stuff about my grades. I know he doesn't care. He doesn't want me to go to vet school. And he wants to know again if you are investing your money."

Yvonne placed the ring on the table. "Your father never asks an idle question about money." She blew air out of her nostrils. "I wonder if he's losing money? Not my problem. However, since we are on the subject of money, I do wish you'd take it a little more seriously."

"I have enough."

"I'm not saying you should switch to a business major. I know you like science, you always have, but why don't you pick a stock and follow it? Learn how the market works. Pay attention to what's happening in the world."

Tootie got up, opened the refrigerator, and pulled out a ginger ale. "Want one?"

"No."

"Mom, money doesn't fascinate me. I think people do terrible things over it. But I will follow a stock."

"Good." Yvonne picked up the ring, slipping it on the third finger of her right hand. "Fits perfectly. I'll see if Violet or Cecil is missing a ring. He's becoming a little forgetful, or so Violet says. I don't really know them enough to see that but if they haven't lost a ring, this is mine. Finders keepers."

CHAPTER 18

That same Friday, Gray and Freddie Thomas sat opposite each other in an office he rented at Old Trail, just to be safe. Gray had met Bill McBryde for a drink down at Shockoe Slip early in the week. Freddie called on her old friend, Sophie Riggs, at the Soliden offices, which made it easier on both of them. Gray dropped her off, then later picked her up.

Freddie liked the office, impressive, views of the James River. People worked but Sophie told her there was unease, worry, since Gregory's disappearance. People kept their mouths shut. There wasn't a lot of office gossip about this unsettling disappearance. For one thing, no one wanted their curiosity to be misunderstood and no one wanted to criticize the missing president, especially since Bill McBryde had been a friend of Gregory's. At least they worked well together, socialized as do most people at the top management level.

Gray asked Bill directly over a whiskey, neat, did he suspect embezzlement? The question didn't surprise the acting president.

He, too, had considered it. Given Gregory's handsome compensation plus stock shares, why steal?

Then Gray asked could there be a revenge motive? Infidelity?

Again, Bill never caught a whiff of same. Gregory and Liz seemed wonderfully suited to each other.

Soliden gave money to many legislators running for state office. Both Democrat and Republican were well supported because the corporation didn't care who was in office, only that their programs not run aground. Anything fishy?

Again, Bill admitted the company had been supporting politicians for decades, not exactly buying them but supporting their runs for office. This eased the way for many projects, including the pipeline. The House of Delegates had been rubber-stamping Soliden projects consistently.

Bill also freely pointed Gray to the entire list of politicians who had enjoyed Soliden's support. The *Richmond Times-Dispatch* had printed everyone's name from recent elections when the pipeline issue blew up.

When Gray picked up Freddie, they compared notes.

Now they sat at two computers, laboriously going through every department's expenditures. They'd get to income later. Bill couldn't give Gray the passwords and stuff he needed to access the numbers, but he authorized the head computer geek to do so, which of course set off a red light in that man's head, sworn though he was to secrecy.

The two accountants had wordlessly scanned and scrolled for days. Nothing jumped out at them. A mistake here or there, nothing unusual in a company that big. The sums were small. None of this looked like embezzlement so much as mistakes, most of which were corrected when the office did its own sweep up.

"Someone wrote a check for a dentist's bill," Freddie noted, "from the marketing department."

"H-m-m. Freddie, we've got a lot still to do, but my hunch is if this is an inside problem, then it's systemic. It's not one department."

"Could be. It could be that Luckham's disappearance and expected death aren't related to the company or to money."

He looked away from his screen, his eyes tired. "I don't know. Money is a powerful motivator."

"You said that Bill McBryde thought Gregory's compensation more than adequate. What, three million per annum plus bonuses?"

"Not bad, but chump change on Wall Street. Never underestimate greed."

"But maybe this isn't about his greed. Maybe it's about someone else's."

CHAPTER 19

Spread over long tables pushed together in Crawford's office, Ronnie, Margaret, Crawford, and Charlotte studied the U.S. Geological Survey topographical maps. Five thousand acres covers so much territory that they studied the maps in shifts.

Crawford pointed to where the house ruins stood. "I think there has to be burial grounds near the house."

"There's the traditional family plot." Margaret pointed to the place. "Sophie is buried there along with everyone in our family except those who fell in foreign wars. An uncle lost at sea during the Spanish-American War, well, a great-great-uncle, but you know what I mean. But everyone who died here is buried here."

Crawford rubbed his chin. "The proposed route sweeps this way."

He ran his finger behind the house, the stable, and outbuildings.

"Given the size of this farm, the number of people working here including the enslaved, the indentured servants, there have to be cemeteries all over." Ronnie held a magnifying glass over the stable area.

"No doubt, but we don't know where they are." Charlotte agreed. "Even if some of the workers were buried at their church, many have to be here. What I don't understand is why aren't those graves marked?"

"I think they were. I remember my grandmother alluding to overgrown sites. My grandfather, whom I really didn't know, didn't care. And you all know how lush Virginia can be. I expect those graveyards are overgrown, deep in the woods. How can you find out?"

"Ground-penetrating radar," Crawford said.

"For five thousand acres?" Ronnie was incredulous.

"If I have to, yes, but I think the chances are the dead will be closer to the house or at least the more inhabited areas. And we have some maps back to World War One." He laid an old map, pulled from under the topo maps, on top of the government maps. "See. Outbuildings are on this map that don't appear elsewhere. Some things are easy to identify. The old draft horse barns, the cattle barns."

"Are you going to restore those?" Ronnie asked.

"No. I will rebuild the carriage barns as they were beautiful. I have photographs of them. Maybe I'll build cattle barns later if I get cattle."

Charlotte swept her hand over those maps on the table. "There have to be Monacan bones. They lived here. Not only will the tribes here fight it. So will a lot of other people."

"An ace in the hole." Ronnie nodded. "I want you all to know, I have to say it out loud, I work for Soliden. They are our client. But you know where my heart is. If you can furnish me with proof of buried slaves, buried Monacans, anything of a historical nature, I can convince them to swerve away from the Chapel Cross area. I think Gregory was leaning that way, but with proof I can convince the new leadership."

"The entire area?" Charlotte was intrigued.

"Surely the Monacans covered much of the land out here. Clear, hard, running water off the mountains, tons of game. It's a perfect environment, so my argument will be, go along or over the Skyline Drive until you find a less precipitous way down and one that doesn't drop right into former Indian territory, into a historic site being architecturally restored."

"The Skyline Drive will set everyone else off." Margaret sighed.

"Yes, it will. Digging along that road right-of-way will delay traffic for years and that park is the most visited park in the country." Ronnie knew his stuff. "But that uproar will shift away from this uproar and Soliden's engineers will busy themselves finding one way up the west side of the Blue Ridge, crossing over the Skyline Drive at only one place that would be perfect and then dropping down on the east side, hence through the Piedmont and to the sea. One way or the other, this pipeline has to reach a major port and it can't be Virginia Beach because of the naval base."

"I thought the end point is to be in North Carolina," Margaret said.

"It is, but that, too, can be changed. If Virginia offered enough incentives, like deepening an existing port, that base would mean permanent jobs. Construction work isn't permanent, so we'll see a spike for the years the pipeline is being dug and then that's it. There will be more company maintenance people but not all that many." Ronnie paused. "However, some jobs are better than no jobs. There are people who need work."

"But are the workers coming from our state?" Charlotte asked the obvious question and one loaded for politicians.

"Some. Whatever state is impacted will have a number hired

to sweeten the deal," Ronnie informed them. "It's how Soliden or any megacompany buys off the state legislators. And the governor."

"Ah." Margaret, a doctor, hadn't considered this.

"So anything you can remember—walks with your grandmother, your father, anything—let me know." Ronnie was sincere.

"I've walked a great deal around the ruins as well as the old outbuilding sites. I was looking for raised ground or depressed grounds, burial size, casket size. I've uncovered nothing." Crawford frowned. "They have to be out there."

"Will you have to unearth some graves for proof?" Margaret hoped not.

"That's the point of the radar. If the remains can be seen, nobody should be disturbed, although if someone wants accurate proof of age, they might want to carbon-date the bones. I'm for a rough estimate, no digging." Crawford folded his arms across his chest. "But I wouldn't be surprised if a legislator wanted physical proof to cover his ass if this comes to a vote. Soliden will lobby endlessly to see that it doesn't."

"This is a lot of effort." Margaret sat down. "You're being forced into this. We can all thank the Supreme Court for this. Remember when they made that decision that private land could be seized for private profit? Goodbye eminent domain if the corporation is big enough. They can take anyone's land, which is the point of this, isn't it?"

"Margaret, money talks." Said a man who knew how loudly it did. "Gregory Luckham has to or had to answer to a board and the board has to answer to shareholders. So if moving the pipeline costs, say, two percent of the profits for, say, ten years, it will cost billions. The profit loss per annum may be as much as two to three billion per year. That's the real issue. Everything is shareholder value, not public value. You and I and everyone else along this route were not consulted. Nor were our elected representatives.

Of course, now it's an issue, but until citizens protested, essentially this was done by executive fiat."

"Payoffs?" Charlotte asked Crawford.

"Too obvious." He smiled for he knew the game well. "A crude way to agree is for the company, any company, to put sums of money in Aunt Minnie's bank account. Not yours, not your wife's or your parents'. Hard cash wakes up most people. Another way to pay off is making sure a legislator's child is accepted at a high-level university or gets a high-paying job once out of that university which will cost about $80,000 per year figuring in tuition, books, clothing. Tuition alone at an Ivy League school now runs about $68,000 per year."

"What about kickbacks?" Ronnie's eyebrows were raised.

Crawford cleared his throat. "Effective if you're careful."

"What do you mean?" Margaret, in many ways innocent to corruption, asked.

"Let's say you manufacture a type of pipe that can withstand the pressure needed to force the gas or oil through the pipeline over hundreds of miles. You have competitors and one might be a Chinese factory that can undercut you. But you work out an arrangement with the union over their wages, you will surely be unionized, you win the contract. You shave off a half a million, more or less, and give it back to the union president as well as the president of the company or the vice president or whoever is in charge of materials. You need to be careful how you do it. Again, Aunt Minnie is critical here." He laughed.

"My God, I had no idea." Margaret was shocked.

"Margaret, have you ever known anyone who served in the House of Delegates or Congress who left office poorer than they went in? Setting aside the Founding Fathers? A vastly different time." Crawford considered all this the cost of doing business.

"They were vastly different kinds of men than we have today," Ronnie added. "Oh, there was a venal one here or there but in the main they truly believed in public service, they cared about the public good. A few such souls are left to us but it's the politics of smash and grab."

"Oh, I hope not. I do hope not." Margaret was ashen faced.

"He's right. These are the times in which we live," Charlotte added. "That's why I get hired to unearth, forgive the expression, histories. It's exciting, in its way, going up against a corporation or the state houses. Everyone pleads that they're doing what they have to do."

"Did you offer Gregory Luckham incentives?" Ronnie directly asked Crawford.

"I did." He said this without shame for as far as he was concerned Soliden was wrong. "I didn't ask him if he had an Aunt Minnie but I alluded to the fact that I could and would be helpful. He was noncommittal. Certainly it wasn't the first time he's encountered such an offer."

"Did you get the feeling he was corrupt?" Margaret looked up at Crawford.

"I got the feeling everyone has a price, including Gregory Luckham." He now sat down next to her.

"I hope I don't."

"Margaret, of course you don't, but the hospital with which you are associated does." Ronnie's voice was low.

"Yes." She nodded.

"No one's trying to buy me off." Charlotte smiled. "I am determined to find those underneath us. Once the snow is all melted we'll begin. I know there are bodies, many bodies, under Old Paradise."

She was right, of course.

CHAPTER 20

Hoofbeats reverberated through the covered bridge as the field crossed over to the other side of Broad Creek. After All, manicured, every building in perfect condition including the covered bridge, loose board repaired, was a beloved fixture. Today, Saturday, sixty-five people, happy to be out, showed up, parked on the western side of the bridge.

The house, painted brick, Georgian, perched atop a low rise on the eastern side. Broad Creek, which flowed throughout the entire county, swept along below the house, hence the covered bridge. Fields, fenced, three-board painted white, extra maintenance that white, had been prepared for spring. Granted spring lay in the future but at the end of fall, the Bancrofts cut down most of the fields, turning over topsoil, be it hay, oats, or even a field of soybeans. When the weather warmed up all they had to do was plow and plant. However, the fields, a good two miles away that abutted Sister's place, were always left in standing corn. The upper ears had been plucked but the lower remained for forage for wildlife but especially the foxes.

Jefferson Hunt Club foxes lived well. Apart from corn consideration they were wormed once a month with wormer sprinkled on the kibble in special boxes. This stopped in March as the wormer would kill the unborn foxes. Those luxurious coats, bracing runs proved the effectiveness of Sister's health and feeding program. If possible, a young fox would be trapped, given a rabies shot, a seven-in-one shot. You never trapped them twice, they were too smart, but there hadn't been a case of vulpine rabies in Sister's territory for twelve years, a wonderful feat. The odd meds put out from time to time, fought off ticks and fleas as well as skin problems.

Sister operated on the assumption that a healthy fox will give you a healthy run. She also operated on the assumption that you were only as old as the horse you were riding, well, she cheated a little but she did convert horse years into human years. Her rule of thumb was five years per human one, absolutely accurate, she didn't know but it worked for her. She was riding Keepsake, a twelve-year-old bay appendix, so he was sixty in human years. Horses, hounds, and people if they stayed fit could just go and go. The Bancrofts, now in their middle eighties, always started out right behind Sister. If the hunt proved long and hard, they fell back to the middle of the pack.

Foxhunters all believe when you stop you die. Keep riding whether it's First Flight or behind but throw your leg over a horse. Face the wind, snow, sleet, rain, or sun. They were all certain one of the reasons they so rarely came down with the flu or colds was they hunted in all weather.

Aunt Netty, a fox edging toward senior citizenship, actually she was there, did not share this philosophy. When the rain slashed sideways or the snow covered everything, she lounged at Pattypan Forge. Huge, abandoned since right after World War I, the forge, operating since the 1700s, evidenced many comforts. For one thing, Sister always filled a big feeder box with kibble, usually once every two weeks. Scraps might be tossed in the kibble.

In her prime, Aunt Netty gave many a merry chase. She was still dazzling for a half an hour, but then she needed to duck in somewhere. Truthfully, Aunt Netty was slowing down. Also she endured a separation from her mate, Uncle Yancy, as they agreed. The owl, Athena, living at Pattypan, called it a divorce, which infuriated Aunt Netty. It was a separation provoked by Uncle Yancy's terrible housekeeping habits. That was Aunt Netty's version.

She'd meandered down to the main house as the morning, brisk, was a great improvement over the last two weeks of weather including the January thaw, which the fox never trusted. The Bancrofts had the best garbage in Albemarle County. Aunt Netty wanted to pry off a garbage can lid. The raccoons got there before she did. Harsh words were spoken. As there were three of the bandits, Aunt Netty retreated. She heard the horse trailers drive in so she headed back toward Pattypan Forge. About halfway there she could hear the hoofbeats in the covered bridge.

Once everyone passed through the bridge, Shaker waited a moment so Sister could count heads. Right behind the Bancrofts, Kasmir and Alida rode, Freddie behind them. Then a large gaggle of people, Walter, Ben, Sam, even Gray was in the mix, Dewey, Bobby, Margaret, Cindy, Skiff, allowed off work today, anyone who could go out did. Guests from Keswick, Farmington, Stonewall, even Bull Run showed up along with a few dear friends from Deep Run. People felt like hunting around today but then again, After All was one of those prime fixtures, plus the breakfasts never failed to impress.

Sister nodded to Shaker. He spoke a few soft words to the pack, then trotted up Broad Creek, the water rushing down thanks to snowmelt. Aunt Netty's scent, strong, set hounds moving in two minutes, if that.

The day, low forties, dark clouds overhead, not much wind, promised good sport. Aunt Daniella and Yvonne slowly followed at a distance. No other car crept along. Most everybody who could was riding.

Aunt Netty heard the hounds. Pattypan, deep in rough woods, gave her the luxury of not having to fly at top speed. However, given the youngsters in the pack, the older red fox didn't underestimate them. She picked up speed, zigged and zagged. Once on a narrow deer trail she paused a moment to listen. Hounds sounded all on so she'd better just get home.

Hounds remained on the "house" side of the creek. Aunt Netty had crossed up ahead by cleverly walking across a fallen tree that had come down in the high winds and snowstorm. She could readily walk across but the hounds couldn't. They had to launch into the swollen creek. Shaker walked up, looking for his usual crossing. It, too, was submerged. He squeezed Gunpowder. The Thoroughbred readily jumped down, water splashing upward, but it did stay out of Shaker's boots. Hell riding with sloshing boots, cold wet feet.

Tootie moved farther up creek; she wanted to make sure if hounds turned left she'd be there, and Betty made the same decision on the right. Both Tootie and Betty rode on decent paths, decent for this mess of woods, but Weevil, like Shaker, battled vines, low-hanging branches, a muddy pothole here and there.

Finally Pattypan Forge appeared. Hounds leapt through the story-high broken windows, the glass long gone as those windows had been broken for nearly a century. However, the forge stood as did huge iron pots, the odds and ends of a once thriving forge.

Aunt Netty's den started at the one side of the forge with openings all over. No need. Hounds couldn't reach her no matter what.

Ardent complained at one of the openings. *"That wasn't much of a run."*

"Maybe you aren't much of a hound," she fired back.

He started digging, dirt flying behind him.

The field, waiting outside, as was Shaker, blowing the hounds back to him, listened to a yip and a yap inside. Hounds stayed put.

Shaker dismounted, stepped over a windowsill as the windows were almost ceiling to ground. "All right."

"She's terrible!" Thimble complained.

He blew "Gone to Ground," which is what they wanted to hear, including Aunt Netty, because then they'd leave.

"Come along. We'll pick up another fox."

"Come on." Dragon followed the huntsman.

As they all filed outside, Athena, the great horned owl who also had apartments all over the place, swooped down from a rafter, out the window, and right over the field, spooking some horses.

Alida, caught off guard, slipped sideways, but Dewey rode right up alongside her, held her up with one arm.

"Thanks." Alida righted herself. Her feet did not touch the ground so no one could say she came off. She didn't, but she sure looked unstable.

Hounds wanted to get on terms with their quarry as soon as possible, as did Shaker. If he returned the way he came, hounds risked running heel. He could correct them—they were good hounds—but why fool with it? The only reason to retrace one's steps is the other ways out of Pattypan Forge, filled with overgrowth, fallen trees, took time as well as cut a few faces. Still, if there was fresh scent, it would be either north, east, or west, so he plunged west. No going south.

Betty, hearing, drifted farther east until she emerged on the gravel road between After All and the Old Lorillard place. Creeping behind her at a distance came Yvonne and Aunt Daniella.

Tootie, remembering a decent deer path, stepped on it. While this took her out of the way she would emerge below the

Old Lorillard place, being in good position for whatever might happen next unless a fox struck out due west.

Noses down, hounds walked with deliberation. A whiff of bear, deer, they ignored. Finally, they, too, emerged on the gravel road.

Cora crossed it, dropping into the woods on the far east side of the farm road. This woods wasn't as thick as what everyone called the Pattypan woods.

Nothing, so she hopped back up on the road, waiting for Shaker.

Once on the road, Weevil at his rear, Shaker cast toward the Old Lorillard place. Uncle Yancy lived there and usually offered a bit of a run until the clever fellow dashed into one of his many places to elude hounds.

Along they all walked, the field out on the road finally. Although a farm road, it was well maintained with crushed rock.

Tootie waited by an outbuilding, which the Lorillard brothers used for extra firewood, a closer one right behind the house. However, one can never stack enough wood in the winter. They could always fill the front-end loader with this, refill the woodhouse by the house if necessary.

Dragon walked over to her, nose to the ground. His stern wagged. He opened. Arrogant though he was, Dragon was rarely wrong. The pack came to him and instead of running toward the house, they ran due west, skirting the Pattypan woods but crossing roaring tributaries of Broad Creek finally bursting out, for it was now a flat-out run, onto the cornfields at the westernmost end.

Sister, keeping up, watched for any sign of movement in the standing corn. Nothing there, but then hounds soared over an old, large hog's back jump. She followed after Weevil, found herself on her wildflower meadow, denuded, charging across, soil relatively dried out, all things considered. One by one First Flight negotiated the hog's back, the first really big jump of the day, while Bobby Franklin had to hurry to a gate, lean over, and try to lift the chain with the handle of his staghorn crop.

Before Sister knew it, she'd passed Tootie's cottage, jumped out of that area over a simple fence, came out onto her back farm road. The fox had headed straight up toward Hangman's Ridge, so hounds followed, as did she. The climb, not precipitous, was steep enough; by the time she reached the large flat pasture on top, the enormous Hangman's tree in the middle, hounds barreled across it, down on the other side.

Galloping down took a tight seat and good balance, which fortunately the Master had but not everyone in the field did. She could hear commotion behind her but she couldn't stop. That wasn't her job. Her job was to stay behind hounds and this she did until down on the other side of Hangman's Ridge they screeched to a stop. She could see Cindy Chandler's fence along Soldier Road, that's how far they'd run.

Hounds milled about. Horses and humans took deep breaths and those who had parted company from their horses straggled down, muddied a bit, last of all, even behind Bobby Franklin, who as usual shepherded everyone and kept them mounted.

Weevil drifted to the side and rear of hounds. They didn't turn. Betty, far ahead, guarded the road. You didn't want a pack of hounds out on Soldier Road without someone stopping traffic. Luckily, there wasn't much, but it only takes one car.

Shaker cast in a circle very slowly. But no scent. Where they waited, the field full of old broomstraw should have held scent, but nothing.

The huntsman was certain they'd been on a fox, most likely a visiting dog fox, but how did he get away without leaving a trace? He scanned the ground for fallen logs, checked the base of a few old trees down low: no dens in the bottom. Nor did he see any holes in the ground or under a large rock here or there.

Once again the magic of a fox foiled them. What a good fox, too. Just ran straight as an arrow.

Shaker turned, rode up to Sister, both of them still taking deep breaths.

"I can cast as you say, but let's walk to wherever that might be. Thanks to all that bad weather, we aren't as fit as usual this time of year."

She smiled at him. "We've been out for two and a half hours. That's enough."

"It can't be." Shaker shook his head.

She pulled out her grandfather's magnificent pocket watch, flicked open the gold cover, held it toward him. He leaned over to peer at it.

"I would have sworn we were only out for forty-five minutes."

"Time changes on a great run. It makes me wonder about all those time theories. A pity Einstein wasn't a foxhunter."

Shaker laughed. "Beats writing on a blackboard. So, Master, what next?"

"We lost a few people running downhill. I would have thought we'd lose them at the hog's back but they all made it. Why don't we go back up, walk past that hateful hanging tree, go down, and you, Betty, Tootie, Weevil, and I can put the hounds up since we're at the farm. Then we can drive over to After All. We'll be just in time for breakfast."

"Sounds like a plan." He tapped his cap with his crop, calling out. "Come along. Come along, good hounds."

"I'd get another fox. I'm not tired," Dragon bragged.

"We'd all get another fox." Diana, his littermate, agreed. *"But we'd wind up with only staff and maybe three people in the hunt field. We haven't had a run like this since before the snowstorm."*

"If the weather stays like this, they'll all be right in no time." Trident smiled, eager as only a youngster can be.

"But the weather never stays consistent on the other side of New Year's," Giorgio prophesied. *"Mark my words."*

Pickens said, *"We can hunt no matter what."*

"Pickens"—Zane walked next to him—*"we don't need to be in a snowstorm like we were at Christmas Hunt. That was truly hateful."*

"Hear, hear." The rest of the pack agreed.

Sister smiled, thinking the hounds chatty.

Forty minutes later hunt staff joined the people at the breakfast. Others were trickling in, having put their horses in trailers or tying them next to them. People changed into their tweed coats, wiped dirt off their bottoms if they could. People had popped off like toast.

Aunt Daniella talked with enthusiasm to Tedi and Edward Bancroft, as they had known one another for most of their long lives, shared many of the same reference points.

Yvonne, encircled by men, chatted amiably as Tootie and Weevil reviewed the hunt.

"How'd you find that outbuilding? I'm surprised you remembered." Weevil complimented her. He'd studied maps as well as asked territory questions.

"If I go somewhere even once, I almost always remember." She looked into his bright blue eyes as though registering them for the first time. "I thought we were on a coyote at first."

He nodded. "Me, too, but then I hadn't heard anyone say they'd seen one in our territory so I figured a red."

"Wasn't Ardent terrific? It's his 'A' line. Asa is the oldest but if you go into the graveyard, well, you've been there, the brass hound in the middle is Archie. Sister tells such stories about him."

He smiled at her. "She loves her hounds. That's why I hunt. I want to be with hounds."

Sister joined Yvonne and the crowd. Gray came next to her, slipping his arm around her waist. Both of them had been raised to not be very physically demonstrative but she glowed—a hard run always made her glow. She looked up at him, thinking as she always did that he was one of the kindest men she had ever known as well as one of the most handsome.

"And then Tootie cut out a back door, two mudflaps." Yvonne continued, then held up her hand, the ring on her ring finger.

"I asked the Van Dorns if they'd lost a ring but they hadn't. I can't imagine leaving Beveridge Hundred. It felt like home the first time I saw it and Tootie has helped me move stuff about. I hope this pipeline threat doesn't upset them too much. But if you've lived somewhere most of your life, a change like that would be hard to bear."

"Hard to bear no matter what," Dewey said. "And the land would drop in value. That, too, would be hard. Plus if I lived where a fox brought me such a beautiful ring, I'd never leave. The fox alone pumps up the land value, hell with the pipeline."

"We'll all probably outlive our money." Betty laughed.

"Maybe not all of us," Dewey rejoined.

"The point is to live long enough to be a trial to everyone," Aunt Daniella, having overheard, called out.

"You've succeeded, Aunt Dan." Gray lifted a glass to her, as did the others, to much laughter.

CHAPTER 21

Crawford walked with the head of the Virginia Historical Society. January 26, cold but clear, allowed Crawford to point out what he deemed important.

"We estimate two hundred bodies in this area alone. The radar has uncovered other burial places but this is the largest here on the east side of this slope. As the land is flat, the slope or hill somewhat protects the site."

"I'm assuming you will remove the debris." John D'Etampes observed the heavily wooded area overgrown with thick underbrush.

"Underbrush but I'll keep the trees. With a little effort this will be a lovely spot."

"Do you plan to exhume a corpse?"

"In order to accurately date the people in here, we will need to do so. What my historical researcher and I are studying now is what spot might be the oldest, what area the youngest? Do these people go back to immediately after the War of 1812? Others much later? Obviously, we have work to do. Personally, I don't want to disturb any remains."

John took photos of the area.

"I have a lot of visual materials," Crawford offered.

"I'll take them, too, or make copies, but this is for me." He took another photo with his phone, then looked up at Crawford. "Big undertaking. Perhaps that isn't the right word."

Crawford smiled, pulled his collar up as the wind edged upward to about twelve miles per hour. The wind changed in the blink of an eye by the mountains.

"The ground-penetrating radar has revealed garbage pits. Dumping grounds. Old wagon wheels, broken bottles, junk, but useful to understanding how Old Paradise was run."

"More buried people?"

"Yes. If you get back in the Rover, I'll take you there."

John climbed in, Crawford slowly backed out, drove over the fields to a rise above a tributary of Broad Creek. He stopped, did not get out but pointed to the land just west of this narrow creek.

"The radar shows a small grouping of people. We've counted fifteen. Charlotte believes these may be the last of the Monacans who lived here, we think, in the summers, moving farther east in winter. Again, we will have to unearth one." He stopped, cleared his throat. "My wife, opposed as she is to the pipeline, becomes squeamish at the thought of digging up old bones. She says we mustn't disturb the dead."

"Many people feel that way. However, it is the only way we can get accurate information about nutrition, health, age. Did these people die of old age? Were they wounded in skirmishes? Could some of them have perished of starvation?"

"Of course," Crawford said. "It's the only way. Marty, my wife, is a spiritual person. Then again, there are people around here who believe this will release the spirits of the dead. There's a fascinating woman, in her nineties, who said to me, 'Don't conjure up what you can't conjure down.' "

"Voodoo." John laughed. "Speaking of conjuring, you all have had your trials."

Crawford cut the motor for a moment, still gazing at the older burial site. "I can't pretend I'm distressed over the Soliden president disappearing. The entire pipeline project is a hideous mistake. But the fellow who was found, he worked for me. He was a decent fellow."

"I am sorry." John had no idea that Rory had been employed by Crawford.

"Bashed in the head." Crawford shook his own head. "No idea. No one has any idea at all. I think"—he said this with conviction—"I think Rory encountered whoever killed or kidnapped Gregory Luckham. Well, killed. Why kidnap him? We'd hear about a ransom by now. I'd ransom his life against the pipeline, were it me." He shrugged. "Has people spooked."

"Small wonder." John looked back out the window as Crawford turned around, pointing out things he felt of interest, explaining the outbuildings, the plan for rebuilding Old Paradise.

"You know, I have to admit, the first thing I did when the radar got here was I had them go over the remains of the house. Well, there is only the columns, which you see, and the basement, which I have rebuilt. As soon as it's warm I'll raise walls again. We have the plans plus this place was stunning. A lot of people took pictures or painted it."

"I take it you found nothing so far?"

"No. But I heard all the stories about buried treasure. Couldn't help myself."

"I did a little research on Old Paradise myself before coming here. From its founding until right after World War Two, money rolled in like the tide. Then it rolled in somewhat sporadically and finally it didn't roll in at all, it rolled out. And two brothers who didn't speak. A strange place."

"Yes. When I saw it I felt an electric current shoot through me. I had to have it. Had to wait out the two brothers. Rented it first."

"You were wise. I researched you, too." John grinned.

"Ah," Crawford replied. "Well then, you know I get what I want."

"Yes. What is it you want from me?"

"A statement from the historical society that remains have been found here, remains of importance to Virginia's history. A press statement and, if you would, a statement here for the TV people. I will arrange and pay for everything."

"Thoughtful. Wise. This will arouse public interest. Remember the excitement when the graves, new to us, were uncovered at Jamestown in 2015? One of the deceased had been a priest, not a pastor but a priest. We are pretty sure of this, which casts a new light on Jamestown. Then again, we will never know everything, will we?"

"No but we can grasp the larger picture. I am, by the way, prepared to give a five-hundred-thousand-dollar donation to the historical society. I need your help and I do support your work."

"Thank you."

The two drove on, Crawford again pointing out this and that while John was already writing the press release in his head.

CHAPTER 22

Low clouds, mercury hanging in the high thirties, promised a decent day's hunting this Saturday, January 27, Mozart's birthday in Austria in 1756. Jefferson Hunt met at Whiskey Ridge, a new old fixture, ten miles south of Chapel Cross. When the hunt was first started in 1887, Whiskey Ridge was an original fixture. Over the decades it remained so until the 1950s, when new owners, opposed to blood sports, ended it. In those days foxhunting was a blood sport, although one rarely caught the fox. But by the 1970s this faded away, until today it's only a memory for those who are old.

The new owners, the Garnetts, new as in the last twenty years, appreciated the fact that foxhunters did not kill and so the old place came back onto the fixture card.

And it was a ridge. One turned right off the two-lane road, drove through some flat pastures, then climbed about six hundred feet up to the ridge. The reward was gorgeous views in all directions, the backstop being the Blue Ridge Mountains. Cold though it was, it wasn't piercing cold, so eighty-some people showed up.

Shaker cast east as there was little wind. The field walked down the driveway their trucks had labored up, pulling those heavy rigs. The ground, soft, wasn't sticky mud. Sister noted it would be slippery in parts but mostly the footing seemed good.

Once in the front pastures, which staff thought of as the flats, hounds began working. Deer had crossed, a rabbit must have wandered out of its warren then hopped back in. Rabbit scent, fragile, wafted up hound noses, which is how they knew this was recent.

"Those little white tails get me," Dasher remarked.

"Come springtime, this place will be overrun with them." Dragon kept his nose to the ground.

The flats comprised one hundred and fifty acres on which the Garnetts grew good hay. No one worried about trampling shoots in January, but by mid-April, conditions permitting, delicious green blades would push through the earth. Good hay contains protein and sugar and tastes wonderful to many creatures.

On the hounds walked, intent. Weevil, behind, noted tracks. He leaned over Midshipman, a young Thoroughbred learning the ropes. The tracks, blurred, became clear as he moved along. Huge great blue herons had walked here, no doubt dabbling in the large puddles as the snow melted. Whiskey Ridge's pond, down low, filled with fish, proved a favorite with the herons, but any body of water, even a big puddle, excited interest. Weevil sat upright again, noticed that a few sterns waved languidly. He decided to move up a bit closer.

"What do you think?" young Aero asked Tatoo.

"A skunk."

"Ooo, wouldn't that be stronger?" the young hound asked.

"Aero, this line is old. You need to learn how to tell time. Water changes scent, wind changes scent, and this line is hours old."

"Well," sputtered Aero, *"what's a skunk doing out here in an open pasture?"*

Tatoo laughed. *"Looking for food or a girlfriend. The skunk was here in the middle of the night. No one to bother him. No other animal is going to kill a skunk."*

Aero puzzled over this when Cora opened, others following. It was the end of January. January and February, the mating months, when the weather is half decent, give you the best runs.

This fox, a male, was moving north and moving fast. Hounds, scent bursting in their noses, sounded like nature's chorus. Bass voices boomed, baritones from darker to lighter, those sweet tenors and then the squeaky yip of a youngster whose voice had not yet changed filled the air.

Thundering over the last pasture, hounds swerved around an abandoned storage building, made from fieldstone so it was sturdy and pretty. Pookah dipped inside to double-check, shot out. No scent in there at all but the young hound was learning to think.

Once around the attractive building they dipped into woods that are called parked out because the underbrush is cleared so the trees stand unmolested.

Pretty as this is to people, it doesn't give cover to foxes or other animals. The fox blew through it in a hurry to get into rougher territory at the edge of Whiskey Ridge. The heavy woods belonged to people living in New York City. Word was they would be moving, but when, no one knew. The land was untended, woods dense, and the fields choking with broomstraw.

The wind came up slightly so the broomstraw swayed. Heading due north, the fox easily squeezed under old page wire, a curse to horsemen. Even the hounds couldn't get through, so Shaker blasted down to the road, hounds following the fox. He then urged Showboat forward.

The next decision was where to duck back into the land. No one wanted to risk running into downed wire. No one wanted to lose the fox either. Weevil, slowing so he could study the edge of the fenced-in mess, found a narrow passage, carefully urged Midshipman through it, walked along hoping he could move along a little faster.

Hounds moved through the woods while Shaker kept parallel to them. Seeing Weevil in the woods gave the huntsman time to find his own way without undue risk. Fortunately, an entire section of the page wire had been peeled back, the half rounds used for posts peeled back with it.

Hounds wedged under bushes, slid by downed limbs. For the humans this was harder. Betty wisely kept on the road, as did Bobby with Second Flight. Sister plunged in and took her chances, as did First Flight.

Hounds screamed.

Reaching the edge of this woods, they followed the wire. Finding no way out they went all the way to the road where they could get under. Shaker wasn't so lucky.

Dewey, not one to hang back, rode up, dismounted, pulled his wire cutters from off his saddle, and cut out a huge section of wire. "The hell with it. When they come down from New York, they'll never notice."

Shaker didn't argue. Dewey was probably right, the absentee owners wouldn't take notice. If they had intended to refresh this fencing, they would have done so by now.

Everyone eagerly moved through the now wide opening back to the road. Hounds, way ahead of them by now, were heading to Skidby, and Skidby lay three miles north of Whiskey Ridge. Hounds, horses were flying.

Some large, jagged rock outcroppings overhung the road. As people passed it they noticed how much cooler it was.

Sister tried to keep Shaker and the hounds in sight, as did Betty. God knows where Tootie was. Somewhere higher and hopefully outside the page wire.

Hounds slowed, scent shifted. It wasn't lost but the fox was playing with them. He turned, ran back south for a few hundred yards, then shot straight up toward the mountains.

Shaker followed. As he climbed up, Showboat stopped. Shaker laid on the whip. Showboat wouldn't move, instead blowing out his nostrils. Shaker, not a hard man, needed to be with his hounds. He raised his arm again. Showboat stood straight up. Showboat had never done such a thing. Shaker slid over the horse's hindquarters, hit the ground, then his head hit a flat rock hard.

He was out cold. Showboat, terrified, ran for the road.

Weevil immediately rode up, dismounted, let Midshipman's reins drop. Midshipman blew out his nostrils, too, but he stood as they had been working on what to do if the reins were dropped and his rider was on foot.

Staff prepares for such a moment, hoping they will never need to perform it. Sister held the field back except for Walter, a doctor, who rode up and also dismounted.

Weevil had taken Shaker's pulse and confirmed he was alive but otherwise didn't touch him.

Betty rode in, called the hounds to her, and held them. She also yelled for Tootie, who appeared moments later to help her hold the hounds.

Hounds naturally go to their huntsman but in a condition like this, they could unwittingly hurt a downed human.

Walter's first thought was Shaker's neck or back. As the huntsman remained unconscious, Walter also did not touch him. Instead he pulled out his cellphone and called 911.

CHAPTER 23

Walter and Weevil waited for the ambulance while Sister turned the field back to Whiskey Ridge. Tootie and Betty followed with the hounds although Tootie had to drift off after Dragon. While not a hound that skirts he was strong-minded, always wanted to be the first. He was skirting now.

Tootie, squeezing Iota, moved outside him to push him back. Determined, he looked up at her, moved back toward where Showboat seized up. Furious, she couldn't crack her whip. She didn't want to set off the rest of the pack. Betty, keenly aware of the situation, slowed from a walk to a crawl.

Sister, turning to look back, didn't see Dragon but fully understood there was a problem with hounds. As they knew her, she motioned for Gray to move up to her while halting the people.

"There's a problem behind. It's Dragon but we don't want the pack to blow up. They're upset. Will you take the field back and I'll get there as soon as I can?"

"Of course."

Sam rode up, a good hand with hounds. "Master, allow me to go with you just in case."

"Thank you, Sam. Whatever is the problem here, the two of us ought to be able to handle it." She thought to herself as they rode side by side, *Thank God for Sam. He's quick-witted and stronger than I am.*

Passing Betty, Sister quietly briefed her.

Hounds wanted to go with Sister but she told them firmly, "No." They knew what no meant as well as "leave it." Ears drooping, they gave Betty piteous and worried looks.

Sister should have paid attention to those looks.

Dragon, trotting now, Tootie still on his outside, stopped about fifty yards above where Walter and Weevil stood. Showboat had come back to Weevil, who held his reins. Walter's angel mount, Clemson, stood like a rock, which certainly helped Midshipman, a youngster. Clemson also calmed Showboat, still a little nervous.

Shaker remained unconscious.

Sister and Sam pulled up next to Tootie, who had just stopped.

Dragon reached down, picked something up, turned to head back down to the pack.

Tootie's face registered disgust. As Sister and Sam could now see Dragon, they, too, were aghast. Dragon, thrilled with himself, was carrying a human hand or what was left of it, cleanly cut above the wrist. The flesh, mostly eaten, still gave off the distinct odor of decay. The bones had been gnawed.

"Let us walk calmly back. He'll carry it with him. We can remove it from him once we're out of here and once I call Ben."

"Sister, why don't I ride ahead and alert Ben?"

"Good idea, Sam. Dragon will walk with Tootie and myself."

Dragon, fearing to drop his prize, did not open his mouth

but obediently followed the Master and the whipper-in, walking between them, head up, tail up.

Tootie said, "There has to be more out there."

"Yes. I expect the smell is what set off Showboat. You'll notice horses don't like dead things. If a deer carcass lays in a field, they'll shy away from it. If they become used to it—say it's out in high grass and we can't see it—they won't eat near it. Showboat is a good animal." She paused. "God, I hope Shaker is all right."

"I didn't see him come off."

"Right over the hindquarters because Showboat stood straight up. He hit hard. His head hit the ground with a snap. Even with his hard hat, that will ring your bell. I was a bit aways but I saw the whole thing." She rode a little more, then said, "Tootie, don't tell anyone what you've seen. We're going to pull up once we reach the pastures, the flats, at Whiskey Ridge. Ben should be with Sam by then, in a car, I hope."

"Yes, ma'am."

"People will be talking enough. This will set off high drama. Never doubt that a situation can't be made worse. The less they know at this point, the better."

"Yes, ma'am."

Her memory unlocked by events, Sister counseled Tootie. "Think like a Master. No matter what goes wrong, you must remain calm. Hounds and horses will feed off your emotions, as will the people. The worst are the people, of course."

"Yes, ma'am."

"Honey, I know you're upset. This is horrific. Occasionally sorrowful things happen in the hunt field. A hound may be killed—I've only lost two in my long career. A horse may drop dead of a heart attack or a stroke just like a person. You have to stay calm. If an animal is injured, the first thing you have to do is prevent them from harming you or themselves but this, well, this I believe, is murder."

"The hand. You think it belongs to Gregory Luckham?"

"I do."

"The rest of him has to be out there somewhere."

"Tootie, yes, but animals eat carrion. He could be scattered all over. Then again, he could have been partially buried, unearthed. This is Ben's job, not ours. We have to keep our mouths shut. Obviously, we inform staff. You all will need to be extra vigilant."

The two women and a very happy hound stopped at the edge of the flats. In the distance they could see Betty on Magellan quietly walking hounds up the drive toward their party wagon. The field walked up also. No one noticed them as they were far enough away, plus everyone had to be talking about the accident.

Ben in Sam's truck, well, Crawford's truck, rolled down that same drive. Sam could hitch and unhitch a truck and trailer in a skinny minute. Ben would have still been working on it so he wisely stuck with Sam. The two men reached Sister and Tootie, stopped, and got out.

Ben knelt down, eye to eye with Dragon who was not going to drop the mangled hand.

Sister dismounted, handing her reins to Tootie. "Dragon, drop it."

He looked at her with baleful eyes. He did not drop the loathsome prize.

She reached for it. Ben grabbed her hand. "Don't. Give me a minute." He turned. "Sam, do you have a plastic bag or an old rag, anything in the truck?"

Sam opened the door, rummaged around the small seat behind the driver's seat, retrieved an oil-soaked rag. "All I got."

"It will have to do." Ben took the rag, the oil smell preferable to decay, knelt down.

Dragon turned his head. Sister knelt beside Ben.

"Good hound. Good hound. What a find."

Dragon, ever responsive to praise, wagged his tail, faced his beloved Master.

"Ben, give me the rag. He's not going to open his mouth for you and you can't force him. He's a powerful animal."

Ben handed her the rag, which she folded over, placing it around the hand. "Dragon, good boy. Good boy. Give it to me. Come on."

With such reluctance he opened his mouth. The hand dropped into the rag. Sister folded it over the mess, patted him on the head as she handed the object to Ben.

"Thank you," Ben acknowledged.

He was about to say something about her composure with something so gross. Then he remembered she had lost her son to a PTO accident, the spinning shaft on the back of a tractor that runs the attached implement. Today those PTOs are covered. In 1974 they were not. By the time she had reached her son, her husband having run up to the house for extra help, he had been strangled by his T-shirt, which caught in the PTO. It spun until her husband could climb up on the seat and cut the motor. RayRay remained in one piece but was nearly torn apart. Strangulation does not leave a pretty corpse.

Sam, a young man when this happened, did not have it in mind, but he knew Sister Jane was tough. He also noticed Tootie, and his opinion of her shot sky high.

Ben carefully placed the evidence in the seat as they heard the ambulance sirens approaching where Shaker was laid out.

"Excuse me. I need to call backup." He fished out his cellphone, then added, "Before you go, tell me what happened."

They waited for him to finish his call, then Sister, Sam, and Tootie recounted Dragon veering off, a mission in mind.

He jotted a few notes down. Ben always kept a thin leather Smythson notebook in a pocket, even while hunting. He then looked up to see the ambulance crew walking up into the woods.

"This has turned into one hell of a day." Sam watched the stretcher being carried.

"We can pray. That's about all we can do." Sister, too, watched.

"Thank God, Walter was there," Ben remarked.

"And Weevil. He did everything exactly correct, as did Tootie and Betty." Sister smiled a thin smile at Tootie. "We have a fabulous staff!"

"What about me?" Dragon felt he performed wonders.

Sister reached down to pet him. "We need to get him back to the others."

They could see the ambulance team carrying Shaker, Walter walking next to him, down to the ambulance. The ground wasn't level so this was arduous.

Once Shaker had been placed in the back of the ambulance, Weevil and Showboat on one side and Clemson on the other waited for Walter to mount. Walter must have said something to the ambulance driver about the sirens with the horses there. The ambulance pulled away and the driver didn't hit the siren until a good quarter mile down the road.

Walter and Weevil walked toward Sister, Tootie, Sam, and Ben. When they reached them Ben thought it prudent to inform them of why Shaker really hit the ground.

"I'll do my best to keep you all up to date." Ben walked back to the passenger side as Sam got behind the wheel. Sam put the windows down because he didn't want the smell to linger in the cab of the truck. Crawford didn't need to know what had happened. As Sam turned to go back to the trailers, the two men were talking about how to get the hand into a box, anything to keep it out of sight. Ben would drive it to headquarters while Sam would take his horse to Crawford's barn. Things were complicated. Sam would have to figure out how to pick up Ben's rig if he couldn't find a free hand to do it from Whiskey Ridge.

The four, horses happy to go back, walked.

Sister said to them, "Thank God for all of you."

Walter, her Joint Master, replied. "You've drilled us enough times."

"Well, I didn't drill you on medical procedure."

"No. Once I get Clemson home, I'll drive to the hospital and stay with Shaker. When I know what his injuries are, I'll call you, then later text the club. The last thing we need are people calling the hospital or you. I'll take care of it."

"Should I call Skiff?" Sister asked. "They are becoming very close."

"That's a good idea. If she's there when he wakes up, it might help. I doubt he will have any recollection at all. I hope his memory isn't impaired, will come back. His head hit the only damned rock on the path."

"As I said—we need to pray."

"We do," Weevil agreed, sobered by events. "Master, do you think that hand belongs to the man who is missing?"

"DNA will tell us that." Walter spoke for Sister, although he, too, could correctly be addressed as Master. "But I expect we all think that is part of Gregory Luckham."

They reached the flats, Sister pulled up. "Wait a moment. Gather round."

Weevil, Tootie, and Walter surrounded her, the horses' noses turned into a circle.

"Tootie, you might want to stay with your mother or have her stay with you. Whoever has killed knows Chapel Cross, knows it well. So well, he, or possibly she, could kill in a snowstorm and get rid of the corpse without anyone suspecting. If she won't agree, then I'll ask Sam to stay with the Van Dorns. Actually, I should ask him anyway. Scratch my request. This will work better. But as we hunt, especially when we hunt again at Tattenhall Station, we'd better be hyperalert."

"We know Chapel Cross. Most Jefferson Hunt members know it, too." Walter stated the obvious.

"That has occurred to me, but I can't think of anyone with enough motive," Sister replied. "Or maybe I don't want to. It's too terrible."

"Crawford," Walter immediately responded.

"Well, he does, but he is not a stupid man. I don't know what we're up against. It seems as though this is about the pipeline, but it does seem so extreme. We're missing something."

Back at their trailers, Dragon put in with the others, the four took care of their horses, then appeared at the breakfast as though nothing else had happened. Everyone asked about Shaker and Walter could tell them he was carefully carried and placed in an ambulance. He made a short announcement that he would send an email once he knew Shaker's condition.

Sister marveled at what good actors they all were. She was proud of her staff. What she couldn't keep from recurring like an unwanted theme song in her mind was, *What am I missing?*

CHAPTER 24

"I guess it's good news." Betty put her chin in her hands resting on the kitchen table.

"No riding. No driving for at least a month. He can't walk the hounds. We can't take the chance of a hound bumping him, knocking him to the ground." Sister looked around. "Any more tea or coffee?"

Tootie and Weevil shook their heads.

"Did Walter give a healing time?" Betty wondered.

"He said after a month another X-ray will be taken but until that month, Shaker has to wear the neck brace. He'll hate it but at least there are no fractures. His skull is intact.

"He has two vertebrae slightly out of line. The brace, we hope, will work and those vertebrae will line up. I expect the brace will be uncomfortable as well as whatever they wrap his neck in. They can't put anything heavy like you'd do for a broken leg. Too painful, plus Walter said he needs something that will give a little, breathe a little. He won't be able to turn his head. It sounds uncomfortable, irritating as hell, but still, it's better than a broken head or neck. Just one of those things." Sister tapped her cup with her fingernail. "What we need to decide is how we will get through the rest of the season. I could just make a decision but I think it's better if we talk it out."

Betty, knowing what was going through her best friend's mind, clarified her position. "Well, I am the senior whipper-in. I am happy to continue in my position. I don't want to hunt the hounds and really I don't think I should."

"Betty, hounds love you. They'll do whatever you ask." Tootie admired Betty, had learned a great deal from the older woman.

"Tootie, that's sweet. I do love the hounds and I hope they love me back, but I am better where I am. I never had a desire to carry the horn. I think I would be an indifferent huntsman. I'm a decent whipper-in. I should stay where I'll do the most good. We have to keep the transition as smooth as possible."

"The field would do as you ask. What good does it do them to complain?" Weevil piped up.

"Not a thing, but people will be people. Whoever hunts our hounds while Shaker recuperates will be subject to intense scrutiny, what my mother called 'the searching eye.' I'm not the least bit worried about our hounds," Sister forcefully stated.

"Well, I, too, would like to decline."

"Tootie, you're young. This club needs youth."

Betty had always wanted a female huntsman, or at the very least to whip-in to one at some point in her hunting career.

"You have no ambition to carry the horn?" Sister directly asked her.

"Not exactly. Of course, I dream about it, but I'm still in school and after this there will be vet school. I have to put my studies first. They don't need lots of people hunting them. At least, I don't think they do. Consistency. Hounds need consistency."

Sister smiled, for indeed Tootie had learned a great deal in her time with Jefferson Hunt. She'd started at sixteen, coming over from Custis Hall. Seeing her grow, deal with the vicissitudes of youth, of her father's treatment of her mother and her, Sister felt protective and proud of Tootie. She also believed you let people make up their own minds.

Nodding at Tootie, smiling, she then turned those penetrating eyes on Weevil. "And?"

He blushed. "I would be honored to hunt the hounds. I've dreamed of it, watched everything when I whipped-in to Toronto–North York, watched Shaker. If you'll take the chance on me, I'll try."

The three women, silent for a moment, then all began telling him he'd be good, a period of adjustment but he'd be fine.

"That's settled then." Sister rose, walked into the library, opened her desk drawer, pulled out an old, bent horn with a bit larger than average bell, returned, and handed it to Weevil. "My husband's."

Couldn't help himself, Weevil put the slightly overlarge horn to his lips and blew "All on."

Golly, on the counter, of course, immediately protested. *"That's awful. Shut up."*

Raleigh and Rooster lifted their heads and howled.

"Sorry." Weevil blushed again.

"Good lungs." Betty laughed.

"Tuesday. Muster Meadow. Tootie, pull up the map on your computer. Weevil, it's on the other side of Cindy Chandler's, maybe two miles down the road toward town. Much easier territory than anything around Chapel Cross or even here. The other good thing is there won't be a lot of people. If you suffer from jitters, it won't last long."

"Yes, ma'am."

Betty chimed in. "It's called Muster Meadow because when men were called to the militia for Virginia to fight the British, they came to be mustered in there. The meadows are flat enough for drills. Hence Muster Meadow."

"Ah." He smiled. "I must learn more American history."

"As long as you know we won." Sister teased him.

"Oh, I think he knows that, but I suggest we write Her Majesty to see if she'll take us back. We aren't doing such a hot job of it." Betty exploded in laughter.

"I am shocked. Shocked." Sister stared at Betty, then she, too, roared with laughter. How good it was to laugh, considering all that had happened.

Sometimes people need to blow off steam or just be silly.

Weevil shook his head and laughed as well.

"Come on, Weevil. Let me pull up those maps. I know where some dens are and I can show you where the property lines are, too." Tootie rose, touched him on the shoulder.

Weevil stood up, horn clasped to his chest. "I will do my best. I wish I could think of more to say but I'm a little overwhelmed." He held out the horn. "I will cherish this."

As they left, Sister and Betty could hear them talking as they lifted their coats off the hooks in the mudroom. Then the door opened and closed.

"Janie, he will try his best. I can't believe you gave him Ray's horn. That horn is over one hundred years old. I remember when he found it."

"England." Sister reached for her friend's hand to hold. "It wasn't doing any good in my desk. You know, I think Weevil will learn quickly and I believe he is our future. I do."

A long, long pause followed this. "I do, too. And Tootie, although it will take her longer. Vet school isn't a piece of cake and then she has to do a residency. Might be years."

"My prediction is she will ace it all. Greg Schmidt has been making noises about retirement now."

Betty interrupted. "He'll never retire. His clients will kidnap him."

"Well, here is what I predict. Tootie, as we all know, is frighteningly smart. When Tootie graduates, summa cum laude no doubt, Greg will snap her up. She'll be right here in the county and she will be learning from one of the best. This county teems with terrific vets but Greg has an eye, I can't explain it, he can see things."

Betty nodded for he was her vet, well, Outlaw and Magellan's vet. "You have an eye, too."

"Oh"—Sister trailed off—"I can see talent. I can't necessarily see a problem before it starts."

The two sat there, Raleigh and Rooster now asleep. Golly wide awake feeling she should be coddled after that piercing blast offended her tender ears. She jumped off the counter and onto Sister's lap.

"We should go to Shaker." Betty changed the subject.

"Yes. This is a face-to-face discussion. He's still a little loopy. They jammed him full of drugs. Walter suggested both he and I speak with him tomorrow. If you could come, that would be wonderful. He'd have his old pals around him."

"Do you think Walter will tell him about the hand?"

"Not right away. He has enough to process. He did ask if Showboat was all right. Walter said he had to put his ear right to Shaker's lips but he told him Showboat was fine, the hounds were fine, everyone sends their love. Oh, Skiff was there and Walter said she was a godsend. She's able to keep him calm because his drugs started to wear off a little and he became anxious. She beeped the nurse, according to Walter, got him more painkillers."

"Why would two out-of-line vertebrae cause pain?" Betty wondered.

"Walter said it's the headache. Once that fades away because he did take a thump on the head, remember, there won't be a lot of pain but Walter said, as soon as he is able, we've got to get him into rehab. Even for walking in a straight line."

"Why in the world—"

Sister filled her in. "Walter said he'll get out of alignment. His body will compensate for whatever Shaker does to favor the injury. And then, let's say he's out of the brace in a month or only has to wear it during the day, Walter said his muscles might go into spasm, especially his back."

"Good Lord."

"I know. This isn't going to be easy."

Betty got up, poured herself more tea because the pot was on the stove. Sister made tea the English way, rarely using a tea bag. She sat back down.

"It will be hard to see someone else hunt the hounds."

Sister agreed. "He loves the hounds and despite that, seeing them run to another person, he will do everything he can to help Weevil. Shaker has a big heart."

"You know something, I think Weevil does, too."

Sitting there in silence, listening to the fire crackle in the large kitchen fireplace, Golly purring, content in each other's company, Sister finally spoke.

"The cadaver dogs are at Whiskey Ridge. Didn't want to bring it up during our discussion."

Betty grimaced. "I don't know how people can do that, although I'm glad they do."

"Ben has divided the area into quadrants. He told me they will work their way back to Chapel Cross, knowing this will take days. I asked him why head north? He said it's a hunch but he thinks Gregory was killed near the crossroads. So wherever the body was or was stashed, even if temporarily, he doubts the killer came as far down as Whiskey Ridge or into the land between that and Skidby, Little Dalby."

"Makes sense." Betty smiled at Golly. "I'm glad I didn't see the hand."

Sister laughed. "Well, it was bigger than King Stephen's hand in the reliquary at St. Stephen's Basilica in Budapest. Looks like a little wizened monkey's paw with rings on the fingers. When Ray and I were in Hungary, it was Communist then, but he'd gotten us permission to go, I never asked how. The basilica is stunning and then there's this reliquary with a hand in it. That was bad enough but there are enough pieces of the true cross in Europe to build a city. Our medieval forebears appear to have been quite gullible when it came to body parts, the nails of the cross, all that stuff."

"Maybe the people were gullible but I don't think the priests and kings were. A holy relic cast legitimacy upon the king, the Church, you name it. What do we have? Nothing."

"You know, Betty, I never thought of that. We have the Liberty Bell, we have copies of the Constitution, but it's not the same. Today, by the way, is Saint Thomas Aquinas's Saint's Day."

"Well, I think they all have a lot to answer for, whether it's Saint Augustine or Saint Thomas. When it comes to women they were awful."

"M-m-m." Sister returned to the search. "Betty, if the dogs find anything, how do we know it won't flush the killer out?"

"Isn't that what we want? This has to be someone we know. I hate to think it but I have come to that terrible conclusion."

Sister thought a bit. "Finding a corpse or part of it if they do doesn't mean it will point to the killer."

"Maybe yes, maybe no, but I would put money on the fact that it will unnerve him unless he has some other plan."

CHAPTER 25

A plume of blue smoke soared straight up into the cold night sky. Gray smoked a cigarette. He'd smoked a lot while in Washington, then worked hard to give it up. Every now and then he needed a puff. This was such a time.

Uncle Yancy watched from the family graveyard. His den there, perfectly comfortable, was not as comfortable as living in the mudroom. The two brothers paid little attention to the mudroom, eager to be inside. A pile of old rags, folded, along with a cardboard box, small, with fabric scraps, partially covered an entrance into the mudroom from outside. The red fox could easily slip in and out, then climb up to the handy ledge over the door into the kitchen. Warmth crept out from the kitchen as well as good smells. Eventually, Uncle Yancy believed he would find a way into the kitchen, eat leftovers, food dropped on the floor, then exit to the mudroom. Now he waited for Gray to finish his cigarette so he could go into the mudroom.

The temperature, 25°F, accentuated the brilliant sky, almost the end of the month. Scarf pulled around his neck, a short, heavy, suede jacket lined with lambskin, warm no matter what, allowed Gray to enjoy his rebellion. Fleece-lined gloves helped, too, and his boots, Thinsulate, kept his feet warm. A lumberjack cap took care of his head.

Summer skies, hazy, while pretty, lacked the hard lines of the winter sky, the stars brilliant, the moon looming two days from full. He looked at the graveyard, Uncle Yancy behind a tombstone. The simple headstones, drenched in silver, always consoled him as a child. He thought, *These are my people.* And they were.

One last long puff, he crushed the red tip underfoot, looked up again, took a deep brisk breath, turned, opened the door to the mudroom. While not nearly as warm as the kitchen the change in temperature felt welcome. He unwound his scarf, hung up the expensive coat, put his gloves in the pockets. The minute he opened the door to the kitchen Uncle Yancy crawled up, slightly moving the rags. Never one to waste time, the fox jumped up on a side shelf and thence to the shelf over the door. One small window in the mudroom allowed him to keep tabs on the weather. He flopped on the shelf, pulling his gorgeous tail over his nose.

Gray walked into the small living room where his brother was reading *The Winter's Tale.*

"Perfect night for this." Sam smiled, the odor of hardwood filling the room.

Gray, lifting his feet onto the hassock in imitation of Sam, folded his hands over his chest. "I need a good book to read but I can't make up my mind."

"You have to be in the mood. I swore I would read Henry Adams's *The Degradation of the Democratic Dogma* but I wasn't there. Know what I mean?"

"I do. You were always the brainy one. I was happy with John le Carré."

"Yeah, but he's really good. Sometimes you just have to be taken away from the day." Sam folded the play.

"I've been thinking about Saturday's hunt. So far no reports from our sheriff. He calls in to Sister. She calls me."

"Are you worried about her being there alone?"

"No. Tootie's not far, Raleigh and Rooster would take care of anyone. And I'll be there Wednesday. I don't see how she can be in danger."

"And no embezzlement?"

Gray shook his head. "Soliden is a well-run company, which is why this public relations mistake over the pipeline is so out of whack. But Freddie and I worked nonstop given that two lives are snuffed out. Obviously, the details are not for public consumption but really, Soliden is a tight ship."

"M-m-m. You liked working with Freddie?"

"Did. It's one thing when you hunt with someone. You get a good idea of their character, their ability to tolerate risk, but this is different. She's sharp." He shifted in the old well-upholstered chair. "So what do we know?"

"Rory was bashed in the head. Dragon found a hand. Left or right? I didn't notice."

"Me neither, but then I wasn't that close. So here's what I've come up with. The snowstorm presented an opportunity to commit a murder that had to be in the killer's mind."

"Right," Sam replied.

"We know roughly the area in which the killing had to take place. From the sight of the Corinthian columns to the trailers. Right?"

"Not necessarily." Sam sat up straighter. "What if Luckham was knocked unconscious himself or thrown down in a manner where he could neither speak nor move. He may not necessarily have been dead," Sam continued. "What if he was left to be picked up later?"

"In that storm?"

"It presents a major problem. My other thought was what if

he was dragged either dead or wounded? If whoever did this moved a bit to the side of the main group, who would have seen him? So he drags the body, drops it where he can find it even in a snowstorm, stores it, so to speak, until he can dispose of it."

"And in the bitter cold, no decay." Gray rubbed his chin.

"He knows the territory. When the time is right, he dumps it or he partly buries it. There are possibilities including dismemberment. I'm thinking how a hand wound up where it did."

"Right. Not near Chapel Cross but not really that far. A body could be dumped in the middle of the night some miles away. Animals tore it up, the hand was carried. This has to be one very cool customer."

"Yes and no. If he or she, and I doubt it's a woman, knows exactly where he is, knows the lay of the land and where it is inhabited and not, thanks to hunting, the difficult part would be retrieving the body or even dragging it into your trailer." Sam stopped. "Granted that's also a big if, but what if Rory saw part of it? Think about that. We still have no idea whatsoever why Rory would be killed. What if he came over to help, sees a limp body shoved into a trailer, and *wham.* Then he's dragged across the street as everyone is frantically trying to get out of there. It's possible."

"Okay. Let's say it is. I left a bit early to get the house ready because I figured Sister would have people there. It would be easier to do a caravan. I was out of there. You were not. You couldn't see, could you?"

"No, but I could hear."

"Talk? Horses loading?"

"Right. I knew that Kasmir and Alida were still there. Makes sense since they were closer to their stable than anyone else and, if necessary, they could have put their horses in one of the Tattenhall outbuildings and stayed in the station. So they were there. I heard Freddie. I heard Dewey's voice as he helped load the Bancroft horses and I only know that because I heard Tedi thank him.

Then I heard a truck motor start up. I assumed it was Dewey after he'd helped the Bancrofts. The snow just came faster and harder. I heard trailers pull out as I was loading Trocadero. Then I heard one go in the opposite direction, the wrong direction I thought about that. I didn't think anything of it. I was one of the last ones out except for staff and then I heard the trailer return. I think it must have been the same trailer once whoever was driving figured out he or she was going the wrong way."

"You never heard Rory's voice?"

Sam shook his head no. "I expect by the time I was untacking he was gone. And I had no idea he was there to help."

"You might be on to something." Gray, boots off, enjoyed the warmth in his feet as both men sat near the fire. "If Ben finds anything, that would sure help."

But Ben and his crew weren't finding anything. Granted, they still had three large quadrants yet to search but with those cadaver dogs and the handlers it seemed something should show up.

CHAPTER 26

True to its name, Muster Meadow's lower acres were made for drilling. Hounds left the flat meadows unaware of the history therein but quite aware of a promising day. Low gray clouds, fluffy, a steady temperature of 42°F with promise of falling later, would have appeared a dull, dreary day to most people yet looked wonderful to foxhunters. Little wind, no rain, sleet, or snow, at least not yet, soft footing. All the snow and moisture, freezing and thawing, dried out the earth, but not so much that one was running on brick.

The meadows, surrounded by woods and higher meadows beyond that, gave foxes chances to observe everything below them, places to scamper, and enough scattered outbuildings to give hounds fits.

Weevil, Betty on his right, Tootie on his left, started out circling the lower pastures. His horn work, a bit garbled as he was nervous, did clear into distinct notes. He thought scent might hold on those lower meadows. Traces of fox clung to the edges but the quarry moved off the lowlands upon hearing the rumble of the big diesel truck engines.

While only two hundred and fifty acres, Muster Meadow adjoined other farms that Jefferson Hunt could use, so it provided opportunities for sport.

Some people took off work to support the young man in his first time carrying the horn. All those people could make a person nervous but Sister, next to Weevil, before the first cast, said to him, "The late, great Fred Duncan who hunted hounds at Warrenton, before that whipping-in to Dickie Bywaters"—she named the man, Bywaters, considered by many to be the finest American huntsman immediately after World War II—"not a man given to lots of gabble. Anyway, Fred said, 'Hunt your hounds and don't look back.' " She smiled at him as he drew a deep breath. "Thank you for taking this on, Weevil, and no matter what, have a glorious time."

He smiled back, white teeth gleaming, tapped his horn to his helmet, Ray's horn, looked down at the hounds who looked up.

"He knows our names," Asa, the ballast, told the others. *"Help him out."*

Pookah looked up at the handsome fellow, his eyes big with wonder. *"His voice is different."*

"Lieu in. Lieu in," Weevil sang out to them.

"Let's do what he says," Diana ordered everyone. *"Come on, we're here to find foxes. It will all work out."*

Hounds moved forward, a hop-a-long pace, noses down. Reaching the farm road curving upward, Parker stopped, moved again, stopped again. He wanted to be sure; his stern flipped a little.

"Whatcha' got?" Thimble came alongside, sniffed then uttered, *"Oooh."*

The others gathered, milling about. Cora held her head up after a deep sniff. *"Take the dog fox."*

Two foxes crossed, conversed, one a vixen and one a dog fox. Perhaps it wasn't romance because he didn't follow her as she dipped down toward the meadows. Then again, did they make a future assignation? Vixens could be highly peculiar when in season. They looked the boys over, not mating with the first fox who came along. Humans chalked this up to where the vixen was in her estrous cycle. Perhaps she wasn't fully ready. The vixen thought otherwise but then humans really had no estrous cycle like other mammals. This explained many of their problems. She, the vixen, had ample time to consider what she wanted to do, with whom she wished to do it, and if she wished to mate at all. Again, humans believe hormones drive everything. Up to a point. A vixen isn't going to mate with a male she doesn't like. For one thing, she doesn't lack for callers. If she likes the fellow, if the dog fox is smart enough to bring food or other gifts, then she may choose him and he will stick with her until the fox cubs are big enough to leave the den. There are dog foxes who stay when the youngsters leave and there are those that go. Foxes do as they please. Humans attempt to make rules about what those foxes are doing.

The hounds, on the other hand, closer to clear thinking, jumped to no conclusions. They could smell that two foxes sat in each other's company for perhaps forty minutes and recently. The scent was lifting off the dirt farm road with packed-down grass in the middle, dead but life was underneath.

The pack headed upward as scent intensified. They spoke at once, began running, and the running turned to flying.

Weevil blew "Gone Away" as Matador stretched out, thrilled to be galloping behind a fast pack.

Up and over an old stone fence probably laid back during the Revolutionary War. A well-tended stone fence lasts forever.

Sister, Rickyroo underneath, easily cleared the three-foot fence. Not all that big but big enough for a first fence. Woke everyone up and that fox led them along the farm road, up through the woods' edge, then away from the woods across a high meadow where a coop with a rider atop kept the cattle in.

Weevil just took the whole thing. Sister, thinking of those behind her, rode alongside, dropped her crop, and lifted the rail with the antler handle, dropping one end to the ground. Then she trotted four strides back, asked her lovely fellow to clear it, which he did, and he took it big. Hounds were running, dammit. He needed to be up there.

Laughing, Sister let him rip. At that moment she was twenty years old, without a care, no husband, just out for the day while at college. The world was in front of her.

And here she was seventy-three without a care and the world was in front of her.

On and on they thundered. This dog fox gave them one hell of a run. He zigged, he zagged, he turned, almost doubling on his tracks but slipping through the woods so no one would see him. He ran through hollowed-out logs—now that did slow hounds down. But they corrected, found where he emerged from the log, and on they ran. They splashed through a hard-running creek, clambered up a slippery bank, shot past the neighbor's barn, horses inside and not at all happy to be there.

The mountains, to their rear, offered no escape but parallel ridges, not high but say five hundred feet above sea level, gave the dog fox opportunities to plunge down, run up, run on the top, then skid down again.

Coops, log jumps, even aligned pickle barrels offered jumps and more jumps. Alida counted fourteen and then the clever fellow dashed through a begabbering, furious flock of wild turkeys, some of whom took to the air; others stayed on the ground and hollered their heads off.

The hounds, now in the middle of the turkeys, couldn't fend them off and those turkeys can hurt you. So the turkeys hopped up and down; hounds ran to get through them.

Dewey, a voice that carried, hollered, "Ware turkeys."

Freddie Thomas hollered back and the people, some with arms over their heads, just wanted to get out of there.

"Jesus H. Christ. Dive-bombed by turkeys!" Sam exploded.

Finally far enough away from the enraged birds, the people stopped for the hounds stopped.

Betty and Tootie, who had seen everything, couldn't help laughing and soon everyone in the field was laughing. Behind them turkey feathers could be seen settling to the ground.

The scent evaporated. The dog fox had ducked into an old hay shed wherein he'd made a nice den, somehow ruining his scent. The turkeys helped.

Tedi Bancroft, who'd kept up the whole time, tears running from her eyes, blurted out, "I am eighty-five years old and I have never encountered anything like that!"

Weevil rode up to Sister and asked, "Madam, is there a way back where we won't encounter turkeys?"

Laughing, too, Sister offered, "I'll ride with you. This will take us longer but we should be unmolested."

"I could have been killed," Giorgio wailed.

"Oh, get over it, pretty boy." Dragon bumped him.

The T's, the P's, and the youngest A's, all fearful, huddled together as they walked through the highest meadows.

Diana, voice consoling, said, *"Next time we'll kill a few. That should do it."*

The hounds chattered about that, the youngsters started to relax, and Weevil sang to them, "Good hounds, brave hounds." Then he called out each hound by name to tell him or her how courageous they were.

Soon those chests were puffing out. Sister, riding next to him, watched with a light heart.

. . .

That evening Sister, Betty, Tootie, and Weevil called on Shaker at the hospital. He would be released tomorrow. They painted a vivid picture of what would forever be known as the turkey hunt.

Brightened him. "Oh, I wish I'd been with you."

"We do, too." Betty sat on the edge of his bed. "Aren't you glad the doctors didn't put a heavy cast on your neck?"

"Yeah, but this thing is a pain in the ass, or I should say a pain in the neck," Shaker answered. "I can't shave."

"You look so butch." Sister teased him.

"The hair on my neck itches," Shaker replied. "I never thought of shaving my neck. I mean I just did it. I am not going to spend the next month without shaving."

"Ask the doctor," Weevil sensibly said. "I can shave you if you can take off the neck brace. But if not, you're going to look like, um, a Viking."

"Thanks a lot." Shaker grimaced. "Well, how did you like carrying the horn?"

Weevil blew out air. "I was nervous. Well, I was really nervous, but then Sister told me what Fred Duncan always said and I looked down at those hounds, they looked up at me, and I thought, 'Just do it.' Shaker, the hounds were terrific. I wasn't sure when they lingered on the farm road leading up to the higher meadows and the woods, but they sorted it out and all I needed to do was keep up."

"Best feeling in the world, isn't it?"

Weevil grinned. "You'll be back out soon."

"Not this season. Do I want to flip the bird at the doctors? Sure. But I want to be hunting when I am ancient, so old you have to lift me up and lift me down." He smiled at the thought. "So I'd better do what they say."

"We miss you." Tootie, never much of a talker, meant that.

A knock on Shaker's door was followed by him calling out, "Come in."

Skiff stepped in, saw the group, smiled. "A party."

Shaker sat up a little straighter as she approached. Sister knew him well, perhaps better than he knew himself. He was in love with her and that love would heal him faster than any medicine. She wondered when Shaker would realize that his life was starting all over again.

Sister's cellphone rang. It was Ben Sidell.

"Excuse me. It's the sheriff." She walked outside the room as Betty, Weevil, and Tootie gave Skiff and Shaker a blow-by-blow description of the hunt.

"Any luck?" Sister asked.

"Yes, but not what we'd hoped. Do you know the Middleburg Tack Exchange?"

"Sure. Mrs. Motion owns it. Very, very good used stuff. Whatever does that have to do with anything?"

"I sent out descriptions of the missing man, clothing last worn, the usual. Well, driving back from today's search I get a phone call and the lady spoke with a sonorous English accent."

"Mrs. Motion."

"To make a long story short, she had a pair of used boots, a man's nine and a half, formal with cuff, Maxwells."

"Boy, are they expensive."

"The name inscribed inside is Luckham."

"What!" Sister put her hand to the wall.

"I asked when they came in. She said she wasn't in the shop but they were left outside the door in a fabric shopping bag. A note run off a computer asked her to sell them and send the money to Mrs. Liz Luckham. The address is a house in The Fan in Richmond."

"That's impossible. Even if Liz Luckham has decided to sell his goods, she wouldn't do it now and she's probably praying, hoping against hope that he's still alive."

Ben, fatigue in his voice, told her, "I called Mrs. Luckham. I described the boots. I did my best to explain all that Mrs. Motion had told me. Liz said the boots sounded like Gregory's but she's not the one who left them at the shop. I told her I'd have Mrs. Motion send a photo to her phone. But it certainly sounds like these are Luckham's boots."

"You all will run fingerprints, of course."

"Of course, but this is either cheeky or odd, I mean odd, someone can't stand to see a pair of Maxwells go to waste."

A long pause followed that. "I see what you mean."

"You know Mrs. Motion. Could she be enraged about the pipeline?"

"Ben, even if she were, she's a highly intelligent, capable woman who must deal with the public. I tell you without hesitation that she would never engage in anything shall we say subterranean. She called you so she did the right thing once she knew who those boots belonged to. I expect she's in a bit of shock."

"She said she called as she had read in the local paper about Gregory Luckham being missing and the boots, recently left, popped right into her mind."

"What's a Middleburg paper doing writing about Gregory Luckham? I mean the *Richmond Times-Dispatch,* sure, but a local paper?"

"A writer did a story on mysteries tied to foxhunting. Stuff about foxhunters saying they've encountered the Gray Ghost, Colonel Mosby. And the president of Soliden's disappearance during a foxhunt was included."

Sister rubbed her forehead. "I suppose I'm glad to hear Colonel Mosby is still riding. A good cavalryman never dies."

"Should we wish for a ghost?" Ben said.

"You know, I think we are surrounded by energies we don't understand but Ben, I'm not worried about a ghost. I'm worried about a flesh-and-blood killer who knows Maxwell boots when he sees them."

CHAPTER 27

The Richmond newspaper spread out on Dewey Milford's leather-topped office desk contained a large photo of the picture taken with ground-penetrating radar at Old Paradise accompanied by an interview with Crawford Howard and Charlotte Abruza.

Betty Franklin bent over to read the article. She'd stopped by to drop off extra fixture cards, which Dewey wanted to send to hunting friends in nearby states. "Looks like he did it."

"Sure does." Dewey pointed to the rows of neatly placed bodies, well, you couldn't see the bones but you could see the rectangles where the deceased, long ago, had been laid.

"Crawford backed up what he said. He has temporarily halted the pipeline route. That doesn't mean people will be buying or selling real estate. Not until this is clear."

"Don't you wonder what would have happened if he hadn't hired Charlotte Abruza? That's a young woman who knows her business. First of all, Betty, there have to be bodies all over this state from before the English arrived and after. If we stop construction every time someone is found, nothing will ever get done. Not that I want to see Old Paradise torn up."

"I never thought of that." Betty pointed to a small rectangle. "A child."

"So many didn't make it." Dewey sat down, motioning for Betty to sit. "Rest yourself."

She smiled. "I will just for a minute. This is my errand day but, Dewey, we hunted hard yesterday."

"And survived aerial warfare." He burst out laughing. "Muster Meadow is such a special place."

"You know, most of our fixtures are." She glanced back at the photo. "I guarantee tomorrow Soliden will issue a statement about considering moving the pipeline so it does not desecrate graves. They can do this to save face. There always were alternative pathways. And business will bounce back."

"True. This needs to be cleaned up, cleared up so people can get on with real estate decisions. Betty, you can't believe how this pipeline issue has affected Realtors, construction companies, suppliers. Everyone is sitting on their hands."

"You're not."

"The development in Green Springs, Louisa County, seems safe. So is the one on Old Lynchburg Road. Going well."

"I couldn't help myself. Last fall before the snows I drove by. Boy, Dewey, those are some big, expensive homes."

"Louisa County is now within driving distance of Richmond. Richmond is coming our way and I predict a few of our easternmost fixtures may be impacted. They certainly will be for Keswick Hunt and even Farmington. We are all going to be pushed."

"Jefferson Hunt is in better shape in the respect it will take longer for people to consider our territory within commuting distance of Richmond." Betty felt relief that Crawford's plan had worked or was about to work.

Dewey smiled. "True, but for all I know I will live to see us hunt the top ridge of the Blue Ridge Mountains." He swiveled around in his chair, pointing to a huge map. "Jefferson is uniquely placed among Charlottesville, Staunton, and Lynchburg. And let's not forget Waynesboro. That town has come to life."

Squinting at the map, Betty shrugged. "We'll do the best we can. Sister and Walter have worked hard to get us new fixtures, well, the members have, as well. Everyone understands how quickly we can lose a fixture. Look what happened when Crawford first rented Old Paradise? He couldn't wait to throw us off."

Dewey laughed. "And his raggle-taggle pack would leave him flat and come to us every time we hunted Chapel Cross. How many huntsmen did he cycle through? Three? Skiff will stick. She and Marty have helped him to see there's nothing to be gained by crossing Sister."

"Ego," Betty simply stated, then added, "But he's somewhat come around. We have a joint hunt in the fall and one in the winter. If our pack follows a fox onto Old Paradise, he follows the centuries-old tradition of allowing the pack to follow the fox onto another hunt's territory. He realized this benefit applies to him as well. Skiff has been over on Tattenhall Station." Betty looked at Dewey, who had swiveled back. "So much time wasted on these things. I've been meaning to ask you, these big homes you build, I'm assuming our people don't buy them."

"Mostly."

"And the new people are all horrified by foxhunting?"

"Some, but they don't know about it. I mean all they know is what they've seen in movies, mostly English ones or *Downton Abbey*. So I've trained all my people to emphasize, underline three times, 'We don't kill.' Mostly it gets through and I always invite a new person to a hunt."

"Good for you." Betty smiled. "Well, let me get rolling here. I'll soon be out of daylight although we've gained a minute each day since December twenty-first. I need those minutes." She stood up, as did Dewey. Then she said, "Did you hear that Gregory Luckham's boots were found?"

"No."

"Middleburg Tack Exchange." She informed him of the rest.

"Great day." Dewey used the old Southern expression although he, himself, was in his forties. "To think that someone would remove boots off a dead body. Well. I'm assuming a dead body. Hey, before I forget, if you know anyone in the market for an SUV, I'm going to sell my Range Rover. I need something smaller, better on gas."

"And before I forget, Thursday we'll be at Jerusalem Field. First time. I'll let you know if I think of anyone wanting a ghastly expensive car."

He laughed. "Usually I can slip away for Tuesdays, not Thursdays, but I'm always curious about a new fixture. And by the way, I thought Weevil did a great job. And thanks for updating us with emails concerning Shaker. So he's out for the rest of the season?"

"Yes. He's taking it about as good as can be expected."

"Got to be hard, and it's got to be hard being replaced by a younger man whom I predict will be brilliant. He's got it."

"He does." Betty agreed. "We can work that out next season. Obviously I will do what my Master tells me to do, but Sister wants this to work out for everyone. She'll do the right thing."

"She always does." Dewey walked Betty to the door. "Thanks for the fixture cards." He paused a moment. "Betty, do you know the size of those boots?"

"Nine and a half."

Dewey looked down at his feet. "Damn."

"Dewey, you're awful."

"I know but still, a pair of superexpensive boots used."

She looked down at his feet, too. "Never work."

CHAPTER 28

"In the fall these meadows are smothered with Jerusalem artichokes, hence the name Jerusalem Field. It's a sea of yellow," Aunt Daniella told Yvonne as they slowly cruised along the farm road.

"Sam mentioned they are new people. Want to foxhunt," Yvonne replied.

"Good. I can't abide it when people move here and this is the country but want to keep their city ways. They come because it's beautiful but then they want things like Noise Ordinance laws." She shook her head. "Will never work. When in Rome, do as the Romans do."

"Until Attila." Yvonne laughed.

"True, but they had one thousand years. We've had two hundred and forty-two years and we're making a mess of it." Aunt Daniella waved her left hand, her old wedding ring and engagement diamond, impressive, gleaming. "I count our beginning to be 1776. So I am ninety-four. How much of our history have I lived?" She said this with feeling. "I have seen systematic mistreatment addressed. Certainly those kinds of things are better than when I was young, but a hell of a lot more is worse. Just get out of people's way. If people talk to one another, we work it out. I believe that because I've seen it."

"I don't know, Aunt Dan. What I see is entrenched interests, be it corporate or racial or gender-based. Now granted, human rights is different than, say, foreign policy, but I think we're screwing up both."

"Well, we always have, but then it straightens out. In my lifetime, foreign policy, I saw Stalin make a fool out of Roosevelt, Khrushchev do the same to Kennedy. Reagan got the better of Gorbachev and for a while the Cold War ended. So it swings and sways, but I am getting old and I'm getting bored. If you're going to be corrupt, then at least be interesting." She let out a peal of laughter.

Yvonne joined her, then asked, "Wind devils?"

A swirl of wind twirled around, then dissipated, a common occurrence near the mountains as tendrils of wind rolled down, often meeting crosswinds at the bottom.

"Sends scent everywhere." Aunt Daniella noticed Weevil trying to figure it out. "There's a lot more to hunting hounds than people realize. He's sitting still. I know he doesn't know what to do about a wind devil but he's not stupid. He's waiting to see what the hounds will do."

"I imagine everyone will be glad when Shaker can follow by car. He can tell Weevil what to do about things like wind devils." Yvonne watched as the hounds cast themselves.

"There they go. They've figured it out, which means Weevil will figure it out. Let them cast themselves. Scent had to be blown somewhere. They'll find it."

Hounds opened running toward a steep ravine. The farmland continued on top of the hill. Aunt Daniella and Yvonne could see a flash of gray horse or a hint of scarlet, but that was that.

"What do you think about the TV coverage of the grave sites at Old Paradise?" Yvonne asked as they waited.

"Good. The historical society added a lot to the seriousness of it. Not that Crawford didn't present himself well and his historical concerns, but the people from Richmond really put it over." She paused. "Why don't we drive down there, to Old Paradise? We're not far and who knows when the field will be back?"

"You don't think we'll get into trouble?"

"I do not," the old lady said with authority.

Jerusalem Field, ten miles from Chapel Crossroads, just on the other side of Close Shave, was close so Yvonne turned around, edged out on the two-lane paved country road. Once she reached the Chapel Crossroads she turned right, cruised a few miles west, then turned left onto the long, winding drive, itself undergoing renovation.

"I can't believe he's got a subfloor over that basement. Half of the county contractors must be here."

"At the Bancrofts' breakfast Dewey Milford was talking about that. Said it was good for the trades but he was needing to hire people from as far as Goochland County."

"Now there's a name, Gooch. A governor appointed by the king, but what I wonder is why he didn't change his name." Aunt Daniella laughed as they slowed, stopping in front of the Corinthian columns. "How I would have loved to see this place in its glory."

"Slaves?" Yvonne raised her eyebrows.

"There were slaves in Connecticut. Slaves were everywhere." She thought a moment. "The DuCharmes, well, how does one say this? The good blood watered down from 1812."

Now Yvonne had to laugh. "See that everywhere. Wasn't that

why the French had the Valois, the Capets the Bourbons, and the English the Plantagenets, the horrendous war between those two branches, and so it goes."

"Mercer, my son, used to say you see it in horses, too. He also said a good mare's first foal isn't usually her best. I told him to be careful as not only was he my first foal, he was my only foal."

"Tootie is mine." Yvonne smiled.

"Beautiful girl like her mother."

"Thank you, Aunt Daniella." Yvonne started the engine again, mostly to keep the heater running. She slowly drove toward the stables, then past the Carriage House.

"There's tape over there." Aunt Daniella pointed behind the Carriage House, just visible in the distance.

"Hey, that's why I've got four-wheel drive. I bought that Continental, which I love, but I wasn't out here two months before I realized I needed, what is it you call some horses, mudders?"

They bounced over frozen ground, stopping in front of a marked-off area. "I suppose they'll dig up some people. But then what is he going to do?"

"He'll have to raise some kind of marker. Create some kind of graveyard."

"But what if it's where the Monacans are or the people they think are the Monacans? Won't Crawford have to revisit tribal burial practices?"

Yvonne considered this. "He doesn't have a choice as I see it. You know, Aunt Dan, this is going to turn into a big project."

They silently looked over the land, a gentle roll at this part.

"I'm willing to bet Crawford has stopped the pipeline or at least stopped this route," Aunt Daniella predicted.

"Good bet." She headed back toward the elegant outbuildings in various stages of reconstruction. "You've been in the stables since they've been restored?"

"Last fall when Tom Tipton was here. All that stonework and then the wood inside, mahogany."

"Lucky horses when the day comes that the stalls are filled."

"That was one grave found early, the one inside the stable. Old Paradise, who knows what's here?" Aunt Daniella then launched into Tom Tipton. "I know that you and your husband built an empire on African American concerns. Marvelous, really, think of the people you reached with first the magazine and then the media empire, but you know, Yvonne, the older I get the more I feel closer to those left of my generation. I don't much care what color they are. When Tom Tipton was here, oh the memories and our reference points are the same. Getting old can make you lonesome. You lose your friends."

"But you are surrounded by people, Aunt Dan."

She nodded in assent. "I am fortunate but it's not the same as your own generation. Maybe you have to get old to understand this and you are far from it."

"I'm in my early fifties."

"Fifty is nothing. Nothing." Aunt Daniella laughed at her. "The late Joe Carstairs used to say that." Realizing that Yvonne had no idea who that was, Aunt Daniella added, "Carstairs Liquor. The heiress. English. Gay. You know there were a lot of fabulously wealthy gay women when I was young and I give them credit. The girls they kept they kept well. Money creates responsibility. I suppose it doesn't matter who you're sleeping with."

"Bet their lovers were beautiful."

"Yes. Ravishing."

"Did any of them try to keep you?" Yvonne's lip curled in a secret smile.

"No, but I wasn't usually taken where I would wind up at parties with the girls. They knew how to have a good time. I'm not so sure people do these days. Oh, there I go again, I really am getting old, but while we're here let's peek into the Carriage House."

"Sure."

Within minutes they parked at the Carriage House close to the restored stables, with still untouched stables behind the Carriage House that housed the driving horses.

The two peeked past the huge door.

"Let's go inside." Yvonne struggled with the door but she got it and the two slipped in. "You'd think there'd be security or something here, so much is going on."

"Most of it up at the house and what is there to steal? Once Crawford has this place up and running, I'm sure there will be security, which I must say is so out of place at Chapel Cross."

They both inhaled the odor of the fresh wood, for the lumber was piled up for future work, as they walked down the extra-wide aisle, peeking into the special parking places for carriages. That's the only word they could think of, parking places.

"He'll buy a Brewster Carriage, I'm telling you." Aunt Daniella stopped to admire an old photograph still hanging on the wall.

"What?"

"The Rolls-Royce of American coaches. Crawford will have to have one and he'll pay hundreds of thousands of dollars for it, too." She looked up at Yvonne, slightly taller than herself. "Every activity has its vertical scale. And let me tell you, coaching is expensive." She walked toward the middle of the expansive place. "The tack room door is slightly ajar." She pushed it open. "Yvonne!"

Yvonne hurried up right behind her. "Aunt Dan, this scares me. It really does."

The two women stepped back into the huge aisle and Yvonne called the sheriff's department. "Hello, may I speak to Sheriff Ben

Sidell? This is Yvonne Harris. I am at Old Paradise and there is another body part."

She was patched through in a second.

"Ben, I'm in the Carriage House with Aunt Daniella. We've found the other hand or what's left of it."

CHAPTER 29

"When was the last time you were in the Carriage House?" Ben Sidell asked Crawford Howard, who had freely agreed to come down alone to the sheriff's office.

"Wednesday, January thirty-first, yesterday."

"Was anyone with you?"

"No. I try to check on work progress at least every other day at Old Paradise. I'd been up at the house so I checked on the Carriage House to see if they'd gotten started."

"What is it you intend to do in that building?"

"Repair and refurbish all the stalls, if you will, for carriages. Like garage bays, roof's good. Flooring is good because the roof held. Anyway, the bays had been scrubbed out. The lumber was still stacked in the center of the aisle. A start."

"Did you go into the tack room?"

"No."

"Nothing seemed out of place?"

"Well, there's nothing in there to be out of place." Crawford controlled himself, although he thought the questions irritating.

"No odor. Decay odor?"

"No."

"You were alone in the Carriage House?"

"I was. The foreman stayed at the big house. Charlotte was outside measuring grave sites. As you know, we found one containing, so far, two hundred graves. No markers. But no one came with me."

"And were you also in the Carriage House during Christmas Hunt?"

"I'd driven down with Rory to check the lumber that had been delivered the day before. Wasn't there long."

"When you drove out, you saw the field?"

"You've asked me this before. After Gregory Luckham disappeared. After Rory was found."

Ben calmly agreed. "Yes, but I am asking you again."

"Couldn't see a thing. The storm obliterated everything but both Rory and I heard the horn."

"You saw nothing?"

"No."

"How did you hear the horn?"

"As I told you, I put the window down slightly. Could hear the horn."

"I thank you for coming down here so promptly. I expected you would have your lawyer with you."

Crawford shrugged. "If I'm charged with anything or I'm a so-called person of interest, I will. But I came alone. I have nothing to hide. I find this shocking. You said the hand had been torn apart. Bones more than anything but remnants of a cotton glove were on those bones, in tatters. That's why I came down. At Farmington Country Club, at Ronnie's dinner, I noticed Gregory's left hand was in a thin white cotton glove. It wasn't a subject of discussion and I didn't ask. My assumption was he had injured it, wanted to cover the injury." Crawford shrugged again. "You'll test those remains, if you can call a hand remains. That will be Gregory Luckham's hand."

"We found the other hand. Actually a hound did. Both these hands are on the west side of the Chapel Crossroads road. We've gone over the quadrants from where the first hand was found. Nothing. So this is important. He's out there somewhere."

"I expect." Crawford agreed.

"I'll be back with the cadaver dogs tomorrow."

"Good," Crawford tersely replied.

"You had good reason to kill Gregory Luckham."

Crawford leaned forward. "Sheriff, a lot of people wanted him dead. Do you think I would be stupid enough to kill him when I can fight by other means and I have? Thank God for ground-penetrating radar."

"Yes," Ben simply said.

"Look, I don't care about Gregory Luckham. He's dead. I had nothing to do with it. I do care about Rory. He was a good hand. Why he was killed makes no sense. Luckham. Makes a lot of sense. People are outraged about the pipeline."

After Crawford left, Ben knew he would be on the phone with his lawyer. Ben didn't have enough to arrest him but he knew that Crawford could make his life miserable, just as he could impact Crawford's. Not that he was in the business of revenge. He was in the business of solving crimes, upholding the law.

Bourbon in hand, Aunt Daniella glumly sat surrounded by Gray, Sister, Sam, and Yvonne. Both women described how they had found the hand.

"That's what I get for being nosy." Aunt Daniella sighed.

"Something like your experience is beyond the norm. Who would have thought of dismembered hands? The other hand was found miles down the road, as you know, but in the general vicinity. You would think the body would be down there somewhere but nothing else, nothing." Sam consoled his aunt.

"Aren't there political careers at stake over this pipeline?" Yvonne asked a sensible question. "If it were Illinois, it would be on the news every night. The public would know what state elected officials were for it, those against."

Gray had a scotch in hand, for he, too, wished for something soothing. "We do know, Yvonne, but apart from this being the most contentious issue in the state, people are riveted by Washington, right now. They might stay on the pipeline for a week or two. People were aroused when a federal judge threatened to sue Red Terry and her daughter a thousand dollars a day if they didn't come down from their tree stand protesting the pipeline. Two non-rich women, a mother and daughter, a thousand dollars a day by a federal judge. Officials hide behind the law obviously, which is what Soliden is counting on. People were outraged."

"But they are more outraged by the president is what you're saying?" Aunt Daniella understood politics as only an old person can. "Let's assume the big company rolls over property rights. What's left of that cuts down trees, imperils public lands, endangered species. Soliden has filled politicians' pockets for decades. I remember those decades. What happens when a major disaster occurs, and it will? I promise you, it will. It might not be a blown pipe. What about mud slides from disturbed earth? Soliden has to go over the Blue Ridge. Everyone will pretend to be shocked by the disaster."

"All those who supported it will turn tail." Sister stated the obvious.

"So my question is: Where is the Democratic Party? Aren't they the ones who care about the environment? Amend that, aren't they the ones who say they care about the environment?" Sam hit the nail on the head.

"Hell, Sam, the Democratic candidates and the Democratic Party in this state had been sucking up money from Soliden for decades, as Aunt Dan said."

"To be fair, Soliden also gives money to the Republican Party," Sister added.

"My point is," Gray continued, "what if someone who believed in the party, who is passionate about environmental issues, killed Luckham?"

"Well, who? Someone in the hunt club?" Sam fired back.

"It's possible that someone planned to kill the president of Soliden. Maybe not at Christmas Hunt but who was there trying to take his measure. Literally, I guess. Well, the storm comes up. A perfect opportunity."

"Gray," Sister responded. "Could happen, but whoever killed him had to know the territory. Otherwise he'd have been left in the open, granted covered by snow for a time. But there was no trace later and whoever killed him had to get him out. I now truly believe the killer is in our hunt club. I don't want to believe it, but who else would know the land?"

A long silence followed this, then Yvonne spoke. "It makes sense that foxhunters would be passionate environmentalists. Just knowing people as I do as a newcomer, I can see that. My daughter is a passionate environmentalist. Kasmir, Alida, Freddie, you, Ronnie, just about everyone."

"Crawford is the best candidate. Not a Jefferson Hunt Club member but"—Sister was fighting a headache, this was all getting to her—"there's no way."

"I keep coming back to what if there's another reason?" Gray rattled the huge ice cubes in his glass.

Aunt Daniella had one of those special ice machines that produced big cubes, maybe not as big as Rubik's cube but big.

"And why his hands? Where's the rest of him?" Yvonne, having seen a hand, thought this more than odd.

"Animals got at him," Gray said.

"Then he has to be out there, right?" Sister asked.

"You'd think the cadaver dogs would have found him if wild animals found his hands," Yvonne replied.

"Maybe that's what we're supposed to think." Sister surprised them. "We're outdoor people, right? We foxhunt. Knowing how some animals feed on carrion, our conclusion is an obvious one. What is obvious to me, again, is this is a foxhunter. And this is someone leading us away from him or her. Like a fox fouling his scent."

CHAPTER 30

Pointing to the large U.S. Geological Survey map, Dewey traced the elevation lines. "You can see how rapidly the grade changes at the westernmost edge of Old Paradise's flatlands. You're climbing the Blue Ridge in a hurry."

Sister, knowing Dewey had the latest maps as well as current information about the pipeline, asked if she could look at the maps. She also wanted an overview of where the hands were found.

Standing next to Dewey in his office, she nodded. "And the ravines are narrower, many deeper. The water can cascade down."

"That's why Binky had his still there." Dewey mentioned a DuCharme now in prison. "Wasn't it Binky?"

"Binky knew about it but it was his nephew, the younger generation."

Weevil, whom Sister had asked to join her, was surprised. "Everybody knew?"

Dewey smiled genially. "Young man, there have been generations of DuCharmes making outstanding liquor for two hundred years. Everybody knew and everybody was smart enough to stay away, most especially the revenue man and the sheriff."

"Why?" Weevil innocently asked.

"Because anyone who troubles a good distiller often doesn't live long," Dewey replied.

"Don't worry, Weevil. You won't be traversing anyone's still." Sister glanced at him as he stood next to her. Then she turned her attention back to Dewey. "You have all the maps for Chapel Cross? I have a few but nothing like you."

"As a developer, I need detailed, up-to-date maps. Look here." He leaned toward a large screen, computer keyboard in front of it, then sat down.

Weevil stood behind him, transfixed. "Did you have this built?"

Dewey nodded. "My trade is like any other trade. The better your tools, the better your decisions and your work. Sister, look here." He pointed to red lines on a topo map of part of Old Lynchburg Road and then blue lines. "The red lines are state roads listed for improvement, usually an extra lane or better turn lanes." He pointed again to blue lines. "If I develop this land on the plat, then this is what I would do, a high-grade asphalt, too. Roads are costly but good roads help sell houses. Now look at this." Photos, large, appeared on the huge screen. "This is the Windsor model." Punched again. "The Kent, the Cornwall. You get the idea. All are set back fifty feet from the road. That's a big setback so the front lawn landscaping must be somewhat in place. The buyer will customize, but the worst thing you can do is sell a house on a plot with rye grass recently sown."

"This is one of your developments?" Weevil, new to the area, didn't know Old Lynchburg Road.

"A solidly middle-class development. Affordable for an assistant professor at the university, an associate could buy a bigger house, but these are in a $200,000 to $350,000 price range. That's now middle class." He looked up at her. "Hard to believe, isn't it?"

"Is. I nearly passed out when the sticker price on the Tahoe was $54,000 loaded. I was going to buy a stripped-down version but Gray told me not to be penny-wise and pound-foolish. He reminded me of how much I am on the road, off the road, etc. So I swallowed hard and paid it."

"Know what you mean. By the way, I'm selling the Range Rover if you know anyone that's interested. Sucks too much gas." He then returned to the computer. "Here, let me show you the development out by Zion Crossroads. First I'll show what it was as raw land three years ago." A photo appeared of scrubland, not a lot of roll to it but a pleasing prospect facing south, which is in the direction of the James River, although miles away.

"Barren."

"Look at it now." A large entrance beckoned into a winding drive, landscaped with rows of Bradford pears. Close-ups of homes appeared, more expensive than the Old Lynchburg development.

"How can you sell more expensive homes there than, say, at Old Lynchburg Road?" Sister was fascinated.

"Richmond. You can commute to Richmond now. Be at the Fan or even downtown in forty-five minutes, an hour if traffic is bad. And if you work on the west end, which now stretches to the edge of Goochland County, you can be at the office within half an hour. This looks good to city workers. They get their taste of the country but on a city salary."

"You must have bulldozed the land, created a roll." Weevil had a sharp eye.

"I did. Visual interest is important. Of course, the best of the best is a view either of the mountains or the James River or both. There are parts of Buckingham County above the James where you can look across and see the Blue Ridge in the distance. Why don't I build in Buckingham?" he asked rhetorically. "It's south of the James, always an issue in Virginia and it's just too far away from Richmond, Charlottesville, although if you work it right you can get down to Lynchburg."

"South of the James?" Weevil asked.

"Wrong side of the tracks," Sister told him. "Dewey, go back to Chapel Cross. First give me the overview."

"I can give you an aerial shot." He brought up the lands abutting the mountains, the crossroads visible although far below. "The lay of the land is gorgeous whether you go north of Chapel Cross for about ten miles or south for ten miles. East you run into Western Albemarle High School. You can do some developments heading that way, Old Trail has certainly been successful." He mentioned a dense development. "But working that way, it just becomes more and more difficult. However, if it were developed, the cheapest house on five acres would be in the eight-hundred-thousand-dollar range. It's a spectacular location."

"Are there road improvements scheduled for Chapel Cross?" Sister wanted to know.

"No. I think Crawford and Kasmir have taken care of that. The DMV is overburdened as it is, so if the two largest landowners had contacted the delegates from our district, an improvement could be pushed back for a decade."

"So you don't have any indication of that?" Sister asked.

"No, but I can show you in detail the proposed route of the pipeline." He tapped away for about three minutes and then the route appeared coming down from the top of the Blue Ridge, down behind Old Paradise, across the lower lands at a forty-five-degree angle, crossing the road, nipping a good part of Beveridge Hundred, and then following Broad Creek east.

"Isn't this floodplain?" Weevil pointed to the route paralleling Broad Creek.

"Yes. That's partly why this route was so stupid. I do think Crawford has solved the problem. Soliden will shift south. So we all owe Crawford and a lot of dead people our thanks." Dewey nodded. "But real estate is still frozen. Until people know the exact route, little will sell or be put on the market. Trust me, real estate brokers are dipping into emergency funds."

"Look here." She leaned forward, placed her finger on land south of Chapel Cross, then placed her finger on the Carriage House.

As the map was large, these were dots, but one could gauge the distance.

"Um-m, six miles? It's hard to tell when the territory is rough. You're pointing out the hands?"

"I am. Now if those hands were found where they were, why can't the cadaver dogs find the rest?"

"If I knew that, I'd be the sheriff." Dewey brought the Carriage House close up. "Damnedest thing."

"I told Ben to check outbuildings, even the old Gulf station. He did. Nothing. There has to be a corpse out there but the dogs can't find it."

"Which means there may not be a corpse out there," Weevil suggested. "Maybe he was tossed somewhere else. The hands were cut off."

"This is a lot of territory. If a body were carried to a ravine"—Dewey brought up a bigger picture of a ravine running down the mountains—"the cadaver dogs would be climbing the mountain. And then again, there's rock outcroppings, sinkholes. That body could have been stuffed just about anywhere."

"It could, but wouldn't the killer have to have driven to get there? You'd think someone would have noticed. The vehicles out there belong to landowners and to the workers at Old Paradise. Someone would have seen something." Sister put her hands on

Dewey's shoulders. "What if the body was dismembered in a safe place? Hands thrown here. Say a torso up by Brownsville." She named a rural area up on Route 810, far away.

Dewey turned his head to face her. "You've seen too many horror movies. Can you imagine the mess, dismembering a corpse?"

Weevil piped up. "Not if it were frozen. It would take an electric saw or a lot of sweat but it wouldn't be a mess."

"Jeez, I hope you two never get mad at me." Dewey shook his head.

CHAPTER 31

Hearing the trucks and trailers, Inky decided she'd stay inside her den this Saturday, February third. Target, under Tootie's front porch, made the same decision. Both foxes lived in dens perfectly placed to know what was going on. The food was good, too. One could saunter into the stables at night, pick up tidbits left on a tack trunk or nibble on sweet feed. The sweet feed rolled in molasses was the best. Both Sister and Tootie put out table scraps. Inky, black as coal, and Target, flashy red, were spoiled.

Living such a good life did attract other foxes for overlong visits. Comet, a gray in the prime of life, paid just such a call last night. Comet created a backup den under the cottage. Fortunately there was so much food, the two males didn't fight about it, but Target resented Comet's dropping in and out. He should make up his mind and stay at After All. Comet, on the other hand, felt he had earned a spacious den near the covered bridge at After All. The den at Roughneck Farm he considered his second home, a condominium. Usually he came over for those extra treats as well as gossip.

"Is it true that Uncle Yancy sleeps above the mudroom door into the kitchen at the Old Lorillard place?" Target asked.

"Says he does. I haven't gone over there to look," Comet answered. *"The good thing about the Lorillard place is there are plenty of escape routes. The bad thing is one is too close to Pattypan Forge. I hate that place."*

"Dark," was all Target said.

"Dark and you have to put up with Aunt Netty."

"Aunt Netty has many opinions all of which she wishes to share." Target laughed. *"Poor Yancy."*

Comet felt the same way. *"I'm going to duck out for a minute and see what they're up to. If I were the huntsman I'd cast toward After All. Always a lot of jumps, the stuff they like."*

"Tell me which way the wind is blowing. I'll tell you how he'll cast," Target promised.

Comet left the den by the front entrance, slipped out from under the stone foundation, full of lots of fox-sized holes. The foundation lifted up the house, or rather the house was rested upon it and the newer portion, the clapboard part, had lattice around the bottom so the notched hardwood logs used as part of the foundation didn't show. Sections of the log had been cut out to make it easy for a human to crawl underneath if something needed fixing.

Sitting perfectly still, the elegant gray observed a flurry of activity. Horses being backed off trailers, humans slapping a rag at their boots to knock off newly accumulated dirt, and, as always, two humans facing each other. Comet watched as a tall lady flipped over one end of a snowy white stock tie, then flipped it under the big square knot. The other side duplicated this so that the tails of the tie crossed over each other under the carefully tidied square knot, a big knot.

What a lot of work, the gray thought to himself.

He could hear half-grown puppies wailing, howling, bitter tears. *"I want to go." "I'm big enough." "I know the horn calls."* The list continued at a high decibel range.

Comet slipped back into the main part of Target's den. *"You should see the people. A real mob."*

"It's occurring to them that the season is flying along. Maybe six more weeks left." He licked a paw. *"They might remember that some of our worst snowstorms happen in March."*

"That and the wind," Comet replied.

"And how bad is the wind and from what direction?"

"Steady but not a great force. Enough to ruffle your fur and it's from the northwest per usual."

Target lay down, paws crossed in front of him. *"He'll cast toward After All and then when he gets into the woods he'll turn either north or south. He doesn't want the wind at their tails."*

As Target predicted, Weevil, hounds, and whippers-in waited while the large field pulled themselves together. Shaker, back from the hospital, talked to people as they rode by. Then he climbed into Skiff's car to follow as best they could by car. Aunt Daniella and Yvonne chose to miss today's hunt, each having other obligations as well as wondering what might happen hunting today. They were happy to miss it.

"Master?" Weevil asked Sister.

Walter, out today, rode tail in First Flight, the best position for a doctor who doesn't mind working on his day off.

"Let's go." Sister smiled at the young man.

"Come along," Weevil called to the hounds, eager to get cracking.

They jumped over the simple coop in the fence line around the pasture behind and surrounding Tootie's cottage and Shaker's. Behind that reposed the large wildflower field so another jump was necessary. This one was three substantial logs stacked as end logs, cut so the large logs could be dropped in. These natural jumps, if you had manpower or a front-end loader, could be easily built as well as inexpensively built. A coop, on the other hand, relied on seasoned planed boards from the lumberyard. That could cost you, plus you had to paint them. However, a coop could be built in a garage and driven to its final destination. This saved many man-hours.

Bobby Franklin led Second Flight to each gate, leaned over, flipped the Kiwi latch, shaped like a comma, a godsend to riders, pushed open the gate from the side of his horse, calling out, "Gate, please."

That meant the last rider in Second Flight had to close the gate accompanied by one other rider. As no horse wants to be left behind when others move off, a companion was good manners as well as prudent.

On all her gates Sister had affixed a small wheel at the free end. This made opening and closing easy until there was snow. Fortunately, the snow melted except for in the ravines.

Dreamboat, behind Diana, said, *"Feels like a good day."*

"Does," she replied.

Before jumping into After All's cornfield, Weevil cast them in the wildflower field. A thin veil of clouds filtered sunlight but kept the temperature from climbing rapidly. The mercury hung at 43°F, good for scent. While 43°F will keep your hands and feet cold if you don't have thin multilayers of socks or tiny little warming footpads, you won't freeze and your feet and hands won't hurt but you'll know it's colder as opposed to warmer.

The temperature bounces created problems of their own. Shooting from high teens, low twenties up into the forties means scent is released but it may not hold, depending on the soil. There's not much vegetation this time of year except for creepers that will survive anything. But cutover fields helped and once hounds could get into the woods, that always helped because it was a few degrees cooler.

All the hounds worked the wildflower field, but nothing.

Weevil popped over the hog's back jump, followed by the field. The standing corn left by the Bancrofts still had a bit of frost on the north side. The harvested stalks farther up had been picked clean.

Weevil slowly drew through as he headed along the edge for the woods.

"Here," Dreamboat called out to the right of his sister.

Didn't take a minute, everyone was on. The fox, whoever he was, proved ungracious because he had moved through the middle of the cornfield so the field had to stay on the edge. Running south, everyone could see hounds as they now flew into the harvest cornfields.

Then, to Sister's surprise, for she thought the fox would cut into the woods at some point, shoot for Pattypan Forge, scent flickered for a moment, then he headed up straight for the covered bridge perhaps a mile and a half away. Out of the cornfield they hurried, along the embankment to the farm road. By now hounds were flat out, scent burning, but no sight of their quarry.

Galloping hard, Weevil reached the covered bridge, where hounds ducked underneath. The fox used the creek to foul scent. Working both sides of the bank while Sister and the field watched, Zane hit the line on the far side of the creek.

"This way," the youngster called.

Soon the pack, wet, shaking themselves, roared out of the creek making straight for the house. After All, an unusual structure, sported four Doric columns in the front but the body of the structure itself was fieldstone. The white columns, doorjambs, and window frames contrasted with beige gray stone.

The original owners, flush with money from the Monroe

presidency where all the boats rose as the tide rolled in, wanted the Palladian look but wanted to be different, too. They succeeded. Subsequent generations of owners reveled in the look, the deep color of the interior floors, heart pine of extra color depth. The current owners, the Bancrofts, honored the original intent.

However, the fox did not. Charlene, the chased fox, a luscious red, merrily led hounds around the house, being sure to step on the sleeping gardens with hopes of creating problems come spring. Charlene knew she had hounds beat, she was ten minutes in front of them, but she couldn't resist tearing up After All a little bit.

She'd pressed her dainty paws on the wrought-iron furniture left outside for the winter. Then she zipped around the dependency, a four-over-four house way in the rear, currently empty, an echo of the main house. Hearing hounds come a bit closer, Charlene turned 180 degrees, zapped through the woods. No one saw her winding up at the cottage, also fieldstone, which Weevil had been given by the Bancrofts for living quarters. This was their gift to the club so a year's rent would be saved. Finding places to rent in the western part of the county wasn't easy and it wasn't cheap. Everyone figured that after a year, Sister would extend Weevil's contract for many years and he would buy himself something suitable.

Charlene liked Weevil as he liked rib-eye steak, which she adored. He'd put the bones out, a few potato skins, butter in those skins, and she gobbled everything. She felt he was her cook. So she enlarged the den at the back corner of the place under the equipment shed. Many entrances and exits added to its practicality. The interior, quite warm, had as its centerpiece a fake fleece–lined jacket, which she took the liberty of stealing. Weevil draped it over an Adirondack chair in the back to air out. He forgot to bring it inside that night so Charlene took it home. Weevil couldn't figure out what had happened to his jacket.

She curled up in it as she heard hounds reach the back lawn.

Dumb twits, she thought to herself.

Dreamboat, first to the cleverly hidden den opening, yelled down, *"You got us wet."*

"You didn't have to go into the water," she called back.

"How else would I find your scent again?"

"You could have found another fox. I'm not the only one. You know as well as I do that Aunt Netty runs Pattypan Forge."

"Aunt Netty is hateful mean." Dreamboat put his nose right at the den's entrance, although most of it was under the corner of the equipment shed, which housed a John Deere riding mower, a weed eater, a few gardening tools hung up neatly.

The other hounds crowded around Dreamboat as Weevil dismounted. Tootie had ridden up to hold Matador.

"Well done. Well done." He praised the hounds, then blew "Gone to Ground."

Dreamboat looked up into Weevil's eyes. *"I smell red meat, cooked red meat. Do you feed this fox?"*

Weevil heard a bark that was Charlene chiding Dreamboat. *"Shut up! I don't want him to stop throwing out meaty bones and furthermore I have a lot of ways to get even."*

"Like what?" Dreamboat sassed.

"Put your nose in my den entrance and I'll whisper my secret to you."

Dreamboat did just that and, like a lightning strike, Charlene whacked his nose and her claws hurt.

"Dear God." Diana laughed, as did the others, for Dreamboat had been snookered.

Even Weevil smiled. Had to give the fox credit. He remounted.

"Tootie, you know this fixture better than I do. Any suggestions?"

"Betty knows more than I do, but if I were you"—Tootie, well educated, used the subjunctive correctly—"I would draw down the creek on the other side, the Roughneck side, even though it's far away. If we run to the Lorillard place, we'll run out of territory fast enough. If we pick up a line that heads west or north, we might get a long run."

"I knew you'd have the answer." He beamed at her, then turned to walk through the covered bridge, Tootie now ahead so she could get in position.

The clouds thickened a bit, good for scent and temperature. Up the creek they drew, northward. A yip here and a yap there testified to game moving but nothing heated up until Weevil reached the good creek crossing. As he asked Matador to go into the creek, low at that point, the pack was already on the other side.

All at once everyone opened. Noses down and then every hound sang out, flying northwest.

Weevil, close behind, ran on a good trail. Sister, maybe thirty yards behind Weevil, heard the hoofbeats behind her. The sound of a large field running hard, hounds in full cry up ahead, made her heart leap. Lafayette, long fluid stride, loved being in front showing his stuff. He was a vision with the long fluid Thoroughbred stride, appearing effortless.

This trail, well tended, no limbs to duck, seemed almost medieval. The pack could have been hunting on a great ducal estate, trees on either side, many conifers, the ground underneath not too hard but not so soft either. Perfect conditions.

A raven or two cawed from branches. They liked encouraging hounds, for crows, blackbirds, and ravens hated foxes. It was mutual.

The woods opened up ahead. Hounds emerged into an open field, not cut, to the north of the cornfields. The old dried grasses swished as they blew through them. The riders couldn't see the hounds, but Weevil, close behind, could see a few sterns. This field abruptly ended at Sister's fence line. Weevil searched for a jump.

"Keep north," Sister called out.

He rode north, loping along because he didn't want to lose his hounds. He was about to do so. Thankfully a brush fence appeared. This was an old steeplechase jump retired from the circuit and Sister, never one to pass up something useful, threw it on the back of her truck years ago. Set it in her fence line. While it was incongruous to see a brush jump in a hunting field, there it was and you'd better take it.

As the Bancrofts had fallen back, the pace a little demanding for them now, Kasmir was the first over, then Alida, then Dewey followed by Gray and Sam, who had dropped from the front just a bit to embolden a guest in the field, not exactly overmatched but a lady not accustomed to territory like that in the foothills of the Blue Ridge Mountains. They all soared over and then it was one after another, really a thrilling sight.

Meanwhile, Tootie ran ahead of Weevil because he had only been in this field once. Betty was already around the bottom of Hangman's Ridge to reach the other side before hounds climbed up. Rock outcroppings slowed her progress. The fox could just as easily turn around. This territory favored the fox. It was rough. They were on a visiting dog fox, which meant anything goes.

Betty, at the bottom of the ridge on the other side, now heard hounds but they weren't moving fast at that moment. Hounds, betwixt and between, searched for a good way up Hangman's Ridge from the southernmost side. There wasn't one so Tootie fell back.

"Follow me."

Weevil did just that as she turned left, worked her way around the bottom of the rocky sides then came out at the farm road, which snaked up to the top. By now hounds hard behind their fox climbed, clawed, slipped, and slid their way to the top of the ridge the hard way. Noses down, they moved as one, but now in a circle, for the fox did not drop over the ridge.

Cora focused, lifted her head for one moment. Startled, she put her nose down. Nothing must keep her from her quarry.

Tootie hit the top of the long ridgeline first, Weevil right behind. They kept their eyes on the hounds as hounds turned and then they stopped cold.

Sister, just reaching the top of the farm road, beheld her huntsman and her whipper-in standing stock-still as hounds screamed past them. *What the hell!* she thought, and then she heard it before she saw it.

A creak, a rhythmic creak.

Looking in the direction where Weevil and Tootie stood frozen, she saw the body of Gregory Luckham hanging from the hanging tree. The rope on the thick branch provided the sound.

Thinking fast, she turned. Kasmir, Alida, Freddie, and Dewey, now on the ridge, also saw the body.

"Hold hard," she ordered. "Kasmir, get me Ben. He's out today with Second Flight."

"Yes, Master." Kasmir turned, threaded his way through the field pinned on the incline, not knowing what was going on.

"Dewey, bring me Walter." As Dewey turned, Sister ordered Alida. "Turn the field back, Alida. Wait at the bottom of the ridge or the farm road."

Then she asked Freddie, "Can you walk with me? If it's too upsetting, I understand."

"Sister, if you can take it, I can." Freddie rode next to Sister.

Neither Weevil nor Tootie could speak and hounds were heard roaring as they tore down the ridge.

"Forgive me." Weevil awakened as if from a trance. "Forgive me. I should never not be with my hounds."

"Weevil, this is a great shock. You two go down the farm road. Everyone will be in front of you, but get by if you can and stay with the hounds. If you can pick them up, do. Shaker is somewhere in the truck with Skiff. Perhaps they can help. Put them up and wait at the kennels. You will need to talk to Ben."

"Yes, Master," they both said and snapped into action, although Tootie was shaking.

Freddie studied the corpse. "No hands. No eyes. No boots."

"We know where the hands are or where they were found. We know where the boots were left. The birds took his eyes."

Walter quickly came up. He, too, was stunned. "Why here? This is insane."

"It may be that. Will you get closer to the body? I find it odd that the body is intact and not decayed." Sister's mind was working just fine.

As the three drew closer to Gregory Luckham, Betty charged up the trail, came out onto the ridge, saw the three even as she heard hounds now below. Then she saw the corpse just swinging slightly in the breeze.

Betty was grateful she hadn't eaten breakfast. Gregory may have been intact but he was hanging, a deeply unsettling sight. Without a word, she joined the three.

"What do you think, Walter?" Sister asked her Joint Master. "He's been dead since Christmas Hunt."

Walter peered intently at the body. He was wise enough not to touch it.

"Preserved. Quite well."

"Like embalmed?" Freddie blurted out.

"I can't touch him. Ben would be angry at me and I do know better. With luck, there may be evidence on this body. But either he was embalmed or he was frozen."

"Then why cut off his hands?" Betty shook her head. "This is the work of a madman."

Freddie, voice low, replied. "Or someone who wants us to think just that."

"Well, it does divert your attention." Sister spoke as they turned, for Dewey was riding with Ben, now at the top of the farm road. Both men stopped for a second, then rode on.

Ben immediately called his forensics team, weekend be damned. Then he asked to be patched through to the medical examiner, who was at her daughter's ninth birthday party.

"Get the body here by tonight. We'll examine it Monday."

"Slow time?" Ben asked.

"Yes, but this is so unusual, best we get to it as fast as possible."

After a few more words, Ben clicked off. "Who found him?"

"Weevil and Tootie hit the ridge first," Sister said.

"I know this is difficult, but if you can, see if you can get as close to your track as possible. When my team arrives I want every inch of this ridge scrutinized as well as the trail up and down. And do me another favor. Wait, after you put the horses up, because this will take time to assemble everyone. If you will, show them the way up."

Sister and the others rode down, Dewey in the rear as backup. Walter stayed with Ben.

Finally Betty asked, "Do you think we're in danger?"

"Only if you get too close to the killer," Freddie sensibly said.

"You have to be nuts to do something like that. Cut off hands, throw them about, then hang the corpse. Nuts." Betty exploded.

"I don't know," Sister's voice, clear, called back. "Dewey, what do you think?"

"I agree with Betty. Makes no sense."

"But it does to whoever is behind this," Freddie said.

"Isn't that what those crime shows determine? What seems crazy to us is logical to the killer," Sister replied.

"Maybe." Dewey sounded unconvinced. "But logic can be part of someone gripped by an obsession. It's still lunacy."

"Consider that Gregory Luckham is dangling from the hanging tree. This is where justice was carried out in colonial times. Criminals were executed here by hanging."

No one said anything, but she opened a door, if ever so slightly.

CHAPTER 32

Holding open the kennel door, Shaker watched Weevil, Tootie, and Betty bring in hounds who had run halfway back to After All on that terrific fox. Skiff walked into the kennel to close the draw pen doors to the inside. This way hounds would first be in the large area where they originally awaited being loaded up. Huntsmen and whippers-in liked to check each hound before opening the door to either the girls' run or the boys'.

The temperature, falling, only made the brace on his neck more uncomfortable.

Shaker and Skiff, at the bottom of the ridge, couldn't drive up the farm road because both flights crowded it and didn't move. That was Shaker's first clue that something had happened. He assumed someone fell off, got kicked, which could happen when mounted and often resulted in a broken leg. Then they both saw riders coming toward them, sliding by the fields, horses' noses pointing up because there was nowhere to really back into to allow anyone to come down in proper fashion.

As soon as Alida saw the two huntsmen, she rode to the truck and asked them to help round up and put the hounds in the kennels. They could all hear the pack roaring to their east as well as Weevil blowing his horn for them to come back.

"What's going on?" Shaker asked.

"No one is exactly sure." Alida glossed over the gruesome discovery.

"Alida, I have hunted with and for that woman for over twenty years, whipping-in before that. Something is wrong and whatever it is, it's major. Did someone break something, is a horse injured, God forbid, is someone dead?"

Taking a deep breath, Alida grimaced slightly, then looked from Skiff to Shaker. "Dead."

"Who? Look, if she needs me, I'm going up there. It's just two vertebrae. I'm fine. It's not Sister. Tell me Sister's fine."

"She is and I'm sure the sight of you would bring her comfort, but Shaker, there's nothing you can do. The remains of Gregory Luckham are swinging from the hanging tree."

"What!" Skiff raised her voice.

"Alida, did you see this? It's hard to believe."

"Shaker, unfortunately, I did see him. No hands. Boots off his feet." Then it hit her, too. "And, well, I didn't think of it at the time, I was too horrified, but he looks, what do I say, fresh. No eyes. Forgot that. No eyes. But he's not deteriorated as one would think. He's gray, that's all, but one loses color in death."

"I can't believe this." Shaker shook his head.

"Honey, don't shake your head," Skiff gently reminded him.

"Damn this thing!"

Hounds bounded up to the kennels and to Shaker. Weevil gracefully dismounted, nodded to Shaker, and led hounds into the draw pen as each one touched their former huntsman's hand. He was near to tears. However, hounds first, so when the last stern waggled into the draw pen Shaker closed the door, listening to the happy sounds inside, the praise, each name being called. He knew as that hound was checked out, Betty would be opening the appropriate door and Diana or Cora or young Audrey would be given an anticipated cookie. Then through the door the hound would bound, a good day's hunting ended.

Tootie was filling any water troughs that needed it inside; each had water heaters in the specially built trough. The outside runs did not yet have those automatic waterers. That would come in time.

Within twenty minutes everyone was curled up on their bed or walked outside just to see why the people were still there.

The field, now led by Dewey, who Sister sent back to get them off the farm road, were walking to their trailers. Dewey asked them to stay after their horses were tended to and reminded them there was a breakfast, go on in, and when Sister came back she would give a report. He rode back, checked the road up to the ridge to make sure there were no stragglers, then rejoined people at the trailers.

Betty, now out of the kennel, spoke briefly to Shaker and Skiff. Then she hurried up to the house to set out the food. Gray, already there, had made coffee and tea. The two friends couldn't believe what Betty had seen. Gray, farther down on the farm road, did not see Gregory.

The forensic squad, led back up by Sam, who Dewey asked to stay, were as prepared as they could be. The photographer snapped away.

Carson Blanton, Jude Hevener, and Jackie Fugate rushed to the scene as well. Ben wanted their eyes and he wanted them to become accustomed to the unimaginable. If they were going to be law enforcement officers, they needed to toughen up.

Sister and Walter quietly waited to the side as the team first examined the scene. Ben soon came over.

"I looked for tire tracks or footprints." Sister watched as one of the forensics men got down on his hands and knees directly under the corpse. "Nothing. Of course the ground is hard now."

"Yes," Ben, almost distracted, replied. "Why don't you go back down? I know you have a breakfast. There really isn't anything you can do. Well, there is something. Obviously, we don't want hysteria. Solves nothing. If you could get the names of those people who saw the corpse, then I could get one of my boys or girl"—he nodded toward Jackie—"to take a statement. Not at the breakfast."

"Of course." She turned Lafayette, who was mesmerized by all this, then stopped. "Ben, think about the hanging tree. This is where justice was carried out. Perhaps this is a message that the killer believes Gregory was a criminal and justice has been done."

Ben looked up at her. "An interesting thought." He turned to Walter. "Why don't you dismount, let her take Clemson, and you stay with me for a bit. I could use a doctor's expertise."

"Right." Walter dismounted, handed the reins to Sister as she walked away.

By the time she reached her stable, Tootie and Weevil were waiting for her. She knew Betty would be helping Gray host things.

"Oh, how good it is to see you." Sister thankfully dismounted. "All of this has been a hideous shock."

Tootie began to untack Lafayette on one side while Weevil flipped up and unhooked the girth on the other.

"Weevil, you stayed with those hounds on full throttle. How did you pick them up?"

He slipped off the saddle while Tootie started on the bridle. "Halfway into the wildflower field where we started they circled, as they did at the beginning. Tootie got in front of them, told them to hold up, and they did. All I had to do was blow the three blasts. Tootie really did all the work."

"They're a good pack." Tootie had the reins on her shoulders, the bridle in her hand.

She needed to wash the bit and she planned to clean the tack.

"You both impressed me. Not everyone could have kept cool under the circumstances."

"Hounds first, madam." Weevil smiled a little.

"Thank God for them." Sister called out to Tootie on her way to the wash stall. "Don't bother to clean the tack. We can do that tomorrow. Let's tidy ourselves up, go to the breakfast, and well, maybe we'd better plan on what to say and what to do."

"What did the sheriff think?" Weevil asked.

"He didn't say, but he also didn't say for us not to report what we saw. The best thing would be for me to make a brief announcement, tell everyone that Ben, the forensics team, and his individual crew are there. Tell them there's nothing they can do and ask who actually saw the hanging tree. Best to put it that way and inform them that Ben will be taking statements today or tomorrow. At any rate, the important thing is to blunt panic. Kasmir and Alida will be a great help with that. Sam and Gray, as well. They are all sensible people, as are you."

"Do you think we're in danger?" Tootie asked.

"I wish I could answer that. I don't know."

"Maybe not danger, but we'd better be alert. Two hands were found in the hunt territory and now this." Weevil placed the saddle on a rack, unfastened the nice thick saddle pad. "Tootie, you shouldn't be alone. No one knows anything. So either you come stay with me at After All or I come stay with you."

"There are people around. Shaker's in his place and Sister and Gray are in the big house. I'm okay."

"He's right, Tootie. We don't know what we're up against. Tell you what. If you all don't wish to be in either one's house, then you can stay in mine. It's big enough. If you don't get along I can stick each of you at opposite ends." She smiled.

"Well." Tootie halted, thought. "Weevil, come here. We have to work hounds and horses anyway. It's more efficient. Sister's given us a way out if we fight."

"Is it true, you don't cook?" His blond eyebrows shot up while Sister observed all this, grateful to have her mind off the hanging tree.

"Kind of."

"Then I'll make bangers and mash." He smiled.

"What's that?"

"You'll have to find out."

"I love bangers and mash." Sister did, too.

"Then I'll make some for you, too." He picked up the saddle, opened the tack room door, and placed it on a saddle rack as Tootie hung the bridle from the big wrought-iron bridle hook that looked like a grappling iron.

Sister, in the aisle, prayed something good would come from all this. Perhaps Tootie would learn to open her heart, to love. She thought of all the rules, rules about age, race, class, the debris of conformity, that people spout about love or even careers. Love knows no age, no color, no anything, really. It just is.

As they walked up to the house, lights shining over the winter landscape, she remembered falling in love with Big Ray. One supposed friend told her Ray was beneath the salt. Granted, he was from a lower class, but she didn't give a rat's ass. And the delicious part was Ray studied, worked hard, became an investment broker, and made a lot of money. Trixie Biglow, the so-called friend, married very well and he turned out to be a worthless drunk.

Smiling to herself, she also steeled herself for the little speech she must give. She glanced again at these two impossibly beautiful young people, realizing she loved them. She was worried and grateful that Weevil was forceful about protecting Tootie although he did this in a gentlemanly way.

Thank God for real men, she thought, and then she also thought, *Love just happens. No rules.* And then it occurred to her that that could also apply to murder.

CHAPTER 33

"A bird in the hand is worth two in the bush."

Sister wrote down what Gray had just said, then she came back with, "Sticky fingers."

"I thought you wanted hand phrases."

Pencil poised over the grid-lined paper, she replied, "I do, but fingers, palms, anything or any part of the hand."

Golly, lying on her side on the kitchen counter, said, *"Paws for effect."*

Rooster, at Sister's feet, corrected her. *"Human stuff, not paws."*

"Just a thought. You and Rooster roam all over. You go up to Hangman's Ridge sometimes." The cat reminded them of their travels.

"Not often and usually with Sister if she's riding up there. I hate it." Raleigh grimaced.

"I do, too. It's creepy. You can hear the dead whisper. Athena and Bitsy"—he named the two owls, one huge and the other tiny—*"say they can see the dead."*

"Bitsy is given to idle gossip and drama." The long-haired cat

now sat up. *"But you can hear the dead and sometimes you can catch a fleeting glimpse, movement."*

Thoughtfully, Raleigh added to that. *"I think some humans can see and hear, too. They say they've seen a ghost and the others pooh-pooh them but for some the ability hasn't vanished."*

"If you'd run up there, you would have found him," Golly posited. *"With your great noses, the hounds' noses, I'd think someone would have known."*

"But that's just it, Golly. Hounds didn't know he was up there until they came onto the ridge. They told me as they got closer they could smell the wool in his coat but not him. He was preserved," Rooster related.

"Why would someone hang up a dead human, preserve him? Wouldn't it make better sense to just dump the body in one of those deep ravines in the mountains or throw the body on I-64 in the middle of the night? That would create a fuss. This seems like a lot of work to me."

"He was mutilated. Hands cut off," Raleigh said.

"I remember when hounds found one in the woods and then Sister told Gray about his aunt and Yvonne finding one. Is that why they're thinking of hand stuff? Seems funny. I mean phrases."

"Is," Rooster affirmed.

"Sister thinks there's symbolism," Raleigh told her.

"Hand to mouth." Gray thought of another one.

"Red-handed."

"That's a good one." He watched her write in her elegant style. "How about a winning hand?"

"See, once you start, things pop into your head." She then said, "All hands on deck."

"An iron fist."

"Oh, that's another good one. Um-m, beat you hands down."

"Bite the hand that feeds you. Maybe he betrayed someone."

"Can't see the hand in front of your face. Well, you certainly couldn't during that storm. Oh, cash in hand."

He smiled. "Cold hands, warm heart."

A knock on the mudroom door, followed by a knock on the door to the kitchen. "Master."

"Come in." She glanced up from her notebook to see Weevil, dish towel around a large plate. Behind him walked Tootie carrying a bowl, also covered.

"Bangers and mash."

"Weevil! You did cook me bangers and mash. Well, let's eat it."

Sister and Gray hastily set the table; the four sat down.

"I didn't make anything last night because the breakfast was so much food. You settled everyone's nerves. You're a good speaker." Weevil complimented her.

"Didn't used to be. Becoming a Master forced me to learn lots of new skills. Maybe the most important one is keeping my mouth shut." She looked at the empty glasses. "Milk, beer, wine, water, tonic water, and, Gray, have I forgotten something?"

"Already at the refrigerator door." Gray teased her. "Nectar and ambrosia." He returned with two bottles of beer, two tonic waters for the ladies, with limes and a cutting board.

Tootie filled the glasses with ice while Weevil cut their limes. "Are you making notes?" She saw the leather-bound notebook.

"We are and we'll ask you for ideas. Here's what we're doing. Coming up with hand phrases." She read what they'd already thought about.

"Carry fire in one hand and water in the other," Weevil said.

"I've never heard of that." Tootie was trying to think of something.

"My mother says that. How about, a dab hand?"

"Don't hear that much anymore, but it means you're good at something. Handy." Sister grinned.

"Did I say beat you hands down?" Gray took another sip of ice cold beer.

"Yes. Another good one. Hand-me-down," Sister said.

Tootie finally came up with something. "Fall into the wrong hands. Oh, got another one. Wringing hands."

"Keep talking." Sister encouraged them.

"One hand tied behind your back." Weevil speared a sausage.

"Whip hand. That should have been the first one we thought of," Gray said.

"Grease your palm." Weevil was liking this.

"Um-m-m, upper hand." Tootie then added, "Hand in the cookie jar. That's one of my mom's whenever she reads about politicians."

"And they're supposed to have their hand on the tiller." Weevil was quick.

"Hand in glove." Gray came right back. "Speaking of politicians made me think of that one."

"Hand in hand," Sister wrote.

"Blood on your hands," Gray added.

Tootie had another one. "And finger in the pie."

"Good one." Sister wrote, then looked up at them. "Play the hand you're given."

"Getting harder." Weevil finished off his mashed potatoes. "Get a handle on it. Not exactly hand."

"No, but it counts." Sister wrote. "The Devil finds work for idle hands."

Gray leaned back. "From my cold dead hands."

"Honey, that's too close for comfort"—she sighed—"not that any of this is comfortable."

"Heavy-handed," Weevil piped up.

"Well, yes. Gray's had to put up with me but I now think so much of what has happened has some symbolism. If we can figure out the symbolism, we might be closer to the killer."

"That's just it, honey, we are close to the killer." Gray was solemn. "That's why Weevil is here. That's why Sam is staying with the

Van Dorns, which he did once the first hand was found." He looked at Tootie. "We don't want your mother alone and we all knew she might not want him in her house. This is the next best thing."

"Is Mom in danger?"

"We don't know, but the first hand was found out there in Chapel Cross. That's where Gregory disappeared and that's where Rory was found."

"I still can't believe his mother didn't come to his service." Tootie squeezed her lime into the bubbling tonic water.

"Tootie, you've never really seen poor whites until you've lived in the South. Many are good, but when they go bad, they're in a class by themselves," Gray warned her.

"Don't you think that's everywhere? The ignorant and the brutal?" Sister scribbled. "And that's what worries me. Our killer is neither ignorant nor poor. He may be brutal. I don't know. One can kill but not be brutal. But this person is intelligent and, in his way, sending the rest of us messages."

"We're not in safe hands," Tootie responded.

That same Sunday evening, Ben Sidell, computer in front of him, was on the phone with the Goochland County sheriff.

"The medical examiner said she'd get on it tomorrow, first thing in the morning."

The sheriff replied, "Liz has asked me to tell her the minute the exam is done. She'll have John Noon Western's funeral home retrieve the body. She wants an Episcopalian funeral. She said she wants him back and she wants his hands."

"Actually, the hands are already there." Ben checked on the dates on his computer screen.

"Damned mess, isn't it?" The Goochland sheriff commiserated. "By the way, she asked for Gregory's ring. She said he wore a ring on the little finger of his left hand. Saint Hubert, I don't know Saint Hubert but I'm a Methodist."

"No ring was found. Saint Hubert is the patron saint of hunters. I'll double-check around here but I'm certain no ring was on that hand, what was left of it, and the white cotton glove."

"I'll let her know."

"Thanks."

CHAPTER 34

Water sprayed off the huge waterwheel at Mill Ruins. The millrace rarely froze at the mill itself, although it did freeze away from it.

February 6, cold, clear, a few clouds in the sky did not look promising, but foxes get hungry and Mill Ruins now hosted more than in the past. James, the oldest, lived behind the mill. Ewald, young, last season made a den in an outbuilding not far from the barn. Both these foxes were reds. Hortensia, a gray, lived in the big hay shed, which she quite liked. Her den, underground, provided protection when needed but she also liked to burrow into the big round hay bales. Sometimes she could hear mice chatter in those bales. The mice could smell her so no little marauder stumbled on Hortensia. Way at the back of this remarkable place Grenville, another gray, had a den in the storage shed.

Inside the large mill the gears still worked, the millstone still viable. Unfortunately, no one knew how to use it. Walter, who had a ninety-nine-year lease on the place, thought about finding a miller to rent it out, but then he considered the traffic on the farm with people bringing their grain. He told himself if he ever retired from medicine, he'd learn to be a miller. At one time this was the farthest-west mill in the county. After the Revolutionary War more people moved west. Numbers forged over the Blue Ridge into the Shenandoah Valley. During the Articles of Confederation people cleared the land, plowed, planted. Once we created the Constitution, more stability, brave souls kept going into the Ohio Valley, land beckoning them. Citizens of the new republic had been promised the vast expanse of that valley would be made safe for them. However, Spain and England fostered other ideas, hoping to pin the newborn nation between the Appalachian Chain, the Alleghenies, and the sea while they took over the fertile valley, hoping someday to defeat us by arms. Monarchies feared this new political entity so they stirred up the tribes, made deals, and blood flowed. Then again, never underestimate one nation's greed for the land of another.

Sister, on Midshipman, hunting him for the first time thanks to Weevil's work, looked west and wondered did Americans truly know their own history anymore? She listened to the *lap, lap* of the waterwheel, knowing that cornmeal, grains kept those early settlers alive. That and being a good shot, bringing down deer. And sometimes bringing down each other.

Being Tuesday, the field was small. Walter always hunted his place and since doctors put in their schedules early, he could do it.

Weevil walked down the farm road, casting hounds behind the mill. James heard the commotion, stayed put. So hounds regrouped heading down the farm road, two large pastures on either side of the solid fencing. Interest here and there but nothing special. On they walked until finally just at woods' edge, Pansy opened. A short run, a couple of bracing jumps, but this was a pick them up, put them down kind of day. Scent just wouldn't carry.

Weevil worried that he wasn't doing enough, didn't know enough, but he was wise enough not to push or scold.

Finally, into the woods, steep decline toward Shootrough, the back of the farm, hounds screamed. Betty kicked it into high gear as did Tootie, who saw a large black shape in front of her. Iota snorted but kept going, closing the gap. A black bear, easily four hundred pounds, rumbled, the whole pack at his heels.

Being no fool, the bear climbed a pin oak, the branches thick so he half positioned himself on one of the big ones, looking down at the hounds.

"I got 'em. I got 'em," Dragon bragged on his hind legs.

His sister, no fan of her brother, sat looking upward. *"You idiot. If he backs down he'll use your head for a step."*

Tootie, close to the hounds, waited for Weevil.

Weevil, swinging his leg over Hojo as the horse skidded to a stop, ran to the base of the tree. "Come away. Come away, hounds."

The field, now thirty yards from the action, held their breath. Sister wasn't worried. Yes, a big bear could break a hound or human's neck with one swipe, but usually black bears want to be left in peace. The only time she ever worried was if hounds picked up a momma and baby.

"Come away."

"I don't want to come away," Dragon sassed.

The pack left Dragon, who, disgusted, dropped to all fours and joined them.

Tootie, now holding Hojo's reins, smiled as Weevil mounted. Tootie, quiet, as soon as Weevil was secure, moved off to her position, which she thought of as ten o'clock on the clock dial whereas Betty was at two o'clock and Weevil was the button on the clock face.

Weevil calmly walked away toward Shootrough. The bear watched, climbing backward once the field disappeared.

Shootrough, once a hunting part of the farm for grouse, had been planted in switchgrass, which grows high, offering good cover for birds, bunnies, foxes. Where the open land met the woods, Walter had planted South American maize in a few rows, which also offered cover but something different to eat.

The switchgrass swayed. He urged hounds to go in. They did, but nothing. The sway was a slight wind. Often Grenville would give them a good run, finally diving into his den at the storage shed. But today Grenville stayed in, feeling lazy.

After two hours of searching, Weevil lifted the hounds, walking back to the mill.

Sister thanked him, Betty, and Tootie for their efforts, which she did after every hunt. Dismounting, she patted Midshipman, removed his bridle and martingale, tossed a blanket over him, finishing with cookies. "What a good boy you are."

"Thank you." Midshipman ate his cookies.

Betty, performing the same things for Outlaw standing next to Midshipman, said, "That was some bear."

"Don't they give off a distinctive odor?" Sister asked.

"Strong." Betty agreed.

Once inside Walter's house, Sister sat down, a cup of tea in her hand. People pulled chairs up as sitting seemed like a good idea. Sometimes a slow day makes you more tired than a fast one. Then again, cold wears you out.

"Everyone have their Valentine's gifts in order?" Betty reminded everyone just as Yvonne and Aunt Daniella came through the door. "It's a week and a day away."

"Did you miss us?" Aunt Daniella asked.

"I'm getting used to you all following by car." Walter offered to fetch a drink for the ladies.

"Well, I overslept," Yvonne confessed.

They all caught up with one another, spoke of the bear, the

hanging tree at the February third hunt, the unsolved murders, the stress of it all.

The door opened again. Ben Sidell arrived. He could have sent the membership an email and he would, but first he wanted to ask about the ring to the hard core, which is how he thought of the weekday hunters. He trusted his powers of observation. Maybe someone would falter for a split second.

After asking about the hunt, he tapped a spoon on a glass. "Folks, a minute. Liz Luckham, Gregory's widow, has asked for his ring. We didn't find one with the evidence we have, but by any chance might one of you have or have seen a Saint Hubert's ring?"

As Yvonne had shown the ring to a few people at After All's breakfast, a few eyes fell on her.

"Saint Hubert?" Yvonne asked.

"Yes. The stag with the cross between his antlers," Ben answered.

She slipped the ring off her third finger, walked up to him, and dropped it into his palm. "Tootie and I found it in the dog box at Beveridge Hundred."

Sam, having seen the ring and heard the story, said to Ben, "She feeds a fox there. He was playing with it."

People couldn't help themselves. They wanted to view the ring so Ben kept his hand open.

Alida picked it up. "How beautiful."

Dewey, his hand open, studied it as Alida dropped it into his. "How did this ring get to Beveridge Hundred?"

"I don't know. But the fox was playing with it in the doghouse. I put toys in there for him."

Ben, hand under Yvonne's arm, took her to the other room to ask questions, ring once again in his possession.

"I don't suppose there could be more than one Saint Hubert ring?" Dewey asked.

"Not likely." Sam kept his eye on the room in case Yvonne might become upset.

"At least, no body today." Dewey exhaled.

"For which I am very grateful," Sister responded. "We might recall that all that has been found up until that gruesome Saturday's hunt has been in the Chapel Cross area. Including the ring."

Weevil spoke up. "Tootie and I have been going over the maps. There are miles between where the hands were found, but that's not inconsistent with animals carrying prizes, edible prizes. What we can't understand is"—he stopped—"well, sorry, it's gross."

"No, go on." Dewey encouraged him.

"Why cut off hands?" Weevil finished.

"In ancient times and even up to the twentieth century in the Mideast, a thief had his right hand cut off or both hands," Tootie added.

Kasmir considered this. "Maybe Gregory Luckham was a thief of some sort. No matter how you look at it, it's bizarre and, well, primitive."

"I say this is the work of a nut," Dewey pronounced.

"I just want it to stop," Betty forcefully said. "How do we know someone else isn't marked? We don't know what this is about. Two people have been killed, one with hands cut off, boots missing, and one killed by a blow to the head. We have no idea why."

"No." Weevil surprised some of the members by his thoughts. "Tootie and I researched the eighteen men who were executed at the hanging tree. Ten had committed murder, two of those killed were stabbed, the others shot. Six stole horses or money. And two had committed rape."

"Serious offenses in any century." Ben, who had rejoined them along with Yvonne, sat down himself.

"Now you hire a big-time lawyer and, well, money talks"—Sam shrugged—"although occasionally justice is done."

"Oh, all you have to do is say the killer was mistreated by his mother. It's always the mother's fault." Betty grabbed a sandwich. "It is," she added for emphasis.

"Do you think all murder is circumstantial?" Sister asked.

"I can answer that." Ben's voice rose. "No. There literally are criminal minds. Granted, I have to be careful what I say, but you all know there are people born without a conscience. That doesn't mean they will kill, but if they do, no remorse. None. Most people feel something, especially if the act was done in the heat of the moment."

"Isn't revenge an exception to that?" Yvonne asked.

"Yes." Ben nodded. "That person feels justice was miscarried or justice will never be carried out. They must redress the balance. Not only is there no remorse—often there is jubilation. But apart from these examples, I believe there is a criminal mind. Obviously, Al Capone had one. Such individuals are usually highly intelligent."

"But are they killers?" Sam asked.

"Some are. Some aren't. But killing usually enhances power or profit. There's no thrill killing. It's business."

"I think that applies to Gregory Luckham. It was business," Sister said.

"Well, what I've been thinking"—Weevil backed up his Master—"is the same thing but in a slightly different way. Hangman's Ridge served as a warning. You can see the tree from Soldier Road if you're looking for it. The hanged were left there, were they not? As a warning?"

Sam, who read lots of history, piped up. "In the earliest part of the eighteenth century they were left as a warning. As time went on, the family was allowed to claim the corpse for a proper burial, except for the two cases of rape. They were left to be picked clean."

"Wonder if it stopped anyone?" Alida mused.

"We'll never know. Why would anyone tell?" Sister smiled at Alida, whom she very much liked.

Sam looked at Weevil and Tootie. "You two did good research. Did you Google it?"

Betty half-laughed. "Of course they did, Sam. They were born with a computer in their cribs."

This lightened the mood.

CHAPTER 35

The U.S. Geological Survey maps, old, edges torn and frayed, covered the kitchen table. Sister, Gray, Tootie, and Weevil bent over them. The maps, forty years old, still proved accurate with topo lines, roads, creeks, and rivers. The maps of the westernmost territories, Chapel Cross, remained unchanged. The ones closer to the so-called home territories were out of date thanks to more roads and development, but still geologically correct.

"Used to be one of Farmington's best fixtures." Sister pointed to a spot on an easternmost map where her territory adjoined Farmington Hunt Club's. "Now, of course, it's a high-end housing development but when Port Haeffner was alive you could ride for miles and miles over lush pastures, some woods. Well, this is progress. So they say."

"I remember the cockfights at the back of Port's farm. My grandfather bred fighting chickens. Illegal now—fighting. You can still breed them." Gray laughed. "I was too little to go in and also a little black boy wouldn't have been there unless he was handling the fighting chickens, but I remember people turning into the drive wearing tuxedos and evening gowns. A different time."

"People dressed up for cockfights?" Tootie couldn't believe it.

Sister pulled over another map. "Did. I was never much for it myself, but at least the fighting cock has a chance. A Perdue chicken never does. Now look here."

Three pairs of eyes followed her finger. Four if you count Golly on the table as she felt her insights would be precious. The dogs flopped on the floor.

"Site One." Weevil put his finger next to Sister's, which stayed on the spot where Rory was found.

Weevil then moved his finger to where Shaker hit his head, Dragon carried the right hand. "Site Two."

Gray's finger on the Carriage House, which of course was clearly visible on the old map. "Site Three."

"Site Four." Tootie fingered the place just behind the dependency at Beveridge Hundred.

"Close enough. I'm not counting Hangman's Ridge right now. Too far. It's Chapel Cross we need to figure out. For one thing, I believe the body had to be there at least for a time."

"Under the snow?" Weevil asked.

"Possibly. I think Gregory was either retrieved, very difficult given conditions, maybe killed near the crossroads. One could somewhat follow the roads if going very slow," Sister posited.

Gray, arms across his chest, studied the four sites. "If the body was left under the snow, which remained for the better part of a week, it would be preserved."

"It would." Tootie agreed. "But wouldn't the killer have to come back and get it? In daylight? How could he find it in the dark under the snow?"

"Good question. It might be possible with a ski pole, something like that. Let's say he had a rough idea where the body was and punched around for it or it was inside something. He would still risk being seen. With the workers at Old Paradise, your mother and the Van Dorns driving in and out of Beveridge Hundred, plus Kasmir and Alida at Tattenhall Station, no way could this be done in the daytime."

"Nighttime would be dicey. People do go out at night. A car or a truck parked off the road might be seen and a person poking around near the crossroads with a ski pole would be a dead giveaway. Forgive the pun." Sister put her finger smack on the crossroads. "I say the body was moved during the blizzard."

"That's taking a hell of a chance." Gray sat down and the others did likewise.

"Yes. So whoever this is is very bold, but we were all in that snowstorm. Nature definitely was on his side. If he retrieved the body that fell near the crossroads, he'd need to carry it back to the trailers. He had nowhere else to go," Sister said.

"Tattenhall Station." Weevil threw that out. "Open a door, throw the body in, come back for it later. There have to be places to hide a body in there. We know there's a huge freezer in there."

"You're right." Gray nodded. "Kasmir outfitted that whole kitchen for the club, but we'd moved the breakfast to Boxing Day so he locked Tattenhall."

"Right." Weevil was disappointed, as he thought he'd found the answer.

"Why couldn't the killer drag the body into his trailer? No one was poking around trailers. Then he could take it home or to a freezer somewhere or even bury it under snow at a safer place." Tootie, like everyone, tried to think of all possibilities.

"Given the rate of snowfall, he wouldn't even need to bury the body. He could dump it somewhere and the blizzard would take care of the rest. He'd have to dump it where he could dig it up without prying eyes." Gray considered where to dump a body so no one would know.

"I think we're getting close. So I think either he threw the body in the woods where we found the first hand, came back later. It would be easy to get up there and easy to hide your truck or whatever. The owners live in New York. If a truck drove up that rutted road in the woods, who would know? That's where we found the first hand. Or as Tootie said, he stashed Gregory in his trailer, then off-loaded him to a large freezer." Sister again pointed to those places on the map.

"Chapel Cross really is the hub of it." Gray exhaled. "And I think Rory saw some of this, which makes me believe the body was put onto a trailer. He never made it."

"I think you're right." Sister agreed.

Weevil, head in his hands for a moment, lifted it up. "We all agree you couldn't see the hand in front of your face, speaking of hands." The others nodded and he continued. "What if he wounded or silenced Gregory in some way close to the crossroads. Rode next to him as Gregory and Pokerface were behind Ronnie. As they all approached the chapel, he pulled Gregory off the horse. Pokerface walked with Corporal to the trailer. So did the killer, who then put his horse up as the snow kept everyone occupied, wanting to get out. He crossed the road, dragged the corpse to the almost empty lot, and threw him inside the trailer. We were all together and staff always parks in the same place. He knew where we were. He knows the drill."

"Yes, he does." Sister quietly agreed.

"Which makes this more confusing and frightening. Why cut off Gregory's hands?" Tootie wondered.

"If we knew that, we'd know why he was killed, I think, but we might not know who killed him," Sister added.

Weevil spoke up as Golly patted his hand with her paw, hoping he might rise and get her a treat. "Maybe we have this a little backward. Maybe the hand in the cotton glove, the left hand, was originally at Beveridge Hundred. The ring came off or was pulled off. An animal dragged it to Old Paradise."

A long silence followed this.

Gray then said, "Well, it is more logical that a hand with flesh would be carried than a ring or that the ring would be stripped off at the Carriage House and carried back. I can't think of a wild animal that would carry a ring. Then again, foxes can be peculiar or birds who like bright things might."

"Do you think my mother should be alone in the house? Sam should come over and stay with her. The Van Dorns' house is far enough away that someone could sneak in and out and she doesn't have a dog." Tootie worried.

Sister, who had risen to fetch treats for Golly, the spoiled rotten cat, said, "Yes. That's a very good idea. Would you like to call her or would you want one of us to do it?"

"I think she'll listen to me." Tootie then pulled out her cellphone. "But if she doesn't, I'm handing the phone to you, Sister, and if she still doesn't listen, Gray will talk her into it."

Tootie dialed her mother as the others listened.

"She believes me but she wants to talk to you." Tootie handed the phone to Gray.

"Fishies. Thank you." Golly gobbled her treats as Gray talked to Yvonne.

"Would you like me to call my brother?" A silence followed this as Gray listened. "Of course. I'll do it right now." He handed the phone back, got up, and walked into the library to call his brother on the landline.

The three looked at one another. Then Sister said, "I'm going to call Ben Sidell and ask him to check every hunt club member's big freezer if they have one. Oh, and while I talk to him, Tootie, pull a bowl of cold chicken potpie out of the refrigerator. I'll heat it up when I'm done with Ben."

"I can do that." Tootie walked to the refrigerator, Weevil with her as he took the bowl from her hands.

"How about I do it?" He looked into the bowl. "I'll heat this up and if she wants a piecrust, we'll have to improvise."

"Oh, Sister will be happy with the insides. Me, too." Tootie smiled up at him as she stood by the stove watching him pull out a big pot, which she indicated was stored in the oven.

After a good ten minutes, Gray came back, observed the impromptu supper, got a wonderful loaf of homemade bread from the bread box. Sister did things the old way: bread boxes; crust made from scratch; real butter, not the fake yellow stuff.

Finished talking to Ben, Sister observed the activity. "Weevil, if you give up hunting, you might have a career as a cook."

He smiled his blinding smile. "Oh, I'd just be a short-order cook. Nothing special."

"Those bangers and mash were fabulous." She looked to Gray cutting the bread in thick slices. "Well, I'll fetch drinks. By the way, Ben agrees. He will check freezers. I told him to get the keys from Margaret to the Gulf station or from Arthur, her cousin. Millie had a big freezer in there. He checked outbuildings but he needs to go inside."

Millie DuCharme, married to one of the DuCharme brothers, ran a little café at the Gulf station for years.

"There's only one problem with the freezer search." Gray inhaled the light aroma of the chicken potpie, a good meal for a cold night. "It will tip off the killer."

"You think?" Tootie stirred the potpie while Weevil searched for fresh parsley in the fridge.

"I do. It means we have part of the puzzle put together," Gray replied.

He was right.

CHAPTER 36

For a Thursday the field proved large. Bugden, a new fixture, drew the people wanting to hunt it for the first time. The land, rolling, pleasant, rested east of After All, nudging toward the border with Farmington. The owners intended to build a bed-and-breakfast catering to the hunting crowd since if you stuck a compass point into the center of the property, made a circle of fifty miles, you could hunt with seven packs. Extend that circle to one hundred miles, more hunts than you can count on both hands. One hundred miles, hauling horses, takes about two hours. In a car it's an hour and a half. The young couple with the bed-and-breakfast dreams might make a living out of this yet.

Jefferson Hunt cleared trails, built interesting jumps, all of which pleased Kylie and Christopher Smith. They currently lived in Charlotte, North Carolina, but would move, start building in the spring. The owners of Mousehold Heath, down the road, another young couple, hardworking, rented them a little cottage on their land.

Sister liked having young people in the mix. She especially liked it when they bought property.

The hunt, a few good runs, ended with everyone at the trailers. Betty's yellow Bronco, per usual, held the food, and Walter's truck, the drinks. As it was cold, everyone outside, this wouldn't be a long tailgate.

Every now and then Ronnie Haslip could hunt a weekday fixture. For Kasmir, Dewey, Sam, and others with flexible schedules or their own businesses, a weekday hunt sparked up the day.

Ronnie swore he did better work after a hunt.

Dewey teased him. "How can a lawyer do better work? Everything is precedent. You don't have to create anything."

"You're too harsh. One can interpret laws in new ways. Nothing really is written in stone."

Kasmir joined them. "My freezers have been investigated. How about yours?"

"I don't have one," Ronnie volunteered.

"I do. Two. One at the office and one at home," Dewey told them.

"Why would you have a large freezer at the office?" Ronnie inquired.

"Big staff. Meetings with clients, construction companies. Best to not run out of cold drinks and thank heaven for the microwave. If we need to serve food unexpectedly, we can."

"Dewey, are you running the microwave?" Ronnie lifted one eyebrow.

"No, I am being sexist and encouraging my secretary to do it."

The three men laughed. Then Kasmir said, "It is unusual. Ben Sidell, and by the way, I am impressed with his work, went through everything at Tattenhall Station. I asked him what he hoped to find. He said perhaps a few threads from the coat. As Gregory wore an old English coat, he had hoped that the dye might leave a mark. No colorfast then. Anything, anything at all.

My freezers were of no help but Ben is determined to solve this and I'm glad he is."

"Might take a long time," Dewey remarked. "Real crime isn't like Netflix, know what I mean? Impulsive anger, that's easy but something plotted out, maybe not." Dewey shrugged. "This seems the work of a looney but a looney with brains."

"True." Ronnie agreed. "I wish I had paid more attention to Gregory. You knew him, didn't you?"

"I'd met him at fundraisers but I can't say as I knew him. You had that explosive dinner at Farmington. That was the first time I'd been in his company without tons of people around. I think fundraising is the second-oldest profession. Soliden is generous to many nonprofits, which meant Gregory rarely got a break. Someone was always besieging him."

Ronnie laughed.

"I admire people who run nonprofits. Even if one has a deep endowment, still endless fundraising. And so many of the nonprofits around here are small affairs, horse rescues, saving a pre–Revolutionary War house, that sort of thing. The director of the nonprofit always has her or his hat in his hand," Kasmir noted.

"Milford Enterprises is nowhere near the profits of Soliden, but nonprofit people work it over pretty good. Given the pipeline uncertainty, I am currently of no use to them." Dewey downed his hot coffee. "I need warming from the inside out. Temperature's dropping. The weather report calls for more snow."

"Saw that." Kasmir caught Alida's eye. She came over.

"Nice run once we got on the other side of that stone jump." Alida smiled. "Sister's right to create a variety of jumps. Although putting together a dry-laid jump takes some doing."

"Does. You take them seriously though, don't you?" Ronnie added.

"Anything solid." Kasmir looked up at the sky. "Low clouds. I think the weatherman is right."

"Well, some snow is one thing. A storm like we had for Christmas Hunt, I sure hope not," Dewey mentioned. "Well, that and everything else at Christmas Hunt."

"You know I was talking to Sister. She brought up something I would not have considered." Ronnie leaned forward. "She said whoever strung up Gregory did it before the hunt, in the dark of the early morning, and he was smart and strong. Probably used a pulley."

"Why would she say that about the early morning?" Dewey wondered.

"Because his tongue wasn't down on his chest." Ronnie added this detail. "She said she talked to Ben, who told her the longer a body is hanging, the longer the tongue gets. Gravity just pulls it down."

"That's a vile tidbit." Alida grimaced.

"Is but it's those little details that often lead one to the right conclusion. At least I hope it does," Ronnie said.

"My conclusion is this is about the pipeline. No special insight there." Dewey put his hands around the heavy Styrofoam cup. "Did you read in the papers where Soliden has moved the pipeline farther south?"

"We did." Alida spoke for her and Kasmir.

"I think Gregory was going to do that anyway." Ronnie threw that out. "He knew what a mess it would be going up against Crawford and you, Kasmir. Two powerful men. Then again, it really wasn't the best thought-out route. Too much floodplain, too many historic properties, and then when Crawford brought out the ground-penetrating radar, that did it, although Gregory was gone by then."

"Why didn't Luckham just say so up front?" Alida asked.

"Corporate politics. He had a board to answer to as well as the drilling company, which wants the shortest route possible. As for his senior management, I expect they were with him," Ronnie answered.

"Ronnie, then why kill him?" Dewey asked.

"Damned if I know."

"What would you do if you did?" Dewey looked at him.

"Go to Ben. Look, what evidence we have points to this being someone in our hunt club or someone close. Sooner or later, he'll make a mistake. They always do," Ronnie replied.

"Just so he doesn't make it during a hunt." Alida pulled up the collar of her hunt coat for the temperature was dropping rapidly.

CHAPTER 37

Pale light cast iridescence over the light snow. Watching it, Sister wondered how that could be. Was there enough sunlight behind the clouds to reflect? Whatever it was, the sparkle was beautiful, as was the stillness.

She, Betty, Tootie, and Weevil walked out the hounds Friday morning with Shaker driving behind. He swore he could drive without messing up his neck. As Skiff was working for Crawford, she could only be with him in the evenings and early morning. But Shaker, like most huntsmen, proved tough and determined. Sister watched him climb into the truck without saying a word.

As hounds walked over the road into the wildflower field, one could hear the soft *click, click* of the snow.

Ardent stood up on his hind legs to bat at snowflakes. The other youngsters thought this was a good idea. Hunt staff laughed at their high spirits.

"I like it when it hits my tongue." Aero trotted forward.

"Melts," Audrey replied.

The older hounds walked along happy to be out, thinking the young ones were silly kids but it did look like fun.

Weevil wore Wellies and heavy socks, as did Tootie. Sister wore Thinsulate L.L.Bean hiking boots but she stuffed her pants into the boots. Betty, feet usually hot, also wore a high pair of boots but these were French Le Chameau, terribly expensive but she'd bought them thirty years ago and they were as good as the day she purchased them.

Betty's motto was "You get what you pay for."

As she wasn't a well-to-do woman, she watched her money. If she spent a large amount, the object better be long-lasting; hence the old yellow Bronco.

Shaker hit the horn.

"Hold up," Sister called out. "He's having a fit. He wants us to come back and walk on the road."

"This is one way to keep him from driving." Betty put her hands on her hips, warm in gloves.

Betty had the secret to staying warm, a high metabolism.

"Madam?" Weevil turned to face his Master behind him.

"If he pounds on the steering wheel, that will be worse than his driving. And here I thought I was being smart. Come on, let's turn around and get on the road."

Tootie smiled, looked over at Ardent. "There will be snowflakes everywhere."

"Good!" The small hound smiled.

"Doesn't take much to make you happy." Dreamboat came alongside the little boy. *"I think I'll try it."*

The two of them hopped along side by side as the humans and hounds enjoyed the spectacle.

Tootie moved forward, reaching the wide farm gate first. The snow, only two inches at this point, didn't bunch up under the gate. Tootie unhooked the Kiwi latch, held the gate; all walked through, then she closed the gate.

A jump was up ahead in the fence line but on foot a gate was easier than climbing over. One never realized the true size of a jump until you tried to get over it on foot.

Sister waved at Shaker, who did not wave back. He crept behind them.

A half mile later they reached the bottom of Hangman's Ridge. Not only did they not wish to go up there, it was a climb on foot, it was creepy. It wasn't that easy on horseback, either.

"Let's hold up for a minute." Weevil reached into the tool apron, short, around his waist, fetching cookies.

Calling each hound by name, he handed the animal a cookie.

"Milk-Bones." Dragon complained.

"I like Milk-Bones." Ardent chewed a large one.

"Greenies. I want Greenies," Dragon bitched.

"Greenies are expensive," Pickens said.

"How do you know?" Dragon smarted off.

"I heard Sister and Shaker talk about costs. We get Greenies for special occasions. You're spoiled."

"Got that right." Dasher agreed.

"Bugger off." Dragon growled, then left the hound circle, veering slightly off the road as the others, sitting, watched him.

"Dragon!" Weevil knew how hardheaded this hound was.

Give him an inch and he would take a mile. Some animals are like that.

"Horn. Deer horn." Dragon grabbed what he thought was an antler piece.

"What the hell?" Betty stepped toward the hound.

"It's a crop, a stag-handled crop under the snow." Tootie wondered how it got there.

"Dragon, I'll take that now." Weevil held out his hand and Dragon turned his head sideways so he wouldn't have to look Weevil in the eye.

Sister walked up to him, grabbed the crop. "Drop it."

He did. *"It's mine. I found it."*

"This is beautiful. Two silver collars." Sister held the large crop in her hand, then turned it. "There are engraved initials on the top collar, the widest collar."

Betty, not worried about the hounds for they were good hounds despite Dragon's attitude, came over to inspect. "G.E.L."

"What's it doing here?" Tootie, surprised as were they all, blurted out.

"I have no idea but I'll stand here, well, wait—that might not work. Don't know when Ben can get here. Weevil, give me your lad's cap."

Sweeping it off his head, he handed it to Sister. She walked over to where Dragon found the crop, placed his hat there.

"I'll get you a new one. You all take the hounds back to the kennel. I'm going to call Ben Sidell from the truck." She hurried to the truck, opened the door, reaching for the phone, an old phone but serviceable, affixed under the dash.

The others could see her dialing as she was talking to Shaker.

Hounds, aware of the emotions, quietly went back to the kennel, where Weevil, Tootie, and Betty put them up.

"We can't all fit in the old hound truck. Come on, get in the Bronco. We can wait on the road for Ben."

The snow continued to fall. Sister and Shaker sat in the truck as the Bronco sat behind them.

Twenty minutes later Ben, driving a sheriff's department SUV, pulled behind the Bronco, cut the motor, got out as Betty, Weevil, and Tootie also got out.

Sister, seeing them, also opened the door.

"Here."

Ben examined the crop. "Show me where you found it."

Except for Shaker, they walked down the road to the spot where Dragon pulled it off the ground, Weevil's hat keeping the deer antler outline in the snow covered.

Ben knelt down, stood back up. "This would make more sense if you'd found it on the other side of the ridge."

"Yes." Sister agreed. "If anyone had driven up the ridge before the hunt here, we would have known. To put the body up he had to come from the other side in the dark. This is almost as if it's been cast aside."

Looking at the crop again, Ben nodded. "No tooth marks. Not that I can see. The team will look it over."

"We found the body. Everyone had to come down this side of the ridge. Well, they went up this side, too. Obviously, there was confusion, distress. Anyone could have walked back here, I suppose, to drop it. What was he doing with it in the first place?"

"Sister, if I knew that, I'd be a lot closer to solving this mess." Ben sighed. "Do you think you'll hunt tomorrow?"

"I hope so. The snow's supposed to stop. We might get a few flurries tomorrow but if there's any way, you know I'll go. It's from Tattenhall Station. I hope you can hunt tomorrow."

"I'll be there."

"It's occurring to me that maybe, and this is a beautiful crop, he couldn't bear to part with it. Then realized he must. Who among us would go up and look at the collars of an old, beautiful crop? Crawford has one with gold collars."

"He would." Ben looked closely at the crop.

"Whoever this is took off Gregory's boots. Apart from knowing quality, he, well, I think he's supremely confident we'd never think of who it is."

Ben leaned against Shaker's truck for a moment and the injured huntsman ran down the window. "Sheriff."

"Good to see you, Shaker. This is odd, isn't it?"

"Odd. Gruesome. Almost like he's playing with us."

"Yes." Ben agreed.

The others crowded around.

Betty asked, "Any luck with freezers?"

"No. I sent out my team. Members of the hunt club have been cooperative. Margaret got the keys to the Gulf station. I'd hoped that might be the place but no."

"Is it possible the body was wrapped in plastic, something like that, so no fibers or hair would come off? Even one strand of hair would do it," Weevil asked.

"It is. This is an intelligent person," Ben replied. "Well, I'll take this back. Who picked it up?"

"Dragon. So there might be his tooth marks but I couldn't see any chewing marks. I don't think any other animal found it," Sister said.

Ben peered closely at the crop. "Cost about four hundred dollars new?"

"Yes, the two silver collars make it expensive. An antique one would be expensive, as well. All the fine braiding on the shaft adds to the cost," Sister added.

"Don't forget the kangaroo thong and the cracker," Weevil noted. "All put together, this is worth about one thousand dollars. That's if it's a staff thong." He looked again. "This one's shorter. Would cost maybe three hundred just for the shorter thong. Must have upset him to part with it, so about seven hundred dollars."

"Arrogant. Didn't think we'd notice and you know what, we didn't. Then he thought better of it," Betty replied.

"Well, we don't go up and inspect people's gear," Sister responded. "It's the arrogant part that scares me."

What also disturbed her was she was observant and logical. She could usually figure things out. Granted, she was not used to solving murders regularly, but still. She felt stupid. A ripple of fear coursed through her. What she didn't know could hurt her.

CHAPTER 38

Powdery snow rested on the ground. Two and a half inches would allow all creatures to easily move. The sky promised more flurries.

Staff eagerly awaited everyone at the trailers to mount up since conditions favored long runs once scent was found. Given those conditions, the fact that the season would be over in five weeks plus morbid curiosity, anyone who was upright hunted today at Tattenhall Station.

"They take too long," Aztec complained.

Outlaw, next to him, snorted. *"Want to take bets on who comes off today?"*

"No." Aztec felt the reins loose on his neck. *"It's amazing some of them stay on. Look at how a few of them have put on weight. If they go off they'll never get back up."*

"Christmas. They stuff themselves like pigs. Not all of them but a few. Then spring draws near and they start these awful diets."

"Luckily, Sister stays the same." Aztec looked around. *"What are they doing back there?"*

"Putting on spurs," Outlaw replied. *"Makes them think they have control. Hey, if I want to go, I'll go. If not, you can't make me. Of course, I love Betty. She never asks me to do anything foolish."*

"Same here but sometimes things happen. Like Showboat locking up. He's a good horse. He likes Shaker. The smell just locked him up."

Outlaw pawed the snow. *"Dead stuff. I'm not saying I like that smell but dead human stuff smells different."*

Aztec considered this. *"Maybe so, but here's the thing. If it's dead, it isn't going to hurt you. I'd be a lot more frightened of a mountain lion."*

Outlaw stopped pawing, started to agree with his friend, then sighed with relief. *"Thank God. They're all mounted."*

"Good day. Just feels right." Aztec moved forward as Sister pressed lightly with her leg.

"Hope so." Outlaw obeyed Betty's instructions. *"We can compare notes back at the trailers."*

Weevil headed for Old Paradise as Crawford, riding up front with Sister, had agreed to a joint meet. He needed to get his hounds out. They hunted well with Jefferson Hounds.

Skiff rode next to Weevil, who carried the horn for both packs. He offered this honor to her but she thought hunting with this large a field would be useful for him.

Shaker, in the car with Yvonne and Aunt Daniella, kept up a running commentary that the ladies vowed never to repeat.

Sam agreed to whip-in, which he usually did for Skiff. He took Weevil's former position as tail whip. He could have stood on ceremony, rode with Tootie or Betty—he was entitled—but he wanted to make sure the pack would hold together.

The first jump in Crawford's fence line, all new stone fencing, was easily cleared. The jump was the same height as the exorbitantly expensive stone fence, except the stone top was six inches lower. On this depression was laid a log. If a horse rubbed the jump, their hooves wouldn't touch stone but wood, which was just a bit more forgiving.

"I'll stay away from the buildings if I can," Weevil told Skiff.

"Good idea. We've got a fox in the old stable. There are others under some of the outbuildings. If we hit a line it's possible we'll wind up at the outbuildings, but no reason to start there."

He nodded, put his horn to his lips, and blew "Lieu in" as well as saying it.

Hounds eagerly rushed to a small thicket in a tight roll of the land near the road. Weevil's idea was to head south, then, after covering all of Old Paradise, to move west to the woods' edge.

No need, for hounds found the scent immediately. Snow like talcum powder flew off horses' hooves. The ground underneath remained frozen although the mercury was to climb into the low forties, so the firmness probably wouldn't last long.

Running hard, hounds hooked left, some jumped over a roll jump while others leapt over the stone fence. Once the work of the building restoration was complete, Crawford intended to return to stone fencing, creating stone fences everywhere. Now the stone was at the road's edge where everyone could see it. He wanted everything in stone, whether a border fence or a small paddock. It would be impressive, beautiful, and cost a fortune. This jump, three feet high, was deceptive, because it was wide, a bracing two feet wide. The horse had to have a bit of scope and boldness to go over this jump. Few had encountered anything like it. Crawford enjoyed creating various jumps.

Aztec saw the wideness, took off just a hair early and big. Sister rode it out. She could have forced him to take off at the spot she thought best, but she truly trusted him so if he took off big, okay.

As luck would have it, the hunted fox had doubled back, so no sooner was Sister over than the two packs turned, heading straight for her. She held up on one side of the fence, as did the field on the other side. Weevil jumped over, then Sam. Sister turned, following him. Aztec picked the right spot. No need to leave early for he now knew this somewhat unusual, new jump.

Once over, Sister effortlessly breezed past the standing field. They turned, falling in behind her, with Tedi and Edward in her pocket, Kasmir and Alida behind them, Ronnie and Dewey and on down the line of First Flight. People placed themselves according to status, not that that was said, their ability and the ability of their horse. Riding tail, Walter again assumed those duties.

Sam, just ahead of Sister, asked for more speed. Sister did likewise for the pack was pulling away. The fox was heading for the outbuilding, visible in the distance.

Crawford, a decent rider but not the strongest, began to fade back a bit. Gray moved up alongside him.

All of a sudden, hounds stopped. They cast themselves, skidding down into a small ravine that opened up on flatter meadows.

In the crevice, the deeper snow slowed them down. Thor, a big Dumfriesshire hound, called out. *"Stay in the crevice. I know this fox. He'll climb out toward the north."*

Sister, on the edge, followed. No point in trapping yourself and others in this fold of the land.

Sure enough, the fox had exited heading north toward the chapel crossroads that lay three and a half miles down the road from this spot. The field was running on the snow-covered pastures. Sister kept her eyes on the pack. This pattern, different, announced a new fox, perhaps a visiting fox. Anything goes.

A light breeze swept down the side of the mountains, enough to make the tree branches sway. Hounds stood out against the snow. Crawford's were black and tan whereas most of hers were tricolor. Weevil and Skiff hung right behind them. Betty, far on the right, was already heading for a jump in the fence line that would put her on Chapel Road. Tootie on the left made for the driveway into the main buildings. She'd need to turn down the road, but she would be in a good position if the fox turned toward the mountains.

A tidy coop beckoned. Hounds soared over it, some simply jumping the stone fence. Then Weevil, then Skiff, a slight gap, Sam on Trocadero smoothly took the fence. Sister, in her eagerness, had drawn a bit close to Sam. She rated Aztec, pissed him off, then when Sam was clear and ahead she urged him over. She could hear the field behind her.

Hounds, up ahead, ran right in the middle of the road, crossed into the churchyard. The entire pack was behind the church screaming while Adolfo Vega cleaned off the steps up to the church for service tomorrow. He leaned on his snow shovel to watch.

Sister paused for a moment. She couldn't lead the field over the front of the church. The ground, still somewhat hard, was dicey enough. If there were any soft spots, she'd tear it up. So she slowed, trotted all the way around the main building, white, so simple, so beautiful. The gold cross gleamed from the blue steeple. Our forefathers exhibited a marvelous and restrained aesthetic sense. Much as she shared that sense, she wanted to get with her hounds, so she squeezed Aztec to trot faster and she looped around all the buildings, trying to keep where she thought the edge of the grass would be. Finally, she emerged at the graveyard, hound at every tombstone or so it seemed. Weevil and Skiff, off to the side, watched.

The two huntsmen couldn't go into the graveyard, nor could Sister. There was enough snow to cover the flagstones. One step on that could be ugly thanks to slippery snow. Worse, the horse's weight could crack the stones, many dating back to the 1820s. The standing tombstones outlined in snow looked either peaceful or mournful, depending on one's temperament.

Shaker's temperament was not peaceful. Sitting in the backseat, for no one would possibly displace Aunt Daniella, he was fulminating.

"That fox will circle. I'm telling you. Those two damn kids better head for the road."

"You know this fox?" Aunt Daniella inquired.

"Yes and no. But the fox, no matter who he is, and it has to be a male as it's breeding season, is smart enough to use these tombstones, so I'm thinking he's local enough to baffle the hounds. He's a red, running straight for the most part. A gray would have turned by now."

Neither of the ladies would refute the color of the fox nor the animal's intelligence.

"There's one of our hounds heading out," Yvonne excitedly said.

"Old Asa. He's dipped in gold." Shaker sat on the edge of the seat.

One by one, the Jefferson Hounds moved out of the cemetery as the Crawford pack began to mingle with them.

Sister and Crawford sat still. No one knew what would happen next, but as if hearing Shaker, Weevil and Skiff had ridden out to the road. Hounds milled about, then a deep roar by Balzac, Crawford's hound, sent them all back to the crossroads.

Crawford, with pride, looked at Sister. "Balzac. A hunting man, you know."

"Yes, I do." Sister smiled for the hound was good. "You've named this hound well."

The two of them turned, fell in behind Sam, and reached the crossroads. Hounds ran right down the middle of the road. Fortunately, there was little traffic out here, but no one wanted to fly on a macadam road covered with snow. Ben Sidell, back with Bobby Franklin, thanked the angels for his horse, Nonni, sure-footed and smart. She stopped for a split second, turned her nose toward the mountain, and Ben, out of the corner of his eye, saw the streak of red shifting through a narrow covert.

Counting to twenty, he then called out loudly, "Tallyho." His hat, in his hand, arm pointed in the direction he had seen the fox, told the huntsman the direction in which their quarry was running.

Second Flight often sees the fox, so Weevil and Skiff, hearing the cry, immediately ramped up the speed heading in the direction of Ben's outstretched arm.

Hounds screamed. Horses were full throttle. So was the fox, realizing he had to get out of there.

Across the snow-covered pastures they all flew, a scene that could have been from prior centuries. Dots of scarlet here and there, tails flying on the weazlebellys, a few hats already swaying on the hat cord behind the ladies wearing derbies. Most people wore hunt caps securely shoved down or even secured with a chin strap. But the die-hards wore their gorgeous shining top hats or reinforced derbies, which usually were quite secure. Derbies banged behind backs. They were all moving far too fast to pull up a derby. Who cared? The pace was too good.

The screaming raised the hair on the back of people's necks. You could tell people about the feeling, but until they experienced it themselves they never quite believed it. Your blood was up, as was your horse's.

For over three and a half miles, those familiar miles, the pack charged hard. The fox made straight for the restored stable, ducked into a hole, as there was a fox who lived there. He stuck right there, deep down as Earl, the proprietor, bitched and moaned.

"What do you think you're doing?"

Breathing hard, the medium-sized red, Mr. Nash, replied, *"Saving my ass."*

The stable fox heard the entire pack, he'd heard them anyway, moved into the deep part of his den, confronted the intruder. *"You can't underestimate those hounds. They know the territory and they have good noses. What did you think you were doing?"*

Mr. Nash followed Earl as he led him through his extensive underground network to come out in a corner of the tack room behind a tack trunk. *"This is something."*

"Better yet, the place is full of workmen and they leave food. Good food. No one thinks to look in the tack room. They know I have a den back in one of the stalls. Every now and then someone fills it up with sawdust and dirt. I just clean it out but I have a lot of ways in and out. But you didn't answer my question. What are you doing here?"

"Looking for a girlfriend. I live up at Close Shave. It's nice enough but nothing like this."

Earl sat on a plush lamb's fleece saddle pad. *"It is impressive. But girls, most of the girls are taken but there's a young one over at Mud Fence. Still close to her parents' den but you could see if she's interested. My experience is the young girls wait a year. They often stick close to home and help with the next litter but you never know."*

"You're not interested?" Mr. Nash was curious.

"Not this year." Earl listened to the two huntsmen speak to their hounds. *"Heading off. Good. Girls, yes, well, I find vixens wonderful, of course, but then they have the babies and you exhaust yourself feeding the little buggers. Taking a year off."*

As Mr. Nash had yet to become a father, he remained silent about that. He cocked his head, hearing the field move off now.

Earl advised. *"Don't pop out yet. Diana, one of the Jefferson Hounds, is really smart. She could double back very quickly and check again. The huntsman trusts her, so she won't be pushed back into the pack. Of course, now there's a new huntsman. Young."*

"Gris told me the regular fellow hit his head over a human hand."

"Ah yes, Gris, the town crier," remarked Earl, who could gossip

with the best of them. *"So you have traveled as far as Chapel Cross before today?"*

"Just."

"You know what amuses me? Heard there was so much fuss over that human hand, another one was found in the Carriage barn. So what's a human part? We can be splayed out on the roadway. Doesn't seem to bother them a bit."

Mr. Nash agreed. *"They are strange creatures."*

As these two became better acquainted, Weevil and Skiff decided to move across the road to Beveridge Hundred, drawing along the way.

A short burst pulled them through the edge of Old Paradise as light snow began to fall. Given their workout no one felt the cold right then, plus most people watched the weather report so they wore their thermal underwear, some layers of silk for others and Sister's favorite trick, wearing an old white cashmere turtleneck over which she tied her stock tie. A thermal shirt, then the ancient cashmere, toasty warm. Her feet and hands, though, tingled with the cold. As Aztec, enlivened, surged forward, she felt that telltale ache in her toes. No matter, the day was too good.

The barn owl at Beveridge Hundred, ears very keen, heard the distant singing of the hounds. At a foot and a half she could take care of herself, not that she worried about hounds hunting her. She liked the hayloft in the tidy small barn, never bothering to build a nest. She was happy on the wood. Given her feathers she stayed warm. One of the reasons she liked Beveridge Hundred was its quiet. The older people rarely walked out to the barn anymore and certainly not in winter. Enough mice kept her full but she especially liked hunting the cemetery at the chapel, full of mice. She thought if they were Christian mice she was sending them to the great mouse in the sky. Why mice liked cemeteries she didn't know, but she took advantage of it. She also liked the stable because she could visit with Sarge, the young fox. He seemed a little naive but he was young. She enjoyed sharing her wisdom of which she thought she had quite a lot.

She flew up to walk along a crossbeam where she could peer out the small louvered slats at the peak of the roof. She didn't see the fox or any fox, but she could see the entire two packs hunting as one heading right for Beveridge Hundred. She looked to the side, she looked down, nothing to entice those miserable hounds. And the doors were closed. Good.

Hounds rushed up to the stable, circled it once, twice. The fox must have done that to throw them off for no den existed in the stable. Then they took off, turning back north in the direction of Tattenhall Station. The people on horseback waited for a moment at the stable. Then they, too, took off.

The owl observed First Flight go, followed by Second Flight. One man from First Flight hung back.

"Dewey, problem?" Bobby Franklin asked.

"Thought I'd answer Nature's call behind the stable." Dewey smiled as he dismounted.

The others moved off, picking up speed as hounds opened.

Dewey, however, did not answer Nature's call. He carefully walked around the stable, peering at the ground. The ground protected by the overhang was not covered in snow. The falling snow was light.

He then tied Bosco to the railing by an old water trough, hurrying over to Yvonne's cottage dependency. He bent over, peering into the bottom of the doghouse, rose, brushed off his knees, hurried back to Bosco, mounted up, and rode off.

Crawling down the state road, Shaker noticed Dewey trying to catch up, as did Yvonne and Daniella.

"Dewey's always been helpful. When Mercer was alive they'd talk about Thoroughbred syndicates and Dewey said he'd try it with real estate. Certainly worked," Aunt Daniella remarked.

"Syndicates can be tricky," Yvonne added. "Victor bought the first television stations with syndicates. We managed with difficulty to eventually buy out the other partners, but what a bitch, I can tell you. I worked the charm offensive overtime."

"Ah, took you two minutes." Shaker teased her.

"He still calling? Your ex?" Yvonne's eyebrows lifted up.

"Not me. He calls Tootie. My prediction is Victor's lost a lot of money. This will take time. Give it another six months or a year. Then he'll call me pretending the divorce was a mistake. I haven't lost money."

"That's good news." The old lady smiled.

"Now what are they doing?" Shaker half stood up.

"Sit down," Yvonne commanded. "If I have to hit the brakes hard, I'll hurt your neck."

"Damn my neck. I am so sick of this." Shaker cursed. "But look at the pack. A tight circle. I want to get out and look for tracks."

"You'll do no such thing." Aunt Daniella put her foot down. "Sister would have our hides if we let you do that."

"There have to be tracks but we haven't seen anything. To hear a roar like that, I expect this scent is fresh." He looked out the window. "Then again, conditions are really, really good. It might be twenty minutes old but no more than that. I've told Skiff to always look for tracks."

"She is." Yvonne stuck up for Skiff, who was looking down.

"Dewey better stop. If that fox shot back straight, Dewey will be in the middle of it. I'd cuss him like a dog. I don't think Weevil will."

"Dewey knows hunting, doesn't he?" Yvonne asked.

"Oh he does, but not as much as he thinks he does. Most people in the field, even if they've hunted for years, don't know but so much." Shaker sniffed. "Never look at hound bloodlines either."

"Well now, Shaker, that's unfair. For most of them that would be like reading Greek." Yvonne stuck up for the field. "What you do takes study, time, and I can't imagine how many packs of hounds you have studied or hunted behind. Most people don't have that kind of time or the eye. Then again, Shaker, this is your profession."

That shut him up for a bit.

Aunt Daniella smiled. "Oh, he has pulled up."

Dewey indeed stood stock-still and Bosco wasn't happy about it.

"Dewey's done well, hasn't he?" Yvonne knew a bit of people's histories but only so much.

"He has. There are quite a few people in the hunt and I've known many of them since they were children who really didn't come from much, but I tell you what, they all went to college and made something of themselves. That's why I was so upset, upset hell, devastated when Sam blew Harvard."

A silence followed this as both Shaker and Yvonne knew the story and both felt and said that Sam had turned his life around. Was he going back to Harvard in his sixties? No, but he lived a useful life. Maybe even a better life than if he had graduated. Who is to say?

Aunt Daniella broke her own silence. "I know. I can't let it go. I should. If my sister were here we could talk it through. Oh, if you could have only known him as a little boy. I'd call him my milkshake boy because he was the color of a milkshake." She took a breath. "Odd but both my sister and myself had sons who were a tad darker than we were."

"Mattered then." Yvonne stopped as the field was circling and she didn't know what they would do next.

"Matters now," Aunt Daniella replied.

"Do you really think it does?" Shaker asked in all innocence.

"Maybe not as much, but it still helps to be light. Momma used to say the whiter we looked, the easier life would be."

"Aunt Daniella, you could have been as black as a true Ethiopian and you would have conquered. Those fabulous cheekbones, your sexual allure. I mean here you are in your nineties and men still turn their heads." Yvonne praised her.

"Well"—then Daniella laughed—"it's not see what you get, it's make what you get worth seeing."

Shaker laughed as did Yvonne. "Seeing what you get. They've turned again. Back to Chapel Cross."

First Flight trotted but slowly, for scent had become spotty. Second Flight, behind, had grown larger as some people from First Flight dropped back, for the hunt had been tiring. Dewey wended his way through Second Flight until immediately behind Bobby Franklin.

"May I go forward to First Flight?"

"Of course."

Dewey picked up a trot, Bosco sure-footed on the falling snow, which was becoming slippery.

Hounds slowly worked in the direction of the old train station. Balzac, next to Tatoo, stopped.

"What?" Tatoo asked.

"He's turned but it's faint." Balzac lifted his head. *"Trudy, check this out."* Then he informed Tatoo, *"She has a bit of a cold nose."*

"Ah." Tatoo understood, for a cold nose could pick up faint scent, which was only a good thing if other hounds could just catch it.

Otherwise the cold-nosed hound would open and not be honored, a frustrating outcome for all.

Trudy put her nose down. *"It's him but he's fading. Curious."*

If this hunt had gone by the textbooks, the line should have been heating up. This fox either possessed mojo or had walked across something to foul his scent.

"He's turned," Trudy called out as her houndmates ran to her.

Crawford's hounds talked among themselves so Jefferson Hunt Hounds joined them as Weevil and Skiff watched.

Walking, the pack continued moving westward across the large pasture, trees dotting the land. They reached the road, Crawford's land across it, in time to see a herd of deer gracefully lope toward the Carriage House in the far distance. Hounds paid no attention.

Sister pulled up as hounds stopped.

"Come on, good hounds. You can do it." Weevil encouraged them.

Banjo, another of Crawford's B litter, turned south alongside the road. He poked around as did his friends for twenty yards, then they opened at once.

Flying. It was 0 to 60 faster than a 911 Turbo.

Ronnie, taking a swig from his flask, nearly dropped his flask, then nearly dropped himself. Dewey on Bosco moved alongside him, grabbed the flask from his hand.

"You'll thank me for this." Dewey secreted the flask in his coat between the first and the second button.

"Took you long enough to get back."

"I lingered."

"Well, we aren't lingering now."

Those left in First Flight hugged the fence line on Kasmir's side for the fox seemed to have run alongside of it.

Five minutes, ten minutes, more people began to falter. Sister and Aztec stayed behind the hounds. Kasmir and Alida, Sam, Gray, Freddie, the tough riders on hunting-fit horses hung in there, but others, due to exhaustion or age, slowed a bit. The fox did not.

They wound up in woods again, the tree branches brushed, dumping snow on them, especially the firs.

Yvonne turned around in the middle of the road. No traffic

so that was easy. Shaker, nose pressed against the windowpane, watched for a flash of red.

Then hounds lost again. Everyone stood, grateful for the break. The snow fell a bit heavier, the sound of the flakes on the pine trees distinct. Snow found its way down coat collars, too.

Sister, alert, trusted her instincts, which told her the fox would return to Beveridge Hundred where he had more choices than being in the middle of a pasture or even crossing over to Old Paradise. Buildings and outbuildings offered escapes as well as scent spoilers, plus this was closer than Old Paradise.

The soft rattle of light wind in the tree branches, the faint patter of the snow filled Sister's senses. Hounds worked to find scent. Standing there, waiting, one was reminded of how ravishing Nature is in her changing wardrobe.

Dreamboat's stern moved. He'd come back out on the narrow path as the other hounds wound around tree trunks, poked noses into anything resembling a bolt hole. An angry click notified Pookah that one of those small holes in the tree trunk was occupied.

"Crabby." The hound stepped back.

Pickens, next to his littermate, smiled, kept his nose down, then heard Dreamboat.

"Here," the reliable hound called out as the others moved to him.

Weevil, trusting Dreamboat, on Shaker's Kilowatt today, watched with rising anticipation. Tootie, ahead but waiting, also listened, as did Betty on the other side. Although easier to see in the woods during winter, the large number of conifers meant there were places where you couldn't see. There was even a stand of large blue spruces, untouched for nearly a century, the snow intensifying their color.

Hounds milled about, a large circle both on and off the path.

"Let's go." Zorro found where the line was still good.

Hounds took off. Humans, full of breath thanks to the respite, followed them.

Scent held; although it faded in and out, it still held. Hounds moved along, trotting. No point running or one would overrun the line. The older hounds knew this and the younger ones had learned it through cubbing in the fall.

The wind picked up. Not strong but about ten miles an hour. Enough to make keeping one's nose on the line an act of concentration. Wind can blow scent. Hounds make up for this by alertness. A stiff wind, though, creates problems. That's when the huntsman has to figure out where the line might be, assuming it's still operable.

Both Weevil and Skiff moved closer, anticipating stronger wind. One never knew this close to the mountains and one never knew about wind devils either.

Hounds steadily pushed. Cry grew louder. The pace picked up. They worked beautifully. Staff was thrilled. The field was happy to be moving on for the wind was starting to cut. A few realized what outstanding hound work this was. So many in the flights couldn't see what hounds were doing. And even then many didn't understand the conditions under which hounds tried for them.

A slow gallop brought them closer and closer to Beveridge Hundred. A few outbuildings promised refuge, or so the huntsmen hoped, but no, fox kept going. But where?

Hounds barreled past the outbuildings. Millie, sitting at the window, saw them. She managed a bark.

Hounds looked up as they passed the old dog sitting in her window seat. She emitted another bark. Hounds filed past the house in a schoolyard line, noses down. Weevil and Skiff behind them stepped carefully. Shrubs close to the house sat amidst buried bulbs. One could just see the edging on those gardens.

The field, forty yards back at this point, also walked carefully.

Hounds trotted slowly. The line was holding but weaving in

and out. Hounds stopped every now and then to check. The fox circled the small barn but did not go into the small dug entrance at the end. Hounds then crossed over the farm road, walked behind the tidy garage for the dependency. Then they headed straight for Yvonne's house and the doghouse. He'd been here, too. Yvonne, waiting at the end of the driveway, didn't want to get in the way. No one knew where this fellow was heading and she thought best to sit on the road.

"You got a fox there?" Shaker asked.

"A visiting fox. I don't think one lives by the houses," she answered.

"But foxes are there?"

"I see them. A gray and then a small red who visits me almost every day."

"H-m-m." Shaker rubbed his chin, wishing he could shave.

Hounds walked back to the small stable, stopped again.

"Fan out. He came back. He has to have moved off from here. He's far enough ahead of us he has time to," Diana paused. *"Found it."*

She opened, whipped around, going straight out the driveway. Hounds crossed in front of Yvonne, Aunt Daniella, and Shaker. Then Weevil, Skiff, and Sam followed. After that it was the two flights and just when Yvonne was ready to take her foot off the brake they all turned, ran in front of her again, turned and headed west again.

"I'm dizzy." Yvonne laughed.

"Clever boy, this fox." Shaker would have nodded if he could. "Yvonne, sit tight for a little bit. I'll give you even odds that he'll turn and if he does, this time we might view."

Ronnie, back at the small stable, had dismounted when the field took off. It was his turn to answer Nature's call. Dewey volunteered to hold his horse. If hounds hit big, Pokerface would have left Ronnie flat. To hell with the human, hounds are in full chorus.

"Thank God for bushes." Ronnie sighed as he relieved himself. "You know, Dewey, I'm surprised more foxhunters don't get bladder infections."

"Bet we do and we don't tell. Come on, hurry up."

"Wait a minute." Ronnie bent down to check a gleam under a tight boxwood.

The Van Dorns, decades ago, planted English boxwoods everywhere thinking the waxy green would show to good effect.

"Ronnie, hounds are opening."

"I found something. Hold your horses."

"I'm holding your horse, dammit," Dewey fired back.

Ronnie, quiet, slipped the cigarette case he had found in the boxwoods into his coat pocket. He mounted up.

"Let's go." Dewey squeezed Bosco and blew out of there.

Ronnie followed, both men pulling up as they saw Yvonne's car. She waved them on.

A jump, not far, allowed them to get over into the southernmost part of Old Paradise. Hounds bellowed now, deep tones, light baritones, basso profundos, a tenor here and there, and a squeal or two from a youngster. Even the female hounds sang out with full, deep voices. For the foxhunters this was as beautiful as Bach's Mass in B Minor.

They galloped, snow stinging a little as it hit faces. Old Paradise, enormous with many open pastures as well as the now-discovered graves hidden in woods, was a foxhunter's dream. On and on they ran, people falling back. Staff thanking the Lord for fit Thoroughbreds underneath them.

This same prayer was uttered by field members. A few crossbreds hung in there, perfectly conditioned. But on long, hard runs and over time, the Thoroughbred usually had the advantage. The animal was bred to run. A Thoroughbred gave you everything they had. Other horses, smarter perhaps, did not.

Hounds, flat out, covered those miles from the jump to the

Carriage House in under twenty minutes. Twenty minutes over uneven ground, patchy footing, a steady wind blowing just enough snow in their eyes to make them squint. Same with the horses and humans.

Those miles on the flat would have been covered faster. In this territory, staff put on the afterburners, snow and mud flying underfoot, rating one's horse to motor down a tricky swale here and there, blowing across small streams for the land was well watered.

Finally, hounds stopped right at the Carriage House. A den entrance by the southeast corner showed where he had ducked in. This fellow, new, had claimed the Carriage House. Hounds dug at the den.

Skiff jumped off, throwing her reins over her horse's neck. As she knew this place better than Weevil, she took over.

She blew "Gone to Ground," praised and petted each hound as Weevil stood by her horse. No need to reach for the reins, the animal was well trained, enjoying the horn notes as much as everyone else including the fox. No more running today.

Dewey, next to Ronnie, at the rear of First Flight, reached into his coat, handing Ronnie back his flask filled with Kentucky bourbon. Before completely handing it over, Dewey took a sip.

"Not Maker's Mark. Umm, you do this. You put in a different bourbon each hunt and if we take a sip we have to identify it. I'll take another. Ah. Woodford Reserve."

Ronnie relieved Dewey of the flask, slipping it in its leather holder on the right front of his saddle. "Is this what you were looking for?" He reached into his coat, pulled out a gold cigarette case, handing it to Dewey with the bold roman initials on the front: G.E.L.

Dewey allowed Ronnie to drop the expensive, masculine cold case in his hand.

Ronnie continued. "You didn't really need to go to the bathroom when you stopped. Why did you do it, Dewey? I can't understand. What was the danger to you? How could you kill someone?"

Dewey stared at Ronnie, put the case in his pocket, then turned Bosco toward the buildings, toward the mountains behind.

"Stop him," Ronnie yelled.

Sister, seeing that Dewey was going to pass her, forbidden on the hunt field anyway, moved out to block him. He pushed by her and tried to backhand her as he picked up a gallop.

Tootie, in the clear on the left, saw this. She saw Dewey try to hit Sister and went straight for him. The hounds were fine. She wasn't thinking about them.

Dewey, now pursued, looked back. He reached farther into his coat where he was wearing a gun and holster well hidden. He pulled out the pistol and fired at Tootie. Missed.

Ben Sidell, in Second Flight, hearing a shot, immediately moved out of the pack to see if he could see what happened. He did. He called HQ for backup.

Weevil, hearing the shot, saw Tootie pursue Dewey. That fast he was flying on Kilowatt. Dewey, chased by two young, superb riders, asked for a bit more from good old Bosco, who was doing his best but the staff closed in. He fired again. Missed again, thanks to the bobbing of Bosco.

Weevil pulled up next to Tootie, yelled. "Go back. I'll take care of him."

"No." She rode right with him.

Realizing he couldn't hit the broad side of a barn in these conditions, Dewey reached the back side of Old Paradise's living places. The old sequestered cemetery was there, the tombstones large and showy. He dismounted from Bosco. He knew the land. If he could stop Tootie and Weevil, he figured he could elude the field long enough to disappear into the thick woods at the bottom of the mountains. He'd take his chances in there.

Ducking behind Sophie's obelisk, he fired again. This time

he was close. Weevil, no fear, urged Kilowatt to untapped reserves of speed while Tootie moved up also. As they neared the obelisk they parted, she to the left and he to the right.

Dewey figured he had them. He calmly rested the Smith & Wesson on his left forearm, staying behind the tomb. He heard hoofbeats but figured he had time to wheel and nail them both. Tootie roared up behind him, snapped her whip's thong around his chest, and pulled. It was enough to throw him off balance. Weevil, now upon him, leaned over Kilowatt's side, grabbing Dewey by the shoulders. Now both men were on the ground. Dewey, enraged, was large and powerful but not quick.

Weevil, strong although not in Dewey's class, grabbed his right wrist, trying to get the gun from his hand. Tootie, now off Iota, joined in. She kicked Dewey hard in the face. The pain made him loosen his grip. Weevil had the gun but not Dewey, who rose, trying to run off.

Not even thinking about it, Weevil fired, hitting him in the back of the leg. He dragged himself forward. Weevil readied to fire again when he heard Ben's voice.

"Hold it, Weevil. I'll take over." Ben reached Dewey, who stopped hobbling.

Sister held the field back at the Carriage House.

Skiff and Betty brought the hounds around and waited, knowing Weevil and Tootie would never leave hounds unless it was critical.

Yvonne drove up and would have known nothing if Ronnie, shaken, hadn't seen fit to tell her. Yvonne drove over the grounds, swung around the back of the house and then the graveyard. She cut the motor, jumped out of the car.

"Tootie. Tootie." She ran to her daughter, being held by Weevil.

The two staff members clung to each other, tears in both their eyes.

Yvonne stopped.

Tootie, a smile now on her face, said, "We brought him down together, Mom."

"She got him first." Weevil released her, shaking a bit, hoping no one noticed.

In the distance two sirens were heard.

"We'd better get back to the hounds." Tootie pulled herself together.

Aunt Daniella and Shaker out of the car now noted, "Skiff and Betty have them."

Shaker, not terribly interested in Dewey, no matter what he'd done or why he'd run, bragged. "Some hound work."

This made Tootie and Weevil laugh. Weevil reached for her hand. She didn't withdraw it.

"I can't believe you jumped him when he had his gun leveled at you."

"But he didn't. You got him with your whip." Weevil, relieved, laughed.

"What were you doing chasing him?" Tootie asked.

"I saw him fire at you."

"You're both crazy," Yvonne blurted out.

Aunt Daniella, genuine emotion coming through, looked at the young people, looked at Yvonne. "It's the Lord's hands, Yvonne. It always is."

CHAPTER 39

"An insanity plea?" Betty questioned on Valentine's Day.

"Standard fare these days," Gray replied, sitting in the library along with Sister, Aunt Daniella, Yvonne, and Sam.

"Do you think he is?" Yvonne's voice rose.

Sister, hands folded in her lap, replied, "My experience with Dewey has been good. He helped out if needed, he was reliable in the field, and he never ran with women, at least not as I can tell. So having him confess to murder, I can only wonder if he isn't insane."

Sam, more cynical, responded. "Sister, he planned out the murder. Cold-blooded. Then he did things that would make people think the killer was crazy."

"And Dewey kept saying the killer was crazy," Gray added.

"To my mind, murder is a crime we all say we abhor, but it has gone on for centuries without much change. This was about money. People kill for money, power, position, and, so they say, love." Aunt Daniella sipped the wonderful bourbon Gray poured for her over those huge ice cubes.

"And it really was over the pipeline but in a way we couldn't have imagined." Sam watched his aunt enjoy her drink.

"Who could have imagined it?" Betty raised her voice slightly. "Who could have thought that Dewey would benefit from the pipeline? We all thought the reverse."

"It certainly underlines our limitations. We see what we want to see. We go along to get along." Sam drank tonic water with lime. "Who would think that Dewey and Gregory were in cahoots? The pipeline just stopped real estate sales but Dewey figured out a way to profit with Luckham as a silent partner."

"Luckham certainly needed to hide." Gray thought the plan clever. "He knew if the pipeline came through Chapel Cross, land values would tank. Horrible, and we thought it would be horrible to Dewey. But just the reverse. Dewey could buy up the land of disgruntled landowners for a song and turn the land into a housing development for an enormous profit. No way would Crawford sell, no matter what, and Old Paradise as well as Tattenhall Station create almost a state park. That would make living here very desirable."

"The right-of-way was 125 feet. A developer could plant trees, things to somewhat hide it plus the homes in the development would not be by the pipeline itself." Sister had heard all this from Ben Sidell. "Plus they'd have those incredible views."

"Gregory had promised Dewey that the energy prices for the homes in this very high-end development would be extremely cheap. He would ensure that the homes could be serviced by the pipeline. This was a plan that could possibly sweeten the pot for this pipeline and future pipelines. It would divide the public, make the environmentalists look selfish, and get state legislators off the hook as they took their campaign contributions from Soliden." Gray stood up to fill his drink, checking to see if anyone else wanted anything.

Aunt Daniella held up her glass. "Well, you never know.

Dewey couldn't have predicted that the outcry to preserve Chapel Cross would be so great."

"What did it was Kasmir and Crawford joining forces to stop it. Then Crawford threatened to find graves and anyone who has had dealings with Crawford knew he would find something, which ultimately he did." Sam paused. "That's what I think."

"The Soliden board was getting nervous. The company wants to start the pipeline now. Years in court isn't the way to do that and Crawford and Kasmir can afford years in court. So why not change the route?" Sister marveled at how money clouds people's minds, how they think it will make them happy. "Dewey confessed to Ben that before the field took off, Gregory told him even though it was not yet public, the pipeline would shift south."

"But Dewey had other developments." Betty threw up her hands.

"He did but he was stretched thin, too thin. And even though those developments were on the other side of the county or the next county, people were sitting on their hands. Dewey needed money. And this Chapel Cross development would have made him millions, big fat millions even after he paid off Luckham." Gray had to admit, it was clever.

"He thought he could buy Beveridge Hundred, I'm sure," Yvonne posited. "He certainly cultivated the Van Dorns."

"And he liked them," Sister said. "Knew them and hunted with them near the end of their hunting days. He also figured he could buy all that land from the New Yorkers. Conservatively he might wind up with about a thousand acres. All the work that Crawford and Kasmir have done benefiting him."

"He just lost it at Christmas Hunt?" Betty wondered. "The boom gets lowered and he loses it?"

"His debts pressed and now his future looked uncertain. All that work, all the preparation, the research, the schmoozing with landowners who would be adversely affected by the pipeline. He would offer them a way out. They wouldn't realize the profits they might realize if the pipeline wasn't tearing up their land, but Dewey could sweeten it. They wouldn't lose but so much. Land appreciates. This would drop the value but it would still be more than when they bought it. It's a good argument." Sister filled in.

"So do you think he's insane?" Yvonne wondered.

"I don't know," Sister quickly replied. "We hear about people, people the neighbors liked, their friends liked, who locked up young women in their basements molesting them for years. No one had a clue. I just don't know. I guess people are capable of anything. We see what we want to see."

Aunt Daniella nodded. "And some people are highly intelligent. They fool us because they know we see what we want to see, hear what we want to hear. Politics is founded on that."

No one said anything. It was too true and too depressing.

Yvonne spoke up. "I will buy Beveridge Hundred. I've spoken to the Van Dorns. They can live there as long as they wish, leave when they wish. Naturally, Dewey's arrest and confession, if you call it that, has disturbed them because over the years he told them not to worry. Then the pipeline route would cut off a corner of their land and they did worry."

"Have they accepted?" Gray looked at his brother, who he suspected knew the answer.

"They have." Yvonne smiled broadly. "I'm the first to admit, I never thought I'd be a country girl and in the South no less, but here I am." She smiled at the small group. "I never expected to like any of you either. You all have treated me with respect, you've helped me with Tootie and, how to put it, I'm happy here."

"Good news. Three cheers." Betty held up her glass.

They chatted, congratulated Yvonne on buying Beveridge Hundred. Then the conversation drifted back to the murders and Dewey.

"Did Dewey say how he did it?" Betty couldn't help herself.

Gray shifted in his chair. He'd been with Sister when Ben came by to inform her of events. "Pretty much like our conclusions. He rode alongside Gregory as they approached the crossroads, hit him hard in the head with the butt end of his gun—a gun we never saw under his coat—pulled him off. The snowstorm gave him his chance. He drove out of Tattenhall Station going the wrong way. Most of us were gone, not staff or Sam but most of the field had made it out. He stopped, retrieved the body, drove to Beveridge Hundred, where he turned the trailer around."

"How did he kill Rory? Actually we know how, why?" Betty asked.

"He says he didn't kill Rory," Gray replied. "Of course he did and of course Rory had to have gotten in the way, but better to be charged with one murder than two."

"He had to have killed him." Sam's jaw clenched. "Rory must have seen him kill Luckham, so Dewey had to silence him."

"Yes. But how can that be proven?" Sister realistically looked at him. "He'll hire the best defense lawyer he can. That lawyer will line up psychiatrists, psychologists, you name it, and the insanity plea will stick. He'll be deemed guilty. He'll go behind bars, but I doubt it will be too awful. He'll be in a place where they think he can be stabilized. Isn't that the word now?"

"What about the cutting off of the hands, the hanging, the boots up to Middleburg, his crop? Stupid stuff." Betty hated the idea that Dewey would be in a country club prison, more or less.

"Well thought out." Aunt Daniella could smell the aroma of great bourbon. "We'd all think this was the work of a crazy person. He thought he could get away with it. I do believe that, but now that he didn't, look at the trail of craziness, if you will. Sending boots to Middleburg Tack Exchange is as nuts as cutting off hands and the rest of it."

"But there are clues. People can't quite cover it all," Yvonne said. "Hands are cut off of thieves. This was about money. And the hands were put where they would divert our attention."

"The crop, the cigarette case." Betty ran her fingers through her sleek hair. "He couldn't bear to part with expensive things, elegant things. Did he say anything about the crop? I mean, here on the farm? The ring? All this stuff."

"The ring he knows nothing about, so it probably was ripped off by an animal enjoying the hand." Gray grimaced. "The crop he said he grabbed, forgetting it was in his trailer. I don't know how true that is, but it does support the insanity plea. Wouldn't a normal person attempt to clean out anything of the victim's?"

"You bet," Aunt Daniella swiftly responded.

"So he realized he had the crop as he came down from the ridge, tossed it aside. He was the last one down of all the field." Gray shrugged. "That's his story. He also told Ben stringing up Gregory in the middle of the night worked up a sweat but cutting his hands off was hard work, too. He relished the gory details. Said he wrapped the victim in large garbage bags, put him in his huge freezer, which he locked. Ben searched the freezers too late. He'd moved Gregory, getting ready to string him up. Said he had him in his car in a sleeping bag. He's a large man, a strong man. He could do these things alone. But he actually was proud of them."

"Sick. Even if he isn't insane, it's sick," Yvonne pronounced.

"Cigarette case?" Sister wondered. She hadn't asked Ben about these items, sticking to the bigger story.

"Ronnie says Dewey couldn't bear to part with it. Twenty-four-carat gold, a sapphire clasp. Ronnie came by my house to visit and to catch up," Aunt Daniella replied. "Dewey had put it in his pocket and I guess it was sort of like the whip: He realized he had to part with it, tossed it during a hunt, I think the one where Dragon found the hand. He said they'd covered a lot of territory, he fell back and pitched it, he thought, under the little stable.

Ronnie doesn't know whether to believe him or not, but he knows he came back for it. Odd. Again, we get back to insanity."

"How did Ronnie know?" Betty would never forget that hunt that nearly proved fatal.

"When he looked at the initials on the cigarette case," Aunt Daniella filled her in, "Dewey had hung back supposedly to go to the bathroom. Ronnie said he doesn't know why but he was beginning to have doubts about Dewey, little things, and he decided to look around that stable. A hunch. How many times have you had a hunch that proved correct?"

"They were hunting buddies. Ronnie knew him fairly well." Sam thought we often know things in the back of our mind before they come to the front of our mind.

"We don't know how this will turn out in court, but at least we are safe. I hope we are safe." Betty smiled then added, "Sister, what are you doing with this lad's cap on the coffee table?"

"I owe Weevil a new one."

"You washed the one you used to cover the crop," Betty said.

"Shrunk."

The back door opened. Two pair of footsteps could be heard.

"In the library," Gray called out.

Shortly Tootie and Weevil stepped into the library.

"What have you got?" Aunt Daniella broke into a huge smile.

Tootie handed a Norfolk terrier puppy to her mother. "I don't want you to be alone. Her name is Ribbon."

Tears filled Yvonne's eyes as she held the adorable puppy to her bosom. She realized her daughter loved her.

"What a beautiful puppy." Sam rose to grab a tissue for her.

They all made noises about the puppy, who was cute and a little sleepy, resting her head on Yvonne's forearm.

Aunt Daniella leaned back, finished her bourbon. A marvelous glow followed but she felt glowing anyway. Love. Puppy love. A parent trying to make up for too much money and not enough time for her child, and the child understanding finally. Then she looked at Sam, handing Yvonne another tissue and oh, she heard Yvonne when she would declare, "I am done with men." Doesn't every woman say that at least once in her life? She certainly had. In Aunt Daniella's case, that promise lasted perhaps a week, but still. As for the ex-husband, he wasn't done with his daughter and ex-wife yet, but for now who cared? He was out of the picture and Sam offered compassion. Eventually Yvonne would figure this out.

Then she studied Weevil and Tootie. Tootie was opening her heart to her mother and to this kind young man.

Aunt Daniella surveyed the room, thinking love comes in many guises. Never turn your back on love. But little Ribbon, well, perhaps that was the best—and it was Valentine's Day.

ACKNOWLEDGMENTS

Donna Packard, my friend and typist for more than thirty years, passed away November 17, 2017. She left behind an adored husband, two grown children, and legions of friends. Working without my wonderful backstop was a sorrowful adjustment.

J. M. Cummings, another novelist, stepped up to the plate so that much did not need to be explained. My handwriting, however, did.

As always, Kathleen King and Dee Phillips, Ph.D., both foxhunting buddies, pitched in when I needed odd bits of information.

I stuck Raymie Woolfe, Jr., briefly in this novel to tickle him. Born July 31, 1935, he died on May 10, 2018, before publication. His bursting onto the steeplechase scene occurred when he was sixteen, winning the Saratoga Steeplechase on Hampton Roads. He was a winner in the saddle and out of it. He also wrote clear, excellent nonfiction. His book on Secretariat in 1981 remains the touchstone. In 2016 *The Doomed Horse Soldiers of Bataan* was published to high praise. There were books in between, and at his death he was writing another.

As to acknowledgments, if I have forgotten anyone, cuss me like a dog.

Speaking of which, my greatly admired, beloved Jane Winegardner, MFH, gave me a Norfolk terrier for my birthday in 2016. She chews my papers. That's all I need, another literary critic.

Couldn't resist putting her in this novel.

May you all be well.

Rita Mae Brown, MFH

Read on for a sneak peek at

Rita Mae Brown's next Sister Jane mystery

SCARLET FEVER

Soon in hardcover and ebook
from Ballantine Books

CHAPTER 1

FEBRUARY 21, 2019
THURSDAY

A flash of scarlet caught Sister Jane's eye then disappeared as a gust of wind blew snow off the trees below. The day, cold, tormented those who thought spring should be around the corner. The calendar cited spring as starting March 20, with the equinox, but the weather gods did not seem to be planning warmth anytime soon.

The winter of 2018–2019 burst pipes, ran up electric bills, sent country people to dwindling firewood piles. Jane Arnold, Sister, master of the Jefferson Hunt, could deal with most of the troubles. It was cold hands and icy feet that she hated.

Another gust of wind sent swirls of snow as trees bent low. Far ahead she again saw Wesley Blackford's scarlet coat as he rode alongside the glittering hard-running creek, ice clinging to the bank sides.

She couldn't see her hounds. Nor could she see the whippers-in, those outriders assisting the huntsman. Sitting on a rise above the creek she peered into the forest, much of it conifers. Behind her stood a small field of riders desperately wishing to drop down out of the wind. Hearing Wesley, nicknamed Weevil, horn to lips, blow hounds forward she turned Lafayette toward the path down. He, too, was eager to move off the rise in the land. As the two carefully picked their way over the frozen ground covered with three inches of snow, more snow slid down Sister's neck from bending tree limbs. Lafayette reached level ground then stopped, snorted. His ears swept forward.

Those behind the master also stopped, wishing she'd move on because some of them still battled the wind. Right in front of Lafayette and his human cargo sauntered Target, a red fox, dazzling in his luxurious winter coat. Looking neither to the left nor the right, he crossed in front of the master, walked to a downed tree trunk secure across the creek, roots upended at the near end. Hopping up, he picked his way over, alighting on the other side.

Now what? No point bellowing "Tally-ho." One should normally count to twenty to give the fox a sporting chance. This arrogant fellow didn't need a sporting chance. Target had them all beat and he knew it. He kept a den on Sister's farm, under the log cabin dependency. Also, chances were that with the wind a "Tally Ho" would be swept away. Still, Sister had to do something so she walked into the blue spruces, firs, and high pines. The space between the trees meant everyone, about fifteen people on this inhospitable day, could fit in. Turning Lafayette's head toward the creek, she waited and counted. If she didn't hear hounds after reaching one hundred she'd move on in the direction she saw Weevil.

"One, two." More snow down her neck.

On she counted as the small field huddled, shoulders up to their ears. A few people wore earmuffs but she couldn't do that. She wouldn't hear her hounds and would most likely mislead everyone.

"Fifty-one, fifty-two." She grasped a heat pack in her coat

pocket while keeping her left hand outside, freezing, because she held her crop in that hand.

As she was right-handed, she mused to herself, perhaps she could afford to lose her left.

"Seventy-two."

Trident shot in front of her without speaking. A young hound, a bit of a kleptomaniac, fast, he stopped suddenly, and put his nose to the ground as his sister, Tinsel, caught up. Now the entire pack, twelve couples today, twenty-four hounds, for hounds are always counted in couples, milled around the tree roots.

Diana, a hound of remarkable intelligence, a true leader, opened while the others puzzled. *"It's him."*

Asa, an older hound, amended this. *"Him, but fading."*

Pickens leapt up onto the large trunk but hopped off, as he couldn't keep his balance.

Parker carefully stood on the trunk, succeeding where his brother had failed. *"He's crossed. Here are his tracks. There's a bit of scent left."*

"We've got to go with what we have." Diana, not fooling around with the tree trunk, jumped into the icy creek, not deep, crossed to the other side, where the scent was a little better. *"Come on, move your asses!"*

The entire pack quickly assembled on the other side of the creek bank, moving with determination.

Sister marveled at their logical powers as well as that fantastic determination so typical of the American foxhound, a hound bred for Mid-Atlantic conditions, conditions designed to make even a saint cuss.

She heard hoofbeats; Weevil came up behind his hounds. She stepped out of the woods, took off her cap, and pointed in the direction the fox had moved in. No need to speak. All it would do would bring up the hounds' heads.

The handsome young man nodded to his master, asked his horse to step into the water, which the fine animal did without a minute's hesitation, crossed, and reached the other side just as the entire pack opened, a sound of exquisite beauty and excitement even to people who didn't hunt. Perhaps it is the sound of our history calling to us.

Sister followed her huntsman and made it across as Betty Franklin, her best friend and a whipper-in, blasted across the creek. The master stood still, for the whipper-in had right of way. Betty hadn't gotten out of position so much as she couldn't find a decent creek crossing. While they all knew this territory, the rains made some crossings treacherous, the silt piling up below. She touched her hat with her crop, a thank you to the master's quick thinking, and charged off.

The field, well trained, now followed.

Sister, up ahead, negotiated a small drift then shot out of it back onto what she hoped was the old farm road. One couldn't see what was underneath the snow and it was easy to slide off the road. Her hope was to look where it was the flattest.

Hounds roared, sang, shook the treetops, bending low as they were.

The riders in the field, most of them experienced foxhunters, for novices often forsook hunting when the weather turned ugly, felt their pulse pounding. The old hands knew the scent had to be red hot.

Scent sticks in a frost or disappears in very cold conditions. The mercury needs to nudge a few degrees above freezing for it to lift and then scent can turn favorable. But today was not a favorable day so hounds had closed with their fox and the scent was hot, fresh for a brief time before the cold ruined it.

Hounds, with their tremendous olfactory powers, could pick up what a human could not, no matter what the conditions. Hounds followed scent but they didn't understand it. In truth no one did. Xenophon, born in 430 B.C., the great Athenian major general, observed it but no one from that time until today truly understood it. Perhaps Artemis did but she wasn't telling.

Lafayette lived for these runs. He and Sister had been a team for eleven years. Both were advanced in years. Didn't mean a thing. He had his Absorbine Jr. rubdowns after a hunt and she had her Motrin. That was their only concession to the years.

Clever, in his teens, Lafayette had an uncanny instinct for negotiating deceptive ground. His hind end slipped a little, he quickly brought up his back legs. Sister stayed in the tack. On they ran. She burst into a meadow, saw the pack at the other end of it, Weevil right behind and Betty to the right. She had no idea where Tootie, the other whipper-in, was but she didn't worry. Staff work was excellent, plus they liked one another.

Diana and Dasher, her littermate, hung a few steps behind two youngsters, Audrey and Aero, who exhibited blinding speed with the recklessness of youth. Of course, they overran the line.

"Stop, you idiots! Get back here." Diana turned in midair, heading west where the sun had not hit the hills, which meant it was going to be even colder.

Betty, in her mid-fifties, an old hand, saw the youngsters overrun the line, not because she could smell scent but she trusted Diana. If Diana or Dasher or any of the older hounds turned then it meant the fox had.

No doubt about it. Riding Outlaw, a solid fellow, Betty reached the outside of the two overexcited youngsters, urging them to turn but not really rating them. No point in scolding. They had figured out something was amiss and were hurrying back to the pack.

Like humans, hounds learn by doing and observing.

Steam rose off horses' hindquarters. People were actually sweating in their heavy coats and winter undershirts. Sister, her eye never leaving her huntsman, reached the other side of the meadow, plunged onto a narrow path, more snow down her neck, and soared over a large tree trunk. High winds had scoured central Virginia last week. Neither she nor her staff knew what lay across paths or how much destruction had been done. Jefferson Hunt covered two large counties. They'd find out when they found out. Work parties, hopefully, would follow. Windy though it was at this moment, at least there were no thirty-mile-an-hour gusts. The wind, too, would blow scent, which is exactly why Target crossed an open meadow. However, a bit to the left of the fox tracks, hounds stuck with it, opening loudly again once in the woods.

Another five minutes of hard running and Sister pulled up at the ruins of a modest house, the chimney standing like an upturned finger, alone, the fireplace visible. The chimney had not fallen down but the rest of the place lay strewn about. Hounds dug at the side of the stone fireplace.

Weevil dismounted, blew "Gone to Ground," praised his hounds.

The fox, deep in his snug den, heard the commotion outside. He knew all the hiding places in a five-mile range.

"I know you're in there," Parker baited him.

Tinsel added her two cents. *"You're afraid to come out. We're ferocious, you know,"* said a hound who was anything but, although she was puffed up from the run.

He said nothing, waiting for them to leave. Target was wise and in his prime.

Weevil called them together and mounted up as Tootie, a young woman, the other whipper-in, arrived at the site. She had also had a devil of a time finding a crossing from her left side of the pack. She took the left, Betty had the right.

"Come along," Weevil sang to them.

Hounds packed in behind him, the whippers-in on each side. They walked back to the trailers perhaps two miles away at Foxglove Farm. Foxglove was a cherished fixture, being in their territory since the beginning of the hunt in 1887.

Coming up to Sister, Harry Dunbar, mid-fifties, trim and tidy with a salt-and-pepper beard and moustache, complimented the pack. "What terrific work on a dicey day. You must be proud."

"I am." She smiled. "It pleases me when people in the field actually pay attention to the pack and know what's happening." She paused. "You've ripped your coat again. Harry, a few more of those and you'll turn into an icicle. The cold has to be stabbing you."

"I'm parading my manly toughness," he joked. "You will, however, be pleased to know I ordered a heavy scarlet Melton from Horse Country. I'll retire this and thankfully be warmer."

"You've worn this coat ever since I've known you, and that's what, since 1990?"

"No, 1989," he said. "I'd opened my shop and you paid me a call, inviting me to hunt. Well, I took you up on it. On the subject of coats, my weazlebelly is as old as this Melton, used when bought, but I save that for the High Holy Days or joint meets. Scarlet is expensive."

He spoke of his tails, which for men are often called weazlebelly, shadbelly for the ladies. Worn with a top hat, the tails reek of elegance as well as dash. Flying over fences in top hat and tails never fails to impress itself upon the memory of those who see it.

"You're right about the expense, but the truly serviceable hunt attire, the stuff that lasts generations, which some does, costs both men and women. Those wonderful English fabrics." She turned to face him fully as they rode. "Could you get heavy English fabric? That dense twill?"

"Marion has worked her magic despite the uproar in England."

Marion Maggiolo, proprietress of Horse Country, made annual pilgrimages to England and Scotland in search of their fabrics, unmatched by any other nation no matter how hard they tried. Given that warmth was now hanging on until later November she also pioneered lighter hunt coats with fabrics from Italy, to keep a rider comfortable on fall days where the mercury might even nudge seventy degrees Fahrenheit. For the old hunters, these high temperatures were confusing. Might have been for the new ones, too.

"When will the coat be ready?"

"Next week, I hope. I waited too late, trying to squeeze one more year out of these tatters. I expect I won't be using the new one until next winter."

"You might be fooled."

He smiled. "You've got that right. I wake up and wonder what season I'm in. Sometimes I even wonder if I'm in America."

She nodded. "I think many of us feel that way. I'm older than you, of course, but I'm coming to the dismal conclusion that it's all smoke and mirrors. No one really knows what's going on."

"Sister, you are not old. You will never be old." He thought a moment. "About no one really knowing what's going on. Honest to Pete, I now think simple competence is revolutionary."

They both laughed, old buddies who had hunted together for decades. Hunting together is not as strong a bond as being in a combat unit under fire but it's strong, partly because hunting can be so unpredictable. One soon sees who has courage, who has brains, and who has both. Truthfully, the horses have more of both than the humans.

Harry reached over, touching Sister's elbow with his crop, stag handle and wrapped in thin strips of leather. "Drop by the store, will you? I've found a Louis XV desk much like the one you and Ray inherited from his uncle. The one that was stolen all those years ago."

"Oh, what a siren song. You are trying to seduce me. Trying to sing that money right out of my pocket."

"What man isn't?" he teased back. "But do drop by. It would be restorative to see you when we both aren't freezing."

She smiled at him, agreeing, then looked ahead, riding forward to Cindy Chandler, an old dear friend.

"What the hell?" Sister blurted out.

Reaching the trailers, Cindy Chandler stood in her stirrups. Booper, her horse, gingerly stepped forward. Sister also stood in her stirrups.

An expensive maroon Range Rover had driven through Cindy's fence by the cow barn. Clytemnestra, huge, and her equally huge son, Orestes, charged about, which set Booper off. No one wanted to tangle with the evil-tempered heifer and her dismally stupid son.

Cindy slid off, handing her reins to Sister. While no one expects a master to perform a groom's duty, these two had been friends for over forty years. Each was always happy to help the other, status be damned. Sister knew Cindy was the only person who could sweet talk Clytemnestra, who actually followed Cindy, her son in tow, into her special cow barn, quite tidy and warmish considering the day.

Morris Taylor, sixty-two, in a T-shirt and jeans, sobbed next to the Range Rover, its nose in a drainage ditch, steam hissing from under the hood.

"I didn't mean to do it."

Sister, now dismounted, motioned for Tootie to come over, handed the gorgeous young woman the reins to both horses, and walked over slowly to Morris, as Weevil, who didn't know the man, approached from the opposite direction.

"Morris, it's Janie."

"Sister, Sister. I didn't mean to do it." He shivered.

As Weevil removed his coat to put over Morris's shoulders, Morris shrank away. "Who are you? Don't touch me."

"It's all right, Morris. He is a friend."

"Who is he? Why does he want to touch me?"

"He wants to put a coat on you," she told the shivering man, who now held on to her for dear life, a life preserver, which in a way she was.

Betty motioned for Weevil to give her the coat, touched her temple. He understood.

"Morris, it's Betty Franklin, your old dancing partner."

"Betty? Betty?" He struggled to place her but didn't shrink away.

"Come on. Let's get you into the house." Sister gently guided him, holding on to his right arm while Betty had his left, toward Cindy's house.

People threw blankets on their horses. Weevil, having pulled his work coat out of the hound truck, and Gray, Sister's partner in life, were already fixing up a temporary fence to keep in Clytemnestra and Orestes for tomorrow, when they would be put out to pasture.

Weevil asked no questions as they worked.

Gray volunteered, "A former hunt club member. Morris Taylor."

"Drew Taylor's family?"

"Brother. Senile dementia. He must have found or stolen the car keys. He's pretty far gone."

Weevil, hammer in hand, drove a nail in the makeshift board. "Hope this holds."

"Let's get another one plus one of her old barrels for a barrier. You never know about that damned cow," Gray grumbled.

As Sister and Betty walked the crying man to the welcoming house, Sister thought to herself, *There but for the grace of God.*

Perhaps.

In the house, having endured the cold for two and a half hours, Sister wrapped her hands around a cup of hot chocolate, glad for the warmth. Today the cold seeped into her bones. Seemed to affect the others the same way. The members sipped tea, coffee, and hot chocolate and a few braced themselves with strong spirits.

A knock on the door sent Cindy to open it.

"I am so sorry to keep you waiting," Drew Taylor apologized.

"No matter, come on. Morris is over there with Betty and Weevil, whom he met today. Chattering away."

Having completed the temporary fence repairs, Weevil and Gray were now inside.

"Had a devil of a time getting a client out the door." Drew blew air out of his nostrils, looked at his brother, sighed. "How much damage is there?"

Cindy released a deep throaty laugh, one that sent men into a transport. "A few fence panels. Don't worry about it. I fear, however, your Range Rover will need to be towed. All the way to Richmond, unfortunately."

He smiled, as he'd always liked Cindy, had done so for decades. "I should never have kept that car."

"You look important driving it."

"Why Rover doesn't open a dealership in Charlottesville I will never know. It's a pain in the ass."

She placed her hand on his forearm. "Morris cried quite a bit. He's afraid you'll be angry at him."

Now noticing his brother, Morris became fearful. "I didn't mean to do it."

Betty stood up but Drew motioned for her to stay seated. Morris now clung to her hand, so she was pulled down.

"It's all right, buddy, but where did you find the keys?" Drew lifted an eyebrow.

Defiantly, his younger brother said, "I'm not telling. You can't make me tell."

People looked at him then away, except for Harry Dunbar, who stared for a minute, shook his head, then averted his eyes.

"Lower your voice, Morris," Drew ordered.

Again a fearful look crossed the not-unattractive suffering man's face.

Sister walked over. "Drew, glad you got here. Missed you during the hunt, which had some good moments."

"And some cold ones." He smiled. "I'll be out Saturday." He looked down at Morris. "Maybe I can find someone to drive him in our old truck. You know, so he can be part of things."

"That's a good idea," Sister agreed. "Morris has always been social and it's not too different now. He seems to remember some of us but not our names. If I say my name he nods."

"There are days and then there are days." He put his hand under his brother's armpit. "Come on. I'm taking you home."

Morris shrugged him off. "I don't want to go home. There are no women at home."

Betty couldn't help it. She burst out laughing.

"Come on."

"I'm not going," Morris refused.

"You know, Morris, you have a point. No women. Men need women." Betty smiled at him. "How about if I walk you with Drew and we figure out how to get some girls to the house."

Morris brightened. "I like to talk to women. I like to look at them. I like breasts."

"Oh God," Drew moaned.

Sister shrugged. "It's all right. He says what everyone else is thinking."

Drew looked around at the small group, noticing Harry Dunbar. A slight sneer appeared on his lips then he refocused on his brother, dismissing the man he loathed, a man he had accused of cheating him and seducing his late mother. Neither charge had ever been proven.

Harry, seeing Drew, turned his back, a maneuver he also used in the hunt field.

To the credit of both men, once the initial uproar had passed, and that was years ago, they did not drag club members into their dislike. The members carefully sidestepped it as well.

What had happened was that Mrs. Waycross Taylor, Missy to her friends, had died, leaving behind exquisite eighteenth-century furniture as well as a few lovely small sculptures from the late eighteenth century, early nineteenth, all English. Neither Drew nor Morris wanted any of it. Neither man had an aesthetic bone in their bodies and their wives were all for the modern, at that time, as well as brighter colors. No silk moire for them.

So Drew and Morris called Harry, told him to pick up the stuff after he gave them a price. He did. Twenty thousand dollars, which sounded reasonable. One small graceful Hepplewhite incidental table alone was worth that, but they neither knew nor seemed to care. So Harry wrote the check, brought a moving van, and took the entire lot, rooms full of fabulous furniture.

A pair of George III giltwood armchairs, circa 1770, sold for nine thousand dollars. The gilt candelabra held by two fetching female figures, breasts exposed and perfect—well, they were bronze-gilded, how could they sag after all those centuries? Anyway, the candelabra had adorned Missy's formal dining room table. The two ravishing ladies stood about forty-six inches high. That included the base and the candelabra, which they held a bit sideways, so their bosoms met the eye. Harry sold the pair for eighty-five thousand dollars. That's what did it. The sons might have absorbed the sale of the gilt chairs, but this, this sent them into orbit.

A few hunt club members at the time felt that the Taylors may have been carried a little fast, to use the old Virginia expression. However, most believed the brothers had been stupid. They could have asked for bids.

Missy Taylor spent lavishly and she could afford to, for her husband, Waycross, a born salesman, expanded the Taylor Insurance business, started by his father. Before there were multiple listings, Taylor got all the big estates, partly due to his prowess in the hunt field. He hunted many of the estates he later sold. Socializing came naturally to him as did easily clearing a stout four-foot fence. Well respected, he increased his fortune. Multiple listings became the norm. It certainly made it easier for buyers and sellers but not necessarily the listing agent. Waycross adjusted, worked well with other firms. The business expanded.

Drew stepped into the business. Morris hated selling, loved science, went to MIT. He wound up working as a nuclear physicist for a private company that built nuclear reactors. He inherited the moneymaking gene, for certain, along with old Waycross's brains. Drew, not so much. He coasted. Taylor Insurance was kept afloat by his agents.

Morris's hopes for his own son were dashed because Bainbridge, now an adult, harbored little ambition and indeterminate brainpower.

Before his accelerating decline, Morris, too, hunted and rode well when he retired, moving back to Charlottesville. Building reactors had taken him all over the country in his prime but when he could he had joined the local hunt. He was well liked and certainly respected, making his decline all the more painful.

Behind their hands many a person whispered, "Why couldn't it have been Drew?"

Weevil, seated next to Betty, rose, walked to where the Shaker pegs were lined up by the front door, grabbed Betty's heavy hunt coat and his own. He returned.

"Thank you, Weevil."

He helped her put it on.

"I could do that," Morris offered.

"Thank you for thinking of it." Betty beamed at him.

Betty, Weevil, and Drew propelled Morris to the front door. Drew lifted his own lamb fleece coat off a peg.

Weevil filled him in. "No coat. Took almost a half hour for him to stop shivering."

"You know, I've an extra in the car. I'll run out and get it." He opened the door and a wedge of frigid air pushed in.

"I don't want to go." Morris's eyes glazed over. "I hate him."

"He's your brother," Betty said soothingly.

"So what? He talks to me like I'm an idiot. I forget things, Betty. I do, but I'm not an idiot. I built nuclear reactors. I know things."

Weevil's eyebrows raised and Betty nodded in agreement.

"You built Three Mile Island. You worked on big projects."

"I remember all that," he said as his brother came back through the door, handing Morris a down jacket.

Betty moved to Morris's right side while Weevil took his left. Both intuited that if Drew touched his brother, resistance would accelerate.

They walked him to Drew's brand-new BMW X5. Had to have cost at least $72,000, with every gadget known to the Germans.

Drew paused for a minute. "Damn, he really did plow through that fence. I'll pay for it, obviously."

"The good news is, Cindy coaxed Clytemnestra and Orestes into their barn and closed the door," Betty noted.

"Thank God the cow didn't attack the Range Rover." Drew exhaled.

Weevil noticed the enormous cow giving them the evil eye from her barn window. "Don't count her out. Best to get the wrecker here before she gets out tomorrow morning."

"Good point." Drew smiled at him then opened the door and slid behind the wheel, while Morris would not close his door.

Betty kissed him on the cheek, closing the door, and Drew quickly locked it.

The two staff members walked back to the house, the snow and ice crunching underfoot.

"When did his dementia start?" Weevil asked.

"I don't truly know. I noticed a change four years ago. Little things. He'd forget a name, lose a reference. The lapses became more pronounced until finally he drove to Roger's Corner." She mentioned a convenience store out in the country. "Didn't know where he was. Roger called Drew. Ultimately he took his brother in and now has a part-time housekeeper. I guess you'd call him that, he's a nurse really, I don't know, but it's a young man who watches him. Morris has a son, but he's not a success story. So far he's not done much for his father. They fight then Morris fights with Drew."

"The nurse must have been off duty today," Weevil noted.

"Maybe. Sad. The whole process is so sad."

They gladly stepped inside, peeled off their coats.

"I didn't think I'd be here so long." Weevil walked over to Sister. "Let me get the hounds back."

"Fortunately, their trailer is closed up and full of straw, but yes, it's a good idea. None of us could have predicted the accident. Better he took out Cindy's fence than one of us."

Weevil motioned for Tootie, and they left together.

The breakfast (hunt tailgates or food at a member's house are called breakfasts, no matter what time the hunt is over) was breaking up.

Cindy said to Sister, "Hope we hunt at Mud Fence Saturday. The weather report is not promising."

"There's time between today and Saturday. I'll worry about it the night before," the tall, silver-haired master replied.

"You're good at that."

"Worrying?"

Cindy laughed. "Not worrying."

"I have Gray to do that for me." She lifted her eyebrows as her partner walked over.

"What?" the handsome man, mid-sixties, said.

"Worry. I told Cindy I don't worry because you do it for me."

"I don't worry. I think ahead."

She looked at him, light brown skin, a thin military moustache gray over his upper lip. "Whatever you say, darling."

He smiled back. "You're up to something."

"Me? Never."

She was, but she would wait to see that desk first.

PHOTO: © MARY MOTLEY KALERGIS

RITA MAE BROWN is the bestselling author of the Sneaky Pie Brown series; the Sister Jane series; the Runnymede novels, including *Six of One* and *Cakewalk; A Nose for Justice* and *Murder Unleashed; Rubyfruit Jungle; In Her Day;* and many other books. An Emmy-nominated screenwriter and poet, Brown lives in Afton, Virginia, and is a Master of Foxhounds.

ritamaebrownbooks.com

To inquire about booking Rita Mae Brown for a speaking engagement, please contact the Penguin Random House Speakers Bureau at speakers@penguinrandomhouse.com.